# nine
# lives

# nine lives

George M. Moser

iUniverse, Inc.
Bloomington

# Nine Lives

iUniverse books may be ordered through booksellers or by contacting:

iUniverse
1663 Liberty Drive
Bloomington, IN 47403
www.iuniverse.com
1-800-Authors (1-800-288-4677)

ISBN: 978-1-4697-5311-9 (sc)
ISBN: 978-1-4697-5312-6 (hc)
ISBN: 978-1-4697-5313-3 (ebk)

Library of Congress Control Number: 2012900901

Printed in the United States of America

iUniverse rev. date: 02/14/2012

# Contents

For Michael, Alicia, and Griffin. Remember to dream.

For De. Remember dreams can come true.

A cat has nine lives: three to play, three to stray, and three to stay.
—Author Unknown

Tybalt says, "What wouldst thou have for me?"
Mercutio responds, "Good king of cats, nothing but one of your
nine lives."
—William Shakespeare, *Romeo and Juliet*

She's had so many accidents with her new car that wonder she's
not been killed.
—Author Unknown

Well now you know that your cat has nine lives. Nine lives to itself
but you only got one.
—John Lennon

# Acknowledgments

I would like to acknowledge the following people who have been inspirational and supportive of my writing. To my wife, De, who has been at my side, always supportive. God knows why, but after all these years, she's still here. To my good friends Marcia and Mark, for all the helpful ideas with my book. You were always there to give me constructive criticism when I asked, and you gave me great ideas as well. To my sons and daughter—Michael, Griffin, and Alicia—you inspired me to write the many things I felt. All of you have helped me in one way or another—though it was Alicia's idea to have a cat spitting up a hairball. To the rest of my family: Doug, if it wasn't for our little adventure I wouldn't have written this book to begin with. My mom and dad have always supported me through thick and thin. The same goes to my relatives who helped me kick this novel off with a bang. There are too many to name, but you all know who you are. Finally, thanks go to the readers. You're the ones who support me. Whether you're my closest friend or a stranger, I will always remember it was you who made this book.

Thank you,

George M. Moser

# STARGAZING

"What's that one up there, Dad?"

"That one is called Leo."

The two of them lay back in the grass, pointing at the constellations up above. Resting on the crest of a hill, they could see the dim lights of houses off in the distance. A perfect night to stargaze, with no moon in the sky on this cloudless night. The only sounds came from the perpetual chirping of the crickets and the hoot of an owl. The sky above was like a dome filled with countless pinholes of light. An occasional falling star streaked across the sky.

"Does it have a story?" The young boy looked up with eyes wide with excitement.

"Oh, does it ever have a story, but it's kind of scary." The man raised his eyebrows.

"I'm a big boy now, Dad. You can tell me."

The man turned to him with a serious look on his face. "Well, I suppose seven is old enough, but you have to promise me something if I tell you, Michael."

Michael rolled over on the grass so he was kneeling beside his dad. He wanted to be close while his dad told the story. It wasn't that he was scared, of course—though he didn't like that one croaking sound that came from the group of bushes to his right. He just loved it when his dad told him stories about the stars, but he couldn't remember one ever being scary. He pressed his face close to his dad and whispered, "What do you want me to promise, Dad?"

"Don't tell your mother."

The two of them burst out laughing, and Michael forgot all about being scared for the moment. It was something only a father and son would understand. It was their time to bond, and Michael understood, nodding his head up and down with excitement. This was their little secret.

"I promise, Dad!"

They leaned back on the grass, and Michael rolled close to his dad. It was comforting when his dad reached around and grabbed him, tugging him close while he told the story. He tucked his head into his side, hearing the slow rhythm of his heartbeat. His dad pointed up to the stars, connecting them with his finger.

"You see the shape of the lion?"

"Uh-huh."

"A long time ago, a man named Hercules was sent to twelve trials. Each one of these tests of strength was dreaded and thought impossible by mortal men. The first of these trials was to slay the Nemean lion."

Michael listened in awe, looking up at the constellation Leo. His dad was always good at telling stories, but he had never told one like this before. He took his time while the two of them lay there in the grass. His dad explained what Hercules probably looked like—all muscles, of course—and Michael imagined the strongest of men standing on top of a mountain.

The lion stood high on that mountain, looking over the small village down below. Michael could imagine the wind blowing through its mane and how magnificent it must have looked. He was the king of the mountain, afraid of no one. The pelt of the great lion was impenetrable, but Hercules did not know this and, like a fool, tried to kill it with his bow and arrows. This made the lion very angry, and Michael found himself pressing his body into his dad even harder.

"Did the lion eat Hercules, Dad?"

"Well, not yet, but if you're scared, I can stop." His dad was good at teasing him.

"No, Dad, I'm not scared!" Michael may have been a little scared, feeling his body tugging at his dad harder, but he wasn't going to admit it.

His dad smiled and continued with the story, keeping his eyes on the stars above. He told of the lion running into a cave, which had two entrances for the lion to escape. The people in the village assumed Hercules would run away after being unable to penetrate the lion's pelt, but instead he ran after him and into the cave. The story became more intense, and Michael's eyes were wide with fascination as he listened to his dad's voice. He explained that Hercules closed off one of the entrances, so the only way out was through him. A fight to the death between the two was evident, hearing sounds of growls that shook the entire mountain. Then there was silence, and the people of the village were certain it was the last they would ever see of Hercules.

"So it ate Hercules?"

"Not exactly."

Michael could not hear any sounds other than the voice of his dad. The crickets had stopped their chirping, and the owl was no longer hooting. Even that croaking sound that was giving him the creeps was silent, and Michael couldn't help but think maybe they too were listening to this story of the lion. His own mouth was wide open as he waited to hear what was to become of Hercules.

His dad explained how Hercules killed the lion with his bare hands. The struggle lasted a long time, but Hercules was eventually victorious, clubbing the animal. The hide was to be returned as evidence that the lion was killed, but when he tried to skin it, Hercules found it could not be penetrated. The only thing that could penetrate the pelt was the lion's own claws, which Hercules used to skin the lion.

"Wow! That was a good story, Dad." Michael looked up with a smile.

"We best be heading off now before your mom starts to worry about you." His dad rubbed his head and smiled.

They gathered their things, taking one last look at the stars up above. Michael helped his dad fold up the tripod that held a small telescope angled down to the ground. He felt good being with his dad and was sad to see the time end, but his eyes were getting tired.

His dad gave him a little piece of advice. "Remember to dream, Michael. Follow your dreams and never be afraid to enter that cave alone."

They hopped in the car, and his dad started the engine. Michael loved the way the car rumbled. He felt his body shake in the soft seat. They pulled out onto the highway and Michael held his hand out the window, feeling the wind glide up and down. The rest of the ride home he dreamed of the story his dad had told him and wondered if he really would ever have to enter a cave by himself. The windows were down, and he felt the cool rush of air blowing through his hair. He imagined himself high upon a mountain, ready to fight the Nemean lion. His dad stepped on the gas and the needle moved up past a hundred. Michael rolled his eyes from his dad to the speedometer with a strong sense of curiosity.

We're going fast, Dad!"

The two of them laughed, and his dad said with a smile, "Don't tell your mother!"

# DREAMS

"Cat? What cat?"

Michael Merlino scrutinized his dreams of distant places pinned to the wall. He reached out with one hand to touch what was so far away, never to be realized. If only the cord on the phone was longer, maybe his other hand could touch the picture of his wife and son standing beneath the star-lit sky. Dreams are just that, a journey of hope barely out of reach that keeps us striving to reach our destiny.

The voice on the other end of the phone had the sound of urgency, which made it hard to concentrate on anything. Rolling his chair closer to the picture of some distant galaxies just out of reach from his outstretched hand, he looked up and tried to smile at the tacks shaped in a smiley face. The desk was a mess, with files piled high and a computer to the side.

"Under the deck. You need to get home now," a woman said on the other end of the phone.

"But why can't you—"

"You know why, Michael. Hurry home." The phone went dead.

Michael was an ambitious young man at twenty-eight years of age, dressed to perfection. The clock flashing on the digital display told that it was six ten in the evening. Standing, he could barely see over the tops of the cubicles. He pulled on a suit coat and grabbed the leather briefcase filled with work he would finish up at home. He was the only one left working in this large empty office on the second floor, filled with cubicles. It was a busy day, but it was time to catch the six-thirty train.

Michael felt his heart sink when he looked down the hall and saw Franklin J. Smith walking toward him. Franklin was a conservative man, who had just turned sixty-three years old and had been with the bank for forty-one years. Ever since graduating from college, Franklin had been a very loyal man to the bank. He was always dressed in one of his typical pin-striped suits with a white shirt and tie, though he had been known to wear a bow tie upon occasion. The man had no sense of humor.

"A little advice, Michael." He paused, tilting his head to one side to see if Michael was listening.

"Yes, sir?"

"First, stop calling me sir. We've known each other way too long now. My name's Franklin." He held up his chin proudly, hands fixed to his tie.

"Yes, sir—I mean Franklin," he answered uncomfortably.

"That a boy." Franklin laughed, patting Michael on his back.

"Thank you, sir." Michael shrugged his shoulders after the pat on his back. "I mean Franklin." Something was different, and Michael couldn't place it. But the only thing that mattered at the moment was catching the train. Recently everything had been about work, and Michael was loyal to the bank, working late hours. He wanted that promotion, and his wife knew this, but why did she have to be so difficult? Michael was annoyed that she wasn't excited about his job. Why wasn't she excited for him? Maybe they could enjoy a candlelight dinner with a bottle of champagne, celebrate a little, and have some fun instead of being so serious about life. He wanted to scream but now was not the time, standing before Franklin, who was always so austere.

Franklin wrapped one arm around Michael, pulling him along slowly past cubicle after cubicle. "Have you ever visited the zoo, Michael?"

This was a strange question, but Franklin often had a reason for his odd questions. "Sure, of course."

"Well, have you ever wondered why they put those signs on the fences? You know, the ones that say *don't* feed the animals'?"

It was getting late, and Michael was sure Franklin had a point. "Sure, it's so the animals don't rely on being fed by people."

"Exactly!"

Michael thought it was a strange thing to be telling him, but time was ticking. That train leaving the station was on Michael's mind. "Sir? If you don't mind, I have a train to—"

"Yes, the train." Franklin smiled. "Socialism." Franklin just looked into Michael's eyes. "Do you believe in it, Michael?"

"Of course not, sir, but—"

"I learned a long time ago that if we feed the animals they will never learn how to survive."

Michael looked up to Franklin, wondering to himself what all this had to do with him and why it had to be now. Jenny was going to kill him for missing the train, but life sometimes gave you lemons and you were supposed to make lemonade, right? "That's very . . ." He paused a moment. Michael was trying to figure out what was told to him. Franklin was always good at bringing up crazy ideas that made him think. ". . . interesting."

"Michael, why is it we feed the animals? Why is it we continue to give things away? How will we ever learn? Tell me, Michael, how do we expect ourselves to grow? Michael, things are getting busy around here, and I just can't keep up with everything coming my way, if you know what I mean."

"Oh, yes, it has been busy around here lately. I like it that way, of course. It keeps me going, you know." Michael was fighting every urge inside to look at his watch.

"Well, son, I have been thinking," Franklin stated.

Frustrated, Michael did all he could to hide the look on his face. He placed his hands behind his back, trying to be humble. A report for the central district was due in a couple days, and he was certain Franklin was going to ask him to stay late and finish it tonight. His head was starting to throb, so he placed a hand to his temple.

"You know Johnson down the way is moving over to the credit division, and Thomas is going up to lending. Well, that only leaves me with a few guys like you around to help me out, and I am losing

Sally any day now because she and her husband are moving to New York. So—"

"I know you want me to help you on the report for—" Michael attempted to cut to the chase.

"Oh, no, no," Franklin started again, laughing this time. "I want you to take Sabastian's desk first thing Tuesday morning. I want you to be my director of the East Coast. I need someone I can rely on, and I cannot think of anyone better for the job than you, Michael. You know, I am looking for you to make some great strides in this company, and I hope someday you remember me when you are up on that twenty-ninth floor."

Standing there with his mouth open, he stared at Franklin in disbelief. Things started to whirl in the room. This was what Michael had worked so hard for, and now that it happened he was speechless.

"Well, Michael, what do you say? Pick up your jaw off the ground." Franklin laughed.

"Ah, yes, I mean no, I mean thank you, sir! I mean Franklin, sir, thank you! Yes, I will gladly take the job! Thank you for your confidence in me. I will do my best to make you happy," Michael finally replied.

"Yes, I know you will, Michael. Now get out of here before you miss that train," Franklin said with a wide smile.

"Yes, sir, and thanks again, Mr. Franklin." Michael ran out the door nearly stumbling on his feet.

---

Michael boarded the six-thirty train just as it was leaving the platform. He sat in his normal spot in the third car, lower level in front. The same guys were there every day, and all nodded their recognition. The seats were flipped over today, facing one another with the hard vinyl green cushions and the silver steel backs. The train had an old musty smell, but he was used to it. No one talked on the train unless absolutely necessary; it was an unwritten rule to leave everyone alone. Michael usually pulled out his newspaper or reports on his way home, getting ready for the next day. Today was different. Excitement was pent up inside him. He was excited about his new job and couldn't wait to tell his wife, Jenny, about what had happened at the end of the workday.

Like most of the people on the train, Michael was a regular and recognized most of the passengers. There was the tall man with dark thick-framed glasses, who always wore a bow tie and got off on the Des Plaines stop. Even the conductor knew Michael by his first name. He would take his ticket, go "click-clack" with his paper puncher, and say, "Yo, Mike," and Michael would nod like he always did. The conductor would go on his way, taking people's tickets.

Then there were the two guys from the exchange, who gambled for anything and everything on the way home, playing a game of greed. One tossed the dice and the other shouted, "You owe me a bill!"

One man stepped on the train, dressed completely in black. Leaning down to clear the doorway, he walked toward the vacant seat opposite Michael. He took the seat and flapped open the *Wall Street Journal*, holding it up to read. Michael looked out the window after giving the man a nod, acknowledging him. The hair on the back of Michael's neck stood up as he felt the weight of the man's stare. Even though Michael never looked at the man, he couldn't help but feel the eyes of the man on him. He looked up several times to see for himself, but the man's face was always behind the newspaper. The thought occurred to Michael to ask where the funeral was, but he decided to keep to himself instead.

Michael pulled out his own books, which he read all the time on his way to and from work when he could. Astronomy was an interest of his ever since early childhood. His dad would sit with him in the backyard and point out the different constellations. At the age of six his dad bought a telescope from Sears. Michael would go out every night if it was clear and search for the one undiscovered planet he hoped someday to find himself. There were a couple of books he loved to read, about famous men like Aristotle and Newton. Hawking was one of his favorites, along with that guy named Carl Sagan, who always made him laugh. "Billions and billions," Michael would always say to himself. Time really flew on the train when he got into his reading about the stars. It was one thing he really loved, knowing there was so much out there yet undiscovered.

The man got off at the Arlington Heights stop, which Michael thought was odd since the man had just gotten on at the stop before. He was quick to get up and had dropped his *Journal*, which was folded over to the help-wanted ads, on the seat in front of him. Circled in red was a large ad that read, "Have you seen this kitten?" It was a cartoon of a black-and-white cat standing up with one paw raised. There was no name or phone number, which made him think the ad was a joke, but why had the man circled it in red?

After that things went as they always did, and the conductor called out, "Crystal Lake is the next stop. Crystal Lake."

# JENNY

Sitting behind a desk full of papers with a phone held to her ear was Jénny Merlino, staring at the pictures of her family on the wall. A bookcase was filled with several folders and boxes of the pharmaceuticals mixed in with more pictures of Michael, her son JR, and herself. She hung up the phone and glared at it with narrowed eyes, realizing the promotion for Michael was great for him and her family but she just couldn't stand thinking about what it would do to them—less time for her and JR, and more time for other things. She was a petite woman, casually dressed for the summer. Rays of sunshine peeked through the windows, lighting up her pretty face. It was hard to imagine someone as pretty as her ever angry.

The smell of dinner filled the air of the kitchen. The countertop was covered with bowls of chopped-up vegetables and ready-to-cook hamburger patties. The door leading off to the family room had laundry baskets overflowing with freshly laundered folded clothes. A pile of medical equipment was stacked up on the kitchen table, surrounded by two settings of plates. A high chair for a small child was at one side of the table.

Trying to balance four different jobs was not easy, but Jenny not only managed but did it quite well. At the age of twenty-seven, she was a smart girl, and working on her master's at Northwestern University in Evanston took plenty of time, including driving back and forth from Crystal Lake, not to mention the time it took for studying and classes. She was very well trained at selling medical defibrillators to hospitals and doctors, which provided a good income for her and Michael. The most important job, of course, was taking care of Michael and their little boy—Michael Jr., or JR. She cooked dinner every night, did the dishes and the laundry, and kept up with the dog, which Michael had wanted most. All of this took time, but Jenny loved every moment of her life.

——————

Jenny grew up in a small town of about a thousand people, just outside of Chicago. Everyone knew everyone, so rumors of course flew. A cheerleader at the local high school dating the football quarterback was bound to start rumors. They were both most likely to succeed, but rumors proved to be too much and the two of them broke up before the end of their senior year. Word spread of Jenny sleeping with half the football team, and her boyfriend at the time, Jake, had fallen for another of the cheerleaders—Jenny's best friend, of course. More and more rumors spread about Jenny. None of it was true, but leaving for college couldn't happen soon enough.

She left for the University of Iowa, where she was determined not to get serious with men for a while and rather focus on her studies. The past haunted her too much, and she spent her first two years of college in either the library or her dorm room. New friends and a large university gave her a chance to start over again. She majored in business and excelled in her classes. Always a leader in the groups she joined, it was hard to keep her hidden even in this large university.

So it was odd when she met Michael her junior year while studying in the library one night. Michael never stepped foot in the library, but some of his friends pulled him on their way home from one of the local taverns. It was a large modern library just off the river, with shelves everywhere on its five levels of floors. Tables sat about with chairs surrounding, and students filled about half of them.

Jenny was hidden at a table surrounded by bookcases when she first heard Michael and his friends. She had heard only a few whispers before the shouting first occurred. Lifting her gaze above the reading glasses she wore and glancing back to her book with a pen in the other hand, she continued to write. She heard a loud shuffle and some shoving, when a book flopped down from the shelves behind her.

"Well, well, well, look what I found." It was Michael, and he was drunk off his ass. Blue eyes stared at Jenny from behind the bookshelves between a slot of missing books. It was actually comical, if not a little creepy, seeing just his face in between the slot of the missing books, and Jenny laughed.

Jenny was hardly amused, though, and turned her back, trying to focus on her homework again. Dressed in shorts and a golden-colored sweatshirt with the image of the school's mascot painted on front and with her hair pulled up in a ponytail, she was as cute as they came.

"I found my girl." Michael slurred his words and pointed through the shelves, shoving more books to the floor. There was more laughter, and his friends grabbed him by the arms, pulling him away.

"Michael! Let's go, man. They're coming!"

Jenny finally saw him being led away from behind the shelves. She couldn't help but smile, thinking he was cute. He wore faded blue jeans with one knee torn and frayed, and a yellow T-shirt with a Hawkeye on the front. He stumbled, tugging his arm from his friends, and stepped closer to her, leaning in close with both hands on his chin and elbows on the table. His head fell, but he was quick to recover, placing his head back in the palms of both hands. He smiled and winked at her.

"Hellooooo, name's Michael and I wanna—" he slurred again, staring into her eyes.

"Shush, you're in the library if you haven't noticed, and you're going to get us all in trouble," Jenny cut in, placing her fingers to his lips. She looked around, half-expecting all of Iowa security to come at any moment.

"Aw, hell, don'tcha worry 'bout them. My brudder is da chief." Then his head fell on the table.

People in the lower level started talking and pointing to the noise. "I think you better run," Jenny told him. Some of the students nearby looked to Michael and his friends with annoyed expressions on their faces.

"Keep it down over there," one guy shouted in a loud whisper.

"Get the drunk out of here," said another in a nasal voice, never turning his head to actually look at Michael and his friends.

His friends grabbed Michael by his arms, but he pulled back, shrugging. "Wait, jus . . . just tell me yer name." Michael covered his mouth and burped.

Jenny winced, smelling the beer on his breath and waving a hand before her face. She looked to the sides and then smiled to him, whispering, "Well, it's nice to meet you, Michael, but if you don't get out of here soon you're going to cause a mess." She looked both ways, making sure no one was looking, and then leaned back to him. "Look for me at Mayflower and ask for Jenny, and you better not be drunk!"

People at nearby tables looked at her disturbed, making noises with fingers pressed to their lips. "Shhh."

Jenny watched his friends drag him out of the library and figured she would never see him again. Who would remember anything, as drunk as he was? She would remember for the rest of her life when he turned and winked at her—feet dragging along the tiled floor and his friends stumbling while holding each arm. Ah, the memories of college life and love.

The Mayflower was an old three-story red-brick dormitory near the center of the campus. Well-dressed that day with hair combed, Michael looked nothing like the slob who had stumbled into the library just last night. Wearing clean blue jeans this time with no holes in them and a nice-looking polo shirt (wrinkled, of course), he held one red rose close to his chest when he approached the door. Jenny heard the knock and opened the door, recognizing him immediately. "Michael!"

Michael's jaw dropped, and Jenny just stood there, swaying back and forth with hands clasped behind her back. "Jenny?" She remembered how she had spent all day preparing the long curls in her hair that smelled like lilac. She wore a pink sleeveless shirt and a bow in her hair, which dangled to one side.

They saw each other every day and talked on the phone late at night. There was never a moment the two of them weren't together laughing or holding hands. She was the serious one and he was the joker. She still took her classes seriously and studied when she could, but he made it fun. They went to football games together and basketball too. Michael would shout about how his girl should have been one of the cheerleaders.

But those days were over for her. She remembered it all and how they would talk on the phone till one fell asleep. Usually it was Michael, and she would laugh when he snored.

As much of a partyer as Michael was at times, he was a very serious person when it came to the stars. Physics and astronomy were his passions, so he would take Jenny out to lie in the grass at night. One of his favorite places was the football stadium, where the two of them would lie on the soft Astroturf. The two of them would lie there for hours, with Michael pointing out the different constellations like his father used to show him. They would make a wish on falling stars, and the two of them relaxed in each other's arms. It was one of the best moments the two of them had. It was Michael's dream to look at the stars and discover new places no man has ever been. On special nights he would bring her to the observatory and use the telescope there. Jenny was very impressed and knew she had fallen in love.

They both graduated from college and moved to the big city of Chicago, renting an apartment together for a while. He started off with a few small jobs while she was highly sought after in sales by a few large companies. Things went well for them, and Michael eventually found the job he had now at the bank. Money was never really on their minds at that point in their lives. They were young and in love. Jenny had started to take classes at Northwestern to get her master's when Michael proposed to her.

Within a year they were married, and things were really going smoothly. Living in the big city wasn't much different from their college days. They had plenty of friends living near them, so parties were plentiful on the weekends. The two of them had each other and explored life in the city for a while. They had their moments of being alone, taking trips to places like London and Paris.

Jenny woke up early one morning and ended up on her hands and knees, hugging the porcelain toilet. The hurling sound was unmistakable, and Michael pushed away the covers and headed for the bathroom, pulling up his shorts. "Jen?" She could still see that soft beam of light beneath the door when Michael opened it and saw her kneeling at the side with puke on her chin. "Aw, babe." He knelt down and put his arm around her, comforting her. Here she was kneeling at the side of the toilet, wearing white panties and a midriff white shirt, and her hair was tangled in a mess. She reached up and wiped the puke from her chin with the back of her hand. "I didn't think you drank that much. I would have—"

"I haven't had a drink in a month." Jenny felt her eyes water and turned back to the toilet and barfed.

Michael just watched, confused, with one hand on her back. He really had no idea what was going on just yet. He took a clean towel and leaned down to wipe her soft teary face.

"Michael?"

"What's wrong, Jen? Is it the flu?"

"I'm pregnant." Those words seemed to come out slowly. The entire world seemed to stop, and Michael's mouth just dropped. She would never know if he was happy or not. Right then Jenny wished she could take those words back. Questions and doubts raced through her mind.

Michael reached over, holding her against his bare chest with the toilet unfortunately pushing against her back. "Pregnant?" Michael asked her, and she just nodded her head, sobbing harder than before. "Really?" He was smiling, but she didn't see it. All she knew was he was going to be mad. "Jenny? Look at me." Slowly she lifted her eyes to him, and he told her, "I love you."

She blinked several times, unsure, and then tugged at him with fingers delving into his side when she just started to cry harder than before. "I thought you would be mad."

Michael laughed, squeezing her back. "Why on earth would you think that? I love you, Jenny."

So their life took another turn, and they headed to the suburbs. The city just wasn't a place to raise a child, so they searched for a home. It would definitely take some adjustment to living in the suburbs, but this was what the two of them had always wanted—a family to call their own, a house with a picket fence, and a big backyard for a garden and a dog to run around in.

———

That was how she remembered it, waking up from a daze. "Damn you, Michael!" She looked out the window at her son, JR, outside on the porch, poking at something in the bush. She grabbed the plate full of burgers to cook and headed outside with a spatula in one hand. "How's it going, my little baby boy?"

JR, who was wearing a diaper and holding a stick in his hand, turned to see his mom. "Mum?" He smiled to her and then turned back to the bush, poking the stick at the branches. Inside the branches something was rustling.

Jenny turned to JR now that the burgers were cooking and looked into his pretty blue eyes. "Kitty cat."

"Meow." A soft purr came from the bushes.

"Don't you worry. Dad will be home soon to save the kitty cat. Poor little guy is probably lost." She repeated the word so JR would learn "cat," pointing at the little cat inside the bushes.

JR watched his mother's lips, listened to her speak, and then turned with the stick in his hand and poked it in the bush. "Cat!" His mom smiled and patted him on the back. JR kept poking the stick and shouting, "Cat!"

Jenny watched JR play with the cat, poking the stick inside the bush, learning its name. Her mind was on the conversation with Michael and what his job was doing to their family. It bothered her that he was spending so much time on something that was so far from his dream. He was losing sight of what really mattered. She sniffed, not realizing at first that she was smelling smoke in the air. She whipped her head to one side, seeing the smoke rise from the grill, and then leaped up to her feet. "Oh no!" She lifted the cover, and nothing but black smoke poured out. She waved both hands to clear the smoke. "Burned hockey pucks again."

# THUNDER

## MERAMEC STATE PARK, WEST OF ST. LOUIS, MISSOURI

A breeze blew through the woods. The pines bent slightly as the skies filled with dark clouds. A storm was brewing, and the cold front was dropping the temperature rapidly. The animals sensed the storm approaching and quickly ran to find shelter. Thunder clapped far in the distance. It was only a matter of time before the storm would echo off the bluffs. The sound of water rushing down the river filled the quiet before the storm.

A woman in a torn white blouse, her face covered in dirt, ran through the woods, swiping branches of the trees. Her faded blue jeans were torn on the right leg, and a wet stain of crimson covered the fabric on her thigh. Her long blonde hair was heavy with sweat, but she ran with such speed that the strands splayed out behind her. Sweat and dirt soaked the torn blouse she wore. Wide brown eyes of fear glowed. Branches cracked while the woman made her way, darting in and out of the pine trees. The soft ground of the pine needles softened the sounds of feet trampling through the darkness.

She could sense something was following, hearing the branches crack in the distance behind her. She continued on her path through the woods and stumbled on a rock jutting out from the ground, falling to her stomach with hands spread and face staring at the ground. A wooden cross popped out from her blouse, and she grabbed onto it, squeezing it with all the strength she had.

"Oh please, God, please help me," she screamed.

She looked behind for any movement and heard a low growl moving closer. She let out a piercing scream and clawed her hands into the dirt, pushing her body back to her feet, and ran. Limping across the forest in desperation, she constantly looked behind her for any sight of that which followed her. The woman looked up into the dark sky, and lightning strikes filled up the forest with an eerie bluish glow. She grabbed the wooden cross and put it back into her blouse close to her heart. Dark brown eyes clenched tight while her dry cracked lips seemed to whisper for help.

She continued on the path, which started a slight incline upward. Wiping sweat from her eyes, she smeared the dirt on her face and clothes. Lightning strikes again gave her images of the forest, but shadows lurked everywhere now. The branches swayed back and forth, but it wasn't the wind that moved them now. Thunder echoed through the canyon, swallowing the sound of what was behind, but this didn't comfort her now.

"Ahhhhhh!" She screamed. "P-p-p-please . . . someone help me!"

She ran, not quite sure if she could sustain this pace, chest heaving and gasping for breath. She knew she must though, because whatever was behind her was getting closer. Deep inside she sensed it, and shivers ran up and down her spine. Like the thunder that erupted and echoed through the trees, the thing behind was getting closer with every step she took. Up ahead through the trees was a dim light. "Oh my God, please help me!"

No answer.

The forest remained silent except for the continual cracking of branches and trees behind her. She ran toward the light, an orange glow barely discernible between the trees, with long shadows moving slowly one way and the other. Stumbling and running through the heavy brush, she saw the light more clearly now. There was an old cabin with a light on the side near the door covered with cobwebs.

"Help me!" she screamed again.

A roar came from behind, and she fell to the ground, screaming at ear-piercing levels in the empty forest. She was shaking and could barely move. Then she started to kick and shuffle along the needle-covered floor of the forest. "Someone help me!" She struggled this time to get up, only to fall again. "Oh my God, help me!" She got up, and streaks of tears ran down her face, making small trails along the dirt on her skin. She started to run toward the cabin, knowing that could be her only hope.

She reached the cabin and grabbed for the door, which was old but solid and had a wooden handle on it shaped in a sideways U. She grabbed the handle and pulled but it didn't budge. "Oh God, please open!" She tried again but to no use; the door still didn't budge. With trembling hands, she began to pound the hard wooden door, whipping her head back to keep an eye out for what was behind. Fingernails scraped downward, leaving claw marks on the door.

She screamed in total exhaustion and fear, "Noooooooooo!" She leaned her head back and arched her body, sensing that whatever was following her was now almost upon her. Any hope she may have had was now almost entirely gone.

She looked around the cabin for any kind of help, movement, or life. There was none. She peeked into the window to see what she could find. Maybe she could break the window, but what good would it do? She could get in, but so could the thing that lurked behind her. There must be a better way. She needed to open the door. Peeking in the window, something caught her eye above the window ledge. It was small and full of dirt, but it looked like "A key!"

She ran back to the door, dirty hands fumbling with the key, found the keyhole, and placed the key in the slot. "You're in luck, Cindy." Pushing the door open, Cindy jumped inside the dark cabin and slammed the door with her back now pressed hard against it. Breathing heavily, her chest heaved up and down and her eyes were clenched tight. She waited. She tilted her head back and began to pray, hearing nothing now but silence.

"I'm safe, I'm safe," she whispered to the silence and darkness of the room.

Lightning strikes briefly revealed a table and some chairs in the dark room. It was brief so she wasn't able to see much, but it seemed like there were shelves and storage as well. Thunder rolled, shaking the small cabin. Cindy felt it with her hands pressed to the door.

"I'm safe," she lied to herself, once again listening for evidence of the beast outside. The door slammed against her body and knocked her sprawling to the ground. "Oh no, you're not going to get me, you bastard."

Cindy threw herself back up against the door, found the latch, and turned it to lock the door. The door slammed again, and this time it made a cracking sound. Cindy was thrown back again, but this time she was still standing. She dug her feet into the ground, pressing back to the door with all her weight—all 118 pounds of her. Both hands pressed to either side, she hoped to keep the door shut. The room was dark and, other than some lightning—which lit it every so often—it was hard to see, so she slid her hand up and down the side, trying to find a light switch.

"Come on, give me some light, God!"

By some small miracle her hand slid over a switch, which she flicked on. Luck seemed to be on her side tonight, and maybe God was as well. She was going to need him now. A small light over the center of the cabin revealed the single room in a very dim yellow light. As she briefly saw before, there was a table with some chairs, a cabinet with some boxes and other items, and a few crates here and there thrown randomly around the room. The door itself had a couple of metal hooks to lock it in place. All that was needed was a bar to slide through the hooks.

"Where the hell is it?" she asked no one but herself in the empty room.

The obvious place, of course, was right next to the door, but nothing was there except a broom. The door banged again with a slam of the beast, and Cindy started to cry again. Trembling with her weak body pressed against the door, she was tired and wanted to give up. She slowly slid down the door when she saw it.

"The bar!" She started to reach for it but found her body leaving the door. As if the beast on the other side knew this, he hit the door with more force than before. Cindy was quick to hold it shut, placing her back again to the door.

"Fuck you!"

Crying and trembling, she reached one hand out to get the bar. Her arm was shaking and her fingers stretched, just barely able to touch it. The bar moved just enough to tilt and then fell to her hand. Quickly she pulled it close to her body, holding it like a good luck doll, and then turned and slammed it against the door, chipping it before slamming it in the hooks that bolted the door. Cindy took a step back, staring at the door.

"Fuck you," she repeated and then raised her right hand and flipped it off with her middle finger. "F-f-fuck you." She couldn't help but laugh hysterically at herself.

There was another slam against the door as wood splinters shot out from the door, but it actually seemed to hold better now. The door was hit two more times, but the bar held it firmly in place. She heard a growl from the outside that was almost deafening. The door slammed inward again and then there was silence. Cindy backed away with both hands held up, as if she were holding it magically shut now.

"Fuck you and all your friends, you bastard." Then she sat down against the wall, curled up in a ball, and hoped the door would hold.

"Please hold for me." Tears welled up in her eyes again. "Please, oh please, oh please . . ." she repeated over and over again. She started to shake uncontrollably and put both hands up against her face, covering her eyes. She felt the wall press against her back, then there was silence.

Cindy opened her eyes and tried to look around the cabin, which suddenly seemed slightly larger than before. On one wall were some tools hanging from hooks. There was a workbench with some rope, more tools, and quite a few empty beer cans. The floor was made of old creaky wood, and there was an old sink in the corner of the room, stained an orange beneath the pump.

Cindy stood up and walked toward the workbench, carefully taking one slow step at a time—as if the floor was made of glass. Watery green eyes judged every shadow in the room. Walking past the window, she caught a glimpse of two large green eyes with long slits of black peering in on her.

"Oh shit!" she screamed and nearly jumped to the ceiling, covering her mouth.

The eyes disappeared from view. She dropped to the floor and pressed her back hard against the wall. She shuffled her feet, as if to move farther and farther into the wall. There was now silence, except for her own voice, which mumbled meaningless words. Time seemed to stand still while she stared at the small fogged-up window, where moments ago the eyes of the beast appeared.

The glass above her shattered with a hairy arm smashing through it, curling and clawing at nothing. Still staring at the window across the way, Cindy was slow to realize there was another window above her. Large curved claws—the size of the pruning shears Cindy used to cut the roses in her garden just the other day—reached for Cindy and slashed her arm in one quick swipe. Blood splattered against the wall as the claws continued to reach for her.

Cindy backed away from the window in pain, holding her bloody arm. She staggered, watching the claws grab blindly for her; yet, it seemed to sense exactly where she was. She backed up against the opposite wall and knocked over some tools. She looked down and saw a shovel and a couple rakes. She grabbed the shovel with her clawed-up right arm and dropped it in pain.

"Ahhhh, damn it!" she screamed as the blood continued to drip from her arm.

She picked up the shovel again—with her left arm this time—and carried it close to the window. The sleeve of the shirt ripped and the blouse tore, revealing more of her cleavage than normal. A soft light highlighted her dirty, bloody, and torn body gasping for breath.

"You son of a bitch." Scared, she felt the warm blood drip down her arm. She hated the feeling of being chased and hunted by some wild beast like an animal. Raising the shovel with both arms in pain, she took a swipe at the claw, hitting it direct on the top of the paw.

The beast roared again, and Cindy covered her ears. It retreated for a few seconds and then came back again, pawing.

"Damn you! Leave me alone!" she screamed. Lifting the shovel, she whacked its arm a little higher this time, and blood flew against the wall. The beast roared again and retreated. Cindy backed up to another wall this time.

Once again there was silence.

Holding that shovel with both hands tightly, she crouched over and stared at both windows. The wind was howling through the broken window, which now had shards of glass hanging from it and the blood of the beast dripping beneath. Lightning cracked, lighting up the room, and thunder followed shortly after, but otherwise there was nothing but silence. The silence continued for what seemed like hours but was only a minute or two. Seconds seemed like hours and minutes seemed like days. Cindy wished it was day now and the beast was gone. She watched the window, waiting for the claw to come back . . . knowing it would come back.

"I'll whack you again, you son of a bitch!" she yelled at the window.

Silence.

Sometimes the worst thing to do to a person is be silent, and Cindy now understood why prisoners were placed in solitary confinement. It was very quiet now. Even the storm seemed to be moving on. The wind had died, and the lightning was moving farther and farther away. Thunder was no longer one count of one thousand but maybe three or four counts away. Silence is sometimes the scariest thing there is. Was he out there still, or had he gone? She knew better.

"You son of a bitch. You come in here and I swear to God I'm gonna kick your fucking ass!"

Silence messed with her mind. Cindy was sitting up against the wall with the shovel in one hand when it happened. The window to her right shattered into a thousand pieces. The beast leaped in with the shards of glass surrounding him. Cindy tried to defend herself. She gave it one more valiant effort. She swung the shovel around with both hands, striking the only light in the room. With a small pop, the bulb shattered. Darkness again consumed the cabin, and the beast tore Cindy to pieces. She let out one final scream but never really knew what had happened. The glass shattered, and the beast was on her so fast there was really no time to react. The claws dug deep into her neck, like a hot knife through butter, ripping her jugular as blood spewed across the room in the dark. She grabbed for something to hold and pull herself away from the beast when his teeth, large and white, sunk into her neck. Staring into the darkness, her eyes were wide with terror and her mouth opened to scream. Silence has a funny way of being dangerous. Blood spit from her mouth when she tried to scream, and the beast closed its jaws, crushing her neck. The beast let out a growl that witnesses later said they heard from a couple miles away.

Her body lay limp on the wooden floor as blood emptied from her and flowed into a nearby drain. Her eyes were wide open. The clawed creature left her body to the scavengers of the night and was never seen again.

All was silent now.

# KITTY CAT

As Michael drove the blue Taurus through the old town, he passed the streets of the old buildings. There was Jack the barber and Tommie's Liquors, which was right next to Tommie's Bar and, of course, Tommie's Restaurant. The middle of small-town America was just an hour outside Chicago. Walking along the sidewalks from shop to shop, people carried bags of items from the stores they frequented. Some of them just hung out at places like Tommie's, wasting the afternoon away.

Michael drove five minutes outside of town to a smaller subdivision that was sparsely landscaped. Large subdivisions with fancy names, like Chateau Versailles, sat in the middle of the cornfields. They had gates or flowers at the main entrance. Traffic was bumper to bumper and moving at a snail's pace, choked off by the few roads that serviced the area. A large flat stone chiseled on the sides, standing erect with the words "Rolling Hills" etched on the face, stood at the entrance to Michael's subdivision with some pretty red flowers surrounding it. The land around there used to be nothing but farmland about ten years ago when, like wildfire, homes started sprouting up everywhere. One after another they all looked the same, sometimes confusing even the owners.

Michael's house sat at the end of the cul-de-sac, with toys scattered everywhere on the front lawn. The car bumped over the curb, and Michael made a wide turn around a child's motorized truck in the middle of the driveway. Balls of every type, including a soccer ball, were dispersed across the lawn. He pulled the car into the garage in between Jenny's minivan and another car covered in the alcove to the left.

There beneath the tarp sat a car given to him by his dad. Pulling away the tarp—like he did most days after work—he revealed a 1966 blue Ford Mustang Shelby GT. Two white stripes ran down the middle of the car with a scoop poking up in the middle of the hood. Running his hand along the side of the car, Michael felt the waxed surface. A white stripe running along the bottom of the car displayed the words "GT 350" on it. Another scoop at the bottom of the door ran into the back, and there was a sloped back window on this two-door car. Michael was always telling friends the car was the cat's meow.

He stepped into the house, smiling at the beautiful silhouette of Jenny highlighted by the light shining through the window. Her blonde ponytail swished back and forth; she did not notice the sound of his footsteps. He noted the kitchen table was set for three and a nice glass vase was in the center with cut flowers of red and yellow.

"Hey, babe." Michael smiled.

"Hey, you," Jenny replied without looking. She kept cutting up the potatoes.

He could hear the sound of the television in the family room, playing SpongeBob SquarePants. He was certain their television was broken because that show was on twenty-four hours a day. A character called Mr. Krabs, a large red crab with a chef's hat, was talking to SpongeBob, the main character—a square yellow sponge with brown pants—and Squidward, a light-blue squid.

"I smell the smelly smell of something that smells smelly," Mr. Krabs said.

Michael's son, JR, was sitting with his eyes glued to the television. Michael was proud of his son and smiled as he watched him bob his head up and down, laughing at the show. JR sat with his back to the kitchen in bib overalls, bare feet, and short brown hair. Michael laughed, so proud to be his dad.

"Squidward, you're steaming. You're like a steamed vegetable, only smarter," SpongeBob said.

JR started to laugh at the television, pointing at it with one raised finger. "Mom."

"So what are you going to do about our little visitor?" Jenny asked.

"Visitor? Does it have anything to do with all the toys outside, or have we decided to open up a toy store for the neighborhood?" Michael responded.

"Well, maybe you should pay a little more attention to your family and stop worrying about our neighbors," Jenny retorted sarcastically.

"I was just saying. I mean, I could hardly make it in the garage without nearly running over Johnnie's little scooter next door. Boy, aren't you a little touchy?"

"I have been working all day around here. I have been making dinner for you, and I have a million things to do afterwards." Jenny's voice became more boisterous.

Michael thought it better not to respond anymore and just go do his thing, but this was still his big day and she wasn't going to ruin it. "You should be happy for me. I just got the promotion I was looking for."

"Promotion?"

"Yeah, babe. A promotion!"

"So you'll be working more, I take it?"

"Aw, Jen, come on. This is—"

"Yeah, I know, I know. I heard this all before. We'll be living it up in fat city before we know it." Jenny stared down and started to slam the knife hard into the potatoes. She was killing the potatoes. Michael was happy he wasn't one of them, but he did a double take, swearing his face was on one of them.

"Jen—"

"What ever happened to your dream, Michael?"

"Jen—"

"You love the stars. It's what we always dreamed about."

"Jen, come on. You know I can't make a living staring at the stars."

"We can figure things out. I have a job now, and we could sell the house."

"Aw Jesus, Jen! What about JR?"

"What about him? It wouldn't hurt him to see his dad around more."

"Come on, babe. I am just being a realist. Astronomers don't make money, and you know Chicago isn't exactly the stargazer's heaven." This was, of course, very true. The lights from the city were so bright it made it very difficult to see more than half the stars in the sky. The entire horizon was lit up from the city and extended its fingers far out to the suburbs, like Crystal Lake and others.

"What happened to those days when you and I would just lie in the grass at night and dream? I loved those days, Michael."

"We were young, Jen. Dreams don't bring food to the table or a roof over our head."

"Just go change, Michael. I told you, we have a cat trapped under the deck and we have to do something." She shooed him off with her hand without looking up. Michael attempted to ask about the visitor, but she kept waving him off. And with that big knife in her hand and the Italian blood she had mixed with a little Irish, there was no way Michael was questioning her now.

"All right, babe, I'll see you in a few."

---

"You didn't feed the thing, did you?"

Jenny looked at him oddly. "I gave it a bowl of milk to try and coax it out, but so far the cat's still under the deck. Why?"

Michael just shrugged it off. "Nah, it's nothing. Just something Franklin told me today. You know Franklin."

In the background the news was on the television. The voice of a newscaster announced, "The police are unable to confirm the identity of the woman at this moment, but we'll keep you updated as soon as we hear more about this gruesome attack. Reporting live to you from Meramec State Park, Missouri—"

"Don't tell me you're starting to listen to the guy."

"No, like I said, it's nothing. All right. Time to get to work. Come, Max!" Michael shouted and opened the door to find the dog outside.

Max—a big, black two-year-old Lab with big paws and floppy ears—came leaping through Jenny's flower garden with his tongue dangling to the side. Michael's eyes went wide as he trampled the flowers in the bed. "No, Max, no!"

Michael held both hands up, trying to stop Max, but it was too late. Max faithfully rubbed up against Michael's leg and then sat at attention to one side. "Good dog, Max." Michael patted his head with both hands, feeling the soft fluff of the dog's hair in his hands, and looked around hoping Jenny didn't see her flowers trampled.

The deck was raised and made of wood, spanning half the length of the house. A grill in one corner had a sign above it—"On the rocks at Merlino's deck"—with a large margarita glass in the middle of it. A couple steps from the yard, the cat was poking out its head from a hole.

"Meow."

"Over here, Max!"

Michael pointed down into the slats between the deck boards. The dog sniffed, making loud noises with his nose, and paced back and forth, trying to find the source. He wasn't trained to look for a cat, but Labs had a natural instinct for using their nose to find things, and Max was very good at it. He barked, and Michael pointed again down to the deck.

"A cat. Get him, Max." The dog barked again.

"What are you doing?" It was Jenny, and she was laughing, but at the same time she was a little distraught.

"We're getting the cat. What's it look like?"

"Don't you dare hurt that cat! Poor thing is just a baby and probably misses its mother."

Michael rolled his eyes and took a deep breath, leaning down to peer under the deck to see what he could find. Did she want him to get the cat or not? There was movement, but it was dark and he couldn't see much at all. The dog was over him sniffing, and his front paws started to scratch at the deck. Max knew there was something down there.

"Well, how do you think we're going to get him out of there?" Michael asked.

"Just don't hurt him."

Jenny turned to Max, leaned down, and began to pet his head, pulling it back and forth. "Oh, you're such a good boy, yes you are."

Max dragged his big wet tongue across Jenny's face. "Ew!"

"Can we get back to work now?" Michael was laughing.

"Just don't hurt the thing." Jenny wiped her face and stepped back inside.

Beneath the deck green eyes stared out from the darkness. A head peeked out, opening its mouth to meow and baring small sharp teeth. It had a small pink nose and soft yellow fur with black stripes running up and down its body. A patch of white in the middle of its body could be seen before it retreated back beneath the deck.

The hunt was on for a while as he ran back and forth across the deck unsuccessfully. Michael poked at it with a stick, and the dog barked. The cat hissed, trapped in a dark corner with two large beasts hovering above it. The two of them were in their element, a man and his dog hunting for a cat.

Frustrated and unable to lure the cat out, Michael took a break and sat on a chair nearby; Max sat faithfully at his side. He needed a plan, because this cat was not coming out as long as a large man and his barking dog were hanging about.

Silently the cat crept out, seeing a chance to break away from the madness. It leaped out from beneath the deck and ran around the corner of the house.

Adrenaline seems to flow through a man's veins when a chase is under way. Bolting upright, Michael and Max stormed after the cat. They chased it around the corner of the red-brick house to the newest hiding spot inside the garage. The dog trampled through the bushes, and Michael leaped off the deck.

The cat managed to find its way along the side of the garage. The dog barked, knowing exactly where the cat was hiding.

Michael lay down on the concrete floor of the garage, feeling dirt and grease slide across his palms. His view was clear beneath the Boss, and he could see the cat hiss at him and then leap up inside the engine.

"Damn cat."

Covered beneath a blue tarp, with hard curves screaming to move a hundred miles an hour, sat the Boss. Michael pulled off the tarp and stepped onto the seat, grasping the wheel. He could smell the age of the car. Vintage had an odor of old, worn vinyl and gasoline. The letters on the speedometer that read lengthwise were worn a dull white. The wooden steering wheel that he grasped with one hand was worn in the parts grabbed the most.

Sometimes during a chase, the adrenaline is flowing and there is not enough time to think things out. Michael turned the key in the ignition and, like thunder to one man's ears, the Boss rolled like Thor. The car rumbled and shook the entire garage in which it sat. His foot tapped the gas pedal a couple of times to goose the engine. Large billows of smoke spewed in the enclosed garage. Any unweary person would have leaped for cover. Instead, Michael was inside just smiling, rubbing a hand along the top of the dash.

"The Boss rules!"

Michael had a crazy idea that if he just started the engine this cat would come running. Instead something dreadful filled his mind. What if the engine started and the cat was so scared it leaped right into the fan?

"Aw shit!"

Clenching his eyes tight, he imagined all the cat guts and blood spewed everywhere, coating the entire chrome engine. Quickly he leaped out of the car and leaned over the engine again. Hanging on the tire by its claws was the cat. The cat was too high for Michael to reach. He needed another plan, so he decided it was possible to reverse the car just enough so the cat would do one of two things. Either it would be low enough to grab or it would run.

Quickly he leaped to the front seat of the Boss, again releasing the brake and dropping it to the floor. He grabbed the large Hurst stick, with one foot on the brake and the other on the clutch.

Shoving the stick into reverse and slowly releasing the brake, he moved to the gas pedal. In synchronicity he moved the two pedals, giving the car juice a couple times and spewing more exhaust into the air. The car shook to one side with each thrust of the gas, and then slowly he released the clutch and the Boss moved backward just a small amount.

Michael stepped out of the car—the Boss still purring and exhaust billowing from the tailpipes. Jenny was going to kill him if she walked out this very moment and saw the garage filling up with exhaust from the Boss. Closing the door he walked around the side of the car and stopped dead in his tracks. There at the bottom of the tire was the cat, still clutching to the tire.

The cat was upside down with its claws dug into the tread of the tire and its tail dangling down. The cat was dead as doornail, still clinging onto the tire with parts of its brain falling out of its skull. A small spot of blood pooled near the bottom of the tire, mixed with a small white blob of the cat's brains. One of the cat's eyes was bulging out, probably from the pressure of the car on its body.

"Aw shit! Jen's gonna kill me."

Putting the Boss in neutral, Michael rolled the car back about an inch or two so he could pick the cat up and dispose of it. With his hands on the side of the opened door, he pushed, leaned his body down, felt the tires rock back and forth, and then quickly reached back to lock the brake again.

"Guess I moved too far," he joked.

He reached up on a shelf and pulled out a large plastic garbage bag and a pair of leather gloves. The cat was still clung to the tire, only now its head was lifted from beneath the tire. Blood was already coagulating, but the brain was still poking out of its skull. With a gloved hand Michael grabbed the cat and placed him in the plastic bag, surprised at how light it actually weighed. Around the neck was a small red collar and a tag that read "Alfarav."

"What are you doing?" Jenny asked, standing at the door.

Michael froze, feeling all the blood drain from his body. Certain his face was as white as a ghost, he stood there before slowly turning around and trying very hard to smile. "Nothing, honey."

Jenny gave him a look he was certain was mistrust but smiled and said, "Dinner is served." He watched her step back inside and close the door.

"Woman. Damn, that was close." Michael laughed nervously, wiping the sweat from his forehead. He pulled off the gloves and pulled out the cell phone from his pocket. It rang a few times before there was an answer on the other side.

———

Dinner was set, with JR sitting at the head of the table in his high chair. Food was mashed all over, including his face and hands. Jenny sat across from Michael, and the two of them didn't look at one another. Of course, Michael didn't want to tell her of the cat being run over by the Boss.

"So did you find the cat?"

Michael looked up, about to tell her he killed it because that's what guys do to cats. "Uh, yeah." Then he decided maybe it wasn't such a good idea to tell her about the cat.

"And?"

"And the cat is gone." He didn't look at her, instead focusing on the food on his fork.

"So he ran off? Did he have a tag? Where did he go?"

"What's with all these questions, Jen? What am I, under investigation or something?"

Jenny was stunned, and things went silent for a moment until JR broke the silence. "Mom?"

Jenny looked to JR, wiped his face, and smiled. "You know, Michael, your work is getting to you."

Michael lowered his head and took a deep breath before looking up at her. "Jen? I got a raise today. I thought you would be happy." He stood up and looked at her, smiling because she was beautiful. Everything he worked so hard for was because of her and JR. He was confused by her attitude and felt something missing. "I need to do a couple of things. Then I am heading out to basketball tonight." And that was it. No talk about the job, no more talk about the cat—thank God for that—and no more talk about how unhappy he actually was with the way his life was turning out.

# Tomb

## July 19, 2008

Approximately two miles north of the Valley of the Kings, located in the Sahara Desert in Egypt, a large group of approximately fifty people was working near an excavation site. Vehicles—mostly beat-up, dusty, tan Humvees—were driving in and out of the site. They were carrying equipment to and from the site. The dust was stirring as these vehicles drove along the sandy roads, leaving plumes of dust in their wake. The sun was beating down on this clear, cloudless day. Luckily, it was only 9:00 a.m. and the temperature was barely over 100 degrees—not too hot considering it would rise to about 120 degrees by noon. There were five tents surrounding the site, four small tents and one large one in the center. Most of the activity appeared to be based around the center tent. The other four appeared to be equipment tents.

The center tent had workers moving in and out of it. Most of the workers were men dressed in long white dishdashas, which looked like long robes. Dishdashas—or thobs, as they are commonly called—are made of lightweight cotton and cover almost the entire body, down to the ankles, keeping the men comfortable in enormous heat. Some were also wearing a headdress, or ghutra¬—a white piece of cloth with a band, or igal, around the head, holding the ghutra in place. The men were carrying many items out of the tent. Some men were carrying boxes, and some were carrying what looked like stone monuments. There were vases, small statues, old tools, and what looked like silverware. There were plates and bowls. There were small vials and large ones too. Some of the vials looked like they actually still had some type of liquid inside. Some were even carrying out boxes overflowing with jewelry. Either men were carrying this equipment or it was being pulled by trucks. The men walked in a line to one of the other tents, where they seemed to be placing the items in a somewhat organized manner.

Most of the men coming out of the main tent were carrying what appeared to be mummies. The mummies were small in size and appeared to be some kind of small animal about the size of a cat. The men carrying the mummified animals split off from the men carrying the other items and walked to another tent. The men placed the mummies alongside approximately two hundred other mummies. All the mummies were what appeared to be cats or small dogs of about the same size. The mummies were nicely organized in rows, each with a piece of paper marking it with a number to keep track of how many, where they were found, and any other pertinent information they may have.

The entire scene seemed somewhat in disarray, with men moving one way or another. Huge lights spread around the scene on tall steel poles hovering systematically around the tents. Cables connected the poles and ran in and out of the tents. A closer look revealed a very organized method of the men placing items, such as vases and smaller, more fragile items, in one tent and jewelry in another. The men seemed to be following invisible lines in and out of the tents.

In the main tent were three men dressed in khaki shorts and beige short-sleeve shirts with beige floppy desert hats. These men were at a table, studying a map and directing some of the workers. One man's name was Marty McAndrews. He was the man in charge of the operation here.

Marty was in his late thirties and had a tinge of gray hair around the temples. He was clean shaven and was the type of person who acted with a bit of arrogance. He had round spectacles on his long face with brown eyes and brown hair. Standing six feet tall, yet weighing only 160 pounds, Marty was what some called gangly.

"I tell you the items in there are nothing compared to what is in that lower level," exclaimed Marty. He pointed to a spot on the map. "We need to blow that crevice open now. When is someone going to get that fan working over here?" He was sweating profusely, with his shirt wringing wet and dark with sweat.

"Marty, we are already treading on thin ice here, running this operation before going through all the necessary channels. We don't want to get too far without getting the proper paperwork," another man with an Egyptian accent replied. This man was in his late thirties or early forties; it was hard to tell, with the weathered face and the beard on the man. The other next to him, an Egyptian man as well, was in his late fifties or early sixties. He also had a long graying beard with dark skin. Both men had a look of concern on their faces. "I helped you with this excavation, but I can't let it get out of control."

"Mohamed, I thank you for your help, but we need to move quickly. You know that," Marty said.

"Yes, yes, I know, I know, but we can't take that risk now. We have already cleared out two of the five upper rooms and will probably have everything cleared by the end of next week. We are risking a huge penalty for this if we are caught," Mohamed replied.

"Mohamed, have I not taken care of you in the past? You know this is a huge opportunity for us, and I have always been able to cover the costs of their small fines," answered Marty in a very arrogant manner. Marty's history was one of being a pompous ass always able to get his way. With his money to back him, not many people could or would stand in his way no matter how foolish the situation may be.

"What is small to you is very large to most. We will continue, but you must realize that this is different than the other times, Marty. Your money will not be enough this time if we are caught, and we could lose more than just—"

Marty cut him off. "Let me worry about the details and keep this project moving."

"Oh, no, no, we mustn't, please, no," the other man exclaimed. He was begging Mohamed not to continue and seemed to be looking around to see if anyone was watching them. Holding his hands to his head, he pleaded with Mohamed.

"It's all right, Abdul. We will work it out." Placing his hands on Abdul's shoulders, Mohamed tried to calm Abdul down, whispering something to him in Arabic.

"But—" Abdul started and then looked up to Marty, quickly diverting his eyes back to Mohamed once again.

"It will be okay. Let's get this moving," Mohamed reassured.

"Agreed," said Marty, clapping both hands together and then rubbing them back and forth. Marty and Mohamed shook hands and continued the planning. Abdul stood to the side in disbelief, shaking his head.

Men continued to move in and out of the tent with items from the dig. Mohamed barked orders to some of the men as they carried items to one of the tents. "You must mark that before any items are moved." Mohamed watched the men bow and go back the way they came. "If we keep this up we are going to have a heck of a fine."

"We will be fine, Mohamed, don't worry," Marty reassured.

Mohamed looked at Abdul and then yelled for his men to move faster. The Egyptian government was very strict and efficient when it came to keeping the reins on illegal digging. He had a worried look on his face.

A closer look at the tent revealed a small hole on the side of a sand dune. The amazing thing was that this hole had not even existed two weeks ago. There was a huge sandstorm two weeks ago that apparently blew away enough sand so that one man happened to stumble upon it. He was studying a tomb near the Valley of the Kings when he decided to take a little detour.

# SHAWN

It was late when Shawn arrived. The moon was full, lighting up the entire neighborhood and setting off an eerie glow. Slowly he pulled up in his old four-door, faded-yellow Chevy that rumbled and spewed smoke out the exhaust—not quite the same rhythmic sound as the Boss. The word "quiet" took another meaning. Most of the lights in the neighboring houses were turned off except for a few. A couple lights did turn on, however, when Shawn's Chevy rumbled down the street with no headlights on. One hand was wiping the front windshield to clear the dew so he could see out the window. Shawn was bent over, peering out the one small clear spot and trying to maneuver down the street. He wore a black leather jacket and a dark baseball hat, trying his best to be inconspicuous.

———

The neighbors hardly noticed Shawn's car driving through the neighborhood but would later recollect the backfire noise a little differently.

The Sullivans were watching the movie *Die Hard* with Bruce Willis for the eleventh time, because it sounded so good on their new surround-sound speaker system. Dan nudged his wife, Lucy, when the gunfire shot back and forth on the screen, feeling the force and not knowing it was actually Shawn's car causing it. "That's some surround sound, isn't it?" Lucy looked up to the ceiling and then shoved Dan a couple times. "It sounds like an earthquake. That better not be my china."

41

The Perwinkles were in bed sleeping when the exhaust popped outside their window. Tommy was lying on his back with his mouth wide open, snoring, and his wife, Betty, had earplugs and a blindfold on. The Perwinkles were used to their son Joey coming home late and making noise.

The Martinsons were lying in bed, watching the news, when they were certain they heard the gunshot. The news was covering a story about gangs in the community and showing clips of drive-by shootings in Chicago, which was a far ways from Crystal Lake. Paul worked in the city and swore he heard gunshots from miles away many times before and would confirm it when he watched the news. Paul had extrasensitive hearing, but it was Holly who heard the exhaust backfire that night. She asked, "Was that gunfire?"

Outside the neighborhood was quiet, and other than the natural light of the moon, everything was very dark. A couple dogs could be heard barking back and forth at each other from another neighborhood far off in the distance. Deer were making way to one of the nearby farmlands to eat their evening dinner. Raccoons and opossums scavenged around in search of a meal. The sound of Shawn's car backfiring scattered many of them.

---

Earlier in the evening Shawn was watching the Cubs game with a Bud Light in one hand and the remote in the other. He wore number twenty-three on his Cubs uniform, which was unbuttoned partially with the word "Chicago" split apart. He was a young man freshly out of college, still living that kind of life. This was beer number ten for him; he was just getting warmed up for the evening. The rule was one beer per inning, and he wanted to stay ahead in case of extra innings. His wife had left him alone over an hour ago, telling him to grow up. He was shouting at the TV about the Cubs blowing another game to the Cardinals when the phone rang.

"Hewo." He had a mouthful of food, spewing chips while he talked.

"Code red. I say code red." Michael was joking, but Shawn knew this was something they needed to talk about now.

"Wuz up?"

"Shawn? Get yer ass over here now!"

"Uh, Michael? Is that you?"

"Yeah, it's me, dumbass. Get over here quick." He paused and then added, "And don't tell anyone!"

"Tell anyone what?" Shawn burped in the phone.

"You're drunk, aren't you?"

"No, I'm not . . . drunk." He burped again.

"Aw shit!" There was silence on the phone, but Shawn paid no attention, munching on some chips until Michael finally continued. "Just get over here and I'll explain later. Leave your headlights off, and I'll signal you."

"What the fuck, Mich—" He crumbled up the bag of chips.

"Just get over here now!"

"All right, all right, just give me ten."

"All right, sounds good, but be quiet!"

Shawn hung up the phone and took one last drink of his beer, draining what was left. He stood, clicked the remote, and swayed a bit. "Fucking Cubs." The room was a mess, with a few empty beer cans and a bag of chips lying on the table.

Shawn was the younger brother of Jenny and still living like he was in college, even after most of his friends had moved on. "Tonia? I have to see Michael for a minute. I'll be back soon, hon," he shouted up to his wife. He grabbed some clothes to disguise himself, thinking of this as some sort of secret operation.

———

Shawn was driving down the neighborhood road, being "quiet" with the rumble of his Chevy. He leaned over the dash to get a better look in the dark with no headlights on. It was bad enough driving in the dark, nearly hitting several deer on the way. Shawn somehow missed them, not knowing they were even there. Luckily no one saw the way he swerved across the white line in the middle of the road. He reached over to the passenger side and grabbed a handful of chips, tossing them to his mouth while he looked for the signal. Then it came, and Shawn spewed out some crumbs. "Michael!"

Michael was hanging on the side of the house with a flashlight in his hands, crouching down against the house with a plastic bag in one hand. When he heard Shawn rumbling down the road, he took the flashlight and blinked it several times, giving him the signal. The two of them were like kids, acting like they were on some sort of secret mission.

Shawn pulled up, as instructed, coming to a stop at the curb, the brakes squealing. Michael ran up to the car, and Shawn rolled the passenger window down. "What's up, Michael?" he shouted, trying to speak over the loud exhaust of the Chevy.

"Shhhhhh!"

"Okay, okay, but just tell me what's going on."

Michael looked around, making sure there wasn't anyone around. It was a quiet little neighborhood, but you couldn't be careful enough. Slowly he pulled up the plastic bag that held the dead cat and the remains inside. Again Michael looked around and then set it on the floor of the passenger seat.

"Dead cat." He pointed a finger at the bag.

"Dead cat?" Shawn shouted again.

"Jesus! What do you know about the word 'quiet'?"

Shawn just shrugged and took a sip of his beer.

"Oh my God! Give me that!" Michael grabbed for the beer can, spilling some on the lap of Shawn. "Now get rid of that thing and I'll explain later."

Shawn shook his head and stepped on the gas, letting out a loud rumble of his car. "All right, man." He waved, pulled the window up, and drove away. Michael was crouching down, waving both hands to stifle the noise and shaking his head. Shawn drove down the road about a block before turning on the headlights. Reaching back with one hand on the steering wheel, he grabbed another beer and then flipped on the radio. Tires squealed at the entrance as the car turned onto the main road and the engine roared. A hand reached out the window, tossing an empty beer can in the air, which bounced several times. Shawn was still in his youth, and rock and roll was what it was all about. He flipped on the radio, cranking the volume and shaking the car inside. Between the loud music and the exhaust popping, this ride was anything but quiet.

There weren't many cars on the road when Shawn turned left out of the subdivision and headed north. The forest preserve was just to the right, which would be a perfect spot to leave a dead body in a plastic bag. The radio was turned on to a local sports channel, and the newscasters were telling everyone to wait until next year for the Cubs. Shawn leaned his head back, took a swig of the beer, and then looked down to the radio. "Hell, they should have given up a hundred years ago." The car swerved over the center line—not that Shawn was drunk, of course, but he was busy listening to the sports talk. "Shit!" Grabbing the wheel with both hands, he spilled beer everywhere. He dabbed the seat with a dirty rag after saving the rest of his beer.

The plastic bag with the dead cat inside was lying on the floor of the passenger seat when it moved. The first time was not much; it seemed like the bump in the road just jostled it, even if the bump wasn't very big. The second and third time there were no bumps in the road and the bag seemed to move more like something inside was trying to get out. "What the hell?" Shawn looked down at the bag, and it stopped. His eyes shifted between the road and the bag while he held a beer in one hand. The bag didn't move again. "Just the bumps." He took another swig of his beer. "Damn, this stuff is good."

It didn't take long to find the spot of the forest preserve alongside the road. He slowed down the Chevy to make sure there wasn't anyone around. Shawn didn't want anyone to know about this, so he had to make the same assurances. He constantly looked left and right and in his rearview mirror before making a sharp turn off the shoulder. Quickly he turned off his car and leaned back in his seat, relaxing. He was safe. He took a long sip of his beer, downed the last few drops, crushed the aluminum can with one fist, and tossed it out the window. "Ah." Shawn hadn't noticed the lights of his car were still on, shining so brightly straight ahead, when a car was heading toward him. He sat there smiling, looking at the car and figuring the driver couldn't see him. That is, until the car drove past him and he was looking straight at them and they were looking straight at him. He shouted again, fumbling for the lights of his car to turn them off. "Shit!"

Reaching over the passenger seat to grab the cat in a plastic bag, Shawn started to laugh and lifted it in his hands. "What the hell is with this cat?" He sat upright and opened the door, stepping out into the darkness and looking both ways. No one was in sight, and thank goodness for the dark clothes he wore. This was, after all, a recon mission or whatever they called it in the special forces, Shawn thought to himself. Hell, he was sorry he didn't break out the full camouflage for this secret operation.

The forest preserve was a small one, but it was a perfect spot to toss a cat in a plastic bag. Shawn would have dropped the cat to the side of the road, but this was after all a secret reconnaissance mission, or whatever they called it. He had to make sure no one saw it ever again, so he walked in about fifty yards instead and then tossed it in the woods. Mostly tall grasses and a few pine trees spread about. A couple larger elm trees with Dutch elm disease and dead branches hung up above. The ground was soft, with old pine needles and sparsely spread patches of grass in this part that no one other than maybe deer walked. The cat in the plastic bag landed about twenty feet farther in. "Well, that oughta do it." Wiping his hands clean, he turned back to the car.

Shawn sat back in the car and reached in his pockets suddenly panicking that he lost his keys. "Shit, shit, shit." He turned and looked up the hill into the dark forest, certain he was in for a long one. "Ah, hell." Resting his hands on the steering wheel, then his head as well, he honked the horn. "Shit!" Looking up, he noticed the keys sitting in the ignition and laughed to himself. "Well, if that don't deserve a beer." Grabbing a nice cool one in the back, he popped it open and took a large sip, with some of it dribbling down his chin.

The car rumbled once he started it, certain to scare any animals that were around. Black smoke spewed out of the exhaust, hidden by the darkness of the night. Shawn turned the lights on and pulled the car in gear. Spitting out the gravel beneath the tires, the car turned onto the road. Some lights were approaching, so he was quick to pull back on the road and drive away. He did his best to keep the car steady this time and not cross the white line in the middle. Hell, he could get a drink of beer after the car passed, he thought to himself.

Shawn drove home that night slightly drunk, weaving in and out of the lanes. Once he parked his car, somehow safely inside the garage, he told his wife, who yelled at him when he walked in the door, that he was called in on some sort of secret rendezvous mission. She rolled her eyes at him right before she tugged him to the bed, stripping his clothes off his body. The two of them had sex so he could, in his words, "work my buzz off."

—·······—

What Shawn didn't realize was that the car passing him was a police car, and the officer had been watching from a distance. It was a good thing he didn't toss another beer can out the window. The officer decided to let him go for now, hoping to discover what Shawn was up to. Had he known Shawn was drinking, things might have been different. *No probable cause,* he thought to himself, watching Shawn drive away in his rearview mirror. He spotted the license plate and called it in to the station.

"I have an old yellow Chevy, license number: Tango Alfa one zero two four niner."

Dispatch Officer Becky Tomlinson responded, "Got it, Steve." There was silence on the radio before the dispatcher came over again. "You know, you do have a computer in your car."

Steve Case put the mic down for a minute and stared at the computer on his dash. "I know that, Becky!" He shouted into the mic, "Just get me the info on it, would ya?"

"Roger that, Steve. The car belongs to a Shawn Williams."

"Great, just keep the info, would ya, Becky?" He pulled the car in drive.

"Roger that, Steve. Will do."

Steve, however, wasn't lucky having the late shift and following guys like Shawn, who left plastic bags of dead cats in a forest. He pulled up to the spot where Shawn had left, making a U-turn in the road, and stopped to get out and search. Pulling out a flashlight, Steve turned it on and walked up to the spot where Shawn had tossed the bag. It was very easy to find, being only about sixty yards from the road. He pulled out some gloves, because he didn't want to ruin the evidence with his own fingerprints.

The high-powered flashlight was locked onto the plastic bag with the dead cat inside, when it rustled about in the leaves. "What the hell?" Steve was quick to put his hand to the gun at his side, keeping the flashlight locked on the plastic bag. He waited a minute, but now the bag just lay there motionless in the leaves. "Just nerves," he told himself.

Leaning down carefully with the beam of his flashlight still held on the plastic bag, Steve reached for the bag with a stick, poking it several times. There was something inside, but what he didn't know was that curiosity killed the cat and satisfaction brought it back. The hand near the gun on his belt reached back and pulled out a small knife instead. A gloved hand poked the bag, gently piercing it with the sharp tip of the blade, and drew down against the ground tearing it enough to see inside. He pulled the bag apart with one end of his blade, and the flashlight lit up the body of the dead cat inside.

The cat was dead, all right, lying there stiff as a board with one eye bulging out and brain spewing out of one side of its head. Steve placed the knife back in its sheath and laughed to himself, wiping a small trickle of sweat from his forehead. "Phew. I really hate this night shift."

That was when the cat's head lifted and turned its head to meow and hiss at Steve. It took him utterly by surprise, and Steve fell back on the ground, dropping the flashlight. It was something Steve would never forget, because he was certain that cat was dead. It was dead. It was stiff and the brain was oozing out the side. The cat spat at him, and Steve swore his eye, the one eye the cat had left, was glowing green in the dark. Things happened quickly, and Steve reached for the gun on his belt, unloading his bullets into the tiny little cat. "Son of a bitch!"

# RELAND

Michael was lying on the couch, watching the Cubs lose to the Reds in the bottom of the seventh, eight to one. A bottle of Budweiser beer in one hand and the remote in the other, he was just relaxing before they headed out to the neighborhood party. The sound of the TV was muted, and music was playing something loud by Tom Petty. Michael's foot was tapping while he leaned back, taking another sip of the beer. Tom was shouting out the verse, "Yeah I'm free, free-fallin!" The Cubs were definitely free-falling late this season, and he muttered to himself, "Damn Cubs."

The news came on, and it was "Johnnie Schwartz, your place for sports." He was dressed in a blue sport jacket and a bright-yellow shirt. Thank goodness for vivid high-definition television today. "And the Cubs are about to be mathematically eliminated from the playoffs."

"Up yours, Johnnie." Michael changed the channel to the soothing sounds of cartoons.

JR was sitting on the floor dressed in a Cubs uniform. Wearing a diaper, he was playing with a baseball and rolling it around in circles. "Mom." His lower lip came up, pressing outward after he said it repeatedly. It sounded more like "Mum" when he spoke, and his body raised when he did, bouncing back on his diaper like a cushion. JR would pick up a hand and point to the television when Michael flipped the channel and looked at him. "Mom."

Shaking his head back and forth, Michael pointed to himself. "Dad." He repeated "Dad" several times, pointing to himself and speaking really slow. "Daaaaaaad. Daaaaaad. Dad. Dad."

JR looked at him, silently tilting his head to one side and taking in every word. The first word and the one word he knew so well was "mom," but not yet had he said "dad." JR was looking at him, about to speak, and Michael could tell the time had come. He leaned over with eyes wide, staring at JR and JR staring at him. Michael held out an open hand, and his index finger flexed back and forth. "Dad?" He waited with bated breath.

"Mom." JR smiled.

"Ugh," Michael groaned.

"Mom."

Reaching up with both hands grabbing his head, Michael let his hands slide down his face, covering his eyes. He peeked out, flexing his fingers wide, and looked at JR, who looked like he was about to cry. JR's lower lip was pressed out, pouting as if he was about to cry. Then he looked up to Michael and smiled, seeing his eyes peek out from his fingers. This brought a smile to Michael's face and he laughed, pulling his hands down to his side again. This was it. JR was going to say "Dad." He just knew it.

"Mom!"

At first he stared in disbelief, but reality hit hard and fast. Michael couldn't believe it and just fell flat on his back, laughing so hard, and shook around, rolling on the floor.

JR was laughing too, which only further instigated the whole situation, so JR just kept it up. "Mom, Mom, Mom," he said over and over with his lower lip pressed out.

Lying on his back laughing, Michael caught movement out of the corner of his eye. He pulled himself up to look at the window, and his laughter stopped as quickly as it had started. There on the ledge was a cat, looking very much like the one he had killed the other day. Before he could get a good look at it, the cat leaped down from the windowsill.

"Max?" The dog came barreling in, sliding on the floor to his master's feet. "Good boy, Max."

JR was watching the dog and his dad, laughing. Then he pointed and said, "Dog." His body bounced like a person with hiccups. "Dog."

"You know 'dog' too?"

"Dog!"

"You're kidding me," Michael said, shaking his head.

Patting his thigh for Max to follow, Michael opened the sliding door and pointed to the outside. "Outside, Max. Go get the cat." The dog looked at him and then the outside, with ears raised, almost like he understood every word Michael said. Sniffing his nose high in the air, Max took off running in the backyard. "Good boy, Max!"

Jenny was upstairs, getting ready for the party and looking as pretty as ever in skintight blue jeans and a yellow button-down shirt. She'd combed her long blonde hair and fixed a bow while sitting in a small chair before a mirror. She turned, hearing Michael shout from below, with an annoyed look on her face.

"Jen?" Michael shouted up the stairs.

"I'm almost ready, Michael."

"Hey, I was wondering. Any of the neighbors get a new cat lately?"

"I have no idea. Why?"

That one word hung there for an eternity. *Why?* A guilty conscience burned inside Michael as he thought back to the crushed skull of the cat. Hoping to sweep the rest of the conversation under the rug, he shouted back, "Uh, just wondering was all."

"I'll be down in a minute."

Michael felt his body sink into the couch as he waited for Jenny to come down the stairs. The television was on and the music still played, but his eyes were on the empty window. It was just a cat, but something just didn't sit right with him. There were no cats in this neighborhood, and now two cats suddenly appeared? He took a long drink of his beer, draining all of it, when Jenny appeared. He looked up and smiled at her. She was beautiful, and quickly the thought of the cat disappeared from his mind.

"Ready." Standing at the bottom of the stairs with one hand on her hip, she was more than beautiful, and Michael felt like the luckiest man there was.

YOU'RE INVITED!
ANNUAL ROLLING HILLS FESTIVAL
3 P.M. TILL WE DROP
PARTY TO BE HELD AT THE SULLIVANS', MARTINSONS', AND PERWINKLES'
CUL-DE-SAC
EVERYONE INVITED, INCLUDING KIDS
BYOB
ALSO? BYOF—THAT'S *BRING YOUR OWN FOOD* TOO.

"You have the invite?" Michael asked Jenny, closing the front door behind him.

"It's a neighborhood party, Michael. We don't need the invitation."

"Well, don't forget last year," Michael joked, and Jenny rolled her eyes.

Last year at the annual festival—which wasn't annual at all, being it was the first party of the neighborhood—they'd had some uninvited guests show up. The party started with just a few friends, gathering for a couple of beers in the front lawn. A few of the neighbors decided to join in, and next thing they knew, there was a party. A party of six people became a party of thirty or more. The music was loud, and most were drunk off their asses. Things were getting a little out of hand.

"Well, hopefully the police won't be showing up this time, and I don't plan on staying up late this time, Michael." Jenny gave him a look before smiling back at JR and tugged his hand. "Come on, JR."

Each of them carried something for the party. Jenny held a platter of cookies and brownies that smelled absolutely delicious. Michael was the drink man, of course, with a cooler in each hand. One was for the beer—and it was loaded heavily too—and the other cooler was filled with soft drinks and juice boxes for JR. Tagging along was JR, holding a small wrapped gift for the neighbors hosting the party. They had walked about a block, hearing the music blasting out some vintage Stones. A nice older couple sitting on their porch waved to them. The maples and oaks were all starting to change pretty colors of red and orange. The landscape was beautiful, and the grasses were still green. Even the temperature was warm for this time of year.

The party was a combined one of the three houses at the end of the cul-de-sac, which included the Martinsons, the Perwinkles, and the Sullivans. Tables were set up with red-and-white tablecloths covering each one and cute little clips shaped like pumpkins holding the corners so the cloths would not flap in the wind. The Perwinkles' house in the center had a larger table flanked by two huge stereo speakers, and Tommy Perwinkle's son Joey at the controls of the iPod blasted the music at ear-piercing levels. Everyone placed their food on a couple of the tables, and coolers of drinks were scattered all about. There were thirty to forty people at the party already, which was a good turnout. Thanks went to the Sullivans for putting up the crime scene yellow barrier tape running the width so no cars would drive down the street.

The Perwinkles were usually the life of the party, having decorated most of it. They were a fun couple in their late forties with three kids who loved to have fun. The apple never fell far from the tree. Their kids were in the police blotter on a monthly basis, but luckily it was never for anything too horrendous. "He was just having a little fun. Not as bad as some of the things I used to do as a kid," Tommy said of his son Joey.

Tall oak trees over a hundred years old surrounded the three houses. The homes were in one of the prettier parts of the subdivision, with a gentle rolling hill and the trees made for a pretty setting. Most of the land in the area was flat, but this part had one rolling hill—thus, the name for the subdivision, Rolling Hills.

The neighbors were a unique type of crowd. Half of them were yuppie types with small kids, and the other half were retired couples with all the kids gone. Most of the people at the party were, of course, the younger ones with either kids in their arms or a beer in their hands. The ones with a child in one hand and a beer in the other seemed to be drinking the most. The iPod was playing John Cougar Mellencamp, which really was appropriate for the scene. "Ain't that America, home of the free. Little pink houses for you and me." There weren't any pink houses, but this was about as American as it got.

"Michael!" Dan Sullivan was wearing a bright-red Hawaiian shirt and shorts. His shirt wasn't tucked in because it would only highlight the beer gut he had. Coincidentally, Dan held a beer high in each hand in salute to Michael for joining the party. Dan and his wife, Lucy, were both in their midthirties. Dan wasn't a drunk by any means, but he told Michael he was a "social drinker." Only on weekends and sometimes holidays or special occasions did he drink, but when Dan drank, he drank a lot. Food was part of the territory, because his theory was that if your belly was full, the beer would not affect you as much as it would with an empty stomach.

The Sullivans were neat freaks, to put it kindly. Everything in their house was meticulously placed, and not a speck of dust could be found. The carpet in the living room always had vacuum cleaner marks running back and forth, and if someone actually walked in there, Lucy would pull out the vacuum immediately to clean the carpet. Michael really thought this was odd. The kitchen was immaculate, not a crumb to be found anywhere. Even their cars were always shiny, and after a rain they would bring the cars to the local car wash. The yard was always perfect, like something you would see in *Home and Garden*. Lucy was a bit neurotic at times, following people into her house with a paper towel in her hand in case they left some dirt on the floors.

The men and women split up into two groups, like at a high school dance, and the kids decided that was a good idea, so they split up into the kids under ten and the kids over. The kids over ten were too cool to hang around with anyone, much less be seen at a neighborhood party, so they hung out in the Martinsons' basement smoking pot and drinking beer they stole from the coolers. The men stood around the fire, talking about the women and other women they didn't want their wives knowing they talked about. The women talked about their kids and the new shoes they bought.

Shawn showed up with his wife, Tonia, dragging a cartload of beer. "You guys need some brewskies?" he shouted, taking a sip of the one in his hand and dribbling some down his chin. Jenny had invited them to join the neighborhood party, knowing her sister-in-law could use some help. Tonia was a pretty girl, pregnant with their first baby. About six months into it, her belly was really showing. She wore a cute maternity skirt that was baby blue, because they knew the baby was a boy, and her long dark hair was curled up with a ribbon tied on top. She was cute as a button, and Shawn rubbed her belly for good luck, of course.

The women were sitting around a table laughing and drinking wine spritzers the Martinsons made. They were talking about their kids and how good they were at this sport or that. Tonia joined them, and all the women started asking questions about the baby. When was it due, and had she picked out a name for the baby? The spritzers were going down smoothly with that sweet taste of lemon.

"What's in this again?" asked Lucy Sullivan, rubbing her nose—a sure sign she was buzzed.

"Club soda, lemon, and lime," Holly Martinson told her.

"No. I mean . . ." Lucy lowered her head for a moment to burp and then pointed to the glass winking to Holly, "what's in it?"

"Club soda, lemon, and lime," Holly answered in an irritated voice.

Paul Martinson was an accountant for the Tyler Henderson and Lloyd firm in Chicago. Paul and his wife, Holly, were in their midforties, with their three kids all in high school and one in college. Michael thought their house was one of the prettier ones in the neighborhood. Well landscaped on the outside, it was the inside that most people never saw. Drapes on every window were always completely closed. Michael once told Jenny it was "creepy to have the windows closed all the time." All the doors were locked as well, so no one could go inside to use their bathrooms. Michael once overheard Holly telling a friend, "I don't want strange people using my toilet and having to clean up their urine and pubies on the seat." The truth was no one was ever allowed inside their house.

Krista Polinsky was dressed swankily and came fashionably late. She wore a black cocktail dress that exploited her cleavage, which wanted to bust out of the truncated dress. On her long, tanned legs were high-heeled shoes, which were hard to wear in the grass. She knew exactly what she was doing when she entered the party, smelling of perfume, and every man's head turned. She was very pretty with dark hair that fell across her shoulders and a black bow on top with large sparkly earrings dangling on either side. She had green eyes and a body with curves that just didn't seem to stop. A real estate agent who sold most of the people who lived in this subdivision their homes, she was always so friendly when it came to selling a home but was typically a rude person if you did not have something she needed.

Joey found some Van Halen on the iPod and clicked the button with Eddie Van Halen pounding on the guitar, but it was David Lee Roth's voice screaming, "Everybody wants some!" that made a few people laugh. "I want some too!" David would yelp like he did. "Whoa!" A few of the guys were too drunk to get it, but the women most certainly did, eyeing down their husbands. Joey was oblivious and started dancing, mouthing the words of the song. In his head, Joey was probably thinking he was David Lee Roth, and he held a microphone to his mouth just to prove it.

Jenny had a look of disgust, watching the way Krista pranced into the party. Michael knew Jenny's feelings and couldn't blame her one bit. Krista never accepted the two of them together, but to him it really didn't matter. He wished Jenny would understand that Krista was no threat to her. She was an old fling from before he met Jenny, and he wished it didn't bother her, but Krista had her ways of getting under a person's skin.

Krista gave Jenny a cold, cruel smile, narrowing her dark eyes with a slight twist of her lips. Michael watched the two react, shook his head, sighed, and rolled his eyes. Some things never changed, and Krista was always the bitch deep down inside.

Jenny stood with eyes still on Krista, giving her a small smile, and flipped her off with her middle finger raised. Michael burst out laughing and turned to see Krista huff and walk away. He was proud of Jenny and winked to her, seeing her give him a smile.

The Perwinkles thought it would be fun to have a few games this year at the party. They prepared some board games and a fortune-teller for fun. One by one each person at the party would go over and sit with the woman to reveal their fortune. An older woman was sitting with the fortune-teller now with a look of concern on her face. The fortune-teller was flipping over tarot cards on the table one by one. There was a glass crystal orb in the middle of the table, which the fortune-teller was waving her hands over, trying to peer into the future.

The men were all standing around a fire burning in a small circular stone pit. Paul Martinson placed another log on top of the heaving fire, because men wanted to see how big they could get a fire before it burned down everything. The flames sparked higher, and one of them joked, "Jesus, Paul! What are ya, a pyro or something?" They all laughed and drank, feeling a good buzz just like the rest.

Shawn was standing closest to the fire with a can of beer in his hand. It was his eighth beer, and the night was early. It wasn't that Shawn was a drunk, but this was their first baby and it meant responsibility. His pants were smoldering with a small trace of smoke actually coming off them, being so close to the fire. He tapped his own ass a couple of times, putting out the possible fire, and then went right back to drinking his beer again.

"Hey, Michael? You never told me what happened with that cat," Shawn blurted out without thinking and then turned both ways, trying to figure out what smelled like something burning.

The look from Michael could have killed. Michael turned back to Shawn and said, "Uh, I don't know what you're talking about, Shawn."

Shawn was not quite drunk this time but well on his way. "Oh, that's right. I'm not supposed to talk about it."

Jenny walked behind Michael, rubbing his shoulders softly, and all the men became silent. "You guys don't have to stop talking. There isn't anything I haven't heard." Each one of them froze, with eyes shifting back and forth at one another. Jenny screamed, "Shawn! Your pants are on fire."

"I know." Shawn had no idea what she was talking about, but he did step away from the fire.

"Michael? Why don't you come and get your fortune told. Come on, it will be fun." She leaned down, kissing him on the top of his head.

"Fortune?" He was nervous. Sometimes people were better off not knowing what the future held for them, but in Michael's case, he figured things were looking up. "Well, I don't really want to have everyone listening in on my—"

"Come on, it's private. No one has to know except you, okay?" She tugged his hand, pulling him up out of the chair.

"All right, it's not that I have anything to hide." He stood, hugged her, and kissed her lips.

Jenny laughed, pulling him along. "It's okay. Come, and I'll have mine done too."

So Jenny sat first with the woman under her little canopy of red and white to the side of the Polinsky house. The woman was dressed like a gypsy, with a ragged skirt and a large belt around her waist. The top was laced together, and the sleeves were puffy, leaving her shoulders bare. A scarf wrapped around dark, graying hair of the elderly woman. There wasn't a way to tell how old she was, but judging by the wrinkles of her face and the frail body of the woman, Michael figured she was probably in her late seventies or maybe eighties. There was a scent of mothballs in the air; either it was the woman's clothes, or that was just the way people smelled when they got old. At the table was a crystal ball, which was covered with a white cloth with tarot cards to one side.

"Greetings, I am Zara," said the fortune-teller. She motioned for Jenny to sit down, holding a hand out to the seat on the other side of the table. Reaching out for the cards with both hands and then lifting her gaze to Michael, she smiled genuinely to him. "If you would be so kind to give us some time alone, please?"

"All right, but be good. I'll be right around the corner," he warned playfully and winked.

Zara, the fortune-teller, shuffled the cards and stacked them to the side, talking to Jenny for about five minutes before starting. The two seemed to be in some deep discussion while Michael watched from the side, seeing Zara hold Jenny's hands a couple times. She would close her eyes and then raise both their hands high. Sometimes humming would come from the woman. She would flip over tarot cards and point to some of them. The fortune lasted for maybe fifteen minutes before Jenny turned to look at Michael and smiled, standing up and motioning for him to take her seat now.

Michael took a seat across from Zara, suspicious but committed to listen. "Ready."

Zara looked up to Michael, holding out her hands on the table with palms up and smiling to him. "Take my hands, please." Michael did as she requested, feeling her old, soft hands take hold of his and then squeeze them tightly in hers. "Now tell me your name and date of birth, please."

Michael could not help himself and laughed, tugging her hands back softly and looking up to her with a smile. He asked sarcastically, "Well, shouldn't you know that?"

"Michael . . ." She paused for a moment to look at the expression on his face. She took a deep breath and said, "You need to be open to me if you want this fortune."

There was a moment of uneasiness between the two, but it quickly faded and Michael smiled and winked at her. "Oh, sure. I get it. Jen told you my name. All right, my date of birth is March 2."

There was silence between the two while Zara slowly closed her hazel eyes and held Michael's hands softly in hers. Zara took a couple of long, deep breaths and seemed to be meditating while she held in the breath and slowly released each one. "A Pisces." Slowly Zara opened her eyes and looked to Michael. "You're a dreamer, and someone will remind you of that more than once very soon. A hard worker, but you have forgotten your real passion in life. A healthy person, and life was going very well for you up to a few days ago, wasn't it?"

So far Michael was still very suspicious about the great Zara, the fortune-teller, and her predictions until she told him about how his life "was" going well. "Actually it's going quite well, thank you."

Tilting her head to one side, Zara closed her eyes once again. "Mmhmm." She licked old wrinkled lips and leaned her head back, tugging Michael's hands about an inch above the table. "You have a beautiful family. Protect them, Michael. Time is running out. He comes from the shadows to warn you. Darkness is his form. Stay away from the other one. She is no good for you."

Zara the fake was what Michael was telling himself, now certain Jenny had put her up to all of this. "Oh, come on!" He pulled his hands back at her words, but Zara had a weird sense of strength for an older woman, and old wrinkled hands tightened around his. Zara's eyes remained closed. Michael's voice was getting agitated at the woman, and he tried harder now to pull his hands from hers. "I don't know what you are talking about. Jenny put you up to this, didn't she?"

"No!" Zara nearly shouted with a raspy voice so unlike the old woman who sat before Michael now. In fact, the voice was now that of a man, and those hazel eyes opened seemingly black as coal. "We will meet again soon." Hands of the woman squeezed Michael's tightly with the strength of a very large, strong man. "Reland," the voice inside Zara said, "you will meet me in Reland." Her dark eyes started to close, and the head and body of Zara swayed around her shoulders. Finally, the hands of Zara left Michael's, dropping hard to the table. Then she grabbed a pencil and paper to scribble a word. While she looked up and not at the paper while she wrote, the pencil seemed to have a mind of its own.

Michael leaped back out of his chair and stood while he stared at Zara, unsure what to think of all this. His heart was pounding, and his hands began to shake, so he stuffed them both in his pockets to hide them. Zara was slouched in her chair, seemingly unconscious now. There on the table was the paper with one word scribbled across it: RELAND.

Standing to the side was Jenny, not able to hear what was happening, so all seemed fine at the time. Her intention to bring Michael to see Zara was only to give herself and Michael some time together and something to laugh about. Never in her wildest dreams had she known what was happening. She saw Michael tug and pull and then stand up, with Zara falling back in her chair. She shouted and then ran over to his side. "Michael?"

Zara started to open weary eyes, which were hazel again, and rubbed them. "Well, I wish you luck." She smiled up to Michael before blinking a couple times. Michael turned and looked at Jenny and then back at Zara, shaking his head.

"Don't ask," he said with a look of frustration on his face.

"What happened?"

"I need a beer."

"Just tell me what happened, Michael." She turned to look at Zara, who sat there in her chair, totally oblivious to being in a trance and talking like some old creepy man just moments ago.

Michael walked over to his beer cooler and pulled one out, cracking the tab on top. The Budweiser can sprayed a mist with a small amount of foam on top. Then he tilted it back to his mouth, taking one very long sip. "Ah!" He wiped his chin and looked at Jenny, who was staring at him now with a worried look. "That woman is a quack."

"What did she say? Tell me, Michael." She stood there, taking his hand in her own.

Michael pulled his hand away and turned to one side. "She pulled this crap on me, changing her voice like she was another person. Told me to beware. Beware!" He held up both hands and spread his fingers, wiggling them now with his eyes as wide as could be, animating himself. He laughed, mocking Zara now. "Funny thing is I almost fell for that shit."

The two of them walked away with Jenny holding his side, and Michael put his arm around her. She leaned her head into his shoulder, and his hand softly caressed her head. They met back up with the neighbors, who were playing games at the fire. Grabbing a single seat, Michael sat first and then Jenny sat on his lap. His arms wrapped around her while the games between the neighbors went on. Everyone was laughing except for Michael, who couldn't get the voice or the warnings of Zara out of his head. Jenny was laughing but would turn and see the look on his face and then give him a big hug or pull herself closer to him. This seemed to settle things down for a while, taking the edge off Michael after his little experience with the fortune-teller.

It was getting late, and JR was now in Jenny's lap, falling asleep. "We're heading back to the house."

Michael was having fun, and the guys pulled him to the side to tell him he had to stay for another. "All right, Jen, I won't be long. Just going to have a couple with the guys."

She nodded and then kissed him. JR waved, barely lifting his tired head from her shoulders.

What Jenny did not see was Krista eyeing Michael down like a lion, waiting for its next meal. She sat with a couple of the guys from the party who dreamed of getting lucky with her, even while their wives were ready to kill the two of them. She was just nodding to the two men, not paying any attention at what was being said. A simple "mmhmm" or a smile was good enough for the two men. Cleavage was gushing out of her little dress, hypnotizing the two of them into a trance. "Excuse me, boys." Krista stood up, not even acknowledging either of the men were even there, and walked straight to Michael like a cat getting ready to pounce on its prey.

Michael had no idea what was coming when Jenny left him with the neighbors. He emptied a beer in his hand, and Tommy passed him another beer can. Holding the can in one hand, he flipped the tab on top to open it with one fingernail beneath it. Michael looked up and saw Krista making a beeline for him. If there wasn't smoke surrounding Krista, then there should have been, because this was like some weird dream to Michael now. The way she was walking toward him and the way she was looking at him was just so unreal. She knew he was married, and yet there she was, her long legs crossing one another almost catlike, and those hips swaying from side to side were just undeniable. The can of beer sprayed open with foam spilling over his hands.

"Hello, Michael." Krista smiled, standing before him in such an alluring way. The rest of the guys took notice, remaining silent and looking back and forth from Krista to Michael. A few of them sipped their beer, acting like the two of them were not even there, but all eyes and ears were on the two.

"Hello, Krista." He placed another log in the fire, which burned and crackled, and then stood and walked closer to her. The perfume on her swirled in the air, and long locks of dark hair curled over her shoulders. He stepped away from the fire, out of range from the others, and smiled up to her. "Good to see you again."

The two of them talked for about an hour alone under a large tree. Michael was excited about his new job and someone to talk to about it. She listened with interest, happy for him and wanting to know all the details. She then talked about herself, which she was good at once she started. She told him how she was number one in sales again. As she tugged her fingers in her hair and twirled them around, it was hard to concentrate, but he listened. The subject of his wife came up in an awkward way, but Krista was good at changing the subject immediately.

The full moon was low in the sky, lighting up the entire neighborhood. The two of them walked along the backyards of the subdivision till the music from the party quietly disappeared, needing no other light than the natural moonlight, which lit up a path for the two to follow.

# DISCOVERY

## JULY 2, 2008

Marty McAndrews had no idea what he was going to find that day. He was driving out to check a coordinate someone had given him as a reference to his studies near the Valley of the Kings. The drive took him a little ways off the main road, which was not like any road the average person would know. The roads he took were barely discernible from the sand that ran alongside them. The coordinate he was given took him off the road and into the actual desert. When his Humvee slipped into a crevice in the sand and got stuck, he thought he was in for a long day. After getting out and checking his Humvee, he discovered he had rolled into something more than just a hole.

Upon further investigation, Marty found a wall of stone with ancient Egyptian markings. Excited by this new discovery, Marty began to dig farther. After an hour—but what had seemed like only a few minutes because of his excitement—Marty discovered the wall was actually a door. It was a very small door with unfamiliar writings, but they were definitely ancient Egyptian. Unable to go any further because of both heat and exhaustion, Marty packed up, got the Humvee going again, and headed back to Cairo. He marked his location with a GPS, which he carried with him. Technology was great in this new world. He was never lost as long as he carried his GPS with him. He knew he would find his door to the unknown again.

Marty knew he was going to have to get a dig permit, and of course that was not going to be easy in Cairo. Getting any kind of dig permit would take years. The Egyptians were not too keen on having their sites dug up by outsiders. Worse, Marty was an outsider from America.

Luckily Marty knew someone who could help him. His name was Mohamed Fahar, and he was a native Egyptian. Mohamed and Marty knew each other from Oxford University. They became very good friends while they both studied at the Institute of Social and Cultural Anthropology. They were both intelligent young men yet from completely different backgrounds. Marty told him about this site, and they knew what they were up against with the government. They both decided to start the dig in secret first. This way they could search the site first and find what they could. If the site was worth the excavation, then they would apply for a permit. They would have a huge head start. If nothing was to be found, then no harm done.

Money was another problem. Starting an excavation like this would cost thousands, and an illegal one would cost more than triple that. More than likely it was going to cost him about a million just to get started. If all went well and Marty found something worth excavating, it would cost him more than just a few million, but the reward could be incalculable.

Marty was from old money, so the financial problem was solved. All he had to do was call his banker back in New York and have him wire a little pocket change. His great-great-great-grandfather, Theodore McAndrews, was responsible for inventing a part for the steam locomotive engine. That may not seem like much, but his grandfather worked with a man named George Stephenson, who invented the steam engine. Theodore patented a small part needed, and Stephenson used this part in every engine he built. McAndrews made millions at a time when millions was something. He ventured off, making railcars and eventually other things as well. The

McAndrews family became legendary, and every offspring (such as Marty) would have more money than they knew what to do with.

Marty had only one interest in life, and that was digging in the sand. His entire life consisted of school and play. He attended and graduated from the finest schools in the world, with degrees in everything from biology to Egyptology. When he wasn't in school, Marty was busy playing. He liked to race cars, boats, and horses. He also played golf, polo, and cards—he was a staple at the club. He collected artwork, such as Picasso and Renoir, like it was going out of style. He was oftentimes called ruthless for his behavior, which he so richly deserved. Marty was tops in his class and would stop at nothing to get what he wanted. A very intelligent man with money was maybe a dangerous combination.

Marty never really worked a day in his life. He was intelligent and busy either in school with studies or out in the field, but Marty never worked. He would oftentimes talk about companies his family owned and controlled, but Marty really did not care about any of them. His only real interests were in things, such as the desert and what lay beneath the ruins of time. All of this was more or less a game to him, as were all the other things he did throughout his life.

Mohamed supplied the equipment and men, while Marty supplied the money. Things were put together quickly, and within a week they were at the site again, working on the dig. Money was never an issue, so this little friendship between Marty and Mohamed was solid in many ways. There was quite a lot of preparation before the dig, with or without a permit. Marty may have had all the money in the world, but without Mohamed this project was going nowhere. Mohamed had to find men skilled in this sort of work—men who would be willing to work in extreme heat both night and day, who would risk working knowing there was no permit. This was not something easily found. The equipment was another thing. Although Marty had the money to purchase or rent, they still needed to use precautions, so they did not tip anyone about the dig site.

The site was excavated slowly at first. They did so with precautions so as not to stir up any interest in the site. Marty grew impatient, but Mohamed kept him calm till they found what it was they needed. Three days it took to open the great door. Once inside, they knew the site was a major find, but had no idea how major till weeks later. Marty wanted in now, and the frenzy could no longer be held back. Marty was too strong, so more men and more equipment came. Everything was moving quickly now. There was a rush to the finish line, and Marty always got what he wanted.

# THE OTHER ONE

Krista led Michael off through the backyards, like the Pied Piper once did leading the children off to the woods. Laughing with dark curly hair bouncing up and down, Krista tugged Michael gently by two fingers through the backyards of the neighbors. The sound of the music from the party was fading now that they were out of the subdivision and into the next. Tripping several times in the high heels Krista wore, she reached down to take the shoes off. She was bent over with her ass pointed in the air and small black panties slightly visible, and it was hard for Michael not to take the bait. Michael knew what she was doing, swaying her ass back and forth a couple of times and pretending it was harder than it looked to pull the small straps from her ankles. Like a fisherman letting the fish take the bait before setting the hook, Krista was good at luring the men in, and Michael was easy prey.

"Do you need some help?" Michael asked, taking the bait—hook, line, and sinker.

Krista's dark-green eyes were glowing under the soft moonlight, which was just rising in the sky. "I . . . I think I will be fine." Setting the hook hard, she stumbled again and fell to the ground. "Ow!" Holding her ankle with legs curled up to her body and sitting in the grass, she moaned and leaned back and forth, playing up the part of a woman injured by the fall.

Michael was gullible, and although he knew what was happening, he ran to her side and kneeled down to look at her foot. He reached out with both hands and grasped her leg, feeling the softness of her skin in his hands. "Where does it hurt?" He couldn't help but stare at the panties that peeked out of her skirt. Legs crossed one over another and the skirt bunched up above curving hips revealed just enough panty to lure him in closer.

Sometimes taking candy from a child only makes you want it more. Krista saw the way Michael's eyes roamed up her legs to her panties peeking out, so she tugged the hem to cover them. Soft eyes looked at him, pretending she was embarrassed, and she lowered them slowly to the ground. She was smooth and slowly looked up—the damsel in distress—and the two of them gazed into each other's eyes silently. Her hand dipped slowly down her leg, touching the ankle that was supposedly hurt. She broke the silence. "Here."

Feeling like the cat with his hand in the fishbowl, Michael felt his face flush. He couldn't believe he was falling for this. "It doesn't look swollen. I should go."

Curling up beside him, tucking in her ankles, and placing her arms around his neck, Krista pressed her nose into his ear. "Don't go." A finger played with his hair, softly swirling it in circles. Leaning back, she arched her body and tugged him close with her arms around him. Her perfume was so intoxicating together with her body, which was alluring. Krista had an aura about her that could pull in any man she wanted. "It's beautiful out tonight, isn't it?"

It was hard not to notice how miraculously Krista recovered from the twisted ankle while she lay in the grass like that. Flashbacks of their days together flooded Michael's mind. "It is beautiful tonight." He would try to change the subject. He and Krista were friends. That was all, and that was where it ended. Leaning back into the grass beside her and finally taking his eyes off her breasts, he looked up to the stars with one hand pointing to the sky and said, "That there is Pegasus."

"Oh, Michael, you always were the dreamer." Krista sighed, leaning into his side and wrapping an arm around his arm.

Michael pulled back, looking down with her arm wrapped around his. "What did you say?"

There was a charm about Krista that most could not deny, but when that hypnotic light wasn't shining anymore, the real Krista came out sometimes. "You mean 'Michael' or 'Oh, Michael'?" She said the word "oh" with lips pursed and voice moaning, exaggerating the word and rolling her eyes.

"No. After that."

Tugging his arm tightly in hers, Krista sunk back to his side, pouting that he wasn't falling for the soft moan of her "oh" just yet. She spoke again, and this time the word just came out—no moan or rolling of the eyes. "Oh, you mean about you being a dreamer?"

"Yeah. You think I am?"

Leaning into his arm again, she nodded while one hand stroked his arm up and down. "Well yes, Michael, you always were a dreamer, staring up at those stars. I never could figure out what you saw in them, but now look at you—all grown up and working at a big bank downtown."

The fortune-teller had told him there would be someone who would remind him that he was a dreamer, but this was just a coincidence. Michael didn't believe in fortunes. He stood and held out his hand to help Krista to her feet. Staring off into the distance, he wondered if he was just a dreamer. "Come on, I'll help you."

Nearly leaping to her feet, Krista grabbed his hand tightly in her own and then started to swing her hand back and forth with his. Pulling his hand, she began to skip along the grass with both shoes in her other hand. "Why thank you! Come on, let's go to my place. I have something I want to show you."

Michael followed along, holding her hand in his own, but he refused to skip like her. "I guess your ankle's okay then?"

"Oh that? I heal fast."

They walked about ten more minutes, cutting through the backyards of some homes till they reached a sidewalk. It was Krista's neighborhood, which was two subdivisions over from Rolling Hills. The homes here were bigger and nicer then Rolling Hills, and the landscape more mature, being it was about three years older.

A man dressed in a long black coat stood at the corner of the road with his hands high in the air. He turned around, and Michael thought he looked familiar, but the distance was too great when the man turned to walk away. Krista and Michael walked to the corner, still holding hands, when he saw a sign posted there. It was a poster of a cat, which read, "Missing, we know you killed him." This struck Michael as more than a little odd. There was no phone number or name, and it was the strangest picture of a cat dressed up in a suit coat, as if he was heading to work at a bank. Michael did a double take, hoping Krista would not see the poster and realize it was a message for him.

They stood at the side door of Krista's house, and she reached down into her purse to take the key out and open the door. It was a red-brick two-story house all lit up with landscape lights around the yard. The yard was meticulously manicured, with nothing out of place. The front door was a large glass, wood-paneled door all lit up from behind and a huge lantern hanging from above.

"Krista? Maybe I should go."

"What are you talking about? Come on. It's a surprise just for you." She tugged him inside, not giving him a chance to escape.

—⁓⁓⁓—

Krista was the number-one real estate agent in the area and for a good reason. Her motto was "Dream of your belle vista. Then call on Krista." It became a household phrase, but it was her looks that every man would remember. Always dressed like a million bucks and driving a fancy little BMW that just oozed the word "success," she was a determined young woman who would do anything for success.

Success always seemed to be a part of Krista's life as long as she could remember. At the early age of eight she was already an accomplished star of the beauty pageants. Her parents were certain she would be the next Farrah Fawcett—or maybe it was Jaclyn Smith because of the dark hair. Her father was a big fan of *Charlie's Angels*. Every year in school Krista was voted most popular. Even the teachers loved her charisma. She knew how to charm, and that was the key to success, right?

It was her freshman year in high school when Krista first met Michael. She teased him, pretending not to care, and made advances on other boys just to make him jealous. Krista learned how to manipulate people early on, and boys were easy prey. She tugged at Michael's heart, and he asked her to the homecoming dance. That was the start of a long relationship between the two, and throughout high school they became the most popular couple.

Their senior year in high school moved fast. Michael was heading off to the University of Iowa, and she was going to the University of Illinois. They both knew it would be difficult being so far apart, but two young people in love sometimes felt they could do anything. They spent all their time together, hoping to make up time for the future, when the two of them would be apart.

Spending all their time together turned out to be a bad thing. Krista did not care about his "foolish" dreams of being an astronomer. She wanted him to grow up and use his skills wisely. She was intent on finding a man who was successful in his life. Michael had a dream of looking at the stars. What she never understood was that success was not about money but more about doing something you enjoyed and being happy about it. Michael learned this about her, and the two of them eventually drifted apart. Eventually they both went off to different schools and lost touch with each other for most of their college days. They would talk during the summers, and Krista would hit on Michael, but he knew it was only a temporary fling for her.

When Michael met Jenny he was never so happy, and word spread back home to Krista. It was by coincidence, of course, when Krista ran into Michael at the summer festival. She looked amazing that day, and Michael was drooling just as she planned. She tried to coax him to come back to her, but Michael just shook his head and told her he was happy now with Jenny. This really hurt Krista, never having been turned down before by anyone. A very competitive person, Krista always had her way.

Time went on, though, and Krista graduated from college and came back to Crystal Lake, joining the real estate team of Jenkins and Murphy. Krista became successful on her own, not having to rely on anyone but herself. She eventually started her own real estate company. No longer did she have time for men, but deep down there was always that voice inside her head that wanted Michael for herself. No one ever turned down Krista, and someday he would come to his senses.

———

Krista opened the door, leading Michael into the large foyer of her home. Stone floors with a gracious area rug and an elegant crystal chandelier above gave a warm feeling walking in. A small table to the side with a crystal vase held flowers. Inside was lit by the lamp placed in the corner. She was meticulous about every detail, and her house was no exception. "Come on in."

Michael looked up at the voluminous foyer and then stepped inside carefully, looking from side to side. "Well, only for a short visit." He was timid, knowing Jenny would just kill him if she knew, but what harm would a little visit do? Looking to one of the other rooms with a painting hanging above a plush couch, he tried to keep things innocent. "It's a very large house."

Krista tugged his hand, pulling Michael up the stairs that curved along the wall in a spiral. She was a couple steps higher, and the short skirt revealed the black-lace panties she wore. Curving hips swayed back and forth, and that ass—oh, that ass—just moved, tempting him. Krista simply pulled the dazed boy up to her room. "This way."

Michael was dumbfounded. He ended up staring at her bedroom like a lost puppy. The bedroom was grand, with a coffered ceiling and a grandiose king-size bed against the wall. A bench sat at the foot of the bed, and two very nice wooden nightstands sat on either side. Candles were lit all over in the romantically lit room, and petals of a rose were spread out on the foot of the bed. Her intentions were now obvious as they were staring at the candles that had wax dripping down the sides. He wondered to himself if that was a fire hazard. "Uh, I think I should go."

She tugged him inside of the bedroom and then wrapped her arms around his neck with one foot kicked up and bent. She leaned up and kissed his lips. Soft hands dragged along the sides of his neck. The sweet smell of perfume was mesmerizing, and Michael knew he was in trouble, but like some sort of siren Krista already set the barbed hooks and was pulling the line tightly. "Why don't you get cozy."

"I really need to go, Kris—" Words did not quite finish when she kissed his lips again. A dense cloud consumed every thought inside his head. He was naive, but she was hitting him over the head with a sledgehammer. He loved his wife, and this had gone too far—you could nearly see the steam rising from the top of his head.

Everything froze except the slim black dress she wore that slid down a curving silhouette in slow motion, pillowing around small ankles. She stood there before him with a sultry look on her face. One knee was bent, and her hands reached up behind, which loosened the clasp of the dress, sending it free-falling to her ankles. Standing there with nothing but black lace panties on, one foot kicked the dress to the side.

Michael's love for his wife and family were too strong, and Krista's obvious intentions were about to be ruined. She moved in close, pressing hard against his body and unbuttoning the shirt that he wore. She pulled it off while Michael stood there, watching and feeling soft hands rub hard against his chest. The soft flickering lights of the candles and the sweet scent of the perfume she wore lulled Michael into a dreamlike state, but the killer was when her nipples rubbed against his chest. Leaning his own head back while she unbuttoned his jeans, Michael had the angel and the devil on his shoulder arguing. The angel of course told him to stop this right now, while the devil just told him to fuck the hell out of her. The devil himself was busy watching Krista with his tongue dangling out the corner of his mouth and was caught off guard by the slug of the angel that knocked the devil out cold. Michael did the same and shoved Krista back with both hands. "Stop!"

Krista stared at him, shocked, and then kept rubbing her hands along his chest. "Come to bed."

"I said stop! I am not in love with you, Krista. I never was."

She stared at him, not believing him and begging him to stay.

"You know I can't."

"You know you love me. Stay." Reaching up, she softly massaged his back with spread hands stroking up and down.

"I can't." He stared at her, grabbed his shirt, and began walking out the door. "I am in love with my wife, Jenny."

"Promise me you'll leave her." A trembling hand reached up, now resting on his shoulder. "Promise me."

Michael turned, feeling her hand on his shoulder, and peeled it off. "Krista, I need to go."

She watched him leave, with her dress still wrapped around her ankles and her breasts bare for him to see—always the tease till the very end. "Promise me, Michael. Promise me."

Michael put his shoes back on, walked out of the house, and never turned back. This was never what he had planned. The night was dark, and the streets were empty. He puked once he was far enough away, wishing he never saw that woman ever again. It was a long walk to his home, and all he could do was think of Jenny.

# STRAY CATS

The sky was so dark that early October night that every star could be seen in the sky. Michael headed home, turned up the collar on his shirt, and wrapped his own arms around himself, feeling the chill in the air and seeing his breath puffing before him. The neighborhoods were completely dark except for a couple of streetlights he passed along the way. A fog rolled low across the grass. Most of the houses he passed had garbage cans at the end of the driveways. It was very late, and he knew Jenny would be asking questions.

He jogged through the neighborhoods using the most direct route he could and cut through backyards whenever possible. Most houses didn't have any fences, but there were a couple that did. Leaping over one of them, he realized too late why the fence was surrounding the house. A dog barked and then a floodlight came on, detecting the motion of Michael running through the yard. He felt his heart beating faster. "Oh, Jesus!"

Blinded by the light, he couldn't tell what kind of dog it was, other than that its bark was low and it sounded very big. He had never run faster than he did that very moment, leaping over the other side of the fence, tumbling to the ground, and landing in some bushes. The dog was barking on the other side, and someone turned a light on inside the house. He crawled to one side and lay down flat on the grass, listening before he was able to run once again. "Remain calm," he kept telling himself. "You didn't do anything wrong."

Lying low on the grass until he saw the opportunity to run, Michel heard the sound of an animal nearby. The dog was still barking on the other side of the fence, but there was something else moving along in the bush. It was very dark, but the floodlight of the house lit up a part of the yard. That was when he saw green eyes staring at him. It hissed, and a clawed hand reached out to him, still hissing. Michael leaped up and ran once again.

"Hey!" a man shouted from the house.

---

The man in the house was Joshua Goldstein, the village jeweler. An overweight man with rimmed glasses, he was standing in his underwear with no shirt on. It was not a pretty sight, with his bald head gleaming under the floodlights and large belly hanging over. He was barely able to see his own toes. A gold Rolex watch with diamonds and rings with jewels on both hands sparkled in the light. A 9mm Glock holding seventeen bullets in the chamber pointed out in the darkness. After a couple of robberies, Joshua was tired of messing around and decided the next asshole who robbed him was going to be sorry and full of bullet holes in his body.

Later that evening the police showed up at the Goldsteins' house, which was all lit up by the security lights and police searching the lot with spotlights. Joshua would tell the police a man attempted to break in to their house, but lucky for him Joshua had pulled out his Glock and the criminal ran. He described the man as dark-haired with a hood over his head. How he saw the color of the man's hair was uncertain in the dark, but Joshua swore by it. The robber was a very large man, about six feet tall. There was no word from the police, the papers said, on any further investigation, but they did remind people to lock their doors at night.

---

Michael did not stop running until he was at the entrance gates of Rolling Hills. He bent over, holding one hand to the stone gate and catching his breath. Headlights were moving up the road toward him, and for a moment he thought it may be the police out looking for him. Stepping behind the wall of the entrance, Michael hid from the headlights till they passed. It was a carload of kids out joyriding, and one had a head hanging out the side shouting something about a girl named Christine.

"She's only the beginning of your troubles."

The party was over—the yellow crime scene tape torn in the middle and dangling to either side of the street seemed to verify that. Passing by the Perwinkle, Martinson, and Sullivan houses, he saw no evidence of anyone loitering about. A few empty beer cans lay on the lawns of these once perfectly manicured lawns. There was something else different too, but he couldn't quite put his finger on it yet. The table where he'd had his fortune told by the great Zara was still standing off to the side, and Michael felt chills run up and down his spine. Who the hell was she talking about? He questioned her fortune of staying away from the other one. *She is no good for you.* He held hands up, feeling frustrated. "Krista."

Continuing down the road toward his house, Michael started humming a song that suddenly stuck in his head. "Stray cat strut, I'm a ladies' cat. A feline Casanova, hey, man, that's where it's at." It was then he realized what else was missing. He stopped for a moment, hearing nothing but silence now. Crickets chirped, and the funny low sound of a bullfrog burped, but there was something else too. He turned, saw nothing on the road, and then continued walking to his home, hoping the smell of perfume wasn't on his clothes.

Something was following Michael home, but he was more worried about Jenny being upset than some wild animal that was probably more spooked and following him. In the distance was his house. He heard the noise of some garbage falling over behind him and a cat whine, "Meeeooooow."

Turning, he saw a cat running off and the garbage tipped over in the road. "Damn cats." He looked the garbage over, making sure nothing else leaped out, but all was quiet for now. "Raccoons are probably out," he spoke to the dark, reassuring himself there was nothing else out there, and then that song came back to him again. "Get my dinner from a garbage can."

Quietly Michael walked up to the house, noticing all the lights off inside. Perhaps he would be able to sneak in without making a noise, but Jenny was a light sleeper. What excuse was he to use when she started in with all the questions about where he had been? None of this really occurred to him until that very moment when he turned the key and pushed open the door. "Uh yeah, uh, Jen? We, uh, I mean I, uh . . . went to the, uh . . . florist to buy you a, uh . . . flower, yeah a flower, but they were out so I, uh . . . uh . . . uh, okay, she tried to seduce me, but I told her no and ran back as fast as I could." Wild thoughts of him panicking flashed through his head. He needed a plan fast because Jenny was not going to believe his story. The door creaked as he closed it softly. What the hell was he going to tell Jenny?

Everyone was asleep, so this was good, and the garbage still had to be taken out. He walked to the kitchen to grab the bag of garbage, wrapped it up, and knotted it shut. Michael leaned over to pull out a new garbage bag for the container when out of the corner of his eye was movement. Nearly leaping up, scared out of his wits, he was afraid it was Jenny standing over him with a baseball bat.

It was not Jenny but a cat instead, crawling along the window ledge and peering into the house. Michael was thankful it wasn't Jenny standing over him with a baseball bat, because she probably had every right to. The cat pressed its face up against the window with eyes that were so wide and black. Arched body and tail curled up high behind it, the cat hissed the moment Michael discovered it. This cat appeared to have a tan color and showed its sharp little teeth through the window. It wasn't that Michael was scared of cats, but this one had such big black eyes—and why was it staring at Michael? Just nerves, he told himself, so he leaped at the cat to scare it off. The cat remained still, unlike most others, which would run off the moment Michael leaped. Instead the cat narrowed those black eyes and made a cry like it was injured before slowly leaping down to run off.

It was really late, and if Michael didn't get the garbage taken out and his ass back to bed soon he was going to be in the doghouse. Tiptoeing through the dark house, he did his best to keep quiet while he gathered all the garbage. He nearly tripped over the dog lying in the middle of the kitchen but caught himself with one hand. "Phew." *That was a close one.* Then something dark ran past the window. It went too fast in the dark, with the soft light of the moon barely lighting up the room. It was an animal, but what kind Michael had no idea. *Probably just a raccoon.* It was garbage night and they would be out looking for food.

Outside, the air was still, with a soft rustle of leaves scattering along the dark streets. Looking down the road while he dragged the two bags of garbage in both hands, Michael noticed how quiet and empty things were at this time of night. All the lights were off except for one streetlight in the middle of their cul-de-sac and the dim light of the waning moon, which was already low in the sky.

Michael first heard the sound of the cat once he reached the end of the driveway, setting the garbage down. All this time his mind was on what had happened earlier tonight and what Jenny was going to do if she ever found out. While worrying about perfume on his clothes and coming home so late, his intuition of being followed by someone or something didn't kick in till just then at the end of the driveway. He turned to the meow, which was high-pitched and whiny, and his eyes tried to focus in the dark light. There was movement off to his right and then another sound of a cat to his left. Were there two cats now? The house looked so far off in the distance, and his feet just froze. A person's mind often played tricks in the dark.

It stood there in the middle of the driveway with its back arched high and one eye glowing, hissing with tiny sharp teeth showing. "It's just a cat," Michael told himself, but he knew better, looking this one over. It was dark so he couldn't be certain, but when that cat turned, it appeared its head was flattened on one side. The one eye was glowing, but the other was milky white, which just sent the heebie-jeebies up and down Michael's spine, reminding him of the cat he had run over. He waved his hands for the cat to run, but it stood its ground in the middle of the driveway.

"Go on! Scat!"

Another sound hissed to one side, and the cans of the neighbors tipped over behind him. Michael turned to see who or what else was there, knowing he had to get out of there now. Turning back to the house, he looked up the driveway to see the cat with the milky eye was gone. Another sound hissed behind, and he whipped around, seeing a cat crossing one foot in front of the other toward him. It was hard to tell the color of this cat in the darkness of the night, but it appeared to be a darker shade. The dark eyes of the cat stared up, and its mouth bared tiny sharp teeth as it hissed at him now. Michael was prepared to kick the shit out of the cat, stepping one foot back.

"Ever play football?"

The claws didn't hurt when they first dug into the flesh of Michael's neck. Maybe it was the shock of being caught off guard and the nerves took time to realize he had been lured and fooled. It was the larger cat with a milky eye that leaped up with claws grabbing hold of his neck. Confused, he stared at the smaller cat walking toward him. Michael would have sworn later that cat had a grin on its face when the other leaped upon his neck. He screamed, reaching back with both hands now and grabbing hold of a heap of fur. One foot kicked out too early at the other cat.

"Ow! Shit!"

The one cat scampered to the side, easily missing the foot of Michael, while the other meowed and hissed, still clawing at his neck. He was still leaning over and spinning around as the cat hung tightly to his neck. A warm sensation came over him, and he felt it trickle down his back. Both hands squeezed the cat and then ripped it off his neck. The cat clawed and hissed, meowing like a rabid animal. Arching its body with back claws kicking, the cat spun out of his hands and then fell to the ground, landing on its feet. How did cats always land on their feet?

"What the fuck?"

Reaching back to his neck and feeling the warm blood trickle down and cover his hand, Michael stared in disbelief at the two cats circling him now. The one cat was bigger and seemed more aggressive than the other, staring at Michael with that big milky eye. Both the cats were hissing and meowing like they hadn't eaten in a month. Michael tried to keep the two in front of him, but they circled around and spread themselves out. He kicked and stomped his feet to keep the two cats out of reach. This was silly, he thought to himself, fighting two rabid cats in the middle of the night.

The cats were too quick, running swiftly around his ankles and clawing with their paws. Michael ran toward the house, hoping to avoid any further clawing or biting of these wild rabid cats. The two of them followed, clawing at his ankles, and the smaller one grabbed hold of his pants. With a swift kick of his foot the cat went flying through the air, but like before it just landed on its feet.

On the side of the house was a shovel that Jenny had used earlier to plant some tulip bulbs around the house. Michael had no idea it was there when he ran toward the house, placing both hands against the brick. Sweat was dripping down his forehead, and his back was now soaked with blood from his neck. Without even thinking, he grabbed the shovel and spun around, swinging it through the air.

The cats backed away, both of them hissing when they saw Michael with the shovel in his hands. The smaller one clawed and leaped in the air. Michael caught him square in his gut with the full blade of the shovel. This same cat went flying through the air, only this time it didn't land on all four feet but his back instead. Not moving a muscle, this cat was definitely hurt this time but not dead. The larger cat watched the smaller cat lie there in the dark grass and then slowly turned its glowing black eye toward Michael. This was really creepy, and it freaked Michael out the way that cat turned its head and started to snarl. It gave a loud, whiny hiss, baring sharp white teeth, and it raised one paw, revealing its claws to him.

Picking up the shovel with both hands and raising it high over one shoulder, Michael stared the one-eyed cat down. Closer it moved, snarling and growling like no cat he had ever heard before. Was it the garbage that was making these cats all crazy, or something else? He had no idea. What he did know was that he was tired and had enough of this nonsense, so he teed up the cat like a golf ball and took a swipe at its head, cutting it clean off its body. Blood spurted out like a small fountain, making a mess of his driveway.

The head rolled a few yards away, finding a resting place in the soft, dark grass. The mouth was still open, and the milky eye seemed to be staring right at Michael.

He leaned down to give the head a double swoop with the shovel when a glint of light caught his eyes. A small dark band that must have been the collar of the cat was now covered with blood. Information was what he wanted, and certainly the collar would have some. Picking it up, he smeared the blood off with a couple of fingers and read the name on the collar.

"Flavara?"

There was no information about who owned it or where it lived—just a simple name like the other dead cat. There was no way he wanted this cat to be found anywhere near his home, so he ran down past a couple of houses and dropped it off in the Sanders' garbage. Better to be safe than sorry, he told himself. The worse part was the head, which rolled back and forth on the shovel while he was running to throw the thing away. The claws of the cat opened and stretched. "Reflexes, just reflexes." He was bothered just the same, trying not to look at that one milky eye that kept staring at him. Holding up his middle finger before closing the lid on the garbage can, he turned back to his house for the other.

"Fuck you."

When he arrived back at the house, the other cat was gone. Of course, this was no surprise at all, but it bothered him. What had caused these cats to attack like that? Was there something in the garbage, like catnip, that was driving them crazy? He cleaned up the driveway, washing down the blood with a hose. It was late and the horizon was starting to light up toward the east. He snuck back inside the house, hoping to get a few hours of sleep before daylight. Jenny was going to be pissed.

# THE BOSS

The Boss was originally purchased by Vincent "Vinnie" Merlino back in 1966 from the Ford dealer in Mount Prospect. The original base price of the car was $2,314, but with the GT-style body and engine plus all the extras, the car totaled a whopping $4,265. In 1966 this was a high price to pay for a car, but Vinnie felt he'd earned it, having just been promoted to sales manager at the time. It was a good year and, besides, what girl wouldn't want to sit beside Vinnie in his new Ford GT Mustang?

The car was delivered, as the brochure said, with a 390 V-8 engine and producing a whopping 320 horsepower, manual transmission, power brakes, power steering, and air-conditioning too! It was a blue beauty with a white stripe running down the center of the car and one on either side. Curves and scoops on every angle of the car turned the heads of anyone who saw it, including the girls who begged to drive with him.

Michael still remembered his dad driving him in the front seat of the Boss when he was just a boy. There were no air bags to worry about or child seats to harness him in—just a simple strap that came across his lap that he held tightly because Dad loved to step on the gas. Michael remembered how his dad loved that car and would keep the windows down as he waved to people when the Boss rumbled by.

Vinnie kept that car covered in a garage later in his life, hardly driving it before his death—a sad day for Michael, having lost his dad at an early age from a heart attack. He left his mom with everything except the Boss, which she could not drive anyway. He it gave to Michael with a note.

Dear Michael,

I guess I won't be seeing you anymore, but I always loved driving with you beside me in the Boss. My only regret was that we didn't drive it enough. Take care of your dreams, Michael, and never give up on them. That's where happiness is. Take care of it for me, and remember I'll be watching you from above.

Love,
Dad

P.S. Drive it!

It wasn't much, but it brought tears to his eyes every time he thought of driving beside his dad in the Boss. So it only made sense that every time Michael drove that car it had special meaning to him. It was more than just a car and more than the history of a Ford GT but the history of his dad and what he meant to him. It was like driving down memory lane, with his dad driving the car and Michael holding his hand out the side and letting the wind drift his hand up and down like a glider. He and his dad would drive fast down an empty road and the speedometer would hit one hundred miles per hour. Vinnie would look at his son with one finger pressed against his lips. "Shhhh. Don't tell your mother." Michael would always laugh. He and his dad would sit back under the stars late at night, peeking out the sides or the front windshield, and Vinnie would point out the different constellations.

---

Earlier that day Michael tried to avoid Jenny. His neck was starting to scab up and the sheets were covered in blood. The shirt from last night was hidden in a corner; he was afraid it smelled of Krista's perfume. His only hope of avoiding everything that happened was Jenny going to class today.

Jenny was already downstairs, dressed and ready to go to Northwestern for her classes, when Michael walked down to the kitchen. She sipped the last drops of orange juice and then set it to the side, barely lifting her eyes at Michael, who looked like a slob. "Have a nice day, and I want to hear all about last night and why the sheets are bloody and you smell like perfume," she said, smiling as if everything was normal, but she did not wait for an answer. Michael was standing there with his mouth wide open and his hair sticking straight up in the air. Taking her purse, strapping it across her shoulder, and then grabbing her books, she headed out the door.

He stood in the kitchen alone and pondered what to do next. The coffee was brewing, and he reached for a cup, hoping it would cure the pounding in the side of his head. He was going to need a whole lot more to get him through the next few days.

What had he been thinking when he followed Krista to her house? Everything just snowballed after the Goldsteins' house and the rabid cats. One hand reached back to his neck, and he winced as he felt pain shoot through his body. If this cat did have rabies, he was going to need shots. That was one problem but not necessarily the most important problem. She had smelled the perfume, which was bad, but how could he lie to Jenny? Perfume was one thing, but explaining how Krista came onto him was quite another.

"Damn it! I am so dead."

Later that morning Michael asked one of the neighbors to keep an eye on JR while he went for a ride. He had things to do, like come up with a million excuses as to why he smelled like perfume and his back was all scratched up. He was selling Jenny short, afraid she wouldn't believe him. Remembering the events of last night, he wasn't sure he could believe it himself. He loved Jenny more than life itself and never wanted to see her hurt in any way. He really wanted to bring JR for a car ride like his dad used to do with him, but the Boss was an older car. He and Jenny decided it was not the best car to be driving their treasured boy just yet.

The doorbell rang, and Michael answered it. A pretty little blonde girl with ponytails was standing at the door. "Hello, Cary. Come on in."

Cary Mendohlson was thirteen years old and lived a few doors down. She smiled and skipped in. "Hello, Mr. Merlino."

"JR is in the family room. If you could just watch him for a couple hours I would appreciate it."

"Of course!" She laughed and then skipped along to the family room.

When Michael pulled the cover off the Boss that day, it shone under the light like it never had before. This was the day his father died, and Michael had requested the day off, deciding to spend it with a memory. The paint job was the original, with only 53,000 miles on it, but it was fading after forty-some years, covered or not. His eyes could nearly see the original sticker still glued to the side window and his dad in the front seat. Every time he looked at it there was a tear in his eyes.

Leisurely running a hand along one side of the car, he imagined how his dad would do the same. He pulled open the door and hopped into the seat. He closed the door with a loud clunk, unlike the newer cars of today that seemed to close like a vacuum with no sound at all. He sat inside, silent and staring at the dash. With his hands on the wheel, he looked out over the scoop of the hood. *Why don't they make cars like this anymore?* he wondered. Like a man in a dream, he reached for the key and then turned it over in the ignition, having to juice it a couple of times before it started. It rumbled like it always did, and his foot gave it a little more gas than he should have, but that was the fun of it, wasn't it? Smoke filled the garage, and Jenny would complain later on when he was home about how the fumes were going to kill them all, but for now he was having fun.

He gradually pulled the Boss out of the garage, like some sort of ghost from the past, with exhaust pouring out from either side. The Boss edged slowly down the drive and over the curb and rolled through the neighborhood. Just like his dad, Michael made sure both windows were down. The neighbors waved to him and he waved back to them.

The Boss pulled up to the main entrance of the Rolling Hills subdivision when Michael turned right. Tires squealed, leaving a trail of smoke flaring out the back end of the Boss. First gear went pretty fast, then he shifted to second and third, and he was flying down the empty street already speeding over the limit when he had to slow it down. That big V-8 roared when pushed, like music to his ears.

This was going to be one of the last drives for the Boss this year, because winter was coming soon. Stored away in the garage under cover, it would go dormant until next spring. Michael tried to drive the Boss whenever he could, but things got busy with a wife, kid, and working late as well. There just wasn't time to do all that and drive a car, but every time he sat inside the Boss, Michael knew this was something special he really had to do.

The streets around Crystal Lake were always busy and the traffic very heavy. He would drive along Northwest Highway or Route 176, waving to people who admired his car, just like his dad would. Some cars would pull up beside him and toot their horns at him or give him the thumbs-up.

Today was different, though, and he just wanted to be alone. Last night was crazy, and Michael needed time to think of the past few days. The cat last night was very strange, but why did two attack? Maybe there was something in the garbage that drove them loony, but Michael knew that wasn't it. Then there was that fortune-teller talking in another voice. He pulled out the small piece of paper with the scribbling of "Reland" on it. Who the hell was Reland, and did it matter to him at all? This was his time to escape from everything for a while. So he decided to take some side roads instead and take it easy, with one hand out to the side patting the Boss on the door. The stereo had not worked in over twenty years, but with the window down and the wind blowing, the sweet engine sounds blew back in his ears like music no one could ever imitate.

———

The first stop was the hospital. He checked in at the emergency room, filling out insurance forms and waiting over an hour before he could get in. The emergency room was quiet compared with later in the night, when it would be packed. A nurse eventually called out his name with a clipboard in her hands. "Michael Merlino?"

They did the normal things, checking his weight and height, and then had him sit down while they checked his pulse and blood pressure. "Everything seems to be fine," said the woman with a tag on her green shirt that stated she was Martha. "So what happened?"

"Well, a long story . . . do I need to get into details?"

"Not unless you did something wrong. Then we're going to have to beat you." She laughed and looked at him. "Just tell me briefly."

Paranoia did things to a person, and Michael swore she knew he killed another cat. "Uh, yeah. Well, I was taking out the garbage last night and this cat attacked me. Scratched me really bad so I—" He stopped himself right before he told her that he killed the cat. Would it be bad that he killed the cat? He figured things were so messed up. Why add to the list? "So I ran inside to check on it, thinking this cat probably had rabies."

"Where's the cat?"

*Now why would she ask about that?* Paranoia struck him deep. "The cat?"

"Yes. Where's the cat? We need it if we're going to check for rabies. If we don't have the cat then we're going to have to give you all the shots just to be safe."

Michael was dead certain she knew he killed the cat. Testing him was what she was doing, but he was not falling for it. "Uh, the . . . uh . . . cat ran off."

Martha sighed and then turned to the door. "Well, you're in for a dose of rabies shots then." She left him sitting there for another twenty minutes until the doctor came in and checked his wounds.

He received a large shot that hurt like hell, and then the nurse bandaged it up. The doctor told him he would have to come back for a series of shots, but it was better than dying.

—⁓⊷⊶⊷⊶⁓—

Michael drove for about an hour in places he couldn't remember. He went far outside Crystal Lake and back, but he couldn't tell you where. Most of the time he was in a daze, dreaming of his dad driving the car, and himself in the passenger seat—the two of them laughing and waving to people while they drove through the town. His dad would juice the engine and then find an empty road, stepping on the gas.

"Don't tell your mother."

Michael never did tell her when they broke the speed limit at one hundred miles per hour. "That's fast, Dad!"

His dad would laugh, letting up on the gas. "You bet'cher ass it is, son." The two of them had had the time of their lives.

It was when he was driving back along one of the smaller streets that Michael punched it and the speedometer hit eighty-five miles per hour on a forty-five that he first saw the cat. One cat leaped out in front of the Boss and Michael swerved to miss it, leaving black tire marks on the road behind.

"Damn cat."

Nothing seemed so odd about a cat leaping out. He looked in his rearview mirror to see the cat disappear, but it was what happened next that really had him scared.

There was a curve in the road, and this was where Michael loved to punch the gas to feel the way the Boss handled. Sure, it was an old car—nothing like the newer ones with the suspension and better steering—but that was what made this car so much fun when he was driving along this stretch. He came to the start of the turns doing about forty-five miles per hour, downshifting, and the car lunged forward and then to one side when he stepped on the gas and feathered it just right, shifting into third. The route had eight turns, and he was on turn number five, coming into a short little straightaway, so he punched it and feathered out the rear.

Michael was concentrating on the road, coming out of the turn into the short straightaway, when he saw something that normally wasn't there.

"Cats?"

He hit the brake so fast, smoking up the front, and the car came to a squealing stop in the middle of the road. About twenty cats filled the street and just stood in the middle. The odd thing was that Michael swore they were all staring at him. He didn't notice at first, but they were not just staring at him; they were coming toward him. This took him by surprise, and he just waited there till they walked up to his car and started to meow. All about the same size but different colors, the cats started to claw at the side of the Boss.

"What the hell?"

He locked the doors quickly, feeling goose bumps crawl up and down his skin. One cat leaped up on his hood, trotting up to the windshield and meowing at Michael. Then it clawed at him, touching the glass. Michael turned on the windshield wipers, laughing when it poked at the cat's face. The cat then hissed at the windshield blade. The cat swatted at it with one paw like a mouse before leaping off to the road.

Michael pressed on the horn and the cats jolted to the side. Then Michael peeled off again, heading down the road. Grabbing hold of the rearview mirror to see the cats scattering and disappear behind him, Michael stepped on the gas and went through turns seven and eight. What he didn't plan on was the police officer waiting coming out of the gate.

---

Chief Marty Dugan was eating his Sausage Egg McMuffin when Michael roared by in his Boss. The coffee spilled in his lap just enough to really piss him off. "Son of a Barbie!" The chief hardly swore, and he promised his wife he would use "Barbie" instead of "bitch." He never liked the Barbie doll anyway and told his wife, who laughed at him and kissed his cheek. Looking up to the radar gun clocking Michael at eighty-two miles per hour in a forty-five, the chief flipped the switch, and the sirens and red lights came on. His Ford Police Interceptor spit out gravel from behind and was quick to catch the Boss, which had a head start on him.

When Michael did stop and pull over to the side, the chief sat there for a while, reading off the plate number and the description of the car to headquarters as well as giving them information on where he was. The chief pulled the car into park and sat there, staring at the old car. He was fifty-five years old, and the car wasn't much younger than he was. Images of his younger days came back to him now so vividly; the car could do that to people sometimes. Those were the good ole days. The chief made a "hmph" before opening up the door and stepping out.

Back in the good ole days he didn't need to wear a gun, and he refused to wear one most of the time today. Chief Dugan hated guns, although he didn't mind shooting them at squirrels and chipmunks once in a while, thinking they were a menace to society. One time he was visiting a friend on a lake and unloaded his gun into the water. His friend asked him why he shot his gun. The chief told him he was fishing, and up came a largemouth bass full of bullet holes.

The chief was older and slightly out of shape, to put it nicely. He was a short and stocky man with a potbelly that made it harder each day to get out of his car. He reached one hand upward to the roof and pulled himself out like a sardine out of its can. He had gray hair and was balding. One hand reached inside for his hat, tugging it on to shield the sunlight from his eyes. Flipping out the ticket book and with a pen in one hand, he walked toward the Boss, leaned over to take a look, and admired the car. He walked up behind to the driver's side and tapped on the door, letting Michael know he was there. Seeing the window down already, he said, "Nice car."

—————

"Officer, I can explain."

"Oh, I'm sure ya can, but I was just wondering, is the paint original?"

"Huh?"

"The paint. Is it the original paint?"

"Uh, yeah, it's the original but—"

"It's a beauty. What year?"

"A, uh, sixty-six, sir, but uh—"

"Son of a Barbie. I thought it was, but I couldn't tell if it was a sixty-five or sixty-six." His eyes looked the car over and fingers snapped. "Boss?"

"It's a 1966 Ford Mustang GT Boss, if that's what you mean but—"

"Yeah! This is a GT? What type of engine? Don't tell me it has the 390 in it?"

Michael was so confused because typically the police yelled, but this guy seemed more concerned about the car than how fast he was going. "Yes, it has the 390 V-8 with 320 horsepower." Things seemed to lighten up, and Michael was smiling. "I take good care of it and cover it most of the time. It's the Boss."

"Don't you get smart with me, son. Do you know how fast you were going?"

How things flipped. The chief was throwing Michael for a loop. One minute he was goggling over the car and the next thing he was back to being the cop, yelling at him about speeding. "Sorry, sir, but it's the name of the car. A Boss Mustang. And I would guess I was going pretty fast. I apologize, but there were these cats."

"Cats? I don't give a hoot about cats, son. Driving eighty-two miles an hour in a forty-five is no excuse. I don't care if there were twenty cats on the road!"

What was this guy, psychic or something? "You saw them too?"

"Saw what?"

"The cats."

Chief Dugan shook his head and pocketed the ticket book. This was when Michael noticed for the first time the chief wasn't wearing a gun on his belt. "Son? We can talk about the cats later, but why don't you pop open the hood of this baby and hop out of the car. I want to check what's going on inside this beauty." He held out his hand and flipped his index finger up and down. "And while you're at it hand me your driver's license and registration too."

"Uh yes, sir." Michael was confused, unsure whether to open the hood first or get his license. He felt like the rug was just pulled out from beneath him. "Don't suppose we can talk about this, can we?"

"What? Ya think I was gonna give you a ticket for doing over forty with this baby?" There was a sparkle in his eyes. "Hell, I just wanna see who owns this beast."

He reached in his back pocket to pull out his wallet and then flipped it over to produce the driver's license inside it. Handing it over to the chief, Michael leaned over to release the latch of the hood. The chief looked at the license and then back to Michael a couple of times, making sure it was him in the picture.

"You live in the neighborhood called the Hills?"

Michael corrected him slightly. "The Rolling Hills. Yes."

"That's what I said. Now come on out here and show me what's under the hood."

Stepping out of the Boss and walking past the chief, Michael raised the hood of the car. He pulled out two clips on either side with pins attached. He leaned down with a hand under the hood, found the latch, raised it up, and then placed the rod up to hold it. Inside was an ancient engine but one you wouldn't see today, with chrome sparkling beneath the sun. Michael stood there with his hands in his pockets, looking up at the chief and then back down to the engine. He stepped back and forth, watching every move the chief made. He was nervous and unsure what exactly the chief was going to ask next. The silence was killing him, so he finally broke the silence.

"So what do you think?"

"Son of a Barbie."

"Excuse me?"

"I said son of a Barbie. My wife . . ." He pointed underneath the hood.

"Uh, your wife is—"

"Not my wife, son! She just doesn't want me to swear is all."

Well, that explained a lot, but Michael was still confused. "Well who's Barbie?"

Reaching up with both hands on the hood and pulling it shut, the chief turned to look at Michael with a straight face. "Son? I'll be watching you." He walked back to his squad car, never turning back to look at Michael or the car until he sat inside, started up his car, and pulled back onto the road again. He rolled the window down and shouted out, "Get a move on now, ya hear?"

Michael was dumbfounded, watching the chief drive away. Halfway raising his hand in the air to wave, he shouted back, "Yes, sir!" Something inside him tingled; he knew this wouldn't be the last time he saw Chief Marty Dugan.

# WARNING

## JULY 19, 2008

Darkness started to descend on the site as the workers continued in the early evening. The sky turned a beautiful shade of fiery red and orange while the sun descended on the horizon. It was a beautiful night in the desert, and the air began to cool again. Dropping to nearly fifty degrees during the night was quite pleasant after being in the extreme heat most of the day.

Marty was examining some of the mummies on a table under a tent. "What is the significance of all these cats, Mohamed?"

"Well, usually the dead buried things they either loved or wanted to protect," replied Mohamed.

"I know all of that, Mohamed. We all learned that back in our schooling days, but this is beyond just a few. We are already at 250 cats and counting! So what is it that is so special about these cats, and don't tell me they are protecting whatever it is we are trying to find." Marty was suddenly agitated.

Mohamed paused for a moment, unshaken by Marty's outburst. Unfortunately, Mohamed had witnessed these outbursts from Marty before, and even though he did not like them, as a very close friend of Marty he was willing to go along with them; of course, the pay he'd been receiving from Marty wasn't so bad either. "This seems to be some type of sacred cat burial ground, Marty. I have never seen anything like this at this magnitude. It may, however, point us in another direction. Usually, pets of one species are buried in a sort of pet cemetery not far from the actual tomb."

"Yes, yes, yes, we know that, but this is different. The artifacts we are taking out of this tomb are exceptionally good, at the very least for someone to just call it a pet cemetery. There is something here, I tell you, and it's not in another location," Marty replied.

"Marty, my past experience tells me that we should be looking in a different—"

"I don't give a crap about your past experience. Have you transcribed what that door says yet?"

"We are getting close, but we need some time."

"We don't have time, and you know that." Marty was practically jumping up and down now with his excitement. His hands were raised in the air, showing the urgency. "I need to know what that door tells us, and I need to know now!"

They both walked over to a huge stone tablet about twice the size of a normal door. It was gray and weathered, with ancient Egyptian writing carved on the flat surface. On the center was a symbol of what looked like a very big cat that was surrounded by many smaller cats. This was the door that Marty had originally found on his little drive to the desert.

"Look here, first. There is this big cat. Next, if you look around the cat, you notice eight smaller cats surrounding the larger one," Marty exclaimed. Marty pointed to the big cat in the center, made a circle around the big cat, and pointed at all the little cats.

"Yes, I know all this, Marty, but did you notice the cats in the upper right-hand corner?" Mohamed asked and pointed to pictures of cats in varying size and shapes, starting with small and going to large.

"Of course I see them, but they don't mean anything, Mohamed. Have you seen this part here underneath the big cat? It looks to me like a big treasure, and I am going to find that treasure." Marty pointed to a section under the cat that looked like gold.

"I see that, Marty, but did you see the other part on top with the big warning? It tells us not to go into this tomb, that we should leave it alone or death will be upon us. I can't quite make out all of it yet, but it definitely is telling us to stay out of the tomb. It says something about locking away the spirit." Mohamed pointed to the top of the door at some ancient writing.

"Mohamed, you haven't even transcribed all of that, and you don't know what it all says. Besides, all tombs have the same markings that you should not open this tomb or the boogeyman will get you. Please spare me, okay?"

"This one is different, and you need to see that. My men are working hard, but they are scared. They can feel it in this tomb," Mohamed said.

"Blah, blah, blah. Just find me the source and we will have what we are looking for," Marty cracked.

A muffled scream or yell was heard from the main tunnel, and some men came running out, hands waving over their heads and swatting at the air. They ran in no particular direction. Some ran left or right while others ran straight ahead. About eight men ran from the tunnel, and although it was getting dark you could see the fear in their eyes.

"Where the hell do they think they are going?" Marty asked.

Mohamed yelled something in Arabic to them, but they continued running. Some other men came out of the tunnel afterward and watched the men run. Mohamed then yelled something to the others who came out afterward. Mohamed ran over to the group of men and started to talk with them. The men were very excited and yelling as Mohamed tried to calm them down, holding his hands out and telling them to relax. The men shook their heads no and continued arguing. Mohamed looked distraught and begged them to wait for a moment. He walked back to Marty, shaking his head.

"Well, what's their problem?" Marty asked.

"It appears that we may have found what you are looking for, but the men do not want any part of it. I think we need to go take a look for ourselves. The men are refusing to go back in. They say nothing is worth the death that will follow if we continue."

Marty watched the men running off in the distance. Their silhouettes scattered over the horizon of the sand dunes. "Hey! Stop, you sons of bitches," Marty yelled to no avail. The men kept running till they disappeared, leaving Mohamed and Marty alone with a skeleton crew. "Screw them. We'll just have to take the whole damn thing ourselves. You have to talk with the others and make sure they don't leave."

"I will, Marty, but this is going to be hard. Until we figure out what is going on here, the men will be afraid."

"Well, I can't think of a better time to check the tomb than now. What do you say? Are you ready to take a look?"

Mohamed nodded and turned to the tunnel. "Ready."

The two of them gathered some items in the tent and then headed toward the tunnel. It was eerie seeing the way the light cast shadows from the tomb in the darkness of the coming night. Marty and Mohamed had no idea what to expect, nor were they ready for what they were about to see. Darkness had so many faces.

# CHAGALL

The buzzer sounded on the alarm clock, and Michael reached up to swat it with his hand, poking out from the sheets. Hair messed up and eyes squinting, he noticed the spot beside him was empty. The room was dark, but light peeked through the slit in between the blinds. It was 5:00 a.m., and Michael crawled out of bed, wondering why Jenny was up so early.

They had not talked since yesterday's brief encounter before she headed off to class. He'd had all day yesterday—including while he was washing all his clothes and the sheets—to think of a story to tell her. If he just told her the truth, maybe she would listen. Why had he been such a fool, following Krista to her home? The last thing he wanted to do was hurt the one person he loved the most. There was plenty of time to think about excuses, and even more time to get rid of the evidence. As Bill Clinton taught us, deny, deny, deny.

Michael needed to come up with two stories that were believable about the perfume and the cuts. The cuts on his back were the easy part; he would simply tell her the guys were drunk and tumbled through some thornbushes. It was the perfume that was going be the difficult one. How many ways were there for a guy to get perfume on his body? This was going to be a tough one.

He turned on the shower, and the room started to fill with steam. He leaned back his head, feeling the water cascading down his head. Michael swore the perfume was still there a day after he saw Krista. It was all in his head, of course, but guilt consumed his mind. The blood washed off, but the scratches really hurt when the soap and water washed across them. Michael stepped out of the shower, dried himself off in the steamy room, and wiped the mirror off to look at the scratches on his back. The scrapes were worse than he'd imagined. It wasn't easy, but he could see how badly infected the cuts were becoming. "Son of a bitch." He took out some hydrogen peroxide and poured it on his neck. "Oh, you son of a bitch!"

Today was his big day of taking over a new position and an elite office at work. He dressed in one of his better suits and picked out his best tie. He was very excited about this job but was concerned about Jenny. This was for her, after all, and he wanted her to be happy. All of this was for her and their son. He made sure his hair was combed perfectly as he looked at himself in the mirror once more before heading out the door. It was going to be a hard day, knowing Jenny was upset, but she would get over it soon. He just wished she was excited about his life.

---

The Ford Taurus was packed with all the things he would need for the new office. The backseat was crammed with boxes of manuals and large manila folders and files. There were personal items too, like photos of Jenny and JR. He backed out of the garage, looking behind at the mess in the neighborhood. Garbage was scattered everywhere, and he hoped the neighbors would blame the raccoons. Clenching his eyes tight because now his head was starting to hurt again, he thought about Krista and the foolish mistake he had made the other night.

He drove down the street, passing the Martinsons', Perwinkles', and Sullivans' houses before coming to the entrance gate of the Rolling Hills subdivision. Turning on his right blinker, he took a glance to his left for oncoming traffic and noticed a poster flapping in the wind. A couple of cars were coming so he had to wait, not paying much attention to the poster till it flapped again. He blinked when he saw a large picture of the cat he had killed the other night.

"What the hell?"

He put the car in park and quickly stepped outside to snatch the poster off the entrance gate. It was a snapshot of the cat, dead as a doornail, with its tongue dangling out of the corner of its mouth. Both eyes—the dark one and the milky one—were crossed off with a big X made with a black marker. "Killer!" was written on top of the sign. Beneath appeared the writing of a seemingly small child: "Have U seen who killed my kitty kat?"

Quickly Michael tossed the poster inside the car, seeing Paul Martinson heading up behind in his Mercedes. The last thing he needed was for Paul or anyone else to see this and call the cops on him. This had to be a joke, but no matter what, he had to get out of there quickly. So he hopped back in the car and pulled out, nearly hitting a car coming the other way because he forgot to look. The driver honked its horn and held up his middle finger high above the roof, screaming out, "Asshole!"

———

The first stop he made was the hospital for another rabies shot. The doctors told him as long as he couldn't find the cat they would have to give him seven shots. The shots were painful as he felt the extra-large needles jab into his hip. The nurse told him it was okay to scream, but Michael was going to be a man. It was his neck that hurt more than anything, and the nurse told him it should get better. She cleaned it for him, replacing the gauze and putting on some antibiotic cream.

He hopped back into his car and headed down I-90 toward the city. It was a long drive as he sat in traffic, which gave him time to think about the other night: the fortune-teller, the cats in the garbage, and Krista. He winced, feeling the pain throb in his neck as he thought of her.

He started questioning himself. Was this what he really wanted? His thoughts went to Jenny and JR. They were always on his mind. How could he make things better with Jenny? He wanted the best for his family. His dreams seemed so far away. He could not understand why it seemed that way with his promotion, but something was missing in his life.

---

Michael turned off the expressway on Washington and headed east into the city. Thousands of people were walking the streets and heading to work in suits and ties. The weather was chilly, and he could see the breath of many along the sidewalks. He took Washington to LaSalle and then turned south to Madison, which was surrounded by tall buildings, one towering over another, each one as pretty as the other.

The parking lot was on the corner of Madison and Wells in this busy part of the city. Each floor was named by a country, making them easy to remember. Michael walked to the elevator and pressed the down button. Looking up he saw each floor with names like Germany and Italy, each with a little flag of the country next to it. His floor was Ireland. The walls of the waiting area for the elevator were painted green, white, and orange for the color of the Irish flag.

It took three trips back and forth from the parking lot to the office with both arms full of boxes. Several people congratulated Michael on his way to his new office, and he thanked them. His arms ached, but the adrenaline was pumping in his veins. The door was surrounded by twenty of his coworkers, who clapped when he first walked up to his new office. He thanked them and felt his face blush when they parted to the side like the Red Sea for Moses.

Everyone in the office was proud of him, knowing the hard work it took to get this office. Some may have been envious, but most were genuinely happy for him and anxious to be working for him. The office was a small eight-by-nine-foot room, but it was private with its own window. A desk was facing the door with a chair behind it, and a credenza on the wall faced the desk. There wasn't much more room for anything else, but it was private and that was what made this so special.

Everyone left a small office-warming gift, like a leather-barreled pencil holder or souvenir paperweights from the city of Chicago, each with a small note of congratulations. A couple of cheap replicas of famous paintings by Chagall and Miró hung on the wall. One of the paperweights was a snow globe of the city with a round wooden base. Michael picked it up, tilted the globe upside down, set it back on the credenza, and watched all the tiny snowflakes inside swirl in the globe. His eyes raised to the wall, not noticing at first the funny-looking cat clock that was hung there—a black cat with a small bow tie and a clock on its belly. The white eyes and black tail comically ticked back and forth, keeping time. There was no note on the clock from the person who'd left it, as there was for the others. Michael poked his head out to see if anyone would take responsibility for the clock, but everyone was already back to work.

"Odd."

Michael settled down behind his desk after a few hours of organizing the files and boxes of his personal items he had brought with him. It was starting to look like his own office now, with pictures of Jenny and JR on his desk and credenza. He took a moment in his chair, resting his arms on top of the desk and admiring the office in silence. This really was his office now, and all the hard work he'd spent was finally paying off.

The phone rang, and he picked it up, leaning back in his brown leather chair that rocked back slightly. "Hello?" The person on the other end of the line was congratulating him and talking about the job. Michael listened, turning in his chair and loving the view out his new window. It wasn't much—just another building across the street—but now if he looked down to the right he could see LaSalle Street. In the heart of the financial district, it was busy with people walking back and forth in suits and ties. Out of the corner of his eye was movement to the left. Slowly he turned, still talking on the phone, and saw a black cat on the window ledge, staring at him with its back arched high. It scared the shit out of him.

"Shit!"

The voice on the other end sounded confused and apologized to Michael. The cat clawed at the window, baring sharp little teeth with its mouth wide open. Then it took off running along the edge to the right.

"Jesus!"

The voice on the other side still sounded confused and kept apologizing that things would turn out better soon. Michael held the phone, oblivious to the voice on the other end, and stared out the window. He tried to look down toward LaSalle, and then the cat was gone. He picked up the phone, still in a bit of a trance, and then shook his head and took a deep breath. "Sorry, Steve. A cat just ran by my window. Must be nerves, I guess, of starting this new job." The voice was laughing on the other side. Then they said their good-byes and hung up the phone.

—————

Michael stayed late that night, hoping to miss most of the rush-hour traffic when he drove home. He packed up a few of the items he would not need anymore into one of the boxes he carried in earlier that morning. The office was dark except for a few lights for the maintenance men and the cleaning crew. He stepped out the back door, and the sun was already setting while tall buildings cast shadows in the alley. Large Dumpsters full of garbage sat along the back of the buildings, and wooden pallets rested to one side. He pulled the door shut, making sure it was locked before heading down to LaSalle Street. Sometimes he would see small movement of rats along the Dumpsters, but not tonight.

Tonight was rather quiet for some reason, and the streets appeared to be unusually empty. He walked down LaSalle Street toward Madison and witnessed little traffic. A couple buses and a few cars passed by, but generally it was very quiet. He decided to take a turn and head east to Clark before turning north again.

The drive home would be long, so he decided to find a snack for the way home. There were numerous fast-food places and delis along Clark Street, so he stepped inside one. The place was empty except for one person behind the counter. Michael ordered a small turkey sandwich to go and waited while the person behind the counter made it. Taking a seat at the counter along the window, he looked out onto Clark Street. A couple cars passed by, but no one was on the street. "Where is everyone?"

"Eh?" The man didn't even look up while preparing his sandwich.

"I said where is everyone? Streets are dead."

"I don't know. Usually quiet this time of night. I was just getting ready to close up myself."

Still, it was more quiet than normal in such a busy part of town. Michael could sense it but had no idea why. He looked across the street at a luggage store, which was turning off its lights. There at the bottom of the window was a cat staring at Michael, hissing the moment it saw him and arching its back with the tail pointed straight up.

"Your sandwich is ready," the man behind the counter called.

Michael turned toward the man and then took another look at the luggage store across the street. The store lights were now all turned off, and a sign lit up in red said "Closed." The cat was gone, and Michael couldn't help but blink several times, trying to adjust his eyes to the darkness. Maybe the lights had been playing tricks on his eyes. He turned back to the man, took his sandwich, and then headed out the door. "Thank you." Looking both ways, Michael was certain there was a cat across the street. A streetlight above his head flickered and then burned out, making it darker where he stood. Then he headed off toward Washington Street.

There at the corner of Washington and Clark was the Picasso in the center of the Daley Plaza. A fifty-foot steel structure crafted by the artist sat silently in the middle. As a fan of Picasso, it was one of his favorites, even if he always thought the gymlike structure was odd. Michael thought this was a perfect place to take a small break and eat his sandwich before heading out in his car. He crossed the street and walked up to the large artwork, sitting along the bottom portion.

A soft sound startled him from behind the artwork, and he turned to see what it was. A few people crossed the plaza, but for the most part it was quiet just like the rest of this odd night. Another noise came from his right, only this time Michael knew exactly what it was.

"Meow."

He turned swiftly, seeing the cat, and spit out the remaining food in his mouth. "You're kidding me." The cat crawled over the side of the Picasso statue and then slid down with both paws spread out in front. Another cat meowed from the left and stepped out of the dark from behind a bench. Slowly this one walked toward him. "This is getting old."

The plaza started to fill with cats from everywhere. Cats of all different types and sizes came from hidden corners and alleys. Black cats and yellow cats walked toward Michael, closing the gap around the Picasso and him. He dropped the sandwich. The thought did occur to leave the box of his stuff as well, but he picked that up in his arms and began to run. Without thinking, he ran east instead of west, disoriented by all the cats, and turned right on Dearborn. He was going south, which was farther away from his parked car. Tall buildings did that to you sometimes, making it hard to know which way was north or south. Every so often he would turn and see maybe twenty cats following him. Where was everyone, and why did the city seem so empty?

Urban legend was that rats in the city were big enough to carry away small children, and surely they would scare away any cats in the area. Never in all his time down in the city had Michael seen cats roaming the area. Rats he had seen all the time, scurrying behind garbage cans in the alleys, but never one single cat. Tonight was different. A huge mob of cats was behind him now. Certainly if there were any rats, there were none to be found. It seemed everyone and everything wisely went into hiding.

Turning onto Monroe and leaping down into the small pit of the First National Plaza, Michael hoped the cats had given up by now. Panting out of breath, he turned to look behind and saw nothing but empty streets all around. Bending over to catch his breath, Michael knew they were still there, but so far there was nothing to be seen or heard. Maybe the little paws of the cats were just tired of keeping up.

"God, I am starting to hate that sound."

Behind him was a very large famous piece of mosaic artwork by Chagall. It spanned seventy feet wide and ten feet deep and stood fourteen feet above him. Surrounded by small rails and well lit from the canopy above it, the Chagall was a very pretty sight at this time of night. This was no time for admiring the artwork, of course, and Michael was much farther from his car than he had hoped.

Standing to run again, he hoped to keep his lead on the pack of cats when something appeared over the top of the Chagall. One by one the cats with glowing green eyes started to crawl over the top, like a spigot was just turned on. They leaped off the top, always landing softly on all four paws. Michael picked up the box and wondered why on earth he was still carrying this box all around. He turned west along Monroe and ran a few blocks till he hit Wells. Then he turned right to head up toward his parked car.

This time he never stopped and never looked back, running the entire distance until he arrived at the parking garage where he parked his car. He was safely inside the building and pressed the up button for the elevator. He peeked out the glass window of the door, but there was nothing outside this time. It was great that the streets were completely empty, but it left him with a bit of unease with no one around. The elevator arrived, making a ding before the doors opened. He happily jumped in and pressed the Ireland button. The doors could not have closed any slower, and he actually pulled them closed with both hands. Once the elevator doors shut and it started heading up, a feeling of relief overtook him. The door opened and he stepped onto his floor, but a strange chill ran up and down his spine. This was his floor, but it hit him like a ton of bricks. What did the fortune-teller say to him in that strange raspy voice of another? It was in his pocket, and he dropped the box to find it. There was a paper that she had marked with a name on it, which he had forgotten until now yet carried with him for some odd reason. He had no idea why, but something told him to keep it. He slowly turning around to look at the wall of the parking garage near the elevator and saw a large sign of the floor he was on—Ireland—only it was missing the "I," so it read just as the paper in his hand had scribbled in black: *Reland.*

He took out the keys for his car, picked up the box, and was ready to run. There was no way he was going to stay for any sort of meeting. Things were really getting out of control now, and he had no idea what was going on other than he was tired of this little game the fortune-teller was putting him through. It was her, wasn't it? Was the great fortune-teller's name Zara? Well, she hadn't heard the last of the great Michael Merlino. First, he had to make a break for it now. He peered out the glass door of the empty parking garage and saw no one.

He shoved the glass door open with one hand and then ran across to his car, which was parked on the ramp. It seemed like he was running in thick molasses. A parking garage could be such a confusing place when everything looked the same, and if you didn't mark the exact location of your car it could take longer than it should. Thinking of the cats and what the fortune-teller told him, he was unable to focus and find his car. He passed car after car, unable to find his own, so he stopped and turned around. It was this level, wasn't it? Or maybe it was on the ramp heading down. He turned to go back the other way, heading toward the elevator.

Standing in the middle of the ramp was a man dressed in a long black jacket and a dark rimmed hat that covered his eyes. He slowly raised his head, revealing dark sinister eyes beneath the rim of his hat. Michael froze, staring at him as if in a dream, and the man raised his right arm slowly, pointing straight at Michael. There was no sound in the empty parking lot. It seemed as if the two of them were suddenly in some kind of void.

"Who are you?" Michael asked.

The dark stranger slowly dropped his hand, not saying a word, and kept his eyes on Michael. A familiar hiss came from the darkness beneath his fedora. This took Michael by surprise. He was unable to comprehend what was happening at this very moment. It was like some sort of time warp; everything seemed to go rather slowly. The man's face was dark because of the hat covering his face, and the darkness of the night made it impossible to see any facial features of the man. A cat leaped up on a car to his right, and Michael saw it out of the corner of his eye. There was another meow, only this came from the left. Michael turned to see another cat slowly crawl in over the ledge of the parking ramp. It seemed the cats had followed Michael the entire way and now were determined to surround him. One by one other cats crawled in from beneath cars and over them, from ramps and stairways. The cats were pouring in and closing the circle around Michael. Some cats hissed, and others just meowed. Slowly they walked to the dark stranger and stood around him. The cats all turned now with their eyes on Michael. Some of them held up their paws, revealing their claws. They scratched at dead air, hissing and meowing. Michael felt like he was in some sort of weird dream.

"What do you want?"

The man remained silent, and all the cats began to meow in sequence. Was it an answer to Michael's question? He had no idea but wished there was someone in the empty parking lot other than him. He cautiously looked from side to side for someone nearby. How could he be the only one to see this? Wasn't there one single person in this large city to witness a strange gathering of cats around this strange man? His eyes turned back to the stranger in black, and he felt a cool breeze blow suddenly from nowhere. He could hear rain starting to drizzle softly outside, and that mixed with the hissing and meowing sounds of the cats before him.

A flash of lightning lit up the parking lot of concrete ramps and also lit up the face of the man. It was a gruesome white color, like dead flesh, and long white hair flowed down and tucked into his coat. The eyes of this man, beast, or whatever it was were similar to cat eyes, with vertical slits of black staring at him. The seemingly dead man's eyes were wide and black. The man hissed and tilted his head to one side. His eyes narrowed, and his mouth was slightly open, revealing tiny sharp yellow teeth that could devour raw meat. Thunder echoed loudly in the city, bouncing off large skyscrapers, and rumbled in the concrete parking lot.

"What are you?"

A cat hissed behind Michael, and he whipped around to defend himself from the unseen terror. Nothing was there but empty parked cars. Michael turned quickly back to the man and the cats before him, only to see nothing at all. Like the flash of lightning that disappeared so quickly, so did this man and his cats. Once standing there before him, now all of them were gone, leaving nothing behind except for the chill in the air that suddenly appeared in their place.

"What the hell?"

Michael stood there, shivering and staring at the empty place where the ghostlike creature and the cats once stood. He saw his car just ahead and the windows were heavily fogged. Still holding the box of things in his arms, he walked closer to his car. Where had this cold air come from? He knew it had to do with the dark man who hissed. He walked cautiously to his car and saw that something was written in the fog on the windshield. He went closer, confused at what was written, and tried to decipher what it was: *Rafalav*. Some of the letters, such as the *f* and the *r*, looked backward, but he was certain that was what they were. He opened the door, placed the box in the passenger seat, and then looked up and realized it was written to be read from inside the car. "Valafar," he whispered—like that just solved everything. What the hell was Valafar? Maybe the question was: who was Valafar? He turned the key to the ignition, started the car, and then flicked the switch of the window wipers, which swooshed back and forth a couple of times and wiped away the wet dew and the word from the windshield.

# Ra Valfa Shake

Nearly a week passed since the late-night neighborhood party. Neither Jenny nor Michael talked much about the events that happened. Michael was busy at work, and Jenny was busy with the million things she had to do. The two of them avoided each other, not wanting confrontation yet. He knew there had to be an end at some point. Jenny kept busy at school and driving back and forth to the university. She was focused on her job, which took plenty of her time. This week she stopped off at the hospital and some doctors' offices, so there was hardly time for dinner. The two settled for carryout and frozen pizza. Michael was busy settling in his new office. This new job was going to take more of Michael's time, as Jenny had warned. Then there was the incident of the cats in the city. The meeting in the parking lot spooked the hell out of him. What was he to tell Jenny? She would think he was crazy or maybe laugh at him. No, he was going to keep this to himself. He would take the train from now on because there was no way he was heading back to that parking lot. Their son, JR, probably had the worst of it. Both parents worked so hard day after day. He played with the babysitter but always asked for "Mum."

The babysitter was a girl named Susan Keng; most people called her Susie. She was a young girl just out of college, still naive about life in general. She was a thin girl with short dark hair, and she usually wore a hat of some type. Today she was wearing a knitted hat of orange and blue, which was pulled down low. Grunge best described her look of baggy pants and a sweatshirt. "Hey yo, JR" was always the first thing she said when she saw JR, who lit up the moment he saw her. The two of them spent a lot of time together during the day, playing games like hide-and-seek. Susie would hide in plain sight most of the time, knowing JR wasn't quite so mobile yet. She would cover her face with both hands, which really made JR laugh.

Michael was home early after a busy first week in his new position at the bank. Franklin said he could use a little time off, seeing bags under his eyes. Franklin assumed it was the stress of the job, getting to know everyone and their positions. "It will take time," he told Michael, not wanting him to burn out early. Little did he know the stress was caused by some rabid cats and a strange man—or was it a ghost?

Michael relaxed on the train. He closed his eyes the entire way until the conductor shouted, "Crystal Lake."

Traffic was normally bad on a Friday during rush hour, but he was early enough to miss the rest of the working crowd. The drive was uneventful and gave him time to think. He made a quick stop at the hospital for another rabies shot. The scabs on his neck and shoulders actually got worse instead of better, but he didn't tell the nurse who asked how he was doing. What was he going to tell Jenny about the other night? Time went by, but eventually they would need to talk. Tonight would be the night.

When he walked into the house Jenny was sitting on the couch, watching a cartoon with JR. The two of them looked so cute. He stood there silently, staring for a while. All his worries washed away in that one special moment, looking at the two of them. Michael didn't notice the dog lying on the side of the couch, who raised his head and barked at Michael when he approached.

"Hey!" His surprise was ruined by the dog.

"Hi, Michael. You're home early." Jenny smiled.

"Yeah, Franklin thought I could use a little time off, and I couldn't wait to see you two."

JR turned and looked straight at Michael and then back to Jenny. He tugged at her shoulder. "Mum?"

"It's Dad. Dad," Michael half-joked.

"Well, glad to see you home early."

114

Michael tugged his tie, loosening it about his neck. Then he sat beside the two and put his arm around Jenny. "Hey, I wanted to talk to you."

Jenny stared at him for a moment and then turned her back to him and kissed JR on his head. "Off with ya." She smiled at JR while he sat on the floor. Then JR placed both hands forward and started to crawl toward some toys. Jenny turned back to Michael, no longer smiling. "Okay. I'll listen."

"Well, uh, first off . . ." Now he was nervous. Maybe he should just let this go. Maybe it was better to just forget all of this, but Michael wanted it over. He wanted to get this out. "A couple of guys and I were out late and went to a bar . . ." So he lied. "So when I realized how late it was I ran home through some of the neighbors' yards and ran into a thornbush." If this was the worst lie in the history of mankind, then it was about to get worse. "And as far as that perfume? It had to be someone at the party or the bar, but how am I supposed to know? I mean it's not like I was sleeping with anyone."

"Oh, of course not," Jenny answered back sarcastically, looking directly at him.

There was no way he was looking at her. He forced a laugh and looked at JR. "Well, anyways, I'm home and I love you, Jen. You know I do." He reached over and hugged her tight. The claw marks on his back were hurting more than ever, and he winced when her hand reached around and touched his lower neck.

Jenny sat there, hardly hugging him back, and looked off in the distance. She knew there was something else, but she couldn't put a finger on it yet. "I love you too," she whispered, because she did. She lay her head back on his.

---

Traffic was heavier now that it was Friday during rush hour. He turned out of Rolling Hills, and the traffic stopped almost immediately. The area had been highly developed recently so there were no major roads to support all the new traffic. Crystal Lake was a small rural town that had exploded in recent years, developing the surrounding farmland. The road system had been built years ago for a smaller population, but now that the city limits and neighboring villages had grown, the streets were outdated. Michael drove the Taurus into town, and it took about a half hour to drive the short five miles to the village. The town of Crystal Lake was busy with commuters riding the train back and forth from the city. The crossing gates raised and the warning bells stopped ringing once the train moved through the town. People were crossing the train tracks dressed in their business suits to either walk home or meet their rides home.

The center of town was a mix of retail and residential buildings. Most were about a hundred years old or older. There was, of course, the main bank of Crystal Lake, but the competition found their way so now there were about eight or nine banks in the village. Tommie's Bar was already nearly filled to capacity with people overflowing for happy hour. Tommie himself was outside handing out flyers for the band that would be playing tonight and gift certificates to Tommie's Restaurant. Competition had tried to come into Crystal Lake for years, but Tommie was always able to keep them at bay one way or another until recently. Now that the younger crowd was moving into the village, they no longer wanted the old neighborhood bar but something clean and new like the big chain from the West Coast called Sherbrock's. America had become one large chain store and shut down the small neighborhood stores and banks. There was no more personal touch now that the chain stores were here. Everything was impersonal nowadays, with e-mail and texting. The younger crowd just didn't want to be involved.

Then there was the Wallace Wagon, which had supplied all household needs for generations. The outside of the old building had a large wooden sign above stating it was in fact the Wallace Wagon. A small glass front with a double wooden door leading into the store was very deceiving. Over the years the Wallaces had taken over all the nearby stores within a block radius and connected them, making this once-small thrift store into a very large community shopping store. It supplied everything from groceries and household supplies to tools and hardware. They wanted to have a little something for everyone.

The owners of the Wallace Wagon were Paul and Mary Wallace. They were fifth generation of the late great Henry Wallace, who was one of the original founders of the area. Paul Wallace was stuck in his ways of running the business because there was never a need to change—that is, until recently, when stores like Walmart opened nearby, offering everything this store sold and more. It was hard competing with such a large company, and Paul Wallace just didn't have the deep pockets of wealth to advertise like Walmart did. Paul's wife, Mary, was an intelligent person who wanted to change the way the Wallace Wagon did business. She wanted to go head-to-head with Walmart, open stores around the area, and eventually franchise the store, but it was too risky. Paul figured Walmart was just a fad and would eventually pass, just like all the others did. Paul wasn't the smartest of the bunch, and some thought Mary just married him because of his money.

Michael stepped out of the Taurus and walked down the sidewalks of the village toward the Wallace Wagon. Most of the parking spots were taken—and all of them near the Wagon—so Michael had to park a couple blocks away. The town was busy for a Friday afternoon. A bell on top of the door jingled when Michael pressed open the wooden door to the Wallace Wagon. "Welcome to the Wallace Wagon for all your family needs. Have a great day!" the boy standing at the front greeted. He was a thin redheaded boy with freckles. A checkered red-and-white shirt and blue jeans made him look like the old television puppet, Howdy Doody.

Michael took a shopping cart and pushed it up and down the aisles. He held in his hand a note of all the items he needed to purchase. Most of the store was filled with household items, but there were some additional items to compete with the bigger chains. He passed a small section of food, where a man wearing a dark suit and a hat covering his eyes stood at a table selling a new diet shake. On the table was a very large blender with a couple of cartons of the diet drink Ra Valfa for sale and a large pitcher of water. Three customers were standing around the table, drinking small cups of the product. A soft melody was playing over the speakers, coaxing shoppers to relax. The melody was soothing and actually put some of them to sleep—like Stan Worthington, who was lying on a couch and snoring in the audio department as the news played on eight televisions simultaneously. There were a couple of nice, thin plasma televisions on the wall with a larger floor television to one side and fifteen different smaller models, six of which were on. Kids were playing a video game on one of the smaller televisions. Two of those boys were shouting while shooting a gun at an imaginary enemy on the screen. None of this bothered Stan, who kept lying there on the couch snoring.

The tools and hardware department was a small section in the back corner of the store. It was put in a few years ago to compete with the large chain stores. On the list in Michael's hand were a few items for his tool chest back at home. He needed a flathead screwdriver, along with a Phillips, and found plenty of them here. There were several different brands and many different sizes. It was really amazing how many choices there were. The eight-piece set was the nicest one, which included a free flashlight with the purchase. He tossed it in the cart. "Nice." It was fall, and he was going to need a rake for the leaves. He found a nice one with a wooden pole and placed it in the basket. He also needed an ax for the wood in the backyard. There were a couple different types, but he wanted one with a larger handle if he was going to be chopping a bigger tree. He found one with a bright yellow handle and placed it in the cart. In the same section was a box of large plastic garbage bags, which were on the list, so he placed those in the cart too. Finally, he needed some duct tape because it was the answer to everything—or so his friends always joked. Every man had to have duct tape on his tool bench, so Michael grabbed three rolls.

The pet section was very large at the Wagon, with four rows of supplies. Anything you desired for your pet could be found here in the pet section. One row was dedicated just to fish, with two rows of both fresh- and saltwater fish tanks. There was an aisle for cat and dog playthings, like dog bones and catnip, and another just for food. No pets were in the store other than the fish, so it caught

Michael by surprise when he heard the sound of a cat. Paranoid, he turned quickly to see a stuffed toy that mimicked the sound of a cat. It was in the cat section with bags of cat food above it. Next to it was the dog section, which was what he was looking for. He grabbed a large bag of dog food and tossed it into the cart. The stuffed cat meowed again, and Michael looked around, wondering if anyone was looking. Seeing no one, he grabbed the cat and then stuffed it beneath some bags of dog food so the sound could not be heard again. Then he started to push the cart again. He laughed to himself, letting the child in him have some fun.

Then he heard the low sound of a cat's meow behind him in the aisles of pets. The meow—low, whiny, and sickly—came from high above. There was nothing in this section that could make a noise, other than the fish and some air pumps and filters that hissed. The stuffed cat was buried beneath the dog food, and Michael wondered if maybe it wasn't buried enough. The sight of the cat standing on top of the shelves, with its body arched and tail in the air, didn't seem out of place at first. Maybe it was another stuffed animal, to create an ambience about the place. The cat had brown fur, resembling a household cat with rounded ears and black tips, but this cat seemed slightly bigger than a household cat. Things did not seem out of place just yet, but it was about to turn ugly. The cat turned his head very slowly, almost intentionally, and that sent shivers up and down Michael's spine. Its movement was almost mechanical, and those eyes—black and dead—stared at him. The cat had one dark black eye that seemed blacker than coal, but it was the other eye that Michael recognized immediately: milky white and spooky as hell. The white globe blinked at him. Did the cat just wink with its milky eye? Michael swore it did. Baring its sharp yellow teeth, the cat hissed, and drool dripped from its fangs. The neck seemed to nod, while the rest of the cat's body was still. The head slipped down like an involuntary flinch or shrug. Then it raised back to its shoulders like nothing was wrong.

"I know you," Michael whispered to the cat.

Leaping over the back side of the shelves, the large cat disappeared without a sound. Michael looked around, holding the handle of the shopping cart. He looked up and down the aisle, waiting for the cat to come back, but there was no sound other than the music coming out of the speakers above. He was certain the cat was going to leap out at any moment from one of the boxes on the shelf. Quickly he started to push the cart down the aisle toward the front, keeping his eyes on the upper shelves. He stopped a couple times because the front wheel of the cart was wiggling, causing the cart to squeak loudly. He gritted his teeth, hating that the cart was giving away his position to the cat. "Shhhhh!"

He heard a crash in aisle thirteen, which was the candy section, followed by a woman's scream. He stopped for a moment to listen and heard some more boxes tumbling. Then another woman screamed, and there were some footsteps running toward the sound. Michael wasted no more time and ran, pushing the cart toward the door. If he had known this cat really was after him, Michael would have dropped the cart right there and ran, but he was not superstitious. Besides, he had killed the other cat.

A voice came over the loudspeaker. "Cleanup in aisle thirteen."

Some more footsteps shuffled across the floor. Aisle thirteen was a mess of boxes and bags of candy spread everywhere. Mrs. Anna Worthington was sitting on the ground against the candy shelves, curled up in a ball and covering her head with both hands. She had just been loading up a supply of candy for her husband, who would later tell her he was running to her side. The cat was in the middle of the pile of candy. It bolted up the moment one of the supply boys pointed at it. The cat leaped up to the top shelf, knocked over more boxes to the floor, and disappeared again.

Things seemed quiet for the moment, but Michael knew better and waited for the other shoe to drop. Straight ahead was the checkout counter, just about eight rows away. If he could just quietly push the cart to checkout while the cat was busy, he could make it. But he stared down to the cart with the broken wheel in front. "Damn cart."

There was another crash, but this one was louder and closer in aisle twenty-five, which was the flatware and glass section two aisles over. Glass shattered, making a loud sound, and the hiss and sickly meow of the cat followed.

A voice came over the loudspeaker. "Cleanup in aisle twenty-five."

This aisle had been Mary Wallace's pet project, with shelves for fancy wineglasses and tulip-shaped champagne glasses. She had worked on the details of this little aisle for over a week, including what it should consist of and how to arrange the glass. The sound of glass breaking was like nails across the chalkboard for Mary.

Michael was not going to hang around for another swarm of cats to crawl out from the shelves or the ghostly man who left messages all around, only to disappear once again. Grabbing the cart full of items on his list and figuring he could come back for the rest later, he pushed it toward the front door. The noise seemed farther away. He heard more crashes behind him, and then another woman screamed. He reassured himself that none of this was his fault.

The man at the blender was pouring out a new batch of the superspecial diet shake into small plastic cups that covered the table. Michael was pushing his cart past when the cat leaped out from behind. It came from above, leaping from the top of the refrigerated section with all four paws spread out and claws ready to dig into Michael's flesh. If it wasn't for the loud "rrrrrraaaaawr" of the cat, Michael would have been totally surprised. Cats normally leaped so silently, but this cat was definitely sick. Michael whipped around, already on alert, and grabbed the cat with both hands. Somehow he grabbed hold of the body, and the cat gnashed its ugly teeth at Michael and clawed at him. Spitting and hissing, the cat was able to claw up Michael's arm pretty well. Blood started to spill, and he tossed the cat hard against a wall. The cat slumped over, seemingly hurt, but Michael wasn't taking any chances.

Slowly the cat lifted a paw, rose to its feet, and stared at Michael with one black eye and the other milky one. Its head lowered, and it leaned down, placing one paw in front of the other. Step by step it walked to Michael, barely showing its sharp yellow teeth. This time Michael looked right at it, and he swore it was definitely smiling. The steps of the cat became longer in stride, and soon it was running toward Michael. It leaped in the air with paws and legs stretched, and Michael instinctively grabbed for the rake in the cart. Like a batter seeing the pitch all the way across the plate, he took a swing and nailed that cat hard against the wall. Quickly he ran to the cat and swatted it again with the rake. The cat did not move this time, and he covered the cat with the rake and then pulled it over to the table with the blender.

The man blending the super shakes had long run away from the scene, leaving the table with the blender and the cartons of super diet Ra Valfa shakes. Mrs. Anna Worthington was watching all of this in disbelief. She would later tell police that Michael was a crazed terrorist attacking a poor innocent cat and caused the whole nightmare at the Wagon. Michael, on the other hand, had his own ideas on what was happening, and he was going to finish it right here and now. Pulling off the top of the blender, he grabbed the unconscious cat with one hand and then slammed it hard into the top of the glass blender. It was obviously a very large blender to fit this large cat inside, which never completely fit. The head went in, and the two front paws. The tail and the two back legs stuck out the top. He placed the blender on the motor and flipped the switch to "liquify." Around and around the cat went at a mesmerizing speed. Blood splattered everywhere, and Mrs. Worthington fainted.

# FELIS CHAUS

Police were called to the scene that evening at the Wallace Wagon. Flashing red and blue lights filled the village of Crystal Lake, lighting up the entire area. Fire trucks at the scene blocked all the main roads and made traffic a nightmare in the small village. All units were called in, because who knew when the next time a small town like this would be able to actually drive the hook and ladder? The roof was two stories high, and the fire chief wasn't going to take any chances. The police called in the rescue crew, not because there was a fire but because people were down in the aisles of the Wagon. Both Anna and Stan Worthington had to be hauled off in an ambulance. A crowd gathered around the roped-off area of the Wagon and tried to catch a glimpse of the mayhem that had occurred inside. Police tried to quiet the citizens down, and rumors spread of a mass terrorist attempt on this small suburb of Chicago. Television reporters started piling in and setting up their communication vans.

Lieutenant Steve Case was the first to be called to the scene, but when he was informed it involved cats, he requested another officer to report instead of him. After finding the cat left in the bag by Shawn a couple weeks back, Steve hadn't been able to sleep much. When he finally was able to sleep, he dreamed about cats that talked and ran after him. "No thanks, guys. I'll sit this one out." Besides, his wife had been missing for nearly a month now, and he was feeling different lately. The two of them had gone on a camping trip down near St. Louis when funny things started happening. His wife Cindy had told him he was talking in his sleep lately, but he just figured it was the stress of working late night shifts. One night the dream of a cat sitting on the ledge just outside his window seemed so real. It was talking to him, and everything seemed fine until the man dressed in a dark cloak appeared out of nowhere. The cat turned and hissed with one milky white eye, and Steve woke up in a cold sweat, happy to be alive. He remembered waking up alone in the tent. His wife Cindy was gone, and after an exhausting week-long search, Steve had headed back home alone. Once he arrived back home things never seemed the same. He tried to cope with his wife missing but found it hard to sleep. The dreams of cats became more real, and when he found the cat in the bag it really creeped him out. No, Steve was going to sit this one out for sure.

---

Michael was handcuffed and placed in the backseat of the squad car. Staring out of the window, he tried to keep his head low so no one would see him. The first thing he noticed was that the backseat did not have any door handles. The seats were a smooth vinyl, and the back of the front seats had a cage that separated the front seat safely from the back.

The police officer in charge of taking Michael into the station opened up the front door and hopped inside. He gave the siren a quick toot and then put the car in drive. People tried to get close to see who was inside, and a line of policemen held them back with arms spread apart. Cameras were flashing, and the camera crews for the news tried to get a peek at the backseat of the car. In different circumstances Michael would have felt like one of the Beatles heading out from a concert tour, by the way people surrounded the car. This wasn't a tour, though, and he wasn't one of the Beatles.

"You caused quite a commotion inside there tonight."

"I didn't do anything."

"Chopping up a poor little cat in a blender isn't anything?" The officer rolled his eyes and laughed.

"You don't understand. Why won't anyone listen to me? I'm innocent."

"Yeah, yeah, yeah. That's what they all say."

"If someone would just let me explain. All I was doing was shopping."

"Shopping for what? Ground cat meat?"

"It was self-defense."

The police officer laughed. "Yeah, tell that to the cat."

They arrived at the station, which was only a few blocks away. Michael remained silent for the two-minute drive. He tugged his handcuffed hands, hating the fact that he was hunched over in the backseat and handcuffed for something that wasn't even his fault. This was the third cat he had killed, but no one knew that other than him. The question was why? What was going on, and why were these cats attacking him? Were the cats related? He had a suspicion they somehow were.

The police station was a small building and inside was a woman sitting behind a switchboard, wearing a headset and talking into a microphone that sat on the table before her. Becky Tomlinson was a heavyset woman who kept tabs on every pulse in the village. The buttons on her blue shirt were bulging, ready to burst. She liked to think it was the muscles that caused this unique situation.

The officer led Michael in by tugging his arm and set him down on a bench. His shirt was a bloody mess, and his face was splattered with crimson stains of the cat's blood. Sitting there on the bench all alone, he looked like some sort of crazy lunatic who had just gone on a wild killing spree. Up on the wall was a corkboard with pictures of wanted people. He looked at the faces wanted by the FBI and came across a funny one that just didn't seem to belong there. It was a picture of a cat with its head locked in a guillotine and a bubble coming from its mouth that said, "Have you seen the man who killed me?"

"Stay here and don't try any funny stuff."

"I'll try not to hobble away," Michael responded in a sarcastic tone.

"Don't you get sassy with me, boy! You're in deep shit right now."

"Had a fun one, I hear," Becky said.

"Nothing I can't handle." He winked at Becky.

The chief walked in and closed the door behind him, silencing the large crowd that was assembling outside. The news media wanted answers on this most recent incident that occurred in this little town. Placing his back to the door, Chief Marty Dugan took a deep breath before taking another step inside. Michael could see by the look on his face that he wasn't in the best of moods.

An officer walked in from the back, carrying the pitcher full of the blended cat with its feet still dangling out the top. Blood was coagulating at the bottom of the pitcher, and rigor mortis was already setting in. The cat was so stiff it seemed to be part of the pitcher now. When the officer held the pitcher to the side, the legs did not bend. A small amount of blood on the top dripped to the floor.

"Where do you want this thing?"

"What in God's name is going on here?" Marty had no idea what was going on just yet.

"It's the cat, Chief." The officer laughed and tugged at a paw that stuck out of the glass pitcher.

"Well, set it down and stop playing with the paw, for God's sake!" That was the second time the chief used the word "God," and a small vein was pulsing on his forehead. The last time he used the word was when his brother-in-law was pulled over for speeding five miles over the speed limit in a thirty-five-mile-per-hour zone. He never heard the last of that one from his wife and was certain to give them all hell at the station. "And God damn it, what the hell is going on?"

Michael was sitting on the bench, watching this display of unrestrained behavior. All he'd wanted was to pick up a few items at the Wagon and head back home for a nice quiet evening. The shirt on him worked like a wick, soaking up the blood, and sent a chill right through his body. He tried to lean forward, but the old cuts on his neck were starting to get worse. Now both hands were cut as well, and he wondered if the rabies shots would help. Recognizing the chief immediately, he groaned, looked to the side, and tugged the cuffed hands behind him.

The chief motioned for the officer with the blender to set it down. Then he raised his chin to the other officer so they could talk privately. The three of them stepped into a room and closed the door, hoping to keep the conversation private. The room was small, with a window across the top half of one wall so a person could see in. The chief raised his hands in the air and shouted while the other two stood there listening. Most of the words were inaudible, but you could decipher "God" more than once. Becky turned her back and held the headphones tightly to her head. Finally they emerged from the room. All three of them stopped and looked straight at Michael. The one officer took the blender to another room to mark it as evidence, and the other officer walked out the back door and placed his hat back on his head. The chief paused, folding his arms across his chest before walking over to Michael. He stood before him for a moment, looking down, and Michael wondered if he recognized him. It had been one meeting—and under different circumstances, of course. Michael was now handcuffed with blood covering his clothes and face.

"I know you, don't I?"

"Uh, yeah. Sort of."

"Sort of?"

"Uh, yeah. I'm the guy who had the Boss Mustang."

"Speeding, you mean," the chief shot right back, immediately correcting Michael when they first met.

"Well, yeah but—"

"And now here you are again." The chief moved closer, pulled out a small key, and placed a hand on his back. "Lean over." He pulled Michael up, inserted the small key into the hole in the cuffs, and turned it. One cuff was unlocked, and Michael pulled the other to his front. The chief then unlocked it as well. "Now, why don't we start from the beginning."

"All right." Michael hesitated. "I was just buying some things for home, when this cat started attacking everyone."

"Whoa, whoa, boy. It's not every day a person shops at the Wagon with a cat attacking everyone." Dugan held up his hands in a slow-down gesture. "Now, again. What exactly happened?"

This time Michael paused, looking at the chief before speaking again. He started at the beginning, telling him how he parked, walked into the Wagon, and shopped for the items on his list when he first heard the cat in the pet section. There wasn't really anything else that he left out of the story. It was short and sweet perhaps, but that was what had happened. Did he tell the chief that he had a weird feeling he was being hunted by cats because he'd killed a kitten? Hell no, and he wasn't going to start with such nonsense now. It was just a weird coincidence that he'd now killed three cats. It was even more of an odd coincidence that all three cats had similar characteristics—like the milky eye, and what the hell was with the neck on this cat? The chief would think Michael was nuts, for sure, so he kept it all to himself. "Look, I was shopping for items on my list." He reached into his pocket to take out the note. "Here, it has a list of the items I was buying before this cat started running around, attacking everyone."

The chief took the note, looked at it, and then raised his eyes to Michael. "An ax? Plastic garbage bags?" Michael didn't see anything odd about that and just shrugged his shoulders at the chief. "Duct tape? Sounds to me like a shopping list for a mass murderer. Boy? I have a lot of questions for you, and I want answers."

Lieutenant Steve stepped back into the room and walked up to the chief with a sheet of paper in his hands. He'd stayed back at the station, away from the whole incident, not visiting the crime scene. He handed the paper to the chief with his eyes set on Michael the entire time. "Chief? This c-c-cat doesn't seem to be a typical c-cat," he stuttered.

"What the hell's wrong with you, Steve? You got a cold or something?" He snatched the paper from Steve's hand and started reading it. "All right, well, get the cat or whatever the hell is left of it to someone who can tell us what kind of cat it is, will ya?"

"Aye, Chief." His eyes, although slightly dazed, were still on Michael as he took the sheet in his hand. "I'll get right on it." He turned to walk out of the room when Michael started to talk about the blender.

"Chief, I was just minding my own business when I walked past the guy selling that Ra Valfa stuff in the blender."

"You mean strawberry smoothies," replied Lieutenant Steve.

"No, I mean Ra Valfa. The guy was selling Ra Valfa. Some diet drink," Michael replied.

Lieutenant Steve started laughing and shook his head back and forth. "Son? You're really a trip. Who ever heard of Ravalva? That man is in there every Friday selling his smoothies, and today it was strawberries." Steve started to twirl a finger around his ears, looking at the chief and motioning with his eyes back to Michael that maybe he was a little nuts.

"It's Ra Valfa, and I know what I saw." But did Michael? The name of the shake was a weird one he had never heard of, it but still he would have known if the guy was selling a strawberry smoothie. That's when it hit him. What did the shake guy look like? A dark suit and a hat was all he remembered now. "I am sure if you find the man you can ask him."

"Chief? Kenny left hours before this incident. I asked about the blender and they told me he had to leave in a rush because his wife called in a fit about their dog. I guess he left the blender there, unable to clean it up."

The room started to spin, and Michael felt sick to his stomach, holding it with one hand. If the guy selling smoothies was gone, then who the hell was the man selling the diet drink? What kind of person sold diet drinks with a dark cloak on? Michael's mind started whirling around, and his hand went to his head. He was certain a man had been there, but this made absolutely no sense. He closed his eyes and started to repeat the name in his head, knowing it was familiar: "Ra Valfa . . . Ra Valfa . . ."

The chief turned back to Michael, looking down to the paper in his hand once again and studying what was written before looking back up to Michael again. "Do you know a man named Shawn Williams?"

Lieutenant Steve bolted upright, as if shocked by a cattle prod. "Chief? I gotta go." He ran off to find out more info on the cat.

Of course Michael knew his brother-in-law, and the chief knew it too, but what Michael did not know was what the chief knew. "Yes, I know him."

"Is he a friend of yours?" the chief toyed with him.

"He's my brother-in-law."

"Ah, I see. Well, he was seen a little over a week ago tossing a bag in the forest. Do you know anything about this?" Dugan kept his eyes locked on Michael, studying his face.

"I don't know what you're talking about."

"Ah, so you're going to deny having anything to do with this."

"I am not denying anything, but if you're trying to put words in my mouth then I am going to say no."

"Well, we checked out the bag, and inside was a dead cat. Now, either you are some sort of cat killer or it runs in the family, and I am not going to be a happy chief if there's a lunatic running around killing cats in my town."

"I'm telling you the truth. That cat attacked me in the Wagon."

"And what about this cat in the forest preserve that your brother-in-law was dumping?" Dugan pulled out the shopping list in his hand, held it out till he could read it, and focused his old eyes without reading glasses. "A plastic garbage bag."

"I don't know anything about that." He took his chance. Certainly the chief didn't know what had happened or he wouldn't be asking these questions. Better to be silent and not answer for now, he figured.

The chief listened but had no further questions at the moment. "All right, you have one phone call, and then you can wait in the cell." Dugan turned and waved to one of the officers. "Take him in."

---

Michael was sitting in a cell of concrete after being questioned by the chief for what seemed like an hour. The cell had one door made of steel bars and a small window above his head with steel bars blocking out any type of escape. He sat on a bench with nothing else around except a stainless steel toilet in the corner and a dim light that was caged above his head. The chief had nothing on him, and Michael made that famous one call to Jenny, who seemed so calm on the phone.

"Hello, Jen?"

"Hi, what's up?"

"Well, long story—I'll tell you when I get home—but can you pick me up at the police station in town?"

There was silence for a moment before she finally gave a short answer. "Give me ten minutes."

He was all alone when a shadow moved across the floor near his feet. The moonlight shone through the small window, adding more light than the small bulb that was dimly lit up above. He turned to see what made the shadow, blinking several times and rubbing his eyes, unsure if it was real or not. Standing on the tiny windowsill was a cat staring down at Michael. Its back was hunched, and its tail was in the air. It was baring sharp little teeth and hissing at Michael. A paw reached up and clawed at the window, baring sharp little claws.

Stunned, Michael looked up at the cat, which started to pace back and forth along the window. It was a small cat looking in, but who knew if there wasn't a bigger one outside waiting or not. He stood up, grabbed the bars of the door, and peered down the empty hallway. Panic started to take over at the thought of being locked up in a cell all alone with a cat outside the window. What if that man dressed in a dark cloak was outside as well? He knew there was nothing the cat could do, but being locked up with no escape did things to his mind. He grabbed the cold steel bars and rattled them a number of times. There was nothing but silence, and the hissing cat paced back and forth.

"Hey! Anyone here?"

He heard a large metal door open somewhere in the distance. Michael was relieved to hear footsteps next. He pressed his face between the cold metal bars to peer down the hallway, hoping to see someone. The footsteps came closer to his cell until he was able to see a man in uniform approaching. He turned to the window and saw the cat pacing back and forth.

"What's up?" the officer asked.

"I know this is going to sound strange, but there's a cat up in that window." He turned to point at the window, but the cat was gone.

"I don't see a thing. Sometimes being in a cell all alone does things to you and you start seeing things." He laughed, turned a key inside the door, and opened it. "Follow me. The chief has a couple of questions before you leave."

They made their way up the stairs to a small room with one window looking into the main police station. The chief and another officer sat down with Michael at the table. He looked around the room, which was empty except for the table and some chairs. A few papers were scattered on the table.

"We have the report on the cat, and things just don't exactly seem right," Chief Dugan stated.

Michael looked up to him, having absolutely no idea what he was talking about. He looked back and forth between him and the other officer in the room. He wanted the chief to tell him now about the other cats, but reality hit and he knew the chief would just place him in a straightjacket. "Oh?"

"Seems this cat isn't from these parts." The chief shook his head and laughed. "A felis chow?" He turned back to the other officer and pointed at the sheet. "Is that right?" The other officer shook his head and the chief tried again. "A felis chaus." He smiled, proud to finally say the name correctly. "It's a swamp cat or jungle cat—similar to a domestic cat, but this thing is from Egypt."

This totally confused Michael, and he held both hands up on the table. "Chief, I have no idea what's going on."

"Neither do I, but I'm gonna find out," the chief snapped back. "I don't know what a cat would be doing here all the way from Egypt, but I would suspect someone stole it from the zoo or something." He stood up, keeping his eyes on Michael. "When was the last time you visited the zoo?"

"If you are trying to insinuate that I stole the cat, you are way off base. I haven't been to the zoo in years, nor have I stolen a cat." Now Michael was getting pissed off. He took a deep breath to calm himself. "Look, why would I take a cat from the zoo and release him into the Wagon, only to kill the damn thing in a blender? Sounds like a book to me."

"Maybe, but I have my suspicions there's more to this story than meets the eye."

Michael just shrugged, remembering the tip he gave himself not to speak any more than he had to. Instead he just remained silent and stared off at the blank wall before him. They had nothing on him, and he knew it—other than some wild cat (from Egypt, no less) that he killed in the Wagon.

The chief stood up, pushed both hands to the table, and slid his chair back behind him. "Your ride's here."

Michael stood up from his chair, slowly following the eyes of the chief toward the door. Standing at the door was Jenny with tears in her eyes. She didn't say a word, and Michael walked toward her. It would be a long drive home, but he was happy to be out of there. He gave her a big hug and then tugged her hand gently in his, feeling the warmth of her body.

He turned before stepping out of the station and gave Chief Dugan a glance. He saw the way he was watching him, analyzing every step that he took. He felt that familiar tingle inside, like he had known the chief for years. The two of them were going to get better acquainted; he could feel it in his bones.

# TREASURE

## JULY 19, 2008

The sky was dark as ink out in the Sahara, with no lights other than the stars that beamed so brightly. Out there a person could see stars one never knew existed. A full moon was nearly blinding in the dark sky. The night creatures that roamed the desert started to come out from small crevices beneath the sands. A couple of scorpions scattered across the table near one of the tents. A swamp cat poked its head out from behind a crop of rocks and scurried after a mouse.

Marty and Mohamed prepared for the journey into the tomb, following the others inside. The tunnel was very small and not for the faint of heart. The claustrophobic would have nightmares in such a long, cramped tunnel that was dark and very hot. The air seemed very restrictive. A large white pipe running along the upper corner of the tunnel provided air inside the tomb, but that was of little comfort. A string of lights covered the ceiling every ten or fifteen feet. The men held onto both sides of the tunnel while they descended to its depths.

The men piled into a large cavern, and Marty held up a light to the room. The men's eyes adjusted to the darkness that revealed many moving shadows. Mostly empty, the twenty-by-twenty-foot room was made of stone with a ceiling about fifteen feet high. Cracks in the walls allowed black snakes to slither in and out of them. Another tunnel slightly larger than the one before lay straight ahead of them.

"Snakes! I hate snakes, Mohamed." Marty bit his lip, trying not to laugh and repeating the famous words of Indiana Jones from the movie.

"This is no time to joke, Marty," Mohamed scolded him.

"Aw, lighten up, Mohamed."

Mohamed motioned with his hand to continue, and the men moved into the tunnel. This time the tunnel was not as long, but it moved downward in a steeper slope. This happened several times as they went from chamber to tunnel to chamber once again. There were five chambers altogether, some larger than the rest and most cleared of items. Scorpions and snakes were the only things left.

They came to the last tunnel that led to the final chamber they had opened. Each chamber had a secret tunnel leading on to the next chamber. Marty was certain there was another tunnel, and now it would seem he was right.

"I told you there was another one." Ducking his head through the tunnel, Marty couldn't control his excitement now.

Mohamed was leading the way now, with Marty breathing down his back. The others stayed close, although they continued to look over their backs. Whatever was down there scared the living daylights out of the rest of the men. The only ones who stayed were Mohamed's best men, including Abdul.

Finally they broke through to the last remaining chamber, lit up all around the perimeter. One by one they crowded around, bumping into each other while they stood there amazed at what they saw. It was a large room, about forty feet wide by twenty-five feet long, with a ceiling of about fifteen feet high. The walls were filled with all sorts of Egyptian writings and colorful paintings.

What amazed them about the room, though, was the light on the other side. A crack in the wall none of them had seen before emitted a soft green glow. Dust swirled in the room, and this only magnified the green light that came from the crack.

"What the hell?" Marty stared in wonder at the crack in a trancelike state.

"Now you see . . . now you see why they run. We should do the same," Mohamed said.

Then the other men turned, ready to run as well, but Marty was quick to shout, his voice echoing throughout the tomb. "Don't you dare leave yet!" They froze in their steps, unsure, but deep down they were ready to run at a moment's notice. Marty turned back to the light now and took a couple steps closer to the crack. He looked back several times while the others stared wild-eyed at him. Closer he crept till finally he stopped only a few inches from the crack. He paused with uncertainty before turning around with a laugh. "It's not what it seems." He turned to peer into the crack, waving a hand for the rest of them to follow. "Come. Come closer now. There isn't anything to worry about."

That was Marty's first mistake, for there *was* something to worry about. Something he would have never imagined lay inside this tomb. The men who were crouched behind Mohamed in fear slowly stood up, timidly looked at one another, and then moved closer. The crack was large enough to see inside, and one by one they looked. On the other side of the wall was green for as far as they could see. The dust made the green appear bigger than it was, and the light seemed to magnify all of this with a light from the ceiling shining directly into the crack.

"Emeralds," Marty said, still staring into the tomb.

"Emeralds?" Mohamed asked.

"Emeralds," Marty reassured him and slapped him on his back. "Emeralds."

# BOBCAT

Wolves are known to hunt in packs, lure their prey into their surroundings, and then kill the outnumbered animal. Once close to extinction, the wolf was reintroduced to the Yellowstone area out west and has come back in strong numbers. In March 2008, the US Fish and Wildlife Service formally removed the gray wolf from the endangered species list. What was once an animal so close to extinction has now become a nuisance to many ranchers.

Coyotes are a little different, hunting mainly alone because they usually hunt small rodents. However, since the development of vacant farmland in rural areas, coyotes have been forced into society more and more and must deal with human civilization. Their food supply diminished, forcing coyotes into the backyards of local communities. The news lately shows more coyotes actually lost in the city of Chicago searching for food. Coyotes have been known to lure small dogs out into the woods only to have the rest of the pack attack and kill the unsuspecting dog. First, one coyote will playfully call to the dog, perhaps running back and forth like a game. The unsuspecting dog will take the bait and follow the coyote into the woods, only to be ambushed by the rest of the pack of coyotes. Changes in environment will do that to all living things finding a way to survive.

Cats are most definitely different with the way they hunt their prey. Lone hunters, they use stealth to hunt their prey. They sneak up on their prey, step with soft paws, and keep their eyes intent on the movement of their prey. Leaping out from a tree or tall grass, cats are very efficient and silent hunters. Most people think of cats as loners. Cats will use this silent technique of hunting in two different ways. First is the stalk-run-pounce technique. The cat's eye is the most important device for sensing prey. It is very sensitive to both daylight and low levels of light, and more so to movement on the horizontal plane and to prey moving. This movement causes the cat to stalk, using the surroundings if it can to become stealth. The cat's body will move very slowly, almost fluidlike, with no sudden movements. It edges closer and closer to its prey, stopping if it must, and remaining completely motionless. Once the cat detects it has been detected or it feels it's close enough, the cat will start the second part of the hunt and run after the prey. It transfers all its weight and energy to its hind legs, leaps up, and chases its victim. To its advantage, if the cat has stalked close enough, it will only have to run a short time before it finally pounces and captures its prey. The other technique is for the cat to hide amongst its surroundings and ambush its prey once close enough. This technique is sometimes used with a run and pounce in the end, but the prey is so startled that the cat hardly has to run far to capture its prey. Cats are nothing like wolves and coyotes and most certainly would never have to lure their prey into a pack of cats.

It was a sunny Sunday afternoon in the first week in October. Most of the leaves had fallen off the trees, while some still had brown leaves on them. Michael collected the leaves with the new rake he had finally bought from the Wagon, leaving piles of leaves scattered throughout the yard. He would collect them later, but thought it would be fun for JR to play in them for a while. The temperature was warmer than usual, nearly breaking the record at eighty-two degrees. Kids were running around the neighborhood in shorts and playing baseball in the cul-de-sac. Not a cloud was in the sky on this nearly perfect October day.

The television was on in the family room with the Mets playing the Dodgers in the first round of the play-offs. There were no Cubs in this year's round, but Johnnie Schwartz swore they would be coming back. "Next year." Michael was on the couch with a beer in his hand, watching the game even though he couldn't stand either team. The inning ended with the Dodgers up two to one, and the news broke in. "This is Ted Baxton with a news update. Keep your cats inside or locked up because there's a cat hunter lurking outside. Seems a man in Crystal Lake is stalking—" Michael was quick to flip the channel and looked around, hoping Jenny was not around to hear that on the news.

"Christ."

Jenny stepped into the family room with JR in her arms. The dog pranced excitedly behind Jenny, knowing he was heading out the door. "Come, Max."

JR was laughing and pointing over to one side at the "Dog!" Jenny pulled the door open to the backyard porch, and Max looked at JR before running out. "Dog!" Jenny smiled at the two of them and set JR on the ground. Crawling out on hands and knees, JR was quick to follow Max outside the door.

Inside the house Jenny and Michael sat in the family room with the television volume blasting the play-offs. With his mind on the game, Michael was oblivious to the cold stares he was getting from Jenny. A bag of chips was on the table, and a cold beer sat on a coaster so the wooden table would not get a ring. The coaster was covering the ring that was already there, made by Jenny's brother, Shawn, who let his beer sit there all night, dripping sweat and rotting the wood. Jenny stood up, grabbed the remote, and clicked off the television.

"Hey!" Michael stared in disbelief.

"We need to talk, Michael."

"But it's the play-offs, Jen."

"This is serious, Michael!" Raising a finger and pointing it at him, Jenny was very serious.

"Okay, okay." He stood up, stepped close to her, and placed a hand on her side, which Jenny was quick to tug off.

"Not now."

"Jen, look, I'm sorry about the police. They just don't understand what happened. Things got carried away. I mean look at me!" He held out his bandaged arms, showing her what the cat had done to him and hoping she would understand.

"It's not just that, Michael. Things haven't been right lately. Ever since you got this new job it's like you're too busy for your family. And you're hiding something—I know it." She was looking straight at Michael, and it reminded him of how the chief had looked at him last night to see if he was telling the truth.

"Jen? If I tell you what's been going on you'll think I'm nuts."

"Try me."

This was his chance to tell Jenny everything, but he was worried she would think he was crazy. He wondered now if perhaps he *was* crazy. The cats chasing him was absolutely ridiculous, and besides, what was he so afraid of? She did not have to know about Krista, though, and that was over anyways. The cuts on his shoulder burned suddenly, only to remind him he had to stop in for another shot for rabies. Why was he so worried about little house cats? The answer came quickly when he felt that pain in his neck and the bandages on his arms to remind him. One cat would be no problem, but there seemed to be many, and they were stalking him. Then there was that man in black who seemed to appear at random. What was that all about?

"I killed the cat."

"I know that." The look on her face seemed to imply she was ready to kill him herself.

"Not that one. The first one."

Now Jenny looked at him, perplexed. "What first one? You killed another cat?"

"The cat in the backyard. The one under the deck. You remember the little kitten a few weeks ago? I killed it." Surely Michael could have gone about this in a better way, but she wanted to know the truth and so he was going to tell her. It probably would have helped if he was a little more sympathetic about it.

"Oh my God! The police and reporters are right about you. I am married to a crazy cat killer." Now tears started filling those eyes of hers, and a small fist pounded his chest. "Damn you!"

"Jen, it's not what it seems." Her fist pounded him again, and he grabbed her tight, pulling her close to his body. "Calm down." His hand gently caressed her hair and held her head tightly to his chest. "The first cat was an accident. It ran up inside the engine of the Boss and—"

"Stop it! I don't want to hear about it."

"Don't worry. The engine didn't grind him up. I ran him over with the—"

Jenny screamed, "No! I told you not to tell me!"

"But you wanted to know."

"I changed my mind." The woman had that right, after all.

"Jen, there's more."

"Oh God. I knew it."

The problem was that the worst part wasn't even out of his mouth, so he started to reconsider. Michael paused and held her tight to his body, softly stroking her silken hair. He rocked her back and forth, feeling the way her body was shaking. He was doing his best to comfort her. Perhaps it was best not to tell her everything. She wouldn't believe him anyways. He was reconsidering telling her about Krista again when the scratch in his neck burned and he winced, rubbing it back and forth. There was no way he could explain the man who seemed to appear in the oddest of places and the cats that seemed to be after him.

"I don't know how to explain any of this, but you have to believe me. I think there's some sort of epidemic that's causing cats to act weird lately."

"Stop it!" She shoved him away with both hands and looked at him wide-eyed. "Michael? I really hate to say this but I think you need to see someone."

"I what? Jenny, you are missing the point. These cats have been attacking me, and I am afraid they are—"

"I told you to stop it! There is nothing wrong with cats, Michael, but there is something wrong with you. I am not going to put up with this anymore." She turned and ran out of the room crying.

Standing there staring at Jenny when she walked away was hard. He listened to her scream while he tried to explain. No one was going to believe him. What was he so afraid of anyways? It was silly to be so afraid of small cats, and the more he thought about it the more he thought Jenny was right. He needed to move on with his life and stop worrying about things like this. He looked down to the remote, wondering what the score of the game was. But that really didn't matter. Besides, Jenny would have killed him. He turned to look outside the window. What he saw made his stomach turn.

—·w··୦·**·୦·⊙·*·⊙·*·w·—

JR was sitting in the middle of a heap of leaves as he and the dog played in it. The dog was running around in circles and barking, and JR was laughing. Leaves were flying in the air, and JR was sitting in the middle, tossing leaves and pointing at the dog. Max would get down on his front paws with his tail in the air and then bark a few times, making JR laugh.

The Rolling Hills subdivision backed up to an undeveloped area of tall grasses and some scattered trees. Most of the area was old farmland, but this was more of an unkempt area. Deer roamed the area a lot as well as many other types of animals, like raccoons and coyotes.

Max was a good dog and, like most Labradors, he loved to hunt and was very good with people. He was a natural for picking up nearby animal scents and being able to find what a person couldn't with his nose. Michael took Max on hunting trips for pheasant in nearby farmland. Max using his nose to find the birds in places people wouldn't. He would run back and forth in the fields, leaping, wagging his tail, and sniffing for the birds. The tall grasses or cornstalks would bounce back and forth while he ran through them, searching for the birds. Once they shot one, Max would stop and watch before bolting to the dead bird. It was really amazing how well Max was able to find a bird lying in the tall grasses. Pheasant blended into the surroundings so well and, without Max, there was little or no chance of recovering that bird. He would sniff the bird, pick it up gently with his mouth, and bring it back to Michael.

The bushes on the edge of the property shook slightly. The wind died down, and the remaining leaves on the trees stood very still. The bush shook again, and Max turned his head toward it. The rest of his body remained still, and his nose raised in the air. JR was still laughing, tossing the leaves around him. Max moved his head slightly to the right, picking up a familiar scent. He turned to the bush, raised one front paw in the air, and straightened out his tail.

A small gray kitten stepped out of the bushes and walked slowly toward the boy. It bounced up and down playfully in the green grass just outside the bush. It looked up and saw the dog, which was as still as a statue at this point. The cat raised its tail, and the hair on its neck raised. The two of them stared at each other before the cat finally let out a small meow.

Max raised his head and perked up his ears the moment the cat crawled out of the bushes. He remained still for the moment, but his muscles tensed, ready to leap into action the moment he saw the chance. Slowly the paw that was raised started to stretch farther forward. Max was a hunting dog, but all he wanted was to play. The cat meowing was like calling the dinner bell, and Max leaped into action.

Dogs were easy to figure out, and Max was no different. He ran toward the kitten with ears flapping up and down. His tongue stuck out of the side of his mouth in a playful mood. His eyes were filled with excitement for finding a new friend to play with. Dogs were simple, and Max would never hurt anyone.

The scene of the dog running toward the small cat seemed like it was in slow motion. A happy dog trotted through the yard toward his newest friend, the kitten. Anyone watching would have been horrified to see a smile on the kitten's face. Max ran into the circle as innocently as a little puppy. Someone to play with was all he wanted. When he came into that circle of cats that were so quick to surround him, Max slipped on the grass with his front paws extended, falling to his belly. He was dumbfounded by the number of cats that quickly multiplied before his eyes.

There were maybe ten cats that poured out of the bush and leaped up on Max's back. All of them were adults, except the one small cat that had lured Max closer to the pack of cats. They were hissing and clawing at his back, sides, and face. Poor Max was in shock, still thinking this was just a game. He tossed and barked, feeling the claws of the cats dig into his skin. Luckily for him, his fur protected most of him. It was the claws at his face, though, that hurt the most, and he yelped several times.

Watching all of this from the sidelines was another cat, larger than the rest. Its fur was thick and spotted, with small tufts on its ears. The face was unique, with ruffs of fur that stuck out on either side. Its face, though, had more than one unique feature, and the most notable were the eyes—dark and black. It was like looking into nothing but never-ending emptiness. That was the one eye, but the other was milky white. Michael would have recognized the eye immediately. It turned its head slightly, which dropped for a moment like it was unattached, and then raised it again.

Horrible sounds of animals were coming from the bush. The dog was barking, but most of the sounds coming from him were yelps of pain every time a cat scratched his skin with its claws. Cats were hissing, spitting, and making wild sounds of attacking cats. Max would grab a cat with his mouth and tug it back and forth. Another cat would leap on his back, and Max was quick to release the cat in his mouth. Confusion set in because there were too many of them. Max leaned down and pawed his nose, trying everything he could to rid his face and body of the cats clawing and biting at him.

The larger cat watched the others do their job, but now was his time to take over. Leaping out toward the dog, every muscle was well defined. It jumped into the air and landed on the back of Max, sinking its claws into his body. Max yelped louder than he had before, because this cat was bigger than the rest. It sunk its teeth into Max's neck, and blood spewed immediately. Max yelped, frantically trying to rid the cat from his back.

Sitting in the pile of leaves was JR, who was watching all of this. His first reaction was to point and laugh at his friend, the "dog!" He watched the dog fetch the small little "cat!" He sat there in the pile of leaves with his legs spread out in front. He was laughing when

Max first ran off to fetch the cat, but when the others leaped out he wasn't so sure anymore. The laughter stopped, and he watched now with curious eyes, wondering what would happen next. It was the sounds of the animals that caused JR to scream first—at the horrible sounds of the slaughter of his best friend right before his eyes. He raised his hand and pointed to his "dog!" Then he started to cry. Screaming loudly and crying saved his life that day.

———

Jenny was the first to hear her son screaming outside, and she ran toward the door. A mother knows the voice of her child. She instinctively ran toward his voice, knowing it was the sound of her little boy hurt. Horror struck hard at the sight of the cats surrounding her boy and attacking Max. She shrieked at the sight, running as fast as she could.

"My baby!"

Michael was only seconds behind Jenny, staring out the window in disbelief. His first reaction was to run and save his child. He saw Jenny running out to save JR, but he also saw the cats—lots of cats, and one very large one this time. None of this was good, so he did the next best thing and ran the other way.

"I'm coming!"

Jenny was screaming with her hands stretched out toward JR, hoping to reach him. Michael fell silent amidst the cats screaming all around her. She heard the sickening sound of wild animals feeding. Had she known Michael ran the other way she would have killed him, but her baby was the only one on her mind. She had to somehow reach him in time before the cats closed in.

"Get away from my baby!"

The large spotted cat was standing over Max's body with blood dripping down its fury ruffs. Hair dangled from its mouth from the bite it took from Max. Hearing Jenny's shout, the cat turned with a sickening grin on its face. Slowly the lips pulled back, revealing those grotesque yellow and now bloodstained jagged teeth. Turning its head to JR and then back to Jenny, the cat knew what she was screaming about and that smile grew even bigger.

A dark shadow covered Max's body. It seemed like a person, but no one was standing near. Covering the body of Max was the shadow of a man. A man with a dark cape and a low rimmed hat stood over Max, but there was no visible image of the man. All the cats stopped in place, standing over the dog, and looked upward to the invisible darkness that covered them. It was the man dressed in black with that hideous white face that only the cats could see. He hissed, leaned down to pet some of the cats, and then disappeared.

The large cat with the small tufts on top of his ears turned toward JR and started to stalk him. The other cats turned, followed the path of the larger cat, and then spotted the prey he was after. Some leaped off Max to follow, keeping a short distance behind the larger cat. Jenny saw this and ran as fast as she could, praying she wasn't late.

The door opened, and Michael stormed out with a large Benelli shotgun in his hands. Jenny may have thought that Michael chickened out and was going to call for help or maybe he was just so scared of cats by now that he gave up. What he did instead was grab the gun he kept in the closet that Jenny yelled at him for keeping in the house. He quickly pulled out three shells, loaded them in the gun, placed a few more in his pockets, and ran back toward the door. He hoped and prayed he wasn't too late, but this was going to end right here and now. He was going to kill every cat in this town, starting with these wild beasts in his backyard.

*Kaboom!*

The shots were heard for miles, they said, when Michael came out blazing. He took a shot at the large cat and knocked his body across the lawn. He was a good shot, but scattering the buckshot was not the smartest of things. He never took the time to think about the pattern of his shot because it was now his child and wife who were in danger. One shot and that cat was thrown to the side, bleeding and mortally wounded.

*Kaboom!*

"Michael!" Jenny screamed after the second blast, which completely annihilated the large cat and left nothing but fur behind. She looked stunned when the shotgun first went off. Things were happening so fast she had no time to react until the second shot went off. She held JR in her arms tightly, looking up at Michael like he was a lunatic with a large shotgun in his hands. He was loading another shell in the chamber. She turned to see more cats scattering all around. "Michael!"

*Kaboom!*

Michael wasted no time picking off cats left and right. The smell of gunpowder was in the air, and the barrel was hot to the touch. His gun pointed toward the cats running back and forth; he blasted what he could. They scattered into the tall grasses and bushes to the side. Michael was focused on the cats, hardly hearing Jenny scream when he looked down to her half dazed, but still looking out to the fields. It took a moment before he realized Jenny and JR were scared half to death. He took another look out toward the fields, making sure there were no more cats before setting the gun to the side.

"I'm sorry, Jen. I had to save you."

Jenny only cried, tucking JR's head into her side. The two of them were shivering, and Michael put his hand on her back and rubbed it gently, but his eyes were still focused on the fields.

He turned to the large cat, never having seen one before, and poked at it with the tip of his gun. Michael was a hunter and was a very good shot, but he mostly hunted birds. He wasn't a big game hunter, but he was certain this was a bobcat. It was spotted with little tufts on the ears. Something glittered in the sun and he knew what it was. He poked it to make sure the cat was dead, and he reached down. There on the cat's neck was a collar just like the other cats he had killed before.

"Ala Frav?" He whispered the name on the collar.

# FLIGHT TO ROCK AND ROLL

The pilot's voice came over the speaker and announced they were approximately one hour and twenty-one minutes from landing. It never struck Michael as strange that the pilot added that one minute to the hour and twenty, but he was relaxed in the soft leather of the seat. "Thank you for flying the Happy and Lucky Airlines," which was one of the largest airlines in the world because they were the only airline that smiled. The paper coasters said so with a yellow smiley face on them and a lucky green shamrock on the cheek of the smiley face.

The plane was a Boeing 737 with three seats on either side of the coach cabin. All the mood lights along the ceiling were on, and half the shades were pulled down, blocking out the sunny skies in which they were flying. Only a handful of seats were filled, but everyone was happy, just as the motto promised they would be.

A stewardess was walking down the aisle with a cart of food. "Would you like the surf and turf or the dried-up old corned beef sandwich?" A pretty woman with a short skirt and a blouse opened wide so her cleavage was gushing out leaned over the man she was serving. "We're running out of the dried-up old corned beef, so why not take two of the surf and turf?" She leaned over to pull out two whole lobsters with the claws snapping, and a button popped off her blouse, shooting over his head. "The lobster tails are delicious." She did a little curtsy for him before moving the cart farther down the aisle.

The lobster tails were good, but the filet was done to perfection. So when it came time to order, Michael asked for the filet. "Well, I'm a meat eater."

"Of course you are." The stewardess was wiggling and shaking that cleavage of hers, bouncing up and down. "Is rare okay with you?"

"That sounds delicious." He looked to the side and stuck out his tongue. Never in a million years would he order his steak rare. The words just kind of oozed out of his mouth, and he was unable to stop it. He licked his lips from side to side, trying to take those words back.

"Mmm, I thought so. I heard about you." The stewardess just smiled and placed a bloody steak on his plate, still dripping red juices.

Everything seemed to be going along very nicely on this flight, and Michael decided to take a little nap. Everything seemed as normal as it could for a flight, but something was a little out of place. Was it the pretty stewardess serving the dried-up corned beef that was out of place? Resting his head on a pillow, he fought to get comfortable in the chair, certain he would wake up with a stiff neck.

Things seemed a little odd when Michael woke up in a seat that was large and furry. The chair was purple and oversized with long, shaggy fur. He rubbed his eyes and looked up to see the seat belt light above was off. Next to it a light was on with an image of a man with a party hat on and a noisemaker poking out of his mouth. Music was playing some really good tunes by Led Zeppelin over the speakers above his head.

The pilot broke the silence and said over the speaker again, "Attention, everyone. I would like to welcome Michael Merlino, who is with us on this flight." Everyone started to cheer.

Now if things weren't odd enough, they were about to get even odder. The person in the seat in front of him was silent during most of the trip. In fact, Michael never saw anyone's face until now. There were people on this flight, right? He saw the stewardess's ass a couple times, wiggling back and forth, but he never saw the woman's face.

149

Of course, he did notice her cleavage, but he blamed that on her blocking his view of the food. He remembered the pilot talking about the time, right? Where were they going to land again? He recognized that voice but couldn't quite place it.

The man in the front row stood up, turned to Michael, and clapped for him. "Congrats, Michael. I am happy for you." Michael stared in awe at the man with long, dark hair standing before him. Was there a feather in his hair? He had rose-colored glasses and a white scarf around his neck. Michael recognized him immediately because he was a huge Aerosmith fan.

"Steven Tyler?"

"In the flesh."

"Wow, this is unreal!"

"Dude, just relax and go with it." Steven Tyler did some weird motions with his arms and hands, stretching them out to the sides and moving them like rubber. Only Steven Tyler could move so fluidly. He reached over his head and laughed at Michael. "It's just a dream, man."

It most definitely was strange seeing Steven Tyler in coach, clapping for Michael, but more was to come. People started rising in their seats and turning to look at Michael. The seat belt signs turned off again, making that little ding noise, and the captain came over the speaker in that very familiar voice. "You are free to walk around the cabin and congratulate my friend." What was it with that voice? There was something so damn familiar about it, but he couldn't place it. The voice was monotone and maybe a little sinister. Whatever it was, he was not going to let it ruin this perfect flight.

One by one people turned around and cheered for Michael; each one stunned him more than the next. A man with slicked-back dark hair and light-blue sunglasses stood in the seat right next to Steven Tyler. He wore small golden hoop earrings in both ears and had a scruffy, unshaved face. He was wearing the blackest of leather jackets. It was Bono of the rock band U2.

Sitting in the seat next to him was a man with a black knitted cap. Michael knew immediately who it was. Wearing a black T-shirt, he stood with a yellow Stratocaster in his hands. His hands ripped a couple of chords and then banged a few notes, screeching at ear-piercing levels. "I feel numb." The lead guitarist for U2 stood there smiling with his guitar buzzing.

"The Edge?"

"Yeah, we're almost there, Michael. Just hang in there."

Across the aisle stood two men with the middle seat empty. "We're saving this one for John and George." That was Ringo Starr talking with a heavy English accent, and the hell if that wasn't Paul McCartney! Paul was dressed with a white shirt with small black polka dots and a black velvet jacket. Ringo was scruffy with smoke-colored sunglasses, a black T-shirt with a big yellow star in the middle, and a gray jacket.

"What the hell is going on?" Michael was talking mostly to himself.

"It's the flight of dreams, Michael." It was Keith Richards of the Rolling Stones, who had a cigarette lit in the corner of his mouth. "Come on, mate. Ya know we all be livin' the dream like yourself."

"We're just happy you finally found your way back, Michael." It was Mick Jagger wearing no shirt at all, and those damn lips could only be his. "All of us here found our dream. That's where this plane's taking us, you know?"

Another man with a black long-sleeved shirt stood. He had a full head of curly shoulder-length hair and brown leather pants with a large belt that consisted of large rings of metal surrounding his entire waist. He had a very serious look on his face, and he stretched his long arms out and then pulled back like he was swimming.

"Jim Morrison? You're . . ." Michael paused. "Dead."

"I don't feel dead."

One of the pilots announced over the speaker, "Who's dead?"

Thoughts were running through Michael's mind. He asked himself, *Why am I on this flight? What was Mick Jagger talking about?* Rock star after rock star started standing up. The plane was full of them. The stewardess handed him a drink, and Michael looked up in awe. "Your drink, Michael, and good luck with your dream!" It was the singer-songwriter Sheryl Crow.

Taking the drink in his hands, Michael slumped back in his soft cushioned seat. He had absolutely no idea what was going on, and now dead men were talking to him as well. Sheryl Crow was pretty and a damn good singer, but why was she pushing the cart up and down the aisle? Nothing seemed right, and yet he was so comfortable here among these people. They all seemed happy, and all of them seemed to have found the one thing in life they loved.

The sky turned black almost instantaneously, and the pilot's voice came over the speaker. "Attention, dreamers. This flight's about to take you for a ride." He started laughing into the microphone like a loony. Lightning lit up the cabin with a loud crack in the air. The lights in the cabins flickered, and the plane began to shake. There was another bolt of lightning, and the plane went into total darkness.

The cockpit door opened up, and two pilots stepped out. A beam of light and smoke poured out from the cabin, and dark silhouettes stood there. No one else was in the pilot's cabin, which meant only meant one thing. These two were flying the plane and stepped out at probably the most critical time during the flight. Another crack of lightning lit up the cabin and the two pilots. Michael stared in shock and shouted out, "No way!"

Both men were dressed very conservatively with suits and ties. They both wore a blue tie with golden dots, although the older one had a smaller pattern of dots. Both men were wearing white button-down shirts and glasses. The older man had a gray suit on with larger framed glasses and receding gray hair. The younger man wore a dark blue suit with smaller square-framed glasses and badly cut short hair.

"Warren Buffet and Bill Gates?"

"That would be us," both answered at the same time.

"They're flying the plane?" Michael stood there wide-eyed and pointing a finger.

"That's right. Can you think of anyone better?" Gates asked.

"I suppose you would feel better if Richards over there was flying?" Buffet asked, and the two laughed and high-fived one another.

"Nice one, Warren," Gates joked.

"I can fly this plane," Keith Richards yelled, fumbling with his cigarette in the corner of his mouth.

"Will somebody please tell me what is going on?" Michael asked the planeload of celebrities.

Now Gates and Buffet moved farther into the cabin of the plane and walked amongst the passengers. The plane started a nosedive, yet everyone seemed calm. Richards was puffing his cigarette, and Gates and Buffet walked along the aisle as if the plane was dead level. In fact, the drink in Michael's hand was level, but he knew this plane was heading downward because everyone's hair tipped forward and he could feel it in his belly.

"For God's sake, someone had better take control of this plane!" Michael shouted.

Thunder clapped, and the lights of the cabin flickered and finally came on again. The faces of Gates and Buffet seemed darker than before. The others stood around the cabin like zombies. Morrison was already dead, so what difference did it make? But the others suddenly had no life left in their bodies as well. He looked up at Gates and Buffet, who seemed to be moving in on Bono. Michael rubbed his eyes to adjust to the light and saw something funny about Gates's and Buffet's faces. Both of them had whiskers, but unlike a normal man's mustache, these whiskers were long and thick. Unlike a beard, the whiskers spread out from beneath their noses about a foot, and there were maybe five long, thick whiskers on either side. They looked like cats. A lightning bolt struck the air, and thunder clapped immediately, shaking the entire plane.

"Weeee!" Ringo Starr shouted, acting like a kid. "We're in for a good ride now."

Gates and Buffet held up both hands—or, more likely, paws—and Bono stood silently, looking straight at Michael. They curled their fingers—or paws—till sharp claws pulled out like tiny knives coming from their sheaths. Holding them over Bono, with Gates on the left and Buffet on the right, they too looked straight at Michael and smiled. This was getting scary. When they smiled, large sharp teeth appeared in their mouths. Their yellow teeth dripped saliva, and Michael could smell their vile breath and wondered why Bono didn't react.

"No!" Michael screamed at the top of his lungs, reaching out for Bono. His mouth was wide open, dragging out the "O" as long as his lungs would allow him.

Sharp razor teeth sunk into Bono's neck on either side, like vampires feeding on their prey. Large claws of a prehistoric catlike creature sliced his torso, cutting him in half. Bono had no time to react or say good-bye because the attack somehow surprised him from behind. Blood sprayed out of his jugular, shooting up like a fountain. His body fell limp to the side, carved up with guts now pouring out. Gates and Buffet looked up to Michael, still holding Bono's lifeless body in their claws. Blood dripped from their mouths, and they smiled, showing those awful yellow bloodstained teeth.

"You're next, Michael," Gates snarled and hissed at him.

"You and all your dreams are finished!" hissed Buffet beside him.

That was when he saw it. The plane seemed to crash, or maybe he just fainted, because everything went dark after he saw the eyes. Perhaps he just wished he fainted, because he could still see everyone. One eye was black like a piece of coal—empty and endless. A person could fall into that eye and never see the end. He knew this eye and knew what the other looked like but tried to close his eyes. Knowing what the other eye looked like, he did everything to look the other way. Both Gates and Buffet smiled with their grotesque smile and blood dripping down their chins. They winked to him with the other eye that was all milky white, and Michael screamed.

"Noooooo!"

Cats started crawling out from beneath the seats, and paws were tugging from inside the luggage compartments up above. Everyone sat in their seats quietly, hardly noticing the cats that suddenly appeared. Cats were crawling out of the pouches in the seats and crawling on the shoulders of Keith Richards and Ringo Starr. A cat was sitting in the lap of Jim Morrison, and one was on the head of The Edge. None of them seemed bothered by the entire incident, and the cats started clawing every one of them. Blood started to trickle down the faces of all the rock stars now.

"We're taking everything you have, Michael," Gates hissed. "Everything!"

"Everyone you love. Everyone you care for," Buffet snarled too. "Everyone!"

The two of them high-fived one another once again but this time with sharp claws, and everything on the plane started spinning. The air became thick, and smoke filled the darkness of the room. Nothing existed anymore because this plane was doomed.

# CATZ AND DOGZ

Michael woke up sweating, and his head was pounding. The alarm was buzzing and rattling on the nightstand beside the bed. Leaping up, he was certain he would see Bill Gates or Warren Buffet. He tossed the sheets from his body and sat on the edge of the bed. The clock told him it was 5:00 a.m. The room was dark except for the red glow from the numbers on the clock. He rolled his head back and forth, making sure no one else was in the room. Shadows moved across the wall, but it was just the branches of the trees outside rustling against the window.

"Jesus."

That was one hell of a dream last night and the weirdest one he could remember. He sat at the side of the bed, holding his hands to his forehead and trying to remember. It had been a very long time since he'd had any sort of nightmare or any dream that felt as real as this one. What was it about, and why had he dreamt it? The cat had been on his mind, and it was starting to take over his life. All the people in his dream were his favorite rock stars from when he was a kid. When he was a kid he'd wanted to be a rock star. "Dreams"—that's what they'd told him, and that's all it was, just a dream. Reality set in, though, when he finally grew up and realized being a rock star was nothing but a dream. The frightening image of Bill Gates and Warren Buffet surfaced, and then they turned into cats? The two of them were probably the most successful businessmen in the world, and yet they turned into the bad guys? Sure, the rock star life was a dream, but wasn't the life of Gates and Buffet more in line with what Michael really wanted in

156

life? A successful businessman was more in touch with reality than a rock star. He would follow the path of an adult and climb his way to success in the banking world.

Lying beside him was Jenny tucked up in the blankets. She looked warm and cozy curled up under the blankets with just her face showing. His hand reached out and softly brushed her hair to one side so he could see her face. She moved slightly but remained asleep, so Michael tucked her in. Sleeping next to her was JR cuddled up in her arms. Yesterday's events had been traumatic for them both. He kissed her cheek and took another look around the room, making sure Gates, Buffet, and the cats were not in the room before leaving them safely asleep.

It had been a long day yesterday, and neither one of them had had much sleep last night. That was probably why he'd had this crazy dream last night. All these things about cats had been running through his mind, and he just wasn't thinking right. Now his dog had been killed by a bobcat, which made no sense at all.

He closed the bathroom door as quietly as he could and turned on the light. In the dark bedroom, only a small amount of light snuck beneath the doorway. He looked at his reflection in the mirror, rubbing his hand up and down the scruffy whiskers on his face. Bushy hair stuck up in wild places, and he looked like some wild man of the woods. He turned to his shoulder to look at the scars, hoping they were healing. But his skin was mostly red and infected, some of it turning yellow and oozing pus. It was not healing; rather it was getting worse, and he winced several times. Another stop to the hospital for his final rabies shot was due.

---

The office seemed quiet when he entered his floor, but something just wasn't right. Usually there were voices talking or laughing about the weekend. The hallway was too empty for a Monday. Walking down to his office, Michael passed a few of his fellow employees. They all seemed to look the other way, which he figured was just a coincidence at first. Some would quickly turn to their desks or maybe grab some papers and lift them to read. That wasn't really unusual, but every single person he passed did the same.

He stepped into his office, placed his briefcase to the side, and settled in behind his desk. Things were not clicking yet when he fanned through the files on his desk, sorting them out, placing each file in stacks, and flipping through each one. He leaned back in the nice leather chair and looked straight ahead at the cat clock, which ticked the tail back and forth.

"I need to get rid of that thing."

He heard a knock on the door and looked up to see Franklin standing there. A gray bow tie with his white shirt probably meant Franklin was all business today, more so than usual. His hands were behind his back, and he looked down seriously at his shoes, which rocked back and forth from heel to toe. It was a little unusual for Franklin to be standing at the door like this, not even saying hello. In fact, it was kind of creepy, and Michael figured it was all business today with Franklin.

"Come in, Franklin."

"Yes, thank you." No "good morning" or "how was your weekend." This was classic Franklin, who felt the company came first.

"How can I help?" Michael's voice broke the moment Franklin dropped the paper on his desk. The headline said, "Cat killer on the loose?" and beneath was an article five paragraphs long about how Michael Merlino was a crazed lunatic and every man, woman, and child should steer clear of his path. "Keep your cats locked up, and please don't let him anywhere near your blenders."

"Perhaps you can start by explaining this little mishap, Michael?" Franklin didn't take a seat like he normally did. Instead he stood before his desk with his hands still behind his back, rocking back and forth on his heels.

"I can explain, Franklin."

"I would hope so." Now his eyes narrowed as he looked right through Michael, just like Jenny and the chief did the other day. What was with everyone lately? he wondered to himself. "And I think it's best you stop calling me Franklin for now."

"Yes, Franklin. I mean sir." One day you're the hero and the next the bad guy.

"I just want to know what kind of person shoves a cat into a blender." He stopped himself for a moment, trying to keep his composure. He had emphasized the word "blender." He looked down to the right and clenched his eyes tight in deep thought before looking back at Michael. "And turning it on—" This time he emphasized the word "on" but stopped again.

"Franklin? I mean sir?"

"Don't cut me off!"

"Yes, sir." Michael was taken back, feeling his body sink into his chair.

"This bank . . . our bank is very well recognized and respected in the community, and although we live in a large city, it just so happens it isn't large at all." His finger stabbed the news article on the desk, confirming his comment.

"Sir, I can explain."

"I don't give a shit about your excuses, young man!" For Franklin to swear was like hell freezing over. Franklin hardly ever raised his voice, but it was apparent he was under a lot of pressure. This was going to be a very long week if this was how Monday was starting off.

"Yes, sir, but—"

"But nothing. You have disappointed me, Michael, and I am going to keep a tight leash on you. Clean up this mess, and hope to God it doesn't get any worse than it already is."

That was how his day started, and it only dragged on as the day went on. Quietly he sat there in his chair behind the desk and stared at the wall. Taking a deep breath, he looked blankly at the clock on the wall. The tail of the cat moved back and forth, keeping time, while the eyes shifted from side to side. He never did find out who gave him that clock, but as each day passed he hated it more and more.

———————

Catz and Dogz We Have It All was filled with everything pets could want and more. It was a haven for the class A animal lover who wanted to pamper his pet to the fullest. There were aisles for your normal pet, like a cat or a dog, but there were also aisles for the very obscure pet. One section was devoted to oddities like scorpions, spiders, and snakes. There was a large section just for birds of many different exotic varieties. The fish section was second to none, with freshwater fish of every type on one side and saltwater fish on the other. They had tanks for fish and tanks for snakes and filter systems and stands of every type. The dog section alone had eight different aisles for dog food, dog toys, dog tags, dog houses, etc. They even had a dog hotel to give him a vacation, along with shampoos, massagers, and an authentic Catz and Dogz We Have It All dog bone. The cat section was their largest section, with twelve aisles of cat toys and food. It was amazing how many different toys could keep a cat happy. What had animal lovers done before this store existed?

Franklin J. Smith was a gold card member of the Catz and Dogz We Have It All store. This required an annual due of eighty-five dollars but included the following: an invite to all special events, which included the annual spring bash sales event by private invitation only (before the public was admitted); a special treat for your pet each month; the monthly newsletter; and a 15 percent discount exclusive for all gold card members. Franklin was a frequent customer of the store, stopping every weekend and sometimes on his way home during the week, like he did this night. Everyone knew Franklin—or Mr. Smith, as they called him—greeting him with a smile.

Tonight he was on a mission to find that one special gift for a very special person. He wanted to give him something that was like no other, so Michael would look at it and say, "Franklin gave that to me. Such a wonderful and thoughtful man." He laughed to himself. He walked up and down the aisles with a cartload of cat food, cat litter, cat toys, and more cat food. He stopped at a very unusual item he had never seen before. It was a clock, but this was no ordinary clock by any means. This clock was a cat clock with a tail wagging back and forth to keep time. He absolutely had to have it. He grabbed it immediately and placed it in his cart.

Franklin drove his Chevy with the large purchase from the pet store in the trunk. The rear end of his car actually tilted downward because he had so much stuffed in back. He pulled up to the front, and the employees helped him load the car, placing bag after bag of cat litter and hoping his trunk was big enough. He managed to fit it all and headed home with a cat bobblehead planted right in the middle of his dashboard.

Headlights lit up the street with large maple trees lining either side of the road. Small red-brick houses sat one after the other, so close neighbors could almost touch one another. He had lived in his home in Skokie for thirty-eight years, almost as long as he had been at his job at the bank. A small brick garage was set back to the side of the house, and he pulled the Chevy in. He stepped out, popped the trunk, and walked to the back to unload it. There was nothing really special about the house and very small yard. Most of the landscape was already cut back for the winter. He looked up to the bay window in the rear of the house and saw a cat perched on the sill inside. Its long tail was wagging back and forth, seeing its owner home with dinner. A concrete stoop led up to the house with a black railing on either side. He stepped up with a large bag of cat food in each hand, and set one down to open the door. Pacing back and forth along the window to the left side was another cat, licking its lips.

The inside of the house was dark, with lime-colored walls straight from the seventies. In fact, most of the walls had the original paint from thirty-eight years ago, when he had first bought the house. When Franklin stepped inside, his feet were immediately swarmed by a wave of cats. Fifteen or twenty cats walked around his feet, rubbing up against his leg. They all knew the moment they saw their owner it was dinnertime. All of them meowed in a soft melody, welcoming him home.

---

The Taurus pulled up to the garage door, and Michael reached up for the remote attached to the visor above his head. He clicked the center button and the wooden door started to roll up. He waited until it reached the top and then pulled the car in between the minivan and the Boss.

Stepping out of the car like he always did, he ran a hand along the curves of the Boss beneath the cloth. Softly closing his eyes for a moment, he stood there with one hand on the car. He took a deep breath and relaxed a little. Past images of his dad and him driving through the country many years ago went through his mind. He remembered how they laughed and the wind blew through his hair. He would hold his hand out the window, feeling the wind. His dad would shout over the loud noise of the wind, "Don't tell your mother!" He would laugh because they broke a hundred on the speedometer. The memories of his dad were good, and he thought about what he had told him in the letter. "Take care of your dreams." The door opened, startling him, and he turned to see Jenny standing at the doorway to the house.

"Michael?"

"Jen!" He felt his face flush because he was caught daydreaming of the past. The words of his dad flashed through his head: "Don't tell your mother!" Was he talking about his wife too? He figured it was all the same and besides, this was their little secret between the two of them.

"What are you doing?"

"Just getting ready to come see you, hon." He never called her "hon" unless he was either up to no good or hiding something. He awkwardly grabbed his things, walked up to Jenny, and gave her a kiss on the lips. She smiled, let him walk into the house, and then followed him and closed the door.

He stepped into the kitchen, and the smell of food was in the air. JR was sitting in his high chair with two bowls of food before him. He smiled, looked up to his dad, and pointed a finger at Michael with pureed carrot mushed on his fingers and cheeks. "Mom!"

"One of these days you'll learn to say 'Dad.'" He laughed, rubbing a hand through JR's hair.

"So how was your day?" Jenny asked.

This completely took Michael off guard, and he stopped for a moment with his hand still on the top of JR. The one question he had thought about the whole train ride home was the one he simply did not want to answer. What was he going to tell Jenny? He never came up with an answer. He'd just hoped it would not come up, since the two of them were not talking as much lately. It did come up, though, and he stared off in a daze for a moment, remembering how angry Franklin was at him, how his job was suddenly in jeopardy, and how it would make Jenny happy. She wanted this, didn't she? She wanted him to lose his job so he could find something closer to home. That's what he was thinking, anyways, with all that had happened recently. It was wrong, of course, but to him it seemed right at the time, so he had to hide the fact that his day wasn't good. He finally turned and smiled. "Everything is fine."

"Good, I am glad." She turned and looked at JR, tears filled her eyes. "He's trying not to think of his friend, but I know it hurts not having him around." Jenny just started to bawl, thinking of their dog and the horrifying way he died. Michael grabbed her tight, but she shrugged his hands off her body and turned back to preparing the food for dinner. "I'm fine!"

"You're not fine, Jen."

"I'll be fine. Now go! Just go and change. I'll be fine." She made a shoo with one hand make him go away.

Upstairs in his bedroom Michael undressed, tugging off his tie and placing his suit up on the rack in the closet. He pulled out some jeans and a sweatshirt with a black Iowa Hawkeye on it. He was certain Jenny was being cynical about his job and started getting paranoid that maybe she knew. Had Franklin called her and told her about his day? Maybe someone else had called her, wanting her to know. Wild things started to run through his mind, but the more he thought about it the more he figured she didn't know. Paranoia was trying to take hold of him, and he just had to calm himself down. *She doesn't know*, he told himself and headed downstairs again.

"I need to check on some things for the office. Just call me when dinner's ready, okay, Jen?" He turned to her and pulled her close, wrapping his arms around her and hugging her body tight. She was quick to tug him tight to her body, lying her head to his chest. She needed this after yesterday more than he would know.

"Okay," she whispered into his chest, softly sniffing. She rubbed her face across his chest so he wouldn't see the tears in her eyes, but his chest was now wet from her tears.

"I am right here." He meant the room next to the kitchen, and he turned to the other room.

The den was dark this time of night, and cold, being at the rear of the garage and at the far end of the house. It was over a slab of concrete instead of a basement, so the floor was colder than the rest of the house. The heat never quite made it this far over in the house. He flipped the switch to turn on the overhead light fixture and the one lamp standing in the corner of the room. He sat down in the chair behind the desk and flipped on the small brass lamp on top of the desk. The computer was already on, with images of their family popping up on the screen saver. When he moved the mouse, the pictures disappeared and the functions on the computer became visible.

Something was wrong with the cats in the area, and he figured it had to be a disease. There had to be a reason the cats were acting weird. Something inside told him there was something else, because these cats seemed to be locking in on him alone. It would not explain why a sand cat from Egypt or a bobcat was here, but he still hoped that was just a freak coincidence. Then there was that man, that strange man in black clothes. That made absolutely no sense at all, and still here he was trying to find an answer. It was a start, and what he needed now was something to begin with.

Hopefully this start would lead to something better, so he typed "cat disease" into the Google search. The screen filled up with all sorts of Web sites for cat diseases, illnesses, and conditions he never knew existed. One made him laugh, and he started to sing the song by Ted Nugent, "Cat Scratch Fever." He would make the sound of the guitar, hammering down "Dah dah dah." There were many types of illnesses that came up, like kidney failure, arthritis, FIV (which was a virus that weakened a cat's immune system), urinary problems, dementia, and digestive problems among many more, but none were the diseases he was looking for, of course. Michael typed in things like "cat acting weird," which pulled up more information about their digestive system. He typed in "cat attacks," and finally an answer came up that seemed related and also might explain what he was thinking. It was an article by a woman who said she was attacked suddenly by her cat. There were pictures of her arm and hand all clawed up by her cat that she had loved for so many years, which suddenly decided to turn on her. It turned out the cat was bitten by a bat and had rabies. It died later, so Michael was happy he decided to get the rabies shots. Maybe there was a large colony of bats in the area that might have caused this. It would make some sense, he figured. Just to test this out, he looked up "rabies and bats" and found most bats don't carry the disease but it could also be carried by raccoons or other animals, such as opossums and skunks. All of these animals were in the area and would explain so much, he figured. Still, there was that man, and what about the other two larger cats? He sat at the computer, holding his face to both hands and laughing, knowing something big was missing.

"Dinner is ready," Jenny shouted from the kitchen.

"All right, I'll be right there."

Michael was about to stand up when he saw something of interest on Google about cats attacking. It was a recent article of a woman found dead in a forest west of St. Louis. There were probably many articles of people being attacked by large cats, but this one for some reason caught his interest. Maybe it was because of the close proximity, but there was more, and his instinct told him so. Apparently it was presumed some large cat attacked her but was never captured. The attack left the girl so mangled they couldn't identify the remains, but authorities were presuming it was the body of "Cindy Case?" That name sounded so familiar, but he couldn't place the face. Supposedly, the article said, she was obsessed with cats attacking and feared for her life. One close friend mentioned her as being hysterical and overreacting to the situation. Drugs were administered to calm her down, and some feared this was what finally broke her down. She cut herself in a hidden cabin far off in the woods. Some thought she planned this whole thing, while others had seen cats roaming near her home recently. Inspectors reported no cats in the vicinity that they were aware of. The last part mentioned she was last seen on a camping trip with her husband Steve—.

"Michael? Are you joining us?"

"Yeah, coming right now." He bookmarked the screen on the computer but was quick to forget about the story. What did a woman far off in St. Louis have to do with cats acting strange and attacking here? Besides, that cat was a large one, and this was a case of small household cats and a couple of strays or escapees.

The three sat at the dinner table, eating silently in a daze. Jenny pushed around her food, eating only a few bites and trying not to look at JR. JR was sitting in his high chair still, finished eating, but was playing with a couple of toys. He was pushing around a couple of toy cars, making a "vroom vroom" sound of a car. He would stop, look outside, and then say, "Dog," and go back to playing with the cars. Jenny tried hard not to hear him, but tears filled her eyes when he mentioned "Dog." Michael's mind was on the cats and what was causing all this to happen. He too pushed his food around, hardly eating any of it.

"Did you ever find out what Ala Frav means?" Jenny asked, breaking the silence.

This turned on a light inside Michael's head, but he wasn't sure what that light meant. All he knew was there was something more to that name than a place or owner. It meant something so much more, but he wasn't sure what. Where had he heard it before? Why did it all of a sudden sound so familiar to him? He stood, picked up his plate, and carried it to the sink. "No, I have no idea." But he did and had to find out why.

Back in the den, Michael sat at the desk and pulled out a sheet of paper and a pencil. He began to write the name that had been on the collar of the bobcat. Scribbling things quickly, he seemed rather excited, and licked the corner of his lips.

"Ala Frav."

Next, he decided to write the names of the other two cats that had collars too. Leaning over and closing his eyes, he did his best to remember. They were not common names, so they would be either too hard to remember or easy because it struck him as odd. Thankfully it was the latter, and he wrote the names down beneath each other.

"Alfarav."

"Flavara."

Immediately he pushed the chair away from the desk, stood up, and stared at the paper. "Son of a bitch!" Jenny was busy cleaning dishes and didn't hear him, thankfully. He turned back to the paper and tapped it several times with the pencil. The third cat did not have a name, but there was something, right? "The shake." He was quick to write down the fourth name beneath the others. It was the name of the super shake that no one else could remember seeing.

"Ra Valfa."

Now things were starting to creep him out, but he wasn't finished yet. Something else was missing. He made a line beneath each word with the pencil. All of them had the same letters, and if you mixed them up they would spell something. But what? He named all the cats, but there was something else he was missing. "Someone," he finally said out loud and wrote down the word he had seen on the windshield the night he saw the man in the parking garage.

"Valafar."

This perplexed him because none of this made any sense. All of the names were connected, but they made no sense at all. Each time he wrote the words down on a sheet of paper and crossed out the letters one by one. They all had the same letters, but he couldn't figure out what they meant. He scrambled them like a word jumble and tried to make some sense, but it spelled nothing other than the words he was already given. There was only one question, but he did not know the answer.

"Who is Valafar?"

# FAMOUS

## July 19, 2008

It took a few hours to break through this opening so they could make their way freely into the tomb. Chiseling and removing stones took time since they were low on men working now. It didn't matter much to Marty, though. He was at the goal and knew it. There were fewer men to pay as well, which suited him fine. The cowards would be sorry, he thought. They worked, not knowing how late it was. They didn't care at this time. You could feel the excitement in the air.

Marty and Mohamed were looking at the walls, trying to decipher some of the paintings, while the men labored to open the room. There was a vast wall with paintings on it and some markings on the side. Large groups of people were lying to the sides of a pharaoh while he walked amongst them. Then there was another with cats all around. There were small cats and big cats, and the men seemed to be at war. The final picture showed the pharaoh standing over the large cat with a spear in his hand.

"I don't get it."

"What don't you get, Mohamed?"

"There was a war. You could see it in the paintings, and the symbols here definitely talk about war. There was much death. I tell you, there may be emeralds in there, but this place is death."

"Mohamed? The only death around here took place five thousand years ago."

"Well, I don't want to be around when it comes back."

Then the men started to cheer, having broken open the final piece so they could get into the tomb. All of them stopped and turned to look at Marty and Mohamed. It was, after all, their dig. It was their right to go first, and who was to stop them? Who really wanted to take the first step anyways? Egyptian tombs were known for booby traps, and none of them really wanted to chance it this late in the game.

"Allow me." Marty moved forward.

It was that fateful step that started it, or for some it was the end. Marty took his very first step on a trick stone that triggered off a series of events. Sand started to shift through cracks that appeared, allowing large stones to slide to the side and others to move. A chain reaction like the mousetrap game, everything moved in what seemed like slow motion. A rumble in the distance moved closer, like a stampede heading toward them. Marty knew the moment his foot stepped down, feeling the weight of his body shifting downward with the stone. He turned to see the others, certain it was his own death and unprepared for what was to come next. Mohamed stood close to his side, not realizing what had happened till he saw the look on Marty's face. A look of excitement turned suddenly to shock and then fear when Marty turned his face.

"No!" Mohamed yelled, shoving him to the side, but of course it was too late.

It was not Marty and Mohamed who were in trouble, though, but the men behind them who had no idea what was about to befall them. A huge stone weighing several tons, for sure, slid down from the high ceiling and crushed all of them. One after the other came sliding down from an opening that appeared out of nowhere. Men shouted, quickly consumed and silenced by the heavy weight of the stones.

Silently now Marty and Mohamed stood staring at one another in awe of the trap set before them. The only sound was that of the final sands still shifting along the stones. Dust filled the room like a dark cloud, making it hard to see. When it started to settle, the pile of rubble could be seen with arms and legs sticking out grotesquely underneath the stones.

Running up behind was Abdul, who had run back to collect some additional supplies. He stood there behind the dust that was settling. He stared with his mouth open at his recently departed mates. His hands fell open and to the side, forgetting the supplies that now fell to the ground. Sadly he looked up to Marty and Mohamed, slowly shaking his head back and forth.

"It's not your fault, Marty," Mohamed tried to reassure him.

"Come on. Inside." Marty waved them on coldly and cruelly. His skin was saved, and that was all that mattered. Now the treasure was closer than ever. Mohamed turned to see the look in Abdul's eyes; the whites of his eyes seemed to glow in the darkness. They both cautiously followed Marty inside, but it was too late. The damage was already done.

Each person had lights that filled up the room. They stood there, shocked once again at the way the room seemed to glow. Green filled up the room, giving off a funny glow everywhere with the lights striking the emeralds. Emeralds were everywhere, filling up this small burial chamber with one large tomb in the middle.

"Unbelievable!" Marty exclaimed.

Marty walked slowly with both hands held out, framing the tomb with both hands. He stared at what was before him, frozen in his moment of glory. A green glow shone on his face, showing his huge smile. The tomb was made of solid white stone, probably some type of marble. It was in the shape of a cat, with its clawed paws crossed over its chest, lying flat on its back, and head tucked in with eyes closed. Neither of them had ever seen anything like it before. No one had ever seen anything like this before. This was the discovery of a lifetime.

"We did it," Marty finally spoke. "We're going to be famous."

But Mohamed and Abdul still weren't convinced. Both of them stared at Marty, not moving any closer to the tomb. None of this was good. The workers were dead, and the others had run for their life. Looking back now, it was good they ran and at least saved some of their lives. Slowly now Mohamed and Abdul walked closer to the tomb. They stood on either side of Marty to gaze upon the discovery they had made.

"Yeah. Famous, all right. Famous and dead," muttered Mohamed.

# KITTY CATS ARE CUTE

Football season officially started the moment the Cubs were out of the pennant race, which was back in August. The season could not have started quicker, so the game between Ohio State and Colorado, two highly ranked teams this year, could not have come sooner. College football was scheduled all day today, with professional football on the schedule for tomorrow.

Sunk deep in the brown leather couch with a beer in his hand was Shawn. A remote was in the other hand as he took a sip of the beer and watched Ohio State score another touchdown, taking the lead back in this seesaw battle. A bowl of chips was on the table in front of him beside the platter of cut cheeses and sausages with a basket of crackers. The family room was small, with the leather couch against one wall and a small table in front. In the corner was an extremely large eighty-two-inch television that was too large for the room, but Shawn was a guy and the most important thing to a guy was the size of the television. A picture of Shawn and Tonia on their wedding day was framed on one wall with posters of Monet lilies framed by a cheap metal brass frame on the other walls.

It was perfect football weather, just cool enough to wear a sweater. Some of the neighbors were outside raking the remaining leaves up into small piles. The smell of leaves burning was in the air on this crisp, clear day. The shouts of the neighborhood kids outside playing football could be heard in the distance.

In the kitchen, Tonia was preparing food for the guests arriving soon. The room had a pleasant smell of her cooking, which included her famous cherry pie for dessert, cooling off near the window. She was dressed in a long-sleeve white sweater with a red-and-white apron covering her pregnant belly. The television was so loud in the family room it was hard to hear anything else. Tonia was in her own little world, happily cooking all sorts of appetizers for the boys coming over.

"Tonia?" Shawn barely turned his head to shout back.

"Yes?"

"I need another cold one."

"Love you too!" Tonia couldn't hear him because the television volume was so loud, so she continued wrapping up the asparagus with pieces of prosciutto.

"Thank you." Shawn had no idea she wasn't bringing him another one and would eventually forget and get himself one later.

The two of them were happy together. They never argued about anything and just went with the flow. Shawn and Tonia were both young and naive and took every day as it came to them, always smiling. They had a small home and lived modestly with no great ambitions in life other than just being happy. A little child coming soon had them both excited and maybe a little nervous, but there was a lot of happy energy between the two of them.

The telephone rang three times before Shawn finally picked it up. He reached over the arm of the couch to the phone, which was resting on the floor beside him. Tonia had no idea the phone was ringing as she hummed a song to herself in the kitchen while she was cooking.

"Hello?"

"Shawn?"

"Uh, yeah? Hello?"

"Shawn!" the voice on the other end was screaming.

"Hello? Who is this?"

"It's Michael," the voice shouted again on the other end of the phone.

"Who?"

"Turn down your TV."

"Oh, yeah. It's awesome! When are you getting here?" Holding the remote in his hand and pointing at the television, he turned the volume down. "Who is this?"

"It's Michael!" he shouted loudly into the phone again.

"Okay, okay. Don't have to yell."

There was a pause before Michael spoke again. "I am getting ready to leave. Do you want me to bring anything?"

"Nope, got it covered." He turned to Tonia and winked at her. He swirled the beer bottle around so she knew it was empty. She winked back to him and then puckered up soft red lips, pretending to kiss him. She turned to the refrigerator, pulled out a fresh bottle of beer for him, walked over to hand it to him, and kissed his cheek.

"All right. I'll see you soon."

There was a click on the other end of the phone. Shawn set the headset back on the cradle. He clicked up the volume to the television again to an almost ear-shattering level. Shawn went back to drinking his beer and watching the game while Tonia went back to preparing food for the boys. Tonia rubbed her belly, knowing the two of them were as happy as could be.

———————

Michael hung up the phone, laughing because he knew Shawn was in rare form. He imagined him there on his sofa with a beer in his hand and the television volume as loud as it could be. He knew Shawn was still living his life as a kid, not quite grown up yet. He had no responsibilities, but that was going to change very quickly once the baby was born. He looked over at Jenny and JR, who were sitting in the family room watching a kids' show on television. Jenny had her arm around JR, and Michael knew she was struggling to get through the events that had happened recently.

"I'm heading over to watch the game with Shawn."

"All right. Have fun."

"I will." He stopped for a moment, looking at the two of them. "You be safe, okay?"

"I will." She blew him a kiss while holding JR tight in her arms. "Love you, Michael."

"Love you too."

"Oh, can you bring that present to Tonia for me?"

"Sure can. I'll see you two later."

JR turned in her lap and waved to him, which brought a smile to his face. He leaned into his mom's neck, cuddling tight and wrapping his arms around her neck. "Mom!"

Michael just laughed and headed out the door, taking the large box wrapped up with an oversized pink bow. Grabbing the case of beer with the other hand, he remembered his promise to Jenny not to try and keep up with Shawn. Besides, police were looking for anyone drinking, handing out DUIs like they were going out of style. He told Jenny he remembered when they were younger and police would take you home if they caught you drinking. She laughed and told him she remembered the police telling her to pour out all the beer and then they followed her home. Things were different now, and it made no sense to drink and drive like her brother, Shawn. They had responsibilities now, as Shawn would soon learn.

Stepping out into the garage, he sensed something wasn't right. There was no reason to feel this way, but there was that feeling you get when you just know someone is watching you. He flicked on the light and saw the minivan on one side, with the middle space empty because he had left the Taurus outside so he could maneuver the Boss out of the garage. There it sat on the side, covered with the blue tarp to keep the dust off it.

On top of the Boss sat a curled-up cat, lifting its black eyes the moment the door opened. The garage door opened and the cat hissed when the light overhead turned on. It stretched its body, back legs first, and pointed its tail. Black eyes stared at Michael, and it hissed once more before leaping off to the side of the Boss.

"Son of a bitch! I'm gonna fucking kill you!"

Michael paused for just a moment, holding the present in one hand and a case of beer in the other. Looking back and forth for a place to set the things down, he saw the cat moving along the back wall. The cat's body was so fluid when it walked, bouncing up and down on its paws. Keeping his eyes on the cat, he set the beer and the present down on the ground and reached to the side to grab a baseball bat. Without looking, he kept grabbing at air, knowing the bat was hanging on the wall close to his hand. The cat seemed to know what he was doing and sat there staring at Michael with those charcoal eyes. Then it hissed. Finally his hand grabbed the bat, pulling the rack and some of the drywall along with it. The cat turned its head, hearing the loud crash, and quickly ran out from beneath the car and headed out the garage door.

"Son of a bitch."

Michael came out swinging the bat, but the cat was too small and fast. Taking the turn around the corner of the house, he ran after it. The cat leaped out of the bushes and into the neighbor's yard, knowing it could easily outrun Michael in the short run. The cat stopped in the middle of the neighbor's yard, turned its head, and stared at Michael. Holding the bat in his hands, Michael stopped and got ready to smash it to smithereens. The cat hissed, once more baring its sharp little teeth, and then ran off hopefully far and away.

Hearing the noise, Jenny came out and stared at Michael, standing just outside the garage with a bat in his hands. He turned and looked at her for a moment but quickly turned back to the cat that was now gone. Questions raced through his mind about why this cat was here and on top of his car. He slowly turned back to Jenny without even smiling.

"Sorry, just wanted to get a little practice in before I went over to Shawn's." He took a swing in the air at a make-believe baseball, but it was a cat he was pretending to hit.

"All right, well have fun."

"I will." He set the bat up against the wall, attempting to cover the hole in the drywall. "And, Jen?"

"Yes, Michael?"

"Be safe. Lock the doors."

She looked at him strangely, having no idea why he would say this. Without a word she just turned to go inside. He watched her standing over the beer and the presents and waited till he heard the door locked from the inside. It wasn't until he heard that sound that Michael could leave her and JR. He knew it wasn't a lot, but a locked door was better than nothing. She would be safe today. He just had that gut feeling, because whatever was out there wasn't trying to harm her and JR, at least not yet.

———————

Shawn was well on his way to enjoying his day when he realized there were a few things he needed to get ready before the boys came over. He wanted a full supply of beer as close as possible so no one would miss a moment of the game. Food was, of course, taken care of by his pregnant and very beautiful wife, Tonia. People would yell at Shawn for having her work like this, but what they didn't understand was how much the two of them loved one another, and Tonia enjoyed keeping him happy. Making the treats was something that made Tonia feel good inside, and she had pleasure seeing the boys happy.

He stood up from the couch, placed a hand on his belly, and burped. Tonia was in the other room and just laughed at him. He swished the beer around in the bottle and winked at Tonia. It was a good day, having his friends over with food and beer while watching a big game on the television. But what was really great was being there with Tonia. He stared at her belly for a moment, thinking of his future as a dad, and took another swig of his beer. Damn, that belly of hers made him nervous.

"Baby? I love you," Shawn told Tonia with a slight slur in his voice, but this time it was purposefully said to be funny.

"Baby? I love you too. Now get over here and give your honeybunch a kiss and a hug."

Shawn walked across the room and grabbed her tight, her belly keeping the two of them apart slightly. They both laughed and looked down to her belly, and he kissed her hard on the lips. She smelled like a sweet spring day, and he smelled like stale beer. They were a very happy couple and had everything to look forward to.

She kissed him back and then smiled at him. His hand reached down and rubbed her tummy.

"For good luck."

He stepped out into the garage and flipped on the light, swearing he heard a funny noise. The garage was a mess with a pile of bikes, boxes, and many other things they hadn't unpacked since first moving into this house. He needed a cooler big enough to hold the beers for everyone coming. Convenience was what he was looking for, because he felt no man should have to get up off his ass and miss one moment of the football game. This reminded him there was a game going on and he had better hurry, so he grabbed the cooler buried under a couple of boxes and a large tarp they used when painting the bedrooms.

Something moved on the other side of the garage. A couple of boxes fell over, and a broom fell to the side. Shawn turned to see nothing and just figured the boxes or broom were just lying awkwardly, ready to fall. There wasn't any reason for him to think it was anything else. He pressed the button to the large garage door, and the noise of the motor lifting the large door masked any other noise that may have been heard in the room at that very moment. He grabbed a couple cases of Budweiser, placed them inside the cooler, and heard the glass clink. Another noise came from behind, but he just ignored it. One by one he pulled out the beers, filling the cooler. He stood happy and figured he could pull this out back and fill it with ice. He pulled out one cold beer, opened it, and took a sip for his troubles and hard work.

Another sound came from the garage, and this time he didn't ignore it. Instead he turned with a beer in his hand to see the strangest thing he had ever seen. Standing in the middle of the garage next to his old yellow Chevy was a cat, but this was no ordinary cat. It was bigger than any cat Shawn had ever seen. He held the beer out in front of him, stared at the label for a moment, and then looked at the cat again. *Shit, this is good stuff,* he thought to himself and took another long sip of the beer. The cat was still standing right next to his car, staring right at Shawn. It was brown with the funniest ears he had ever seen—large, black, pointed ears with fuzzy little tufts growing out of the tops.

"Aw, what a cute little kitty cat."

Shawn took another sip of his beer. He was certain it must be a pet of a neighbor's that had somehow run off. Now if he could coax it in, maybe he would get a reward. This cat was no normal cat and certainly worth a lot. He leaned down, motioned with an open palm, and then curled his fingers.

"Come here, kitty, kitty, kitty."

The cat raised its head, and those pointed black ears lifted before it slowly took one step toward Shawn. One front leg crossing the other in an imaginary line. The brown tail curled back and forth while it stepped closer to Shawn. Dark black eyes were wide open when Shawn realized the one was milky white.

"That's odd."

The cat rubbed up against his leg and started weaving in and out of his thighs. It was the biggest cat he had ever seen and reached more than halfway up his legs. It reminded him of a small mountain lion. Then he began to wonder. Was it a mountain lion? If it was, then it was just a baby. He looked down and saw a collar around its neck. It was definitely a pet if it had that collar around his neck. The cat seemed pretty well mannered, coming up to him and rubbing his leg like it did. Most definitely it was domesticated, he figured. *Probably one of those really fancy expensive cats too, with those funny-looking ears.* His reward was going to be big with this cat. The cat stopped and looked off to the side, and Shawn followed its eyes.

Walking toward him were about twenty other cats—gray cats, brown cats, striped cats, and just plain old white and black cats. All of these cats walked in synchronicity with one another toward Shawn. Heads were low and their dark-green eyes stared at him, never taking him out of their sight. Every single one of the cats' tails was moving back and forth like a mechanical coil curling. They spread out and made a circle around him, and that was when the large cat with that one white milky eye bit into his leg.

With the windows of the Boss open, the wind was blowing through Michael's hair. His left arm lay on the side of the door as his hand tapped the steel. The beer was hidden in the backseat of the car with the present and extra-large pink bow covering it. He loved the sound of the engine and figured this would be one of the last days to really enjoy the Boss before winter hit.

The ride was good for him even though it was a short drive from his house to Shawn's. He needed time to go over things that were bothering him. The cat sitting in the garage was very troublesome to him. The thought of Jenny and JR sitting at home worried him, but he was happy knowing she'd locked the door when he left. She wouldn't go outside today and probably not for a while after what had happened the other day. It was traumatic for the two of them. He wondered how the cat got in but figured it must have crawled in when he pulled out one of the cars earlier. His one regret was that he didn't shut the garage and lock the thing inside so he could kill it. Why had he become so obsessed with cats, and why were these cats scouting him? That's what they were, he suddenly realized, scouts or sentries for the one who kept coming back. Was the cat coming back? He'd never thought of that before, but certainly each cat that attacked had some distinct characteristics similar to the others. The flinching of the neck was odd, but it was always that horrible milky eye. That wasn't a coincidence—he was certain of that. How many cats were out there with a gross milky eye? What bothered him even more was the kind of cats that were showing up. What the hell was a cat from Egypt doing here, and how many bobcats were in this area? If there was a breakout from a zoo like the police chief had suggested, then they were specializing in milky-eyed cats. None of this made any sense, but he was certain they were related. Finally, what did this man dressed in black have to do with all of this? Were they his cats, perhaps? The man looked sick himself with that pale white face.

He stepped on the gas, and the Boss revved into high gear. He watched the speedometer rise from forty, past the speed limit, to sixty miles per hour. Images of his dad filled his mind while he listened to the music of the exhaust and engine. "Don't tell your mother." He started to laugh, pressed the pedal all the way to the floor, and felt the Boss push his body into the seat of the car. He wanted to hit a hundred just like his dad used to do. He wanted to go back to those days when he sat beside him, waving his hand in the air outside the car. The car now moved past eighty miles an hour, and his left hand was still out the window. He felt the wind blow it up and down. Keeping his left hand flat while the wind blew beneath it, he could remember when he did it as a boy and his dad was driving the car. He turned to the passenger seat, imagining JR sitting beside him. "Don't tell your mother." He laughed and then looked at the speedometer, which hit one hundred miles an hour. Some curves were ahead, and he slowed down, loving the sound of the engine when it downshifted. The sound of the car backfiring was music to his ears.

He imagined his dad buckled in beside him, still looking the same. He was young and handsome with dark hair blowing in the wind and waving at the girls. He turned to Michael and smiled. *God, he had such a beautiful smile.* Michael returned the smile and was happy to imagine him there. He looked to his dad—though he really wasn't there—and asked, "Dad? What do I do? I need your help."

His dad just laughed, but it was genuine when he did. It was funny seeing him in the passenger seat beside him. Michael waited for his answer, knowing he really wasn't there. It felt so real, though, and Michael wanted to reach over and touch him. Then he spoke with such authority. The sound of his dad's voice seemed so real. "Drive it, Michael."

The Boss backfired, and Michael woke from his daze. Blinking several times, he was certain his dad was really there. He reached over to the passenger seat and felt the warmth of the seat. That feeling was quickly lost when he looked ahead. His eyes widened, and his hands gripped the steering wheel so tight he was certain he saw a ghost.

Shawn always told Michael he could hear the Boss a mile away or farther. It had that distinctive sound like no other. Two or three miles was a long ways off to hear a car, but even farther if the sound you heard was perhaps the one thing that could save you. With a low roar and gears shifting, the sound of the Boss was like no other.

He first felt the warm rush in his leg when the cat bit into his thigh with sharp teeth, but it was the claws that dug into the sides of his body when he really started to scream. Wearing blue jeans helped when the cat bit into his leg because of the thick material; however, the thin cotton shirt was no match for the sharp bladelike claws that sliced through his flesh like a hot knife through butter.

"Help!"

When the large cat attacked, it was like a feeding call to the others, and all twenty cats leaped up to Shawn's body. Scratching his arms and clawing his neck, they were little but the claws and teeth still hurt. He wanted to reach down and fight off the big brown cat, but the twenty others kept him busy as well. There were cats on his back and cats on his neck. Blood was soaking the shirt he wore.

"Michael? Help me!"

Michael pulled up in the Boss, the tires squealing when the car came to an abrupt stop in the driveway. Shawn reached out with one bloody hand, asking for help, and Michael leaped out of the car. Some of the cats leaped off of Shawn and ran toward Michael. He clashed with the cats, which leaped up to greet him, and tossed them to the side with both hands. Some he would kick, and the cats now hissed and made that sickening meowing noise. He fought his way toward Shawn, but the cats did all they could to keep him off balance.

"I'm coming, Shawn! I'm coming!"

Shawn was overtaken and fell to the ground. It was simply too much to take anymore. The big brown cat with the pointy black ears crawled up between his thighs and walked up his stomach. It flexed its claws in his belly while it stared down at Shawn with one black endless eye. The other cats were biting and clawing his arms and hands, keeping him busy while the big cat prepared to end it. The cat turned and looked at Michael with one milky white orb, and the head began twitching. Michael tossed a cat to the side with three others still clinging to his legs.

"No!"

Shawn saw the big brown cat with pointy black ears turn its head slowly back to look into his eyes. Its mouth was wide open, and drool dripped down sharp, jagged, yellow teeth. The cat almost looked like it was smiling. Nothing else mattered now. He hardly felt the clawing and biting of the smaller cats now because he could see what was coming next. Michael ran as fast as he could, but it would be too late. Both of them knew it.

A dark shadow appeared over Shawn's body, and for the first time, Shawn saw the man dressed in a long, dark trench coat with a hood over his head. Michael could not see the man standing there but noticed a dark shadow over Shawn's body. It was the face that frightened Shawn more than anything. Never had he seen anything or anyone like him, with long white hair and a face he was certain was dead. Those eyes of the man were those of a cat, and the man hissed as Michael ran up the driveway.

"Who are you?"

Shawn screamed his last words, and the cat sunk its grotesque, yellow, jagged teeth into his neck. The man dressed in black whispered a name, but only Shawn was able to hear. Blood squirted out of his jugular, and his eyes rolled back. His mouth dropped open as he coughed up blood and his head dropped back.

Michael was too late when he reached him and saw Shawn lying there, clawed up and his entire body bitten by cats. The cats all ran off, and the dark man with that lifeless face disappeared. Michael grabbed Shawn and held his body against his own. He rocked him back and forth, knowing there was nothing he could do but hold him. Michael cried and held Shawn's lifeless body tight against his chest. "It's me . . . Michael," he repeated over and over, holding his friend tight until the police came. They had to pry his hands from his friend when they finally arrived.

# INTERROGATION

The entire neighborhood was flooded with flashing red and blue lights. The entire police force was crowded in the small subdivision, including two ambulances, three fire trucks, a hook and ladder, and one emergency control vehicle. Police were marking the perimeter of the crime scene with yellow tape. Camera crews were just arriving and setting up their satellite dishes for live coverage. A crowd of people from the neighborhood surrounded the house as close as they could. Police tried holding the public back, raising their hands in the air. Some people stood on tippy toes and others on the backs of friends, trying to see what was going on.

Kevin Beck was the first to make the call to the police. He lived across the street from Shawn and Tonia but usually kept to himself. He was seventy-seven years old and lived alone. His wife had died a few years back, and Kevin had hardly stepped out of the house since then. Things were generally very peaceful in this neighborhood, he would tell police later on. Kevin was a lonely man who sat in his living room, reading often and keeping an eye on the neighborhood. Since his wife was gone, his life was very mundane. A little excitement would have been nice, but this was taking it to extremes.

"This is 911. How can I help?"

"I need the police here now!"

"Okay, slow down, sir. Who am I speaking to?"

"Just get me the police fast!"

"Sir, I can do that, but I need to know where and why."

"Oh, God. It's a bloody mess. I—I—am not sure what it is, but the guy across the street is bleeding to death."

"Okay, sir. Do you need an ambulance? I thought you said you need police."

"Yes, I need an ambulance and police."

"I have dispatched both police and an ambulance."

"I haven't even told you where I am."

"We know where you are, sir. Can you tell me what happened?"

"Well, my neighbor. He's a young guy. Look, I just looked out my window and saw him lying there in some guy's arms. I think they killed him."

"Who killed him?"

"Oh, God. I think I am going to have a heart attack."

"Sir? Hang in there, the ambulance is on its way."

The phone went silent, but she could hear Kevin gasping for breath. He was the only witness to the cats, and now he had a heart attack. Facts sometimes get construed in ways that are not the total truth. A man told the police they killed him but couldn't finish explaining he meant the cats. The tail wags the dog, and in this case it was very true. Everyone jumped to conclusions because the only thing anyone saw was Michael holding Shawn—the two of them sitting in a pool of blood. The cats were all gone from the scene, and no one saw them except for Michael and Shawn. Kevin died before the ambulance arrived and was the only other person to see the cats. Of course, there was the man dressed in black, but he was gone too.

---

Hearing the sirens, Tonia stepped out of the house. She was busy preparing things for the boys and turned to see Shawn was gone. Never in her wildest dreams had she thought they were coming for him. Standing at the front door, she saw the two sitting in the middle of their driveway in a pool of blood. Everything flashed in front of her now, and she screamed before falling to the ground and fainting. When the police arrived, they thought they might have a double homicide. Poor Michael was pulled from his friend and cuffed immediately. Tonia woke up to see him hauled away and could only imagine her brother-in-law had killed his best friend. The ambulance came and took Tonia. The EMT was afraid to give her sedatives because of her pregnancy.

---

The police placed Michael in the backseat of Lieutenant Steve's squad car. Steve paced around the scene several times, asking a few people some questions before finally walking back to his car. There was something different about Lieutenant Steve Case today. Michael didn't notice because he was in a daze after watching his best friend get killed by a sick cat. Other people knew it, though, and stepped back when he walked past them. There was an aura about Steve today that seemed to tell people to stay away. Dark sunglasses hid Steve's eyes, but you could tell by the look on his face he wasn't happy about the events.

"You're in a shitload of trouble now, boy."

Michael was slumped in the backseat of the car. He didn't respond to Steve and just stared straight at the seat in front of him. This was becoming a familiar sight from his perspective, but today he was not as talkative. His best friend had just been killed, and Michael was numb. Blood soaked his clothes, and his face and hands were coated as well.

Some people noticed a change in Steve, but they couldn't say what it was. He never wore sunglasses until today, and maybe that was it. He seemed more sure of himself for some reason. He lowered his head to look inside the squad car with his eyes just barely above the glasses. A finger pushed up the new dark sunglasses on the bridge of his nose, and he stood up. "Quiet now? Well, you're gonna be singing once I get you back to the station, jackass." Steve pounded his fist on the roof of the car and then walked around, started the car, and took him to the station.

Michael tripped into the station with his hands cuffed behind him. Lieutenant Steve gave him a nice little shove on his shoulders from behind. When Steve opened the door to let Michael out, he didn't waste any time and pulled him out by the hair. He gave him a cheap shot to the ribs and then grabbed him by the cuffs, shoved him forward till he was in the station, and gave him one last shove. Watching this grand entrance was Becky Tomlinson, who was sitting in her chair behind the front desk with her headset on. Michael was soaked in blood just like the last time he visited the station, only this was different. The blood on his hands was that of a human, and if he could talk right now he would have said it was his best friend's blood. Steve couldn't help but give Michael a nice warm welcome to the station by giving him a couple of punches in the side after he pulled him out of the car.

"Book him."

"For what?" Becky asked, looking at Michael's familiar face.

"Murder."

Becky raised an eye and tilted her head to one side. Never in its entire history had there been a murder in this small town. She saw that Steve was very serious and then turned to see the look on Michael's face. She had seen that look five years back when the Quinlan twins were found in the lake. Their father had taken them out fishing that bright sunny day, only it might not have been so bright and sunny for the father. His daughters had just turned twelve, and he was excited to spend the day fishing with the two of them. The eldest—by fifteen minutes—had caught a fish, and the two of them stood up excitedly on the small rowboat. There was a rope attached to an anchor, and it was coiled around on the floor of the boat. When the girls stood it rocked the boat back and forth, capsizing it and tipping all three into the warm July waters. The rope was around the girls' feet, and when the boat capsized it tightened around both of their ankles. The anchor fell to the bottom of the water, which was only eight feet deep but just deep enough to keep the two of them beneath till they could no longer breathe. Becky remembered the look in the father's eyes that day when he was brought into the station when they rescued him. He had been diving down to rescue his daughters for an hour straight when they finally dragged him out. He was in shock, having lost both of his daughters, and it was the exact same look in Michael's eyes now. No, this was not murder but a loss of someone close instead, and she knew it.

"Murder? Steve, are you—"

"Don't argue with me, Becky!"

"I'm just saying I know that look—"

"Stick with the phones, Becky, and do as you're told!"

Steve had never acted this way in his entire career as a police officer. He was usually a quiet man who took orders from everyone. Reaching up with one hand, he pulled the sunglasses from his eyes. There was something wrong, and Becky recognized it immediately. Was it the sunglasses that did it? This was definitely not the Lieutenant Steve she knew, but whoever he was scared the hell out of her. There was something about his eyes that caught her attention, but she feared looking at them. They were dark and endless like nothing she had ever seen before, but she promised she would pray tonight. *His wife,* she thought to herself. *He's acting this way because his wife is missing and they found that girl in St. Louis. He shouldn't be handling this case if it has anything to do with cats.* "Steve—"

"One more word out of you, Becky, and I'll charge you with insubordination. Now book him!" Steve was wired.

———

Becky processed Michael for murder, as she was ordered to do. She took all his information that a police officer does in such a situation. His valuables were taken and placed in a baggy marked with his case number. They took a nice photo of him too, placing him against the board with horizontal lines running across it. A front shot and two side portraits would look nice on his mantle at home. He was even allowed to hold a chalkboard that stated his name and number on front.

Steve brought him down to a cell where he would spend some quality time alone. Unlocking a few doors on the way, Steve kept a tight hand on the back of Michael's hands. It was dark, with only a few lights up on the ceiling that were caged in wire mesh. The walls were all plain, and each door had a small piece of glass with wire mesh in between. Breaking out of this place was not an option. When he came to the cell, Steve shoved him in. Then the weirdest thing happened Michael would never forget.

Steve hissed, "No one is here to save you now."

Michael just stared at him in disbelief. His mind and body were numb to all the verbal and physical abuse he was taking, but that hiss awoke him from his slumber. He stood up on the bench, narrowed his eyes, and looked straight at Steve for the very first time. He remembered Lieutenant Steve, but the last time he had seen him the man was stuttering. This was a different person, but it didn't quite click just yet. This man scared Michael, but he was also pissing him off. This wasn't the way you treated a person after his best friend was just killed before his eyes.

"Who are you?"

"I'm your worst nightmare!" Steve hissed again.

The chief opened the door, looked at Michael, and stared directly at Steve. He heard him ask Steve who he was, uncertain of what was going on, but he knew it couldn't be good. He was shaken by the whole incident and took a moment before walking into the cell. Steve was oblivious to the chief standing there and took one step closer to Michael. The chief was quick to place a hand in front of Steve, stopping him cold in his tracks. Sometimes nerves got to a police officer, and the chief figured the whole episode of his wife missing and that girl recently found in St. Louis was messing with him. "I don't know what the hell is going on, boy, but you're in a shitload of trouble."

Steve nodded his head and stared at Michael with a cold, cruel grin on his face. He placed the dark sunglasses back up on his face, covering his eyes. His facial features seemed to be sneering at Michael now. The chief looked back and forth from Michael to Steven and placed one hand on Steve's chest, pushing him back.

"Steve? You wanna head upstairs now."

"But, Chief."

"Now!"

"I'll be seeing you, boy," Steve hissed.

"And what in Barbie's name is with those sunglasses, Steve? We're inside."

Steve paused for a moment, not answering the chief. He then walked away and poked at the bottom part of his new shades so they were high on his nose. He stopped for one moment to turn and look at Michael, giving him one last grin before leaving. The chief watched this and then turned back to Michael, waiting for the door to close before he spoke again.

"Do you want to tell me what happened?"

"That guy's an asshole."

"Steve? He's a pussycat."

"He's been beating me ever since he took me from . . . from . . ."

Michael broke down, unable to finish. He thought he was coming out of it for a while there. The beatings and the verbal abuse were one thing, but when Steve hissed, it brought out the anger inside him. Now he thought about his friend again, and the memory of what happened came back to him. His world started to spin out of control, and finally he started to cry.

"All right, all right. Take it easy."

"Is this how a person is treated after his best friend is killed?"

"Michael? Can I call you Michael?"

"Yeah . . . sure."

"Michael, your friend was killed, but I need answers. Can you do that for me now?"

"Sure . . . sure, Chief." He was fighting back tears, and his body was shaking.

"All right then, why don't you tell me what happened."

Michael told him about his day, how they were all getting together for a party to watch some football games. This, of course, could all be confirmed by many people, including both their wives, who were now in hysterics. He explained to the chief how he drove up and saw Shawn in the middle of the driveway with cats surrounding him. Cats were everywhere, and one large cat was attacking him. The chief seemed to keep a straight face, but this was hard for anyone to take. Michael told him about the cats and how he was attacked himself. He showed him the fresh claw marks on his hands and arms. Finally he told him of the large cat that killed Shawn. He broke down at this point and held his face in his hands. There were some parts that he kept out, though, because it would be foolish of him to tell the chief everything. He was beginning to like Dugan but had to be careful of what he told him. The chief would think he was a lunatic if he told him of the milky white eye and the shadow over Shawn's body.

"Well, that's an interesting story, Michael, but I have a problem with it."

Michael looked up from his hands with teary red eyes and sniffed. "What's that?"

"We have a witness, but he never saw any cats."

"You son of a bitch! There were cats there!"

"Well, we shall see."

Michael was dizzy, unsure if he should stop talking now and ask for an attorney or scream. *This was just a wild dream*, he started to say to himself. There most definitely were cats and one very large one now. Cats had killed his best friend, and if the police weren't going to help then he would do this on his own—right after he was able to get out of there, of course. Dugan was the only person he could talk to, and even he didn't believe him.

"Your friend Shawn was seen a little over two weeks ago getting rid of some evidence. A police officer—" He stopped and motioned toward the door. "Lieutenant Steve, to be specific, found what your friend was trying to get rid of. It was a plastic bag, and inside this bag was a dead cat. Now, can you tell me about this cat, Michael? I have asked you about this before and you denied knowing anything about it, but I think you do know something, don't you?"

Michael was silent for a moment before shaking his head. "I don't know anything about it."

"Ah, we'll see. Here's the problem. It just seems like a weird coincidence that your friend Shawn was getting rid of a dead cat, and now he is suddenly found in his own driveway sliced to hell in his best friend's arms. No cats seen anywhere in the area, but his friend swears cats killed him. I don't know what's going on, Michael, but I am going to find out."

"I didn't kill Shawn."

"Well then, Michael, we have a problem with a wild cat now, don't we?"

Michael couldn't have said it any better and just smiled at the chief.

# CAT FIGHT

Jenny was quiet most of the day, preparing to visit the funeral home. Dressed all in black, she was still finding it hard to imagine her brother, Shawn, was gone. To make matters worse, she had to deal with Michael and all his crazy stories. She was torn between her husband, who had become so obsessed with his new job that now he was seeing cats everywhere, and her brother, who was killed by God knows what—or who.

She thought about taking JR to the funeral home to visit but decided it would be best to leave him home this time. It was a closed casket, and she really didn't want her son to experience something so traumatic. She called up the sitter, Susan, who would come to pick him up soon. This was better, she told herself, and knew it was the right thing to do. Besides, she needed time alone; she was an emotional wreck herself. It would be good for him to have some time to play and not see his mom crying.

The doorbell rang, and she looked toward the door and saw the face of Susan peeking in the glass transom on the side of the door. JR turned and smiled the moment he saw Susie's face peeking inside. She wore a yellow-and-black-striped sherpa-style hat. She waved one hand in the transom window, seeing the look in JR's eyes. The ball on top of her hat bounced up and down. A cute girl holding up a bag of goodies in one hand, she loved to play with JR and would always bring some new toys or stories to read to him while she took care of him.

"Hello, Susie."

"Hello, Mrs. Merlino. I'm sorry about your loss."

"Aw, you're a sweetie. Come on in."

"Susie," JR said, only it came out more like "Soo zee," with a pause in between the "soo" and the "zee." It was a start, anyways, of a two-syllable word that made his mom proud and happy. He still needed to work on "Dad," which Michael hoped would come someday.

"Yay!" Susie reached out and grabbed him from his mother's arms. JR nearly leaped into hers with his arms open wide as well.

"I know you'll take good care of him. I shouldn't be too long."

"Yes, Mrs. Merlino. Take your time. JR and I will be fine."

"Thank you, Susie."

Jenny leaned in, kissed her boy, and waved good-bye to Susie. She really didn't want to leave him, but she needed time alone. Sitting inside the minivan, she checked the mirror and stared at her eyes. They looked horrible and tired, so she pulled out some makeup but knew it wouldn't cover the feelings she had inside. Silently she sat there in the minivan, holding back the tears before finally pulling out of the garage.

She headed to the Wagon to get a couple items for her brother's funeral. She would stop at the Wagon first and then head over to the funeral home. Traffic was light this time of day, but it didn't matter to Jenny today. She was in no rush to go anywhere, wishing all of this was just a dream. Her life was suddenly swept away in another direction of which she had no control.

---

Krista was sitting at the small makeup table in her room with a mirror lit up in front of her. She was applying powder to her face with a large facial brush. She turned from side to side, looking at the mirror to make sure she looked absolutely perfect. Scrunching up her bright-red lips, she applied another coat of lipstick. This was a typical routine for her whenever she headed out the door. She never knew who she would bump into, and today she was heading to the Wagon. She stood up and checked herself in the full-length mirror, making sure the clothes she wore looked perfect. A hand fluffed up her dark curly hair and then gave it a shake to see how it fell. She practiced this a couple times as she posed in front of the mirror.

The image of her bed was reflected in the mirror, and she turned to see it there in the center of her bedroom. A flashback of her and Michael came to her, and she stepped over to the edge of the bed, imagining him lying there. She dragged a finger along the edge of the bedspread and pranced around it like she was being seductive. She had a plan to get him back somehow. He would leave that wife of his after realizing the woman she was, and the two of them would live the life she planned for them. She knew what was happening in his life, but none of this really mattered to her. To her it was destiny that these things were happening to him. It was destiny to break him and Jenny apart. He would come to his senses and realize what he missed. Then he was all hers and she would make him beg to come back to her.

The drive to the Wagon was a short one in her plush little Mercedes. Traffic was light, but she wanted the entire road to herself, weaving in and out. She checked her makeup while she drove and constantly checked her phone to see if anyone called. She honked her horn several times at people on the road. How dare they drive on the same road as her!

Along the way she passed a large billboard in the middle of a cornfield with her picture on it. "Dream of your belle vista and then call on Krista" was at the top of the sign with her phone number beneath. A small portion of the billboard was dedicated to the vacant land that was to be developed, but it wasn't about the land, was it? It all had to do with her. She was the reason things sold, after all. The picture of her was in the center, of course, taking up most of the space on the billboard. She started to hum her little motto while she drove and waved to people in the cars she passed. It was another bright, cheery day, and sales meant everything to her.

---

The doorbell jingled when Jenny entered the Wagon. The old wooden door creaked and the few people working inside turned to see who it was. The boy at the front greeted her with the phrase that was embedded in everyone's head within a twenty-mile radius: "Welcome to the Wallace Wagon for all your family needs. Have a great day!" He was the same freckled kid who'd greeted Michael that glorious day when the special protein shake man decided to lend his blender to him. Jenny hardly noticed the boy because her head really wasn't with it this day.

—··················—

Shopping in the women's clothing department—or, to be more specific, the lingerie section—was Krista Polinsky. Some may have figured that the Wagon was not exactly the first place a person would think of buying lingerie, but they had one of the best selections and prices around. Besides, it was good business to shop there for Krista. She met many customers coming in and out of the Wagon just by spending a few dollars there.

An upbeat style of music was playing on the speakers, giving the place a little spark. There was nobody lying around or sleeping near the video department, like Stan Worthington, although he was seen strolling about in the lawn and garden section. Shopping carts were moving back and forth in the aisles, making it hard to move at times in those crowded spaces.

Mary Wallace was checking the aisles when she saw Krista shopping in the lingerie section. She was one of Krista's customers and was searching for a new home in the area. A stickler for details, Mary had become a very demanding customer for Krista. One day she would want a house with a large kitchen, but when Krista showed her the perfect house with a large kitchen Mary would tell her it was too big. Krista finally thought she had found the perfect house that had just been listed on the market. She called Mary, picked her up in her Mercedes, and took her to the home she had found. Mary took one look at the house and said, "It's too old." Krista wanted to pull her hair out—Mary's hair, that is. Mary was very much into the details of what she wanted, and sometimes her husband Paul wished she would just stick to the basics. The two

196

of them often argued about how to run the Wagon. Paul was old school, and Mary wanted to change everything. Krista had no idea what she was getting into, but Paul certainly did. He let the two go off on their own to search for the "perfect home."

"Krista?"

Krista turned, knowing the voice, and groaned deep down inside. Mary was probably the first customer she ever had that she regretted. Never had Krista worked harder for a customer. "Oh, hello, Mary."

"Any news on the housing market?"

"Nothing yet, but I am going to check out some new listings tomorrow."

"Oh really?" Her nasal voice accented the word "really" with a cynical voice. "Where?"

"The west side of the lake has two—"

Mary was quick to cut her off. "I never liked the west side of the lake. The east side is so much better."

"I'll see what I can do."

"Please do."

With that final dagger in Krista's heart, she turned and walked away. This was going to be the hardest commission Krista had ever worked for in her short career. Right now she was regretting it, knowing she wasted way too much time on it. She only hoped one day she would look back to this and laugh about it. Holding little black lingerie in her hands, she looked at the price tag, sighed, and tossed it in her basket. "I should get a discount for this."

Shopping in the aisle next to the lingerie was Jenny, who was looking for something black to wear in her hair. She was too busy trying on different bows or wraps in her hair to notice the voices coming from the aisle next to her.

Krista did notice Jenny when she was pushing the shopping cart around the corner, and she couldn't help but be a bitch. She quickly grabbed the black lingerie she was buying and held it up to her body. She knew exactly what she was doing and pretended she had no idea Jenny was there. She posed with the lingerie with a sultry look on her face. Krista waited for just the right moment when Jenny turned the corner. She waited until she knew Jenny was close enough to hear her talk and see what she was doing. Krista was a conniving little bitch who would stop at nothing until she got what she wanted.

"Oh, this is nice. I think Michael is really going to want to rip this one off me like he did last time," Krista said to herself, although she was really speaking to Jenny.

Jenny stopped dead in her tracks, turning to that evil little voice. She was in no mood to start anything, but this bitch was stepping on the wrong girl and at the wrong time. Slowly she looked straight at Krista with eyes that burned. Fingers clenched the bar on the cart she was pushing.

"That fits a sleazy tramp like yourself. Well, only next time you should place a tag on yourself that says 'slut'!"

"What did you call me?"

"You heard me, you bitch, and if you don't stay away from Michael I am going to make sure you wished you did."

"Oh really?" She laughed nervously.

"Really," Jenny reconfirmed.

Krista just had to push it, though, being the total bitch she was. She was used to getting her way, and this was not going to be any different. She twirled the lingerie in her hands, teasing Jenny while she batted long lashes and acted innocent now. "He told me you don't have what it takes to please him."

Jenny didn't respond but pushed the cart to the side instead. Krista stared in disbelief as Jenny stormed toward her. As if in slow motion, Jenny's eyes grew rageful and Krista dropped the lingerie. Krista got what she wanted, but maybe it was a little more than she expected. Jenny grabbed Krista by the hair with one clenched fist and pulled it hard. Krista screamed, and that cute, innocent look on her face was lost to one in agony.

"You little bitch! I told you to stay away from him!"

The two of them grabbed and shoved each other back and forth. Clothes on the shelves fell to the ground, and racks were pushed over as well. Between the two of them screaming at each other and the noise of things falling over, it sounded like two cats fighting. And that was exactly what witnesses later said it was.

"You bitch!" Krista screamed.

"Slut!" Jenny shouted back.

"Maybe he likes it!"

"Tramp!"

They went back and forth, pulling and scratching at one another. People would have put money on Krista any other day, but today Jenny was not to be denied. She had Krista down on the ground and was pounding her with clenched fists.

"You . . . stay . . . away . . . from . . . my . . . Michael!" She shouted with every punch.

"Cleanup in aisle thirty-two," the voice shouted on the speaker above.

———

Krista was clawed up pretty well, but Jenny had a few scrapes and bruises too when the police finally arrived. Both of them were entangled with arms and legs wrapped around each other. Racks of clothes and boxes on the shelves were thrown all over the place. The aisles were littered with items knocked over during the fight.

Police got the call from Stan Worthington, and when they arrived they had to pry the two women apart. It took three officers to end the fight, an officer holding one woman back and the third in between. Stan was nearby, waiting on his wife when he heard all the commotion in a nearby aisle. He seemed pretty excited and gave a play-by-play description of the fight when he called in.

"This is 911. How can I help you?"

"Uh, yeah. This is Stan Worthington, and we have a heck of a fight here in the Wallace Wagon."

"All right, sir, I will dispatch a police officer. Can you describe what's happening, please?"

"Sure! The blonde is beating the shit out of the dark-haired one. Oh! She just gave her a right uppercut."

"So there are two women fighting?"

"Yep, two women. It's a good one. Oh! The dark-haired one is a cutie, but she's getting pummeled right now."

Krista was worried this would ruin her relationship with Mary Wallace. Once the police arrived and broke up the fight, she turned to see if Mary was around. Standing to one side was Mary Wallace with her arms folded, but what Krista didn't know was that business started to pick up because of the fight. People crowded into the store, making it one of the busiest days of the year. The entire week was busy after that, with rumors going around that this was the place to be. Mary looked at Krista, gave her a thumbs-up, and walked away, confusing the hell out of Krista.

Jenny was in another mind-set and wanted to beat the living tar out of Krista. She had been waiting for this moment for a very long time. It took police officers ten minutes to cool her down. She pulled and tugged, wanting another round with Krista, but the police shook their heads and held her strained body back.

Chief Marty Dugan arrived on the scene and decided it was best not to press charges. He talked to all parties involved, including Mary Wallace, who was completely excited over the whole event and found no reason to belabor the event.

# SPRINGER

Michael was back at work after an extended weekend of hell. He had seen his best friend killed by a pack of cats, he was interrogated by the police and beaten, his wife was depressed, and now he had Franklin to deal with. The job of his dreams had quickly become his nightmare, and now he wondered if things would have been different if he could do something else. Nothing he could do would make things better; he was certain this was his future. It was what he did, and he was good at it, too. He certainly wasn't going to be an astronomer.

The phone at his desk started to ring, and the small display lit up, telling him it was Franklin on the other end. He hesitated before picking it up with one hand and placing it to his ear. There was a time not long ago when everything was going so well. Michael was moving up in the world and Franklin was there to help him. Now it was spiraling out of control, and the last person he really wanted to talk to was Franklin.

"Hello?" His voice was hesitant.

"Have you seen the newspapers today?" The tone of Franklin's voice was sarcastic.

"No, sir, but I can explain—"

"Explain? Son? You could explain a lifetime and never repair the damage that you caused."

"Yes, sir, but—"

"In all my years with this bank never have I had the pleasure of meeting a total disaster!"

"Yes, sir, but—"

"This bank will not be dragged down by an incompetent little imbecile."

Michael held the phone away from his ear, listening to Franklin scream. Every once in a while Michael would nod and say, "Yes, sir." Had Franklin no compassion for what happened in his life right now? Had the bank really taken priority over his best friend dying and his family shaken by the whole incident? Apparently it had, and this was not what Michael had signed up to do.

After a long talk, with Franklin giving him life's little lessons, Michael hung up the phone and leaned back in his chair. He clasped his hands behind his back and clenched his eyes tight, hoping all this would just go away. Franklin was the one person who he always made fun of for giving him life's little lessons, yet Michael took most of what he said seriously. He was a wise man, but none of this was making any sense. It was like he was another man now. Maybe it was all the pressure. Maybe it was because Franklin saw Michael failing after giving him the reins to run the business. Was it that he had worked so long with Michael only to see his own work become a failure? It was silent in the room, which was nice, and he needed that so much right now. He sat there in silence, trying to get rid of all the wild thoughts inside his head. A ticking sound broke his concentration, and he opened one eye to see the cat clock hanging on the wall and staring directly at him. The tail wagged back and forth, and those eyes of black and white were laughing at Michael and mocking him. Every day that went by he hated that clock more and more.

"I hate that thing."

---

It was a long day for Michael at work, and he came home hoping to relax. He changed out of his suit and into some jeans and a sweatshirt. In the past Michael would have run downstairs to see his wife and kid, but things were definitely different lately. Instead he just lay there on his bed, staring up at the ceiling. He really wanted to do absolutely nothing and just closed his eyes again. This was becoming a habit now, and he opened his eyes slowly, hoping it was all just a bad dream.

Michael knew he had to step on eggshells when he walked down the stairs to the family room. He tried to be compassionate toward Jenny, but his own mind was spinning as he tried to keep up with all the things happening to him as well. Jenny was taking this very hard, and he had to find a way to help her get through this. He brought home a large vase of yellow daisies and tried to help out with cooking the dinner. He helped with the laundry, though the colors bled into one another and the clothes were wrinkled when he folded them.

The little fight at the Wagon was really uncalled for by that little bitch, Krista; he was going to have to talk to her. The pain from the scratch on his neck was feeling worse than ever. He took a couple of aspirin for the pain, but he was going to need something stronger if it didn't heal soon.

His job promotion was the start of all the events that had happened recently—from coming home late and killing the cat, which somehow caused these crazed cats to come back. They haunted him in ways that were destroying his life. The killings of his dog and best friend were the worst of the things that happened so far. His job was in jeopardy, but what worried him the most was what was to come next. Would this ever end? The most important question running in his head was: how could he end it? He knew deep down this would eventually end, but he was afraid it would have a devastating effect on his life—a disastrous effect on the ones he loved.

"What do I do, Dad?"

No answer.

He sat down on the couch in the family room and clicked on the television. With the remote in one hand, he changed channels from one to another. The news was too much for him, and he just wanted to relax now, so he leaned back on the sofa and placed his feet up on the table before him. Looking back at Jenny and JR made him smile. He loved the two of them. He would do anything for those two, and he knew if this thing he was worried about ever tried to harm them he would lay his own life down to save them.

A voice on the television announced Jerry Springer as the next show. Michael was daydreaming and did not bother changing the channel. It was a rerun of an earlier show about people, like Michael, who worked during the day but really needed to see other people whose lives were worse than his. On the bottom of the screen was a banner that stated, "Man Warns Cats Are Evil."

Jenny was in a horrible mood after her incident with Krista and the police yesterday. Scratches covered her body and, although she had the better part of Krista, it still hurt in certain spots. A long red scratch ran down the side of her cheek. Michael knew she was having a hard time dealing with things at the moment. She was short and snappy at any comments. Now was just a time to leave her be and get some mental rest.

People started shouting on the television. The camera zoomed in on a man with darker skin. The camera switched from that man to Jerry Springer, who held a microphone in one hand. Springer turned to the audience, smiling with his wire-rimmed spectacles. The crowd was shouting and pointing fingers at the guest.

"I tell you this is very real," the guest told Springer.

Michael stared at the television, but his mind was on something else. His day had been rough at the office with Franklin, and things were not much better on the home front. The camera spanned the audience, showing them laughing and jeering at the guest. Springer tried to play the neutral host; it was obvious he was prodding the audience with every comment or facial expression he made.

"So you're telling me we should all be afraid of cats?" Springer asked the man incredulously and then turned to the laughing audience. Raising his eyebrows without saying a word only fired up the audience even more.

Jenny seemed agitated by the sound of the people shouting and jeering on the television. "Why do people go on shows like that anyways? Can you turn that off, please? It's driving me nuts."

"They will kill us all if we don't do something about it now. You must trust me about this." The guest was pointing a finger at the rambunctious crowd.

"So you're telling me these cats . . ." Springer asked him, emphasizing the word "cats" and dragging out the "s" like he was hissing, "are going to kill us all?"

"Read my book. It will explain it all." The guest held up a book. "Valafar will be our demise. Remember! I warned you all!"

Springer laughed and put an arm around the guest. "Well, thank you very much for joining us, Mohamed." He turned to the camera and smiled to the audience. "That was Mohamed Abdulah with his new book out called *Valafar, Cats and Our Demise*. You don't want to miss this one." The crowd cheered, and Mohamed stepped away, shaking his head.

"Jenny?"

"What is it, Michael?"

"You have to see this, quick!"

Michael watched the television in shock. This was the first time he'd heard of anyone with a connection to cats attacking. The hiss in Springer's voice was what had first caught his attention. It was the name Valafar that made him nearly scream at the top of his lungs. What was the name of that book? He wasn't certain he could remember that part, but what about the author? This was serious, and he had to find out why this man was so upset. Who was this Valafar, and why was he in Michael's life right now?

Jenny stepped into the room and stared at the television. The show was over, and now the caption on the bottom said, "Man with woman parts is pregnant." She was pissed off before, but this was going to put her over the edge, for sure. "Michael? You have to be kidding me."

"No, no! Jen, the show before that. It was about the cats." Michael pointed to the television.

"It's Jerry Springer, Michael. Get serious, would ya?" She rolled her eyes at him.

"Jenny, the man on the show was talking about cats attacking people and—"

205

Jenny nearly fell over when she burst into tears. Michael was so excited about the show and the book that he had forgotten all about how sensitive Jenny was right now. It took him a moment because he was so wrapped up in the book and cats that he missed the part when Jenny bent over sobbing. He ran to her finally and grabbed her tight with both arms around her and hugged her tight. She just placed her head into his side, and the two of them remained silent for some time. He carried her over to the couch to let her recover and turned the television off. JR was watching his mom and dad step off into the family room and lifted one finger and pointed to the two of them. "Mom!"

⸻

Michael sat at the desk, moving the mouse around in his hand to start up the computer. The screen flickered on, and he clicked the Internet button on the bottom. Jenny was in the other room, cuddling up with JR, and he thought it was a good idea to just let her rest awhile. The book was fresh in his mind, and he needed to see if there was any information about the cats he had seen.

He first typed in "Valafar" in the Internet search because it was the one word he remembered. It had been one of the words on the windshield in the parking lot. There was not much online, but the name of the book did come up: *Valafar, Cats and Our Demise.* He clicked on it, and a picture of the book came up on Amazon.com with a picture of the author. His name was Mohamed Abdulah, which Michael wrote down beside the name of the book. He clicked the order button for the book and typed in all the information to have it sent to his house in about a week. He clicked back in the history of the search to see what else he could find about Valafar. He was amazed at the several links he found. There were, of course, many unrelated items, but some struck him as most unusual and very unsettling. The name appeared to be of a demon, specifically a grand duke of hell. He researched this for hours that night, totally captivated by what he found. This demon commanded ten legions and a very strong demon of hell. What caught his interest mostly was one definition that described him as appearing in the shape of a lion.

Something moved along the window and Michael was spooked, certain it was a cat coming back. He whipped around in his chair to see nothing but some leaves blowing in the wind along the deck. It was getting dark outside, and the wind was picking up. He turned to the family room and saw Jenny and JR smiling at each other now. Still holding him in her arms, she seemed to be doing well right now. This made him happy, but he had to figure out what to do next.

There was not much on this Valafar, and all of it seemed to pull up the same information—the grand duke of hell and a demon who commanded ten legions. What concerned him the most was the part about him appearing as a lion. He clicked more links and finally found some new information. It was a picture, and sometimes a picture speaks a thousand words. There staring at him was a picture of the dark man—the man in a dark cloak or the man of death. It was him, Michael was certain, and goose bumps broke out on his skin. The eyes were those of a cat staring at Michael, so lifelike he swore it would leap out of the screen and grab him. The skin was white like that of a dead person, but who the hell was this person?

The description called this person a "wraith," or a keeper of the afterlife. He was a ghost, and Michael would agree with that since this man seemed to appear and disappear out of nowhere. Why was he appearing in Michael's life right now? What did he have to do with the cats? It frustrated Michael, and he searched the Internet for hours. Finally, something had confirmed this thing's existence, yet it told him absolutely nothing. The picture only confirmed to him there really was a person. Was this Valafar a person, a ghost, or a keeper of the afterlife? What did that have to do with him? The more he searched, the more frustrated he became. The book would help, he hoped. It would provide the answers that he needed.

# VALAFAR

## JULY 20, 2008

They worked through the rest of the night and into the early morning, carting out all the emeralds they could manage, but it was the tomb that concerned them the most. While Abdul was busy shoveling in loads and loads of emeralds and carting them back and forth, Marty and Mohamed worked on a winch system that would propel the tomb up and out to daylight. With just the three of them it was not easy shifting the tomb to an angle good enough to clear the opening, but once they did, the pulleys and cables would do most of the work.

The wind was blowing and the sky was growing darker once again, with lightning striking in the distance. A sandstorm was brewing off in the distance, and if they did not work faster now all may be lost. On the horizon the sky was filled with sand, and a great cloud of dust swirled all around. It was a slow mover, but it was heading straight for their camp.

"We have to move now!" yelled Marty.

The three of them worked double-time, trying not to look at the storm because they knew it would slow them down. Every second mattered, and they focused on getting the tomb inside the wagon to be hauled away by the Humvee. Mohamed and Abdul would drive the one Humvee that carried the wagon behind with the tomb, and Marty was to drive the other Humvee loaded with the jewels.

Mohamed and Abdul drove back to Cairo once they loaded up the plane and saw Marty off safely. Mohamed was driving because Abdul could not think straight after the long night they'd had. Abdul sat in the passenger seat, still mumbling about death and curses, and held his head in both hands. The roads grew crowded with heavy traffic the closer they came to the city. There were plenty of people walking along the streets. In the markets, canopies over the merchandise covered it from the hot sun. Old cars and trucks barely moved, and several honked their horns now and then.

They were at an intersection, held up by a couple of men arguing at each other in the middle of the street. One would raise his hands in the air, and then the other would shout back. People were getting agitated in their cars and honking horns. The sun was beating down early in the afternoon and would have cooked a dozen eggs on the top of the cars. Most people just wanted to take shelter, knowing the day was getting near its peak.

It seemed the two men arguing both had trucks vacated in the middle of the intersection. The green truck was hissing, with smoke pumping out of the radiator and a puddle of water beneath the hood. The faded yellow one had a smashed side, and the door was hanging off a hinge. Meanwhile, cars kept honking, moving nowhere any time soon.

"It seems we are going to be awhile," Mohamed told Abdul.

"It's okay. Just glad we're out of that place." Abdul seemed more relaxed than he had been earlier.

A large building was under construction overhead. It was fenced off so people would not get hurt, and all the precautions were taken care of for the safety of the public. A crane was lifting a heavy steel I-beam and starting to swing it to a portion of the building. Men stood up on the beams—high in the air like acrobats—waving hands for the crane operator to bring the beam closer.

Mohamed leaned back in his seat and placed the car in park. It was going to be awhile, so he rolled down the windows and turned off the car. He unrolled a pouch of dried fruits and handed it to Abdul, who looked up to Mohamed and smiled.

"I guess I got a little carried away."

"No, Abdul. It's understandable. It's over." He patted his back in reassurance.

That was when things went terribly wrong. A strong gust of wind swirled dust in the air. Mohamed remembered seeing a man walking nearby suddenly thrown back by a force, knocking him to the ground. At the time he did not think too much of it till it was too late and he just rested back in his beaded seat and closed his eyes. The crane overhead tilted to one side, and the beam it carried began to swing back and forth. The construction workers on the beam were directing the crane operator and starting to shout to others down below. The crane was strained and began to creak loudly, tilting to one side. The beam took a nosedive toward the ground. The reel that held the cable and the beam clicked a couple times and began to smoke and whine from the strain. Because of the sudden gust it could not hold the tension anymore. The beam came crashing down in what the papers would later say was a freak accident. Never had they seen high winds like that appear out of nowhere, strong enough to damage a crane. Yet it did, and the heavy steel beam came crashing down right on top of Mohamed and Abdul's Humvee, crushing every part of Abdul. The end of the beam came down upon his head. Reports came in later of a hole in the ground about five feet deep. The remains of Abdul were hard to find, being smashed like a pestle would crush a pill in a mortar. The top of the Humvee had ripped shreds of steel pointed down to the ground.

Mohamed was luckier, only losing his right arm in the freak accident. It took the rescue crew half an hour to get to the accident site and another hour before they were able to pry Mohamed out of the wreckage. He was unconscious, luckily for him, but during that time he was shouting out something about cats.

The Boeing C-17 Globemaster III traveled across the ocean, making its way across the States. Marty sat in the back with the cargo, never taking his eyes off the treasure he had found. It was a long journey, and Marty slept most of the way, dreaming of his future of being famous. The plane was enormous; it was the same type used by the military to transport troops and cargo, including airdrops from the large back door.

Mohamed stayed in Egypt to take care of things while Marty took the tomb back to the States. They had argued for a very long time about the laws of taking such a valuable item out of Egypt, but Marty wouldn't listen. It was Mohamed's job to keep things quiet and cover the tracks of the dig site. With the sandstorm hitting, this was not going to be hard at all. By the time he got back to the site, the sandstorm had already passed. The dig site was completely covered, without a trace of anything going on other than a few straggler tents. The rest would have to be found later once they went through all the permitting, which would take months if not longer.

Marty traveled across the Atlantic, stopping in New York and customs, without any incident. Things went smoothly, considering what was inside, but again Marty had his connections. Again they were off to the West Coast, where Marty would meet some experts who would examine what he had found. A couple of hours into the flight the sky started to fill with ominous clouds. The plane bumped a little at first. Then about fifteen minutes later the plane really started to jump. Marty woke, blinking his eyes like a drunken fool with drool dripping down the corner of his mouth. He wiped it with the back of his hand and then grabbed hold to stand. The plane shook again, and he wobbled, grabbing now with both hands, and then made his way to the cabin to check on the status of the plane.

"Everything is okay, Marty, but you might want to buckle up. A bit of turbulence for the next half hour, but everything is okay," the pilot told him.

"Bah! You do realize what's on this plane, don't you?" Marty snapped.

The pilots nodded, assuring him everything would be all right, and then turned back to the controls of the plane and flipped a couple switches. "Yes, sir."

Marty went back to check on the stone tomb, making sure it was secure. He could not keep his mind off it. He kept wondering what was inside. Everything had happened so fast when the storm came, and they loaded all they could before it hit. He stood before it, wiping the top where a label was etched upon it.

Marty placed his finger under each picture—a snake, arm, lion, arm, snake, arm, and then a red eye. It wasn't a complicated message to read.

"Valafar."

Marty looked it over and scratched his head, having no idea what Valafar was or what it meant. His only conclusion was that it was the name of whoever was inside. They could not open the tomb earlier because of the storm, and the weight of the top was enormous for one man to move. He had searched the sides and the top many times before, not seeing anything that would help to open it or give him a clue as to what lay inside.

The plane jolted to one side, and Marty fell to his knees and slid to one side of the plane. The tomb, which was strapped in, managed to remain in place. He placed one hand to the floor to push himself up when he noticed a small lever sticking out of the side of the tomb that hadn't been there before. "What the . . ." Marty slowly crawled to the tomb with one hand reaching out with palm held up and facing the tomb. His eyes were wide with excitement, and gently his hand touched the lever; he was careful, as if touching something hot. Unsure what it was or where it came from, Marty was careful but knew this lever—no matter where it came from—opened the top. He pulled the lever to one side, but at first it did not budge. "Well, for fuck's sake." He grabbed it with both hands, pulled it harder, and leaned his body back. He heard a snap, and the lever finally gave way. Marty fell again to his ass, but the lever now had pulled. He heard a hiss and stared in amazement while white smoke poured from its sides along the edges of the top. It had been sealed for thousands of years, and was finally able to breathe right before his eyes. Gently the top turned on its own. It seemed to move on a pivot. Again, Marty rose to his knees and crawled, in wonder to be the first to look inside this tomb that had been closed for at least five thousand years, if not more.

He placed both hands on the side, pulled himself up, and looked inside. With eyes wide and full of wonderment, he stared into the tomb, blinking several times. "Valafar." Lightning struck outside, shaking the plane again. He stared in awe at the mummified remains. Again, Marty spoke the name: "Valafar . . . Valafar." Three times he spoke the name, and three times lightning struck. Three times was etched on the side of the tomb of the forbidden one to be awaken. Three times his name was spoken to release what lay inside. On the third strike the plane dove. Marty tried to hold tight to the tomb but couldn't and fell to the front of the cargo.

His eyes went wide again, seeing darkness loom around the tomb. The plane was screaming now, diving to the ground. Marty lay there with his back to the wall and both hands held up suddenly in fear. He had no consciousness of the plane suddenly crashing to the ground; all thoughts were on the tomb. Darkness consumed the cabin, engulfing it like black ink. Marty's scream was the last thing the pilots heard before they too were engulfed in flames.

---

## The Daily Star of St. Louis, July 22, 2008

A plane crashed just outside St. Louis late last night during a violent storm. The plane, a Boeing C-17 Globemaster III, was owned by Marty McAndrews, a wealthy anthropologist, who was one of three passengers on board, all of whom did not survive. The FAA is considering this flight an accident because of the storm but will be doing a full investigation. The storm was an odd one, meteorologists are saying, which seemed to have just appeared. "It wasn't predicted," said TV weatherman Steve Sunberry. "The skies were clear as could be, perfect for flying. It must have been an odd collision of the highs and lows." The plane crashed in a remote area of the forest so no other damage was reported. Nothing was found other than scattered debris of the plane.

# DEATH OF A FRIEND

It was another crappy day at work for Michael, who felt the pressure of upper management at the bank. The newspapers were having a ball at his expense. The media was starting a frenzy over the crazy "cat killer" roaming the neighborhoods. Animal rights activists were talking about protesting. He arrived very early at work, hoping to catch up on lost time before everyone else arrived. The bank was dark except for a few lights here and there. Even the janitors were home sleeping in bed. The sun was still waiting to rise, and the moon was low in the sky, giving off the only natural light in the darkness of the halls.

The funeral for Shawn was later in the morning, and Michael was dressed already in a dark suit with his polished black shoes and a white shirt. It was hard to concentrate on his work while he thought about his friend. He thought about a lot of things, including his wife and child. Were they in danger? Things were tough right now, but he needed to focus on what really mattered in his life.

The clock on the wall was ticking its tail back and forth with both eyes shifting from side to side. Michael was shuffling through some papers, but the ticking of the tail was really bothering him and those eyes were so menacing. They may have been moving from left to right with every tick of its tail, but he knew better. Those eyes were looking at him. The sound of the ticking became amplified inside his head. He stood, sighed, and looked around to see no one. Then he walked closer to grab the clock from the wall. Just as he was about to yank it from the wall and smash it, the phone rang. The

215

clock kept ticking, and the eyes moved back and forth with that smile on its face, laughing at Michael.

"I'll be back for you."

It was Franklin bright and early, ready to give him hell. He paused and looked back to the clock on the wall, which only smiled at him while the phone rang again. His picked up the phone and placed it to his ear. *Saved by the bell,* he thought to himself as he stared at the clock.

"Good morning, Franklin."

"Don't lie to me. You know today sucks."

When Franklin said the word "sucks," the "s" dragged on for a really long time. Why was it that everyone sounded like they were hissing all of a sudden? He sounded nothing like the Franklin he had known all these years. Franklin always had something intellectual to say, but "You know today sucks" wasn't going to be one of his most memorable quotes or inspirational speeches.

"What's wrong?"

"Wrongs? Who said anything was wrongs?"

He swore Franklin said "wrong" with an "s," but when he said it a second time Michael was certain something just wasn't right. It sounded like Franklin had a lisp, but he wasn't going to question things right now.

"What can I do for you, sir?"

"You're falling behind, boy. I wanted that report on the riverside branch days ago, and now it's Thursdays."

There it was again—that lisp in his voice, or was it a hiss? The cats were getting to him. Certainly it was not a hiss. Franklin was a respected man, after all.

"Yes, sir, I know. I had a death in the family, but I'll make sure I get that report to you tomorrow."

"Tomorrows?"

"Yes, sir. I have a funeral to go to now, but I came in early to—"

"Son? You're going to get me that report first thing tomorrow or your ass is mines!"

Before Michael could even respond, the phone went dead. This was so unlike Franklin, but Michael figured it was all the pressure he was under from the press. He had never seen him like this and was probably upset because of all the events that were taking place. Michael finished up his work and headed home.

—⋯⋯⋯—

The funeral was today, and the cars were lined up in procession at the cemetery. A black hearse was at the front, and the rest of the cars followed with small orange stickers taped to the front windshields. A very large crowd gathered around the plot in which Shawn was to be buried. It was a dark, cloudy day with scattered showers. Small pools of water collected on the streets and dew on the landscape. The cemetery was an old one with large mature trees shading many of the areas. A wrought iron fence surrounded the perimeter.

The ceremony was very sad, of course. Shawn's pregnant wife was left all alone. It was a closed casket, which really made it worse. Tonia had to be pulled away from the casket when they started to place it in the hearse. She laid her body on top and grabbed it with both arms spread over the casket. No one wanted to be the one to take her from her husband, so they waited an hour before she finally calmed down. Eventually the funeral director and his men were able to coax her from the casket, but they still had to pry her fingers, which were locked onto it.

It started to rain hard at the ceremony, and many pulled out black umbrellas. Some wore raincoats, but Michael just stood under the rain, not even noticing his beautiful new suit was being ruined. Water dripped down his lapel, but he hardly noticed. Mud was sliding down the edges of the freshly dug grave. There was a canopy over the grave, but so many people made it impossible for everyone to get beneath. Michael just stood there outside of the canopy, feeling the rain pelt his face, until Jenny tugged at his hand and pulled him to be at her side under the canopy. It was muddy at the edge of the grave, and Michael's shoes were caked with mud when he stepped closer to the grave.

217

It was hard to see far in the distance because of the heavy rain, but Michael swore he saw a cat sitting next to a tree. It was a black cat sitting beneath the tree, wagging its tail back and forth. He could see its green eyes staring directly at him. This infuriated him because he knew somehow this cat was related. His hand tightened around Jenny's, and she looked up to him and then off to the distance to see what he saw. She saw nothing but the rain pouring down on this day. He looked from side to side, wondering if anyone else had seen the cat, but no one seemed concerned. When he looked back to the tree, the cat was gone. Was it just an illusion? Maybe it was the rain and his mind playing tricks on him.

The priest stood over the grave and blessed Shawn's casket. He spoke about how it was a tragedy to lose such a good, happy person. People started sobbing at the loss of Shawn. Jenny and Tonia became terribly upset, crying for the loss of their brother and husband. Jenny had Michael to grab onto his side, but Tonia had no one to hold onto. Tonia had no one after this day was over, and although she had friends and family to support her, once this day was over she was all alone. Her hand went to her belly, holding it gently, and tears streamed down her cheeks.

Slowly the casket was lowered into the hole, and thunder cracked far in the distance. Rain dripped over the edges of the canopy, and the crowd started to leave. Slowly cars departed, and only the closest of relatives remained. Tonia stood all alone, staring down into the grave.

Jenny took a rose and placed it in JR's hands. He smiled to his mother and kissed her cheek, hugging her tight with the rose held in one hand. He looked down to the grave and smiled, tossing the rose on top of the casket. JR smiled, looked down to the hole, and said, "Shawn."

---

Michael arrived home that night exhausted from another long day. Running into work for half a day before the funeral took its toll on him. Pulling into the garage tonight, he hardly took notice of the

Boss beside the Taurus. He stepped out of the car and moved more like a slug than the happy person he once was. Today was something he would never forget, but the events that led up to it would haunt him forever. He turned to the Boss before entering the house and asked with a blank look on his face, "Why?"

Nothing. No answer. Did he really expect one?

He smiled when he entered the house, giving both Jenny and JR a kiss on the forehead, but even the two of them seemed different than they normally did. He needed something to make him smile; the two of them were the most important people in his life. Never would he allow anything to happen to them. The two of them were the reason he worked so hard and the reason he lived. They were the most important people in his life, and he would do anything to keep them safe and happy. He felt like he was failing both of them as the days passed away. Somehow things needed to change, and he was determined to make it right.

Michael dressed in his casual clothes again and looked about his room. It felt so cold and empty there for some reason. It was dark outside, with the clouds and the storm, so he turned on the lights in the room. He just wanted to relax, so he sat there on the edge of his bed, staring off in a daze. Too much had happened, and he tried to comprehend the most recent events. All he wanted was for his family to be happy. He wanted Jenny and JR to be happy with their house and their lives. He wanted the best for them, so he worked at the bank and tried to provide the best of everything for them. He was happy too, wasn't he? It was what he had wanted. He went to school so he would be successful at what he did. He was no longer a child with dreams but a man who had responsibilities now.

"Dream," said that voice inside his head.

One thing scared him more than anything. What if this thing that was haunting him came back for his wife and child? He knew the answer immediately. He would protect them with his own life, because that's what a father and a husband did. He would kill whatever was threatening them. Then he thought of Shawn, and tears welled up in his eyes because he was too late to save him. He would have protected Shawn had he known, but now he started to doubt himself. How could he? Would he be able to save his wife and kid, or would he be late like he was with Shawn? No matter what happened, he promised himself that he would protect them till his dying breath.

A shadow moved across the window, and Michael knew immediately this wasn't leaves blowing across their two-story bedroom window. He ran to the window and the cat was sitting there, arching its back high and hissing and clawing at the window.

"You son of a bitch! I am going to fucking kill you!"

Jenny was downstairs and heard him screaming at someone. "Michael?" her shaky voice shouted up to him.

"Everything is okay," but it wasn't. Michael felt a mix of fear and anger as he stared out into the dark, rainy day, wondering what another cat was doing at his window. He was safe inside for now, anyways. The doors were locked, and everyone was inside for now. He knew they couldn't stay inside forever, but for now they were safe.

When Michael walked down the stairs he was smiling, but the look quickly changed to shock. There at the bottom of the stairs was Jenny holding JR in her arms. Beside her was a large suitcase, and Michael knew what this meant. She was leaving, but he had no idea where. Things were stressful and there were some problems lately, but surely they could work them out. He looked at Jenny and saw tears in her eyes but also a determination that this was final.

"Jen?"

"I'm leaving, Michael."

"What do you mean you are leaving?"

"I am taking JR with me until you can figure out what you're doing, Michael."

She looked down to the suitcase and JR holding both arms around her neck. JR lifted his head from Jenny's neck and turned to look at Michael with a serious look on his face. "Mom." Never had

JR said "Dad," and now the two of them were leaving him at a time he needed them the most.

"Don't do this, Jen. Things are going to get better."

"No! They are not going to get better until all this nonsense stops, Michael." He reached out to hold her, but she was quick to swat his hands from her side. "You have your job now, Michael, and God knows what's going on with the cats in your head."

"Jenny, you have to believe me. The cats are real."

"Yeah, maybe Krista will believe you. She told me you like to rip off her lingerie." She picked up her suitcase and started walking toward the garage. It was a low blow, but he deserved it.

Out of the corner of his eyes was movement along the window. He turned just in time to catch a black cat hissing at him before it leaped down to the ground. They were everywhere now, and he couldn't leave Jenny and JR all alone and helpless. She had no idea the dangerous situation she was putting herself in. His attention was now on the cat at the window, and he yelled at the top of his lungs like a lunatic.

"That bitch!"

"So it's true," she huffed and kept walking toward the garage door.

"No, it's not true!" The pain in his neck was throbbing like it never had before. He leaned back, arching his body, and reached with one hand. Jenny saw this, shook her head, and then stepped out into the garage to place JR and the bag inside the minivan. He was confused on which to pursue: Jenny or the cat. Looking back to the window, he saw nothing again.

"Where are you going, Jen?"

"I'll be at my parents' until you figure out what you need to do with your life, Michael."

He wanted to pull her back inside. Would she be safe? He was concerned because he knew this cat had plans for him and everything that he loved. He loved Jenny, and he loved JR, so naturally he was scared for their safety. He knew no matter what he told her he would look like a lunatic to her.

"Jenny?"

"What?"

"Just be safe."

She looked at him for a very long time, and he wondered if she was going to tell him she made a mistake. She would tell him she would stay now and everything would be okay. Instead she just grabbed hold of the door and started to pull it shut so she could drive the car far away from her crazy husband. "I will." The door slammed shut, leaving him alone with no one except the pesky little cats.

"Dream," the voice inside his head whispered. "Dream."

# CARACAL

The weekend was finally here, and Michael should have been happy. The weekend would be filled with football games on Saturday and Sunday. The weatherman said he couldn't remember an October with such nice weather but warned winter was around the corner. Friday night was always the time to unravel and forget about things for a couple of days.

Sitting in his house that night, he had never felt so alone. It felt so cold and empty without Jenny and JR to light up his night. He made himself a bowl of cereal for dinner but hardly took one bite; the cereal became soggy. It was strange how the house seemed dead without the two of them there anymore. He sat down on the couch and turned the television on, hoping to pass the time. The phone was next to him, and he instinctively reached out to call his friend Shawn. Nothing was going right, and he broke down and started to cry. Shawn was no longer with him, and now his wife and son were gone as well. His job was being tugged away, and he was certain it was only a matter of time before he lost it. Why was everything being pulled away from him now?

Michael tried to take his mind off things by keeping himself busy. He tried to watch some football games, but every game seemed to be a blowout. He picked up a book but couldn't concentrate enough to actually start it. He opened up the garage, stared at the Boss, and thought he would relax and think about happier times. None of this soothed the pain of losing his wife and kid.

He decided to go for a walk in the neighborhood to get his mind off things. He pulled on a warm leather coat. Even if the weatherman did say it was pleasant, Michael knew the nights were getting colder. He just needed to relax and get his mind off his wife leaving him and taking his son, and his best friend being clawed to death before his very eyes. If only he could forget about reality and the responsibilities he had.

The sun was going down over the horizon, and the sky lit up like it was on fire. All the trees were bare now, with all the leaves bagged and gone. Things seemed pleasant, but they always were before any storm arrived. He walked along the streets of the neighborhood, keeping his hands in his pockets. The wind blew stronger now that the sun was setting in the west. Many of the houses in the neighborhood were decorated for Halloween. One house had a sheet strung up on a tree, looking like a ghost, with a cardboard skeleton sitting on a bale of hay. Fake spiderwebs stretched across some bushes with a giant wire—and fur-covered spider sitting in the center of it. No one was out except Michael, who seemed to be the only one brave enough to enjoy this pleasant evening. He figured they were all inside eating dinner and enjoying time with their families, unlike himself.

Something caught his eye up ahead, but it disappeared behind some bushes. It was dark but there was still a small amount of light to allow him to see it was a brown animal. Michael knew what it was. He looked both ways, as if checking to see if traffic was coming, before crossing to the other side. He was still amazed not one soul was outside on this perfect night in the neighborhood, but then neither would he if his family were still around. He ran toward the bush, but when he looked behind it there was nothing there.

"Rrraaaaaaawr." It was a cat calling. Never would he like that sound again. It was creaky and sounded like an old wooden door that needed oiling. He nearly jumped before turning to the sound, knowing what it was. Sure enough, standing up against the Sullivans' house was the biggest cat he had seen. It was brown with long, pointy black ears and little tufts on top of each ear. One eye was black as coal, but when it turned, its milky eye winked at him. It was the cat that had killed his best friend, Shawn, and it was smiling at him, he was sure. Again it made that sound from hell before arching its body and hissing at him. "Rrraaaaaaaawr."

———

Two cars were sitting in the driveway of the Sullivans' house. The dim light glimmered on the shiny waxed surfaces of the two cars. Everything at the Sullivans' was meticulously kept, including their cars. The landscape was well manicured and the flower beds all cleaned up for the winter.

The cat ran off when it saw Michael coming after it, and leaped up on the cars in the driveway. It didn't seem to be in any kind of hurry, knowing it could run much faster than Michael, and it sat on the top of the BMW in their driveway. Michael was about fifty yards from the cat when it arched its body and stretched out its arms. He could see the giant claws extend from its paws and dig into the roof of the car. Oh, the Sullivans were going to be pissed when they pulled their nice BMW back into the garage. The cat stared at Michael with one dark black eye and the other, of course, was milky white. Slowly it pulled its paws back with a scraping of its claws along the metal of the car. Leaving marks, he was sure, was worse than any key job they would get from some jealous kid. The sound of the claws dragging slowly across that steel, like nails on a chalkboard, screeched in his ears. The cat spat, and leaped to the other car, sliding across the Mercedes with soft paws. The cat raised its claws again to stop itself from sliding and scratched the other car as well.

Michael knew he was at a disadvantage, seeing those claws dig into the metal skin of the cars. If he was going to chase after this monster, then he was going to need a weapon. The cat somehow knew this and lowered its head, baring those grotesquely sharp, yellow teeth that drooled and dripped on the roof of the car. Michael couldn't say for certain, but he would swear that drool was acid. He heard it sizzle on the roof of the car. He recognized the body language of the cat and quickly started looking back and forth along the house for something he could use. It was dark and things didn't always appear as they were. It was fall, though, and he knew there had to be something they used to clean this sterile house. Maybe someone from high above was there to answer Michael's call, because never in a million years would the Sullivans have left a rake on their lawn. Yet there it was, lying near the bushes out by the street. Perhaps they just forgot it, but it was surprising nonetheless. None of that mattered to Michael as he ran toward it and grabbed it with both hands. Whipping it around like some sort of Japanese ninja, he almost looked like he knew what he was doing.

This started a whole series of catastrophic events that neighbors would talk about for years. Michael was so intent and filled with rage that he went straight for the cat that was sitting on top of the car. With the metal rake held high above his head, he slammed it down, trying to hit the cat. But it leaped up and jumped to the ground. A loud bang was heard when the rake smashed right through the metal, poking several holes in the hood of the car.

"I am going to kill you!"

It took three tugs to pull the rake out of the hood of the car, but finally it pried free. The cat ran up the branches of a large bush in front of their house. Michael sliced away the branch on which the cat was sitting, but the cat was quick and leaped up to another branch. Again Michael sliced away. This happened until there were only two branches left on the mangled bush. The cat leaped off the bush and to a tree next to the house. Again Michael sliced away at the trunk of the tree and the branches, but the cat crawled up too high for him to get. Frustrated, he took a swing and the rake went right into the window of their living room. The window shattered with a large crash, and glass scattered everywhere. The cat leaped up into the window and stopped on the ledge, staring at Michael. It hissed before leaping into the house. Michael ran after it with the large rake in his hands. He shoved the rake inside the window and then swung it back and forth to make sure the cat wasn't hiding on the sides to attack. He saw it run off into the house, and Michael leaped up, pulling himself into the house. With the rake in his hands he ran after it, now inside the Sullivans' house. They entered into the dining room, and the cat leaped across the table, scratching up the glossy finish with its claws. It knocked the crystal candlestick holders over, shattering them on the floor. Lucy Sullivan was going to be pissed when she found out about this, but the worst was yet to come.

The cat ran off into the living room, leaving prints on the freshly vacuumed carpet. Michael was right behind the cat, holding up the rake and standing at the border of the carpet to the living room. Like at an invisible fence, he stopped and stared at the cat, which climbed up on top of the nice white sofa with pillows laid all about it. He looked at the vacuum trails on the carpet and the white couch, both now marked with the muddy tracks of the cat. Carefully, Michael took a step into that room and left a muddy print on the carpet. It was the beginning of the end for the Sullivans' perfectly manicured room.

<hr />

The Sullivans were watching a movie that night with the volume of their surround sound turned up very loud. Dan told his wife, Lucy, that *Die Hard* had to be loud to get all the effects. The walls were shaking, and Lucy was concerned the paint was going to start chipping. The room was downstairs in their finished basement so no one would be bothered by the special effects of the movie room. The volume was so loud they couldn't hear anything upstairs either, like a crazy lunatic Japanese ninja. They had watched *Die Hard* eleven times before, and never had it sounded so good. The bad guys shot the window out, and Lucy swore when the glass broke it sounded so much like her own Waterford crystal breaking. There was thumping and running, and the sound went from one side of the room to the other. Dan was so impressed with his seven-speaker surround sound system he kept nudging his wife, Lucy, pointing to the speakers on the walls.

Lucy had spent the day cleaning the house. The living room was dusted and the carpet vacuumed. She would know if anyone dared to walk in the living room. The trails in the carpet were like a sign that told weary wanderers to stay out. The crystal sparkled and the wooden floors were swept. She was proud of this house—if ever someone actually stepped foot inside.

Dan was drinking a beer when the first crash came. He looked up at the ceiling with wide eyes and smiled. He loved the way the movie sounded so real. It was his surround sound system that was doing that. When Bruce Willis shot a bullet to the right, Dan swore he could feel the bullet zip right by on his right. Little did he know that the actual shaking and noises in the house were real.

"That's some surround sound, isn't it, Lucy?"

"What?"

"I said that's some surround sound, isn't it? I feel like I'm in the building!"

This time Dan shouted louder. Lucy smiled back to him but didn't say anything. She looked about the room, glad it was only the movie. Had she known there was a wild cat upstairs and Michael—the crazy lunatic ninja—she would have fainted.

---

Michael was so intent on killing that cat he hardly noticed the noise of the movie playing down in the basement. An earthquake could have shaken the house and Michael would not have paid any attention to it. He was set on killing the cat that had killed his best friend, and now he had it cornered. It arched its back and hissed at him, lifting a paw to show its claws. Michael flicked the rake several times, showing the cat he had his own claws too. The two were staring at each other, anticipating one another's next move.

The fight was on, and the cat leaped at Michael first. It ripped up a couple of the pillows, and feathers flew in the air. Michael was slow. He whipped the rake around and missed the cat, hitting some of Lucy's fine Waterford crystal that she had collected from their recent trip to Ireland. The cat stopped and dug its claws into the rug beneath its feet. It started to pull and rip at the rug with its claws. Michael turned and slammed the rake down hard into the floor.

Swinging the rake back and forth, Michael was determined to end the life of this cat any way he could. He knocked off paintings from the walls, leaving large rake marks in the drywall. He chased after the cat, running through the first-floor rooms. He smashed the living room glass table into smithereens, with glass and wood flying everywhere.

The cat was busy clawing everything it could grab hold of. It leaped onto the sofas, ripping up each one. The cat was hissing, with its body arched and hair standing tall. The cat tried to swipe its claws at Michael in defense.

Michael had the advantage of being bigger than the cat, but the cat was quick and able to run and leap so much faster. He was able to corner it in the dining room, smashing the crystal chandelier hanging from the ceiling. The cat hissed, arching its body, while cornered in the room, and Michael moved in for the kill. He stepped closer with the rake held across his body, ready to slam it hard into the cat if it moved.

The cat ran straight up the wall, digging its claws deep into the drywall. Michael followed it and took a swing, as if with a baseball bat, and hit the cat over the wall into deep left field. The prongs of the rake dug into the side of the cat, nailing it to the wall. It was a quick and effective way of killing the cat, leaving it dangling on the wall with the rake holding it there. Blood dripped down the side of the wall, leaving a pool of blood on the floor. The head dropped back with its mouth wide open, revealing those sharp and gnarly teeth. The milky eye was open, and it stared at Michael.

Five cats were dead, but the hair stood up on Michael's back, telling him there would be more.

# WRAITH

## 10,500 B.C.

The rock band AC/DC once wrote a song called "Hell Ain't a Bad Place to Be," but it was very likely they never saw it. The desert was well over one hundred degrees, and with a clear sky there was nowhere to hide from the scorching sun. The sand baked all day beneath the sun, burning one's bare soles if they were left uncovered. Nothing lived in the desert unless it was of another world.

High above the desert was a man standing over the large formation of slaves below. Overseeing the work to be done, he stood admiring what had been accomplished. The slaves were shackled and chained, only able to work in small areas. There were thousands of men with dirty, sweaty bodies laboring beneath the hot afternoon sun. Some had hammers and chisels in their hands while others carted off crushed rock in small wagons on dirt pathways. Activity was high with a swirl of dust in the air coming from the workers below. The man stepped out from the shaded area that protected him, and he basked in the warmth of the sun. A large black cape covered his entire body, hiding his features from the sun.

Surrounding the area was water everywhere. Palm trees shaded areas along the water's edge like an imaginary oasis. The area seemed desolate with the scorching sun and winds that beat upon every living thing, yet somehow there in the middle of this godforsaken place was paradise all wrapped into one. The water seemed crystal blue, sparkling beneath the sun. Baskets of food were carried on the tops of slaves' heads toward the upper part where the man stood. In front of the man was a very large formation of stone being carved. Workers labored with tools, carving the limestone. Standing over the men were creatures holding whips in their hands. The creatures were larger than the men, standing over them wielding the whips. They cracked the whip when the slaves slacked off in the slightest bit, making a hiss in the air. It was obvious that men—at least in this part of the world—were ruled by this man up above, and the creatures were his minions. Screams of men below followed the crack of the whip and the sound of the leather upon the flesh of men. This place had to be hell.

This was the age of Zep Tepi, which the ancient Egyptians referred to as the golden age. It was the first time of Osiris and was well before the creation of the pyramids. It is believed that the three great pyramids of Egypt were directed toward the three stars of Orion, and the great pyramid itself has its main shaft pointed directly toward the meridian of Orion. Osiris is Orion, and this was the age of Zep Tepi. It is believed that the great pyramids referred to this time in history for a reason. It was the beginning of the age of Leo. The lion constellation rose into the sky due east and in perfect alignment with the sphinx.

Slightly east of the great carving of stone were workers pouring in and out of a tunnel like ants. They carted off crushed rubble in carts while others rolled empty carts in. This area was lush with palm trees, and water flowed down into a pool beneath. It was surrounded by hell, with large, endless dunes of sand.

On either side of the entrance to this tunnel were two great statues of giant lions, protectors of the abyss of darkness. Ancient Egyptians believed that the doorway to the afterlife was protected by two lions called Aker. Legends were told of these two lions guarding an underground duct or stream. Behind the lions was a large mound or pyramid and under it was a large oval chamber that was sealed of air and gas. This chamber was presumed to hold ancient secrets of those who ruled during the time of Zep Tepi. That time was now, and that chamber appeared to be right in front of them. It was called the House of Sokar in Rostau. Sokar was a hawk-headed deity that was identified to Osiris, and Rostau was the name of Giza in ancient times.

The man looked over the work of his slaves, mastering the great stone before him. It was nearly finished, with only minor carvings needed to the face. His face was covered by the dark hood he wore, shading him from the light of the sun. The whole statue measured 240 feet long and was over 40 feet high. The body of the statue was a lion resting beneath the sun. Lying in the sands with paws stretched forward, the sphinx was nearly completed in the likeness of its ruler.

Carts carried loads of emeralds down a path of dust. The man watched with interest while these emeralds were shipped off. Cart after cart heaping with emeralds was hauled away. A guard stood over the men, hauling the emeralds down into the tunnel. The supply seemed endless, and the emeralds glowed a bright green in the light of the sun. No man dared touch any of these, or his hands would be sliced away.

All was going well for the great ruler of Rostau while he watched the great sphinx carved in his likeness. Both hands reached up to pull the hood back, which revealed the resemblance to the great sphinx that lay just beneath. The sun shone down on his face, revealing the features seen on the sphinx below. He was no man of this or any known world, but it would explain the beasts that ruled men of this time. He had a face of a lion and so too did the sphinx below.

---

The man or beast sat on his throne, which was a large chair carved of stone. Small ornamental carvings of all sorts of species of cats covered the stone chair. One large lion was on the center of the back of the chair. The room was large, with stone steps leading up to the perch upon which his chair sat. It overlooked a large room with columns on either side. Surrounding the chair were two very large cats lying to his side. Around them were many smaller cats of different species, either standing or sitting near his side.

Slaves, manacled to each other, were dragged in on a leash by a beast. The beast held a whip in one hand and snapped it over one man's head. The men stumbled into the room and looked up to the man in his chair. Their eyes were wide with fear as they realized where they were. Their faces were covered in silt and sweat. The whites of their eyes gleamed in the soft flickering light of the torches that lit the room.

"These are the men," the one leading them in told the man in the chair.

Slowly the man rose from his chair and stood high above them on his perch. He was three steps above them, yet he seemed taller even if he wasn't on the perch. The men beneath him started to tremble, looking to one another for reassurance but knowing no one could save them now. He stepped down from his perch and stood before the men in shackles, standing taller than any of the slaves. The guard pointed to the floor, and obediently they all bowed down to their knees. There were three men kneeling now, each one shackled to the next. Their legs were shackled, and a chain ran to the next person. They bowed their heads and clenched their hands, shaking before this man.

"These are the men? The ones who stole from me?"

"Yes, master," his minion hissed.

"What made you think you could get away with my emeralds?"

The men were shaking, their heads lowered. These men were nothing but slaves to this man with nothing to look forward to in their lives. The slaves had nothing to live for other than working for this man. Their lives were his to take any time he wished if they displeased him in any way. The emeralds were so hard to resist, and they thought that if only they had one, they would run and find a better place to live. What fools they were for not realizing there was nowhere they could run from this man. They turned and looked to one another, afraid to say anything. One motioned upward with a nod of his chin, and another looked up to him.

"We were mistaken."

"Oh, you were mistaken!"

He hissed now and raised his hands in the air, standing tall above them. Thunder clapped in the near vicinity on this clear day while he held his hands high above him. He leaned back his head and looked up to the heavens. Something was happening, and the men curled up their bodies beneath him, knowing their lives were on the line. He walked around the men, with the bottom of his cloak dragging on the ground.

The man stepped before the slaves and lowered his hands to his sides. Thunder boomed again, and the cloak about his body started to transform. His shape leaned over with his back arching until the man was standing on all fours. His hands and feet transformed into large paws with claws six inches long. Its head changed only slightly into the figure that was shown on the sphinx. Its head turned, and the mouth of the beast opened, showing off the biggest, sharpest teeth these poor men would ever see. It roared, and the sound echoed off the stone walls before the beast ripped into the three shackled men.

The beast transformed again into the man it was before after ripping each one apart. He pulled up the cloak and hood again, covering its body and head. The three men lay there at his feet, dead as dead can be. One man was flinching, but it was only involuntary nerves that caused it. He stepped over the pile of slaves and was escorted by a small parade of cats behind him.

He walked through several chambers until he came to one at the far end of the palace. He waited at the entrance before entering, holding out his arms to either side. A large beast stepped next to either side and helped him take his cloak from his body. They pulled it away, and then he stood there with his dark catlike eyes staring into the darkness of the room before him. He motioned them off and stepped inside while the others waited outside. This was his ceremonial room adorned with emeralds everywhere. It was sacred and for no one other than himself. The door closed and he was all alone with one large chair for him to meditate. He stepped up to the chair and sat, closing those eyes to meditate.

He heard a crack, and his eyes flashed open wide. Something wasn't right, and his claws pulled out from their sheaths digging into the arms of the chair. There was another crack and then a small ray of light filtered into the torchlit room. Rays of light filtered in and covered him. The beast howled, knowing he was betrayed, and reached up helplessly with body arched and spread. Spears burst through the walls, piercing his body in twenty different places. There was nowhere for the beast to run, and the ground started to shake. Spears pierced his body over and over, with blood spilling from his body. It was like the magician's trick of disappearing in a box of swords, only this one had no escape. He howled the fiercest sound anyone had ever heard. Spear after spear came bursting through the walls till the beast dropped to the ground.

The door opened and men burst in, poking and prodding the beast again with spears. They were careful, knowing this beast had powers none of them understood. They lifted him upon a large cloth and then covered his body to lift him out.

This was the start of the revolution of men over beast. It was the beginning of one species and the end of the other. Once the leader was killed, the others fell easily, having no one to follow or lead. It was only a matter of days before the downfall of this beast and its followers. Strong yet outnumbered and with no leadership anymore, the beasts were killed and men took over.

Earthquakes shook around the world as the door to hell was closed. Rumblings followed great shifts in the sands. The entire area was being transformed, and the great sphinx was suddenly surrounded by a river that ripped along the sides. Erosion tore the sides of the sphinx for hundreds of years before finally drying up and being buried by the surrounding desert sands. The doorway to hell was closed but not without one last shout.

They took him to a place down low in a cavern, hoping the beast would never be found. A large tomb made of stone lay beside him, and they laid him on a table. They wrapped him up with cloths and mummified his body. Placing the beast in the tomb, the men took hold of the stone top and placed it over the tomb. On the side of the tomb was the name of the beast that lay inside. It was a warning to any who might uncover his body someday that the beast was to remain undisturbed. Cartloads of emeralds poured into the room, which glowed a dark green until they sealed it off. No one would enter this tomb again until the year 2008, when a man named Marty would discover the tomb of Valafar.

This was the change of power between good and evil and the beginning of human civilization. The sphinx was a reminder to all that Valafar had been their ruler. Once they mummified his remains and hid him in a chamber, they hoped it would never be found again. The men climbed the sphinx and started carving off the face of evil and replacing it with the face of a man.

——————

The dark man had waited a very long time for this coming of age. Soon his time would come again to rule what was once his. The date of his formal change would happen on the night before All Saints' Day, otherwise known as Halloween. It was the festival of the dead, and the doors of hell would be open once again.

He sat on top of an old grave monument in the middle of the village cemetery, looking down at the headstones beneath. This was his town now, and soon his power would extend to the farthest reaches of the world. It was only a matter of time, and there was only one person standing in his way.

Michael Merlino had killed him five times now, but that would be the last. Valafar was getting stronger now, and his henchmen would serve him well. Michael Merlino was the only one who could stop him. With four lives left, there was no way Michael was going to be able to stop Valafar before his time came and the gates of hell opened to the world. The sacrifice would be complete, and Valafar would kill Michael and anything or anyone he loved.

Valafar looked over the village with dark eyes glowing in the night. He would visit his newly appointed servants and give them a test of their abilities. There was work to be done, and his reign of the world would come again. This was one thing Valafar was certain of, and he had only one obstacle left. No mortal was going to defeat him anymore. He would be more careful until his power became overpowering. One by one this world would fall into his hands again, and night would cover the entire earth until there was no light at all.

# LIEUTENANT STEVE

Lieutenant Steve pulled into his driveway, lighting up his small house in the country. It was along a rural road with cornfields surrounding the entire property. An old subservient house to the main farmhouse used way back in the days when the farmer had workers living on the farm to help. Now with all the mechanical advances there was no need for help. Things changed, and the house became an old run-down place. Steve met the farmer on a routine call one day and asked about the house. He offered the farmer to fix it up if he could stay at the place and call it his home. The farmer agreed and told Steve he would be responsible for the utilities and, of course, it was nice to know there was a police officer around. Some of the kids who drove past it said the place was haunted. In the days before Steve was staying there, kids often used it to drink and party. This was one good reason to have someone living there—and who better than a police officer? The house was all alone on the east end of the property. The paint was peeling, and it needed a new roof. The chimney on the side could use some tuck-pointing, and the weeds around the house consumed it.

He stepped out of the squad car, grabbed a couple bags, and carried them to the house. The driveway was crumbled asphalt, and weeds grew all around. The stairs leading up to the house were old, and one step was broken. The stairs creaked with every step he took toward the door. Leaning his shoulder into the door—which was not locked—he pushed it open. Inside, the paint was peeling, and the ceiling sagged with water spots all around.

There was a lot of work to be done with this old house, but that was the least of Steve's concerns right now. He set the bags on a table in the kitchen, which was the only piece of furniture in that room other than two metal chairs. A dim lightbulb dangling from some wires was the only source of light in the room. He walked to an old beat-up refrigerator in the corner of the room and grabbed the metal bar to open it. The light came on inside, showing the refrigerator empty except for a case of beer that was half empty. He grabbed one, twisted the cap off, and flipped it to the floor. He took a long drink, leaning back his head and closing his eyes. There was an old stove next to the refrigerator with a yellow exhaust hood above it that had not been used in over twenty years. The gas line was connected, and this was one of the many things Steve was going to get right on and repair until something else became more important.

The place was in shambles, and he sat down on the chair, still dressed in his police uniform. Sipping his beer, he started to unbutton his shirt and undress. He pulled off his belt and set the gun on the table. He leaned back with his shirt off while he drank the rest of his beer. There was work to be done and he knew it couldn't be put off, but none of it had to do with the house. The old linoleum floor was yellowing, but it had a trail of mud going back and forth from the back door to the table at which he was sitting and then another trail going to the bedroom in back.

He set down the beer and walked back to his room, which had a small bed and a pile of clothes. He stripped to his briefs and grabbed a dirty pair of pants that was covered in mud and pulled them on. Sitting on his bed, which had streaks of dirt on it, he pulled a pair of boots on his feet.

"Back to work."

———

A week earlier, Lieutenant Steve was sitting in his house all alone. It was Friday night and he was hoping to get some work on the house accomplished that weekend. There wasn't much he could do outside this late in the season, so he figured he would work on the inside walls first. This was going to be a long winter project, but he was hopeful to make some progress and lighten up the dreary place. The ceilings would have to wait because of the roof leaks, but that would come in the springtime.

The house never bothered him until recent events gave Steve the creeps. Finding that cat in the bag had given him nightmares lately. He had recurring nightmares of cats surrounding him outside his house. At first he couldn't remember his dreams but knew they were nightmares about cats. He would wake up in a cold sweat and cover himself under the blanket, crying out his wife's name, Cindy. He often slept with his gun beneath his pillow and left the small light on at his bedside. The dreams he was having always had some type of cat in it. These cats would surround him and his house, but that was all he could remember.

The old farmhouse had cats running around. The farmer liked to have cats because they would eat the mice, he told Steve one day. There were many cats roaming the old house and, since his dreams, Steve didn't like it. They were all around the house, lying on the steps and on the roof. The cats were in the weeds and under the house, meowing when he walked around it. He couldn't remember any cats when he first arrived and started to fix up the house. Maybe it was the time of year and they just wanted to be closer to the house for the winter. He thought about that and shook his head, knowing he would have seen at least one or two cats if that was the case. No, these cats didn't appear until he started having these nightmares. It wasn't until he saw that cat in the bag come back to life and he shot him.

Steve went to bed one night and had another nightmare, but this one seemed so real. He could remember everything about it when he awoke and covered himself under the blankets, not coming out until the sun rose and light filtered through his window. Everything about it seemed so real; he could even smell the man. This time there was a man who reeked of death. Steve would never forget it. The dream started off with him sitting at home in the kitchen. He was painting the walls when a light appeared along the edges of the refrigerator. He remembered opening it, but like a fool he was screaming inside at himself not to open it. It was like watching a horror movie when you know something bad is about to happen yet the actor does it anyways. Steve was in a dream and opened the door anyways. There on a shelf was the dead cat he had shot in the bag. Its eye was bulging out, and its brain fell out of its head. It jumped to its feet and looked at Steve, who just stood there watching. The cat started to talk, and Steve acted like this was perfectly normal.

"Hello, Steve."

"You know my name?"

"Of course I do. You shot me after all." The cat winked its good eye at Steve.

"Oh yeah, I'm sorry about that."

"No need to apologize, Steve."

"Well, you scared me."

"Aw. Well, you can do me a favor now and I'll forgive you."

"Really?"

"Really."

"Well, what is it you would like me to do?"

"You seem pretty good with that gun of yours."

"You think so?"

"Oh, I know so." The cat rubbed its bulging eye.

"Well, thank you very much."

"You're welcome. Now, about that favor—"

Everything about the dream seemed so real, up to the point when he told him of the favor. He remembered everything so well and knew the cat told him something, but this part just went blank. Maybe it skipped because that's the way dreams are, but he was certain the cat told him something. He just couldn't remember what it was.

The next part of his dream was so vivid and real he was certain the man who visited him was still standing at the side of his bed when he awoke. Steve was sitting on the edge of the bed when the man in black appeared. The man was dressed in a large black cloak covering his entire body, so Steve could not see any part of him. Even his face was hard to see. He wondered if there was anything beneath the cloak as he stared into the blackness of the hood. There was a flicker of light that must have been his eyes, but that was all. Otherwise the only thing he remembered of the man was that horrible smell on him. It was death, and maybe that was who this man was, he thought to himself. Yet there he was talking to him like he had known this man for years.

"Hello, Steve."

"H—hello," Steve stuttered.

"I am your master. Is that understood?"

"Yes, master."

"You will do as I command. Is that understood?"

"Yes, master."

The man stood there and began tapping his toes, his arms folded across his chest. Staring into those lights inside the hood, Steve felt like he was being hypnotized. The man stood still, and Steve could feel his own heart racing. He was afraid of what he was thinking. Why was he so silent? he wondered to himself, and then the man broke the silence.

"Then why have you not begged me for an order?"

Steve fumbled with his hands, looking back and forth. This caught him by surprise, as he did not having any clue what to say to the man.

"Uh . . . would you like me to do something for you . . . master?"

The man studied him with eyes that glowed inside the hood. He did not beat Steve this time but certainly would in the future.

"Yessssss," he hissed. "There is a man. I want you to find this man for me."

"All right."

The man slapped him hard across the face with the back of his hand. Steve's head jerked to the side, and his mouth gaped open wide. The sting was felt and should have woken Steve if this was real, but it was just a dream, right? He held the side of his face and, like a fool, turned back to look into the hood. It was then he saw something he never wished to see again because it scared the hell out of him. Quickly his eyes dropped to the floor. He was afraid for his life. He trembled but just couldn't help himself and looked up once again.

"All right? How is it you address me?"

"Y—yes, master. Who is it you want me to find?"

"Michael Merlino."

Steve was lying in bed covered in sweat, certain the man in black was standing over him. He pulled the blanket over his head, feeling his feet dangle out the bottom, and curled up in a ball. He waited silently beneath the blankets, afraid of the man in his dream. This wouldn't be the last time he saw this man, and now he knew why he was afraid of cats.

---

Steve was standing over the kitchen table with the heavy bags lying on top of it. He reached inside, pulled out the items, and set them on the table: leather work gloves, a couple extension cords, and a couple large work lights with clamps. He examined each one, took off the tags, and pulled the gloves onto his hands. He placed the extension cords over his shoulder, took the lights in one hand, and walked to the back door.

Pressing open the back door and stepping down the old wooden steps, he looked out into the darkness of the yard. It was hard to see now, so he walked over to the side to find an outlet. He uncoiled the extension cords, connected one end to the outlet, and tossed the rest to the side. He took one of the lights and connected it to the other end of the extension cord, lighting up the backyard. He stood there holding up the light for a moment and looking at the huge mound of dirt that was before him. To the side of the mound was a black hole, and he shone the light on it and lit up about twenty by fifteen feet. He stepped into the hole, which just covered his knees, so it was only about two feet deep at the most. It was a large hole, though, and the pile of dirt stood about four or five feet high in places, with scraps of weeds from the topsoil showing. In the center of the hole was a shovel that he was using to dig the hole. He picked it up and started to dig again, tossing the dirt to the side.

Cats started appearing around the hole, and that was the thing Steve hated the most. Crawling out from every angle the cats surrounded the hole. He could never figure out what it was about the cats, but they seemed to be watching every move he made. Some sat on top of the mounds of dirt, and others paced back and forth. If Steve had been around twelve thousand years ago, he would have understood. The cats were watching him and making sure he worked.

Beyond the dirt and resting on the ground were some old wooden crates. Chained and padlocked, the wood of the crates looked ancient—at least a century old—but somehow still very strong. They were wrapped with large metal bands, like a pirate's treasure chest, and guarded by more cats. Some cats sat on top of the chest while others kept an eye on them from nearby. Whatever was in those crates was precious to Valafar and all the cats roaming about.

# THE WOODS

Michael knew it was only a matter of time before the police would be after him. This was the fifth cat he had killed, and the Sullivans had to be pissed. No one saw him, but it was obvious he was the only one in the entire area who had a problem with cats. The local cat killer was on the loose. Lock your doors and make sure you know where your cat is. Michael Merlino was on the prowl. A house wrecked, with one large dead cat hanging on the living room wall with a metal rake holding it up, would surely bring the police knocking at his door if they weren't there already. Things like his fingerprints or maybe torn clothing from his shirt never crossed his mind. He was a man on the run now, and he was scared of what to do next. Like a little kid who broke a window when playing baseball, he had no idea why he was running just yet. He needed time to think, and a police station was the last place he wanted to be.

He took off and found a hotel just outside of town. Running was probably the worst thing he could have done, but he had a feeling this wasn't over by a long shot. He paid the man at the front desk in cash, so there was no way of knowing where he was. The man behind the desk asked no questions and handed him a key to the room, grumbling the number. It was *that* type of hotel, Michael guessed, which was fine for him tonight. Never had Michael thought he would be staying at the Sleep Inn Crystal Lake, but tonight it would have to do.

He walked up the stairs to find room number 232. The hotel only had twenty-four rooms, with twelve on each floor. The wooden steps leading up to the second level creaked, and the light was dark with one floodlight over the small parking lot. A neon sign on top of the roof was lit up in red and said it was the Sleep Inn. It had a man sleeping in a bed and a stocking cap on. Michael turned the key and entered the room, which smelled musty like a basement. That was odd, of course, since it was on the second floor, but he wasn't going to complain about it tonight. He flipped on the switch and looked at the room, which had one twin bed and bright-yellow shag carpet from the seventies. That explained the musty smell; it was probably the original from when this inn was built.

He settled his things, which weren't much since he just ran off and never went home that night. He had purchased a toothbrush and toothpaste from a local drugstore, but that was all he had other than the clothes he wore. He flipped on the switch to the bathroom, and a yellow light came on above the sink. A dark film coated the sink, and yellow stains marked the linoleum floor. After washing up and brushing his teeth, he settled on the bed to relax. Turning on the television straight from the seventies, which sat on the dresser in front of the bed, he waited for the tube to warm up before the picture appeared. At least they had cable; he was excited about that and turned on the news before going to bed.

"We have a breaking story out in the burbs. Ted? I'll send it over to you."

"Thanks, Kurt. Although police are not saying just yet, it appears there was a struggle here at this home in Crystal Lake."

The camera zoomed in on the Sullivans' house, showing the entire lawn and house ripped up. Michael stared at the TV in disbelief for a moment. He knew this was going to happen, but actually seeing it on the news made it all real. Police cars were parked outside the house with spotlights lighting up the neighborhood. Lucy Sullivan was in the background, strapped into a gurney with an oxygen mask strapped over her face. Her husband, Dan, was walking alongside her when the camera crew approached him, holding the microphone up to his mouth.

"Mr. Sullivan, can you tell us what happened?"

"I'll tell you what happened! A gang decided to wreak havoc in our house. Look what they did to my wife." He pointed down to Lucy, who was lying on the gurney, rolling her eyes behind the oxygen mask.

"What did they do to her? Do you know which gang it was?"

"I am lucky she is alive. I don't know which gang it was, but I keep telling the police we need to do something about gangs in our neighborhoods."

"What did you do?"

"We hid in the basement while they ransacked our beautiful house and left that cat inside our house. Some kind of sick satanic ritual. Oh—oh my *god*!"

"Cat? Mr. Sullivan?"

Dan turned to his wife, who suddenly decided she didn't need to be on the gurney. Lucy was pulling off the oxygen mask and pointing at her once-well-manicured lawn that was now ripped up. She screamed and pointed at the house and the damage she saw. The paramedics held her back down on the gurney, placing the oxygen mask back on.

"Well, that's all we have for now in Crystal Lake. Looks like a new frenzy may have started with cats. This is Ted Flurry, bringing you everything in a hurry. Reporting live from Crystal Lake. Back to you, Kurt."

In the background was Lucy Sullivan, struggling with the paramedics to keep her on the gurney. Dan Sullivan was doing his best to help, but Lucy was frantic over her garden in front, which was completely torn up. Dan Sullivan turned and saw his BMW gouged by the claws and screamed in the background before the news cameras shut off.

Michael turned off the television and lay in bed, staring up to the ceiling. It was bad but he started to laugh. Everything was out of control, and he knew the police would be on it very soon. He wondered if Dan would be his friend once he knew it was him who had caused the mess. He turned off the lights and closed his eyes, because he was going to need the rest.

"Gangs and a cat frenzy. What's next?"

Michael pulled his car into the neighboring subdivision and parked it. He knew the police would be watching, so he was careful and ran through the backyards to his house. The neighborhood next door was large enough with a small park beside it. No one was going to see his car parked there for a while. He was just worried about driving around, but the police department wasn't a large one. Jumping over bushes and hiding behind trees, he made every effort not to be seen. He traveled only a couple blocks and spotted his house.

Sure enough, there was a squad car sitting out in front of the house. It wouldn't be hard to sneak into the house with the police sitting out in front. The officer was in the front seat, leaning back with his hat covering his face. Things were slow, and he wouldn't be expecting Michael to sneak around the back.

There was a spare key hidden beneath a rock that he picked up. Quietly he stepped up to the back door, making sure no one saw him while he opened the door. He turned the key, opened the door, and then quickly stepped in and lowered himself to the floor.

He ran up the stairs, making sure no one could see him from the outside and always careful that the police officer outside couldn't see him. He stepped into his bedroom, grabbed a small suitcase, and placed some clothes and necessities inside. The phone was flashing, which meant there were messages, and he hoped one would be Jenny saying she was coming back.

He picked up the phone and listened to the messages, but none were from Jenny, as he'd hoped. There were a couple messages from neighbors asking if everything was all right, but none from Jenny, which made him worry. He picked up a picture of her and JR together and stared at it awhile before taking it along with him.

Still he needed a place to stay, and hopefully all of this would go away. He flipped through notes and found Krista's number. Jenny would kill him if she knew, but it was someone he could trust and someone who would help him hide for now. He dialed the number and heard it ring a couple times before her voice answered, all chirpy.

"Hello, it's Krista, how can I help with your belle vista?"

"Krista?"

"Yes? This is Krista."

She sounded way too bubbly for Michael, and he was seriously thinking about hanging up. He imagined her in some short little skirt skipping around. He held the phone out and winced before pulling back to his ear.

"It's Michael."

"Michael!"

"Shhhh. Yeah, it's Michael, but you have to be quiet, okay?"

"I knew you would come to your senses, love."

"I didn't come to—" He paused and winced again, knowing he couldn't blow her off completely just now. "Look, I need your help. Can you help me?"

"Absolutely, love!"

"All right, listen. I need a place to hide for a couple days. Any ideas?"

———

Lieutenant Steve stepped out of the police squad car with his gun pulled from its holster. It was dark in the woods, so he pulled out the flashlight on his belt and held it in his other hand. He swiped back branches, which swatted back at his face, and the light flickered all around. Bent over and trying to point his gun and flashlight all at once was hard. The branches kept swatting his face and his neck; trying to run through this jungle wasn't easy.

"Steve!"

A familiar voice was calling his name, but he had no idea who the woman was. She sounded pretty, so he kept running through the trees and hoping she was as pretty as her voice sounded. His face was getting all scratched up, but none of that mattered because he was going to rescue someone. Damn if he wasn't going to get the best reward when he saved this pretty woman. He stopped and leaned over, tried to catch his breath, and pointed the flashlight into the thick jungle of branches.

"Steve! Please help me!"

There it was again. He started to run again, shoving branches to the side and breathing heavily. It was a forest thick with pine trees, and the smell of the needles was so vivid in his mind. He started to climb a hill, pulling at the dirt with his fingers, to reach the top. He looked down and saw his clothes were ripped from all the scrapes of the trees. He stopped along the way to listen for that voice but also to regain his breath. He was panting now, but something inside told him to keep going. A bolt of energy burst through his body, and he somehow ran like never before.

The sky was dark, and a soft wind started to blow, bending the pine trees to one side. Lightning flashed in the sky and a soft rumble followed. The weatherman didn't say anything about a storm. Steve couldn't remember a forest in the near vicinity of his house which sat in the middle of a cornfield for miles around. He kept running to the voice and trying to navigate his way, wondering what a forest and hills were doing in his yard, which was flat and covered with corn.

"Help me! Please help me!"

He was getting closer to the screams when lightning struck again, lighting up the entire sky a brilliant white. He could see through the pine trees. Once the lightning was gone, his eyes had to adjust again to the blackness of the night. He fumbled with his flashlight. He was holding his gun in the other hand, pointing it left and right, certain something was going to jump out because he had seen this dream before. This was just a dream, wasn't it? Everything seemed so real, but he had been here before, chasing this girl who was running in the forest. He sniffed the air of pine trees and smelled something different. It was the perfume of the woman, and he ran toward it.

"Steve? Help me!"

He looked up on top of the hill and saw a small cabin with an image running around it. She was so close now, and his heart was pounding. Something felt funny inside, and he ran up the hill again when he sensed something else. Someone else was there, and he had no idea who or what, but it was dangerous. His hand tightened on the gun, and he pointed it toward the cabin. There was only one image that disappeared in the cabin.

"Rrrrrrrrrrrrrr!"

"What the hell was that?"

"Jesus, Steve! Help me!" the woman shouted.

Steve froze and looked up the hill, having no idea what made that sound, but it frightened him. The gun was shaking in his hand, but he knew there was a woman in trouble and he was a police officer. It was his duty to save her, wasn't it? Slowly he crawled closer, inching up the hill.

"Who . . . who's there?" the woman asked.

Things went silent and he moved closer to the house. He could see a light turned on, and he inched his way closer. That voice was so recognizable, but he couldn't place it yet. The storm was getting closer, with lightning striking hard and the sound of thunder filling the air. Finally approaching the door of the cabin, he pounded on the old wooden door.

"Hello? What's going on?"

"You stay away from me, you son of a bitch!"

"Cindy? It's me, Steve."

"Come any closer and I'll kill you!"

This was really confusing him, and he walked around the side of the cabin. A small window was there, and he tapped his gun on the side. Something was really weird when he looked at the gun, because it was replaced by a claw.

"Damn you! Leave me alone!"

He tried to tell her it was only Steve, but a different sound came out of his mouth. At first he looked around, pointing his gun into the forest. The gun wasn't there anymore and he shouted again, but the only sound coming from his mouth was a growl like nothing he had heard before.

"Rrrrrrrrrrrrrr!"

His hand—or claw, as it was—smashed into the window and reached all around. Something inside smashed it up and he screamed, pulling it back. Blood was dripping and he screamed—or growled—again, staring at his hand. He looked at his hands and wanted to scream again. Held before him was the biggest claw he had ever seen, and it was on his very own hand.

"I'll whack you again, you son of a bitch!"

Steve looked up to the window, hearing that voice inside, but remained silent for a while. Everything was really confusing him, and he wondered if maybe it was the mushrooms he was growing. This was just a dream, he kept telling himself when he scratched his face with the claws, drawing blood. If it was a dream then all of this was way too real for him.

"You son of a bitch! You come in here. I swear to God I'm gonna kick your fucking ass!"

Steve couldn't take it anymore and leaped up into the window. The woman was very pretty, sitting in the corner up against the wall with a shovel in her hand. He tried to speak, but another growl came out of his mouth instead. Then his clawed hands came down upon her, ripping her body to shreds.

"Where's Michael! Tell me where he is!"

The woman couldn't answer, but Steve kept slicing her body up with his claws. Now he bit into her neck and realized he had the biggest teeth that would make Little Red Riding Hood scream and run into the arms of the big bad wolf if she could. Things started to spin in his head. He tasted the blood that spurted out of the girl's jugular and dripped down his throat. Looking up with a blood-covered face, he growled.

"Where's Michael!"

---

Steve was lying in bed covered in sweat and mumbling in his sleep—something about finding Michael. He kept turning his head from side to side. His hands were grabbing at the air above him like he was clawing at something that wasn't there. His head was snapping back and forth, and his teeth were gnashing.

"Wake up!"

Franklin was standing over him, slapping his face back and forth. He was dressed in a white shirt and a blue bow tie and looked like he was ready for work. It took a moment or two for Steve to wake while Franklin kept slapping his face and shouting for him to wake up. He finally woke up, and in a daze Steve stared at Franklin and looked around confused. Sheets covered his body, thankfully, because all he was wearing were some briefs.

"Wake up, you imbecile. I know where he is."

"You do?" He blinked and rubbed his eyes. "And why does everyone keep slapping me?"

"Yes, I do." Franklin told him and then slapped him again. "Because you're an imbecile. Now get dressed."

"Who's Cindy?"

"Your wife."

"My wife?"

"Yeah, you dipshit. You killed her on your camping trip near St. Louis. Now clean off that dirt and blood on your hands and face."

Steve held his hands up to his face and saw they were covered in dirt and blood. Franklin looked at him, disgusted, and wiped the blood from his own hands now after slapping him. The sheets were covered with dirt and blood as well. His face had a claw mark running down the side of his cheek. A strange taste filled his mouth, and his tongue rolled around, tasting the fresh blood on his lips.

"I feel sick."

"I feel sick looking at your sorry ass."

"Fuck you."

Franklin slapped him hard across the face. "Don't talk back to me." He looked around the room, which was a mess. Mud covered the floors of the dingy room. "You had better get moving on that hole in the backyard."

"Well, I could use some help."

"I don't dig holes."

"Why not?"

"Because I'm smarter than you, dick wad."

"Oh."

# RENDEZVOUS

Krista walked in the door, tired from her day of searching for the perfect house for the Wallaces. She woke up early in the morning, having mapped out some areas in the village in the hope of finding a needle in the haystack that wasn't listed on the agent's multiple listings. A call came in on her cell phone, and the person on the other end asked if she would come see their home to list. The house was along the lake, and Krista knew immediately this was the one that would sell. The house had everything the Wallaces requested, and this time she was not going to play along with Mary Wallace. This time she had a plan to get Mary to leap at the house whether she wanted it or not.

The plan was simple but would require some assistance. That was where Michael came into the picture. It was the takeaway theory used by many people—take something away from a person and she wants it even more. Krista had a plan to show this house, which she felt was the perfect house for the Wallaces. But she knew their tendency was to knock it and Krista would have to search for another. But what if something different happened with this house? What if this house had another buyer who was anxious to purchase it before anyone else? Krista's mind was running with all sorts of ideas as she figured out the perfect way to do this. What if she showed the house to the Wallaces, who would tell Krista something was wrong with it, and then Krista would tell them it wasn't available anyways? She would hold that piece of cheese right in front of their face and then take it away. Krista was certain the Wallaces would realize someone else wanted the house and that would cause them to come running back to buy it.

She was wearing a white button-up collared shirt with a short black knitted skirt that fell just above her knees. She wore a small white belt around her slim waist and black high-heeled shoes. Her hair was pulled up with a large white bow holding it in place. The slight smell of perfume would have seduced the strongest of men. She was determined that today she was not going to let him go.

The house was one of the prettiest in the area, sitting on the lake with its own private dock. Built in the early twenties during Prohibition, it had many secrets inside. It was a large framed white house with a large refurbished kitchen that Mary Wallace was looking for. The house was old, and Krista knew that would be a problem, but everything inside was remodeled. The only thing that wasn't new about the house was the foundation on which it stood. Inside were marble floors and wooden staircases refurbished from a time gone by. Some of the items inside—like the stairs and chandeliers—could never be duplicated. This was definitely the house for the Wallaces; they just had to be pushed a little.

Krista pulled up the winding driveway that was gated at the front. Large hundred-year-old oak trees lined the driveway on either side. The view of the lake was marvelous from the driveway. The house was situated perfectly high on the hill with the lake as a backdrop.

Inside the house Krista walked around, planning her walk-through with the Wallaces. She stepped in the foyer, which had a gorgeous crystal chandelier hanging from its two-story ceiling. She walked through the living room, opening up the secret wooden door that had been used to hide the liquor during Prohibition days. The house was in perfect condition, and she made sure every detail was in place. Every room had magnificent views of the lake, with large clear windows making this house one in a million. She knew the Wallaces would have to take it.

Once upstairs in the bedroom, her eyes lit up as she stared at the antique bed sitting in the center, with large posts and a canopy overhead. She walked around the bed, making sure everything was perfect. She had Michael this time, she was certain, because he needed a place to stay. She figured that was just an excuse to get back with her—that was how her mind worked. He wasn't going anywhere this time.

The house was vacated after the death of the woman who owned the home. It had been in the family for generations, but times were difficult and the remaining members decided now was the time to let go of the house. There was a long history in the house, but now it was time to move on and leave it to someone new. Little did anyone know that history was about to happen once again in this beautiful old home.

⁓⁓•◦❉◦•⁓⁓

Michael was constantly looking in his rearview mirror for any signs of someone following him. He was constantly scanning the horizon for police cars to avoid. He was paranoid, and for good reason, since the news broke out on the radio about a crazed cat killer stalking the area—mainly a guy named Michael Merlino. This whole thing was out of control, but he desperately needed another day or two to work things out. The problem was he had no idea what exactly needed to be worked out.

He was to meet Krista at the house on the lake she was about to list. It was the perfect place to hide from the public, from the explanation she had given him of the house. It was secluded from any neighbors, which sounded good.

His mind was on Jenny and JR when he pulled up the driveway and saw the gate before him. Not hearing a word from them was really bothering him. The back of his neck never hurt so bad as it did at this very moment; the scar seemed to be more infected than it had before. He looked up to the house, wondering what Krista was up to, and the pain in his neck became unbearable.

The window rolled down, and he reached his hand out to punch the button on the gate. He waited a moment before hearing Krista's voice crackle over the small built-in speaker. He winced hearing her voice because the pain in his neck burned even more.

"Hello?"

"It's me. Open the gate."

"Me who?"

"Krista, don't play any games. I'm not in the mood."

"Aw, you're no fun!"

She buzzed the gate and the phone went dead. Slowly the large black wrought iron gates opened wide to either side. He pulled his car in and saw the house at the end of the winding drive. It was a very pleasant setting for a house, and he hoped to be able to relax there. The car pulled up to the circular drive, which had a nice red-brick planter in the center full of plants and beautiful mums. The house was prettier than he'd imagined, with a large porte cochere over the front entrance. He pulled his car under it and sat for a moment, looking around the yard. This was a dream house, and he wished things were better. Someday it would be nice to have him and Jenny live in a place like this, raising their boy, JR.

From inside the house Krista watched his car pull up the driveway. She opened the door and posed at the top of the stairs like some model in a magazine. She stood with one hand resting on the side of the door, one leg bent, and her head tilted back. She must have practiced this pose before. Michael would have to admit she was beautiful, but he was tired of the drama that came along with her. It was all about her, and nothing else mattered. Anyone else was just along for the ride.

Michael stepped out of the car and saw her standing at the door. His mind was on other things, and he turned, not paying any attention to the sultry way she looked. Where was Jenny, and why hadn't she called? He needed to relax and was worried Krista wasn't going to allow it.

"That's all you have?" she asked, squishing her lips, disappointed he did not have a large suitcase for a long-term overnight.

"Yep."

"Well, you're not going to need much anyways."

She took his hand and elegantly led him inside the house like some fancy hostess showing off her house. One hand tugged his hand while the other was hoisted above her head, showing off the foyer and the chandelier above.

"This here is the main entrance of the house."

"Krista? I'm not buying the house. Get over it."

"Aw, you're no fun!"

She pouted, pressing out her lower lip, and then tugged close to him, kissed his lips, and dragged a hand across his head. She worked fast, and Michael knew she always got what she wanted. He looked at her and shook his head, upset at the way she was handling herself.

"You know I am only here to rest and get a little breather, right?"

"I know. Now come, let's take a look around and get you comfy."

Michael wanted to strangle her because he knew Krista well. Her meaning of the word "comfy" meant sleeping naked in a bed. Reaching around to the back of his neck, he wondered why it hurt so badly.

She led the way through the house, showing off the different rooms. She pranced around the house like she was the belle of Crystal Lake. They walked into the living room and looked out at the view of the lake. Krista stood in the middle of the room, twirling around in circles and playing with her skirt. Krista was always flirting, and there was never a moment when she wasn't selling herself.

Like déjà vu, she brought him to the master bedroom and slowly opened the double doors. It was a gorgeous bedroom with a large sleigh bed in the middle. It had a high coffered ceiling, a sitting room to the side with a fire going in the fireplace, and a couch in front of it. Petals of red roses were spread over the bed, and candles were lit everywhere. Her intentions were obvious, and Michael shook his head.

"Krista?"

She didn't say a word but just pressed him to the bed. With both hands on his chest, she took control and leaned over him. She slowly batted her long lashes and smiled up at him. She walked two fingers up his chest to the tip of his chin. Her body arched above him, pressing her breasts hard against him, and her long silken hair dropped down across her shoulders and rested on his chest.

"Krista? I'm serious."

Still she didn't say anything and tried to unbutton his shirt. She kissed his chest, nibbled at the buttons, and tickled his skin with her hair, which dragged across his chest. A good salesperson never stops even when the person tells them no. When Michael told her "no," the word just slipped through her ears and she continued smiling up to him and kissing his chest.

Michael lay there on the bed and realized he had made a mistake coming there. He was naive and was trusting of most people, but she wasn't going to stop until things went her way. His neck was aching, but now it was his head that was throbbing. He sat up and shoved her off himself. "Ugh. Krista? Do you have any aspirin?"

"I have something better."

"Krista!"

"Okay, okay." She rolled her eyes, turned with a huff, and headed to the master bath. "You're really not being fun, Michael." Acting angry and being angry were two different things with Krista. She walked to the bath, shaking her ass back and forth as wide and slowly as she possibly could.

Now Michael rolled his eyes and lay back on the bed. This was not his idea of relaxation and getting away from the world. His mind was on Jenny now, and he wondered where she was. He would have given anything to talk with her again. He couldn't help but watch Krista walk to the bath and feel an urge to toss his cookies. This wasn't right and he knew it, so he would end it immediately. Somehow he needed to find Jenny and get her back as soon as he could.

---

Outside prowling the grounds was a large four-legged creature with its tail curling back and forth. Large brown paws stepped lightly in the soft grass, making absolutely no sound at all. Its body moved all in one fluid motion, stopping at the slightest sounds in the yard.

It leaped over small obstacles with no effort at all. Following this animal were twenty smaller cats. Like a herd following the shepherd, they stayed close to the larger beast. They stayed together like a school of fish moving in synchronicity with one another.

The house was lit up and reflected in the lake, and the large creature stopped, taking in the scene. Standing in the backyard of the house under the floodlights that lit up the yard, the creature could be recognized as a large mountain lion. It froze and stared at the house, studying it for any movement. Up above the cat saw what it needed and turned back to the herd of cats behind him. The small army of cats surrounded the mountain lion, waiting for their orders, and the mountain lion made a low growl. Quickly and quietly the herd of cats ran to the house with their orders.

——————

Ten minutes with Krista, and his head was already pounding. Michael rolled his eyes shut, wondering if it was the right choice to come there. He could hear Krista ransacking the drawers, searching for any type of pill. The sound of medicine cabinets opening and the frustration in Krista's voice made him laugh. Boxes and bottles were being tossed, and he imagined she probably didn't care if she found aspirin or vitamin C as long as he started paying attention to her. He opened his eyes for a moment and saw her standing in the bathroom, surrounded by bottles on the floor. She was examining one bottle and seemed pretty happy with her discovery. *Please let this nightmare be over,* he thought to himself.

Krista turned toward the bedroom with a look of disappointment on her face. She sighed, looked at Michael lying on the bed, and slumped over. She seemed to be planning, and a lightbulb went off in her head. She straightened herself up once again. She stripped off her clothes, revealing the black lingerie. Jenny would have recognized the chemise she had purchased from the Wagon.

Stepping out of the bathroom and posing for him like she did before, she stood at the doorway with one leg bent and an arm over her head with her hand placed on the doorframe. She leaned back her head and let that long, dark, curly hair fall behind her. The flicker of the firelight highlighted the soft, sensual curves of her body. She waited for him to notice her, because who wouldn't notice this beautiful woman in lingerie standing at the door? She looked over to the bed. He was just lying there with his eyes closed, resting on the bed. A little prompting was needed, so she said in a dramatic voice, "Your aspirin."

Michael opened his eyes slowly, hearing her voice, but his mind was on something else. He did not look at her but instead just motioned with his hand for her to come closer. She looked at him and rolled her eyes, letting out a sigh and hoping he would hear it. She walked over to him with shoulders slumped, the glass of water in one hand and the Midol PM in the other.

"Your aspirin." This time she moaned with a very soft, soothing voice, hoping to grab his attention.

She definitely grabbed his attention, but it wasn't the voice that jerked his head. Michael turned, finally seeing her dressed in the lingerie. His eyes went wide. It wasn't excitement that he felt inside but shock instead. There was no doubt she looked fabulous, but he did not want her. He was married to the woman he loved and knew this had to end. She was dressed in a black chemise that ended just below her slim belly, with the tiniest matching panties. Spaghetti straps held it up on her shoulders, and her cleavage was gushing out. Slipping in beside him in the bed, she reached up with one hand and pulled the bow from her hair. Long, dark, curly hair fell across her shoulders, and she shook her head back and forth, letting the scent of her hair intoxicate him. There was an overwhelming scent of her perfume that suddenly filled the air. He grabbed the glass of water from her hand and swallowed the three Midol PM she gave him.

"I'm going to need something stronger," he said, shook his head, and covered his face with one hand.

Krista did not waste any time and started to undress him. Both hands went to his shirt and pulled it from his body while she kissed his lips. Most men would have succumbed to the intoxicating lure of this siren. Her hands went to his chest, sliding them up and down. She wrapped her body tight around his, pressing her breasts against his chest.

"Krista?"

"Yes, Michael?"

She kissed his chest with wet lips and slid her body down his chest. Soft brown eyes looked up at him with a smile to seal it all. Hands like velvet tugged his body to hers, and she lowered her eyes to his chest.

"This isn't going to work." He rolled to the side of the bed.

"What do you mean it's not going to work?" Krista stared in disbelief.

"It's not going to work. You know it's not going to work."

"What's not going to work? Michael, you're not making any sense."

"Stop it! I don't love you. I am a married man, and I love my wife."

"You don't love her, Michael. You love me."

The pain in his neck started to burn again, but this time he didn't care. The scar on his back was grotesque and he realized what a pain in the neck Krista was becoming. He looked up at Krista, who was bringing on the tears, but he wasn't falling for any of her games.

"It was a mistake that I came here."

"You son of a bitch! You're mine!"

"No. I'm hers."

"Are you breaking up with me?"

"We were never together."

He stood up and walked to the master bath, closing the door behind him. Krista sat in the bed, pulled the sheets up against her body, and stared at him in a state of shock. Inside he locked the door, looked around, saw the mess she had made looking for his aspirin, and sat on the toilet. He needed time to think, and Krista wasn't helping.

A noise came from the French door leading out to the balcony. The drapes were closed, so Krista got out of bed and walked over to see what it was as she stood barefoot in her lingerie. It was dark, and she saw nothing at first. Then the noise came again. Down by her feet she saw the cutest little cat and smiled. She unlocked the door, opened it, and then leaned down and reached out to the kitten with one hand. "Aw, what's a cute little kitty cat like you doing in a place like this?"

The cat stepped inside and walked around Krista, rubbing its body against her bare legs. She sniffed, rubbed a hand across her nose, and then reached out to pet the cat, which nuzzled against her hand. Another cat appeared on the porch and meowed, which was odd, but she smiled and reached out to pet that one as well. She leaned down with her ass pointed up, barely covered by the smallest of panties. She picked up the kitten and held it in her arms. Another cat leaped over the railing of the balcony, and then one leaped down from the roof and stood on the railing. In all there were four cats now. "Hey, Michael? Your friends stopped by!"

―――――――――――

Michael heard Krista, but it was all gibberish to him now. The reason he had come here was to have some quiet time to think, and now he had this nymphomaniac who could do nothing but think about sex. Did she say his friends were here? Whatever it was, he just sat there on the toilet ignoring her.

More cats started to jump up on the balcony from every different angle. Some came from up on the roof, and others crawled from beneath the porch. Krista was suddenly surrounded by fifteen cats in all. They walked around her legs with their tails in the air. The sound of purring filled the air, which made Krista a little uncomfortable now. "Michael? I think you should come see this."

"What is it, Krista?"

"Cats."

One word from hell was all he needed to hear. Sitting on the toilet, he stared at the shower in front of him, certain she had something else. Resting his head between his hands, he began to massage his temples. He opened his eyes and saw a bottle of the Midol PM sitting on the counter. She did say "cats," didn't she? He promised himself he wasn't going to fall for her seductress games. "Hey, Krista? What kind of aspirin did you give me?"

"What difference does it make? I really think you should come out here, Michael." Things moved quickly after that, and Krista had no time to think. One of the cats leaped on her back and dug its claws into her neck. The small kitten that was purring in her arms turned and hissed at her. The other cats walking around her feet suddenly lurched up with their claws and teeth, grabbing and biting her.

"Michael!"

———

While Michael was trying to think, locked away in the bathroom, the larger cat was prowling beneath, waiting for the signal. When Krista screamed, the mountain lion seemed to know its time had come. It leaped up on the balcony and paced back and forth, watching the smaller cats do their job to distract her for the moment. Krista was in shock, hardly noticing the mountain lion that was looking at her like its next meal. She was pulling cats off her body, turning and twisting, when she stopped and heard the mountain lion roar. Everything seemed to stop—including her heart—and she shrieked louder than before.

"Michael! Oh God, Michael! Help me!"

The mountain lion took its time and played with its new toy. It slashed one large paw across her body, tearing the lingerie. She was bleeding from small bites and scratches from the smaller cats, but when the larger cat slashed at her she dropped her mouth in horror. Cats are known for playing with their food, and this cat was no different. The reason cats play with their food is to weaken their prey before the kill. The slash across her chest was a good start to weaken her, and the smaller cats did the rest. This wasn't in her plans for the evening, and the lingerie was ruined, but worse was her beautiful body had a gash across her chest. She grabbed herself and felt the warm rush of blood on her hands, which she lifted to her eyes. Then she stared at the mountain lion, which was glaring at her with one grotesque milky eye.

———

Michael snapped out of his trance when Krista's piercing scream for help sent shivers down his spine. Something was wrong, and he leaped up to open the door. He unlocked it, pulled it open, and stared in disbelief at the scene unfolding before him. It was so surreal to see the cats attacking her. He started thinking back to what had led up to this. He remembered Krista yelling about his friends coming and something about cats. He was too busy to listen to her and was too pissed at her to believe her. He thought it was a ploy to entice him out of the bathroom. The mountain lion, with its milky white eye staring at him, slapped him out of his slumber.

"Krista!"

She turned to him slowly, with cuts and bite marks all over her body. That beautiful body in lingerie was cut and bleeding, and tears fell down her face. She looked at him, knowing he was too late. The large cat paced back and forth along the railing. Cats crawled all over her body, digging their claws into her skin.

"I'm sorry, Michael. I love you."

The black eye of the mountain lion stared at Michael with that endless dark hole leading to no place other than hell. He swatted Krista across her back, and her body fell helplessly to the floor. Blood spilled from her body, and her hands clenched tight to the floor as she tried to pull herself from this hell. Michael ran out from the bathroom toward the sitting room and the fireplace. The cat was smiling, and Krista figured Michael was giving up and running for his life, but what the two of them did not see were the fire tools next to the fireplace. He grabbed a fire poker and turned toward the beast.

"You son of a bitch. I'm gonna send you back to hell!"

The mountain lion watched him, with one foot reaching out and clawing Krista. He put his weight on her back while she kept clawing to pull her body away from him. The cat grinned at him, knowing he was too late, and pulled back its gums, which showed the jagged yellow teeth. Drool dripped down from the mountain lion's chin to its latest victim, whose life was about to end.

"Michael! Save me! Please save me."

He ran toward the cat with the poker raised in his hand, but it was too late and the two of them knew it. The cat opened its mouth and showed off its large jagged, yellow teeth, dripping with saliva. It slowly leaned down and sunk its teeth into Krista's neck, biting her jugular vein. Blood spilled down her neck and out from her mouth onto the floor. Her life ended as she lay lifeless on the ground.

"No!"

The poker rammed into the side of the cat, piercing its ribs with a crack. The cat shrieked unbelievingly at what just happened. The hooked end of the poker pulled from the cat, ripping out a portion of its flesh with a sickening crunching sound.

"Rrrrrrrrrrrrrrr!"

The poker rammed inside his body, breaking ribs and piercing several vital parts. The cat tried to swat at Michael, but the poker swatted at his paw, knocking it to the side. Then the hard steel of the poker slammed into its skull forty-seven times.

---

A police car sat just outside the gates, waiting in the dark. Inside, with the window pulled down, was Lieutenant Steve peering up with binoculars pointed at the house. It was quiet that night as he sat in the dark. Nothing ever happened in this part of the neighborhood. The binoculars were pointed at the front of the house, but Steve knew if he was going to catch Michael he would have to make his way to the back.

A large wrought iron gate surrounded the property, which Steve would have to climb. He stepped out of the car and walked up to the tall gate, calculating how to climb over it. He grabbed it with both hands and pulled his body up and over the wrought iron gate with spikes on the top. He was able to pull his body on top, but once he tried to pull himself over, one of the sharp spikes ripped into his leg. He screamed and fell to the other side, landing with a thump.

"Ow, that hurt like a son of a bitch!"

Without a search warrant he would need a good reason to climb the gate. His leg was torn very badly, bleeding through his pants. The house was still a good distance away, but he figured he could make it if time was on his side. Then the sound of screaming and that horrifying sound of a beast sent shivers down his spine. A thought came to him, and he grabbed the microphone attached to his shirt.

"This is Lieutenant Steve. Officer down. I repeat. Officer down."

# JAIL CELL

Police stormed the house after getting the call from Lieutenant Steve that an officer was down. Every available man from Crystal Lake and neighboring communities raced to the scene at 25 Lakewood Drive in Crystal Lake. In all there were eleven different authorities at the scene, including the state and county police and the local SWAT team. The house was lit up like a Hollywood set straight from the movies, with large spotlights hitting the house from every angle. The SWAT team rappelled into the house from the roof, breaking through the windows. The outside of the house was surrounded by the state and local police, standing ready behind squad cars, with rifles and guns resting on the roofs and hoods of the cars for balance. Snipers waited patiently behind trees, wearing camouflage to make it hard to see them. A small army of men with guns raised or pointing toward the house stormed the front door, breaking it down with the battering ram they carried.

Inside was Michael Merlino standing over Krista with the fire poker in his hand. The mountain lion was lying dead to the side. Krista lay in a pool of blood, barely clothed, with her head turned to one side. Dead eyes stared blankly to the side. Michael heard the police enter and just dropped the poker to the ground. He was in shock as he stood over Krista, trying to comprehend she was really dead. He started to cry and felt tears run down his face. She was not his lover or his wife, but she was a friend just the same. He felt responsible for her death, just like he did with Shawn's. He clenched his eyes tight and wished it all away. His legs started to shake before finally giving out and dropping to his knees.

The police heard one of their own was down, and everyone on the police force wanted a part of the action. When they saw Michael standing there with the poker in his hand, fingers became itchy on the triggers touching them. Had Michael not dropped the poker or dropped to his knees, the trigger-happy police might have filled his body with holes. Instead they raced to him and handcuffed his wrists behind his back. They roughly pulled him to his feet and dragged him down to the squad car waiting below to take him into the station.

News cameras arrived on the scene, trying to capture all the live action for their viewers. Michael being led into the squad car was all the action they could get. It took hours before the coroner and all the forensic crews were able to get all the information they needed. The news crews had a deadline to hit the evening news so ran with the video of Michael being dragged to a police car with his hands cuffed behind him and placed inside. News vans pulled up and surrounded the police cars, which surrounded the house. Ambulances and fire trucks were just pulling in after the news vans arrived.

"Looks like another murder for the Crystal Lake cat killer," an overjoyed Ted Flurry announced to the viewers. "Whether the police be able to keep this killer behind bars after tonight is yet to be seen, but it's been a bloodbath here tonight. Reporting to you live first on the scene. This is Ted Flurry bringing you everything in a hurry. Back to you, Kurt."

Emergency crews poured out from their vehicles, opening up the compartments on the sides and doors on the back. A couple men lowered a gurney to the ground and started to wheel it toward the house.

---

Steve limped into the station with his leg all bandaged up. He wore his newly acquired sunglasses that covered his eyes because the moon was very bright. Becky Tomlinson watched him walk in the station that night. She laughed to herself, but the moment their eyes caught one another she was quick to lower them to the operator board before her. Whatever happened to Steve since his awkward days, she had no clue, but there was definitely something different and her instincts told her to stay away.

"Where is he?" Steve barked at Becky.

"Where's who?"

"You know who, damn it! The cat killer. The asshole I am going to personally crucify once I get my hands on him."

"You mean that boy? They brought him into interrogation."

Steve wasted no time with Becky, storming off to the interrogation room. She let out a sigh of relief, happy to see him gone.

Inside the interrogation room was Michael sitting at the table with one officer standing guard at the door. A mirror hung on one wall and reflected the side of his face. The only thing in the white room was a long table and five chairs spread out along the table. The officer was silent, standing to the side, and kept his eyes on Michael the entire time. He seemed nervous having such an important job of watching over a man suspected of murder. Michael was nodding off; the Midol PM pills he'd swallowed were taking effect.

Steve opened the door and stared at Michael from behind his dark shades. The door closed behind him, and the guard turned to Steve.

"I need some time alone with this one."

"I am under strict orders to remain here until the chief gets back."

"The chief just told me to take over for you."

"You sure, Steve? Because if he finds out I left my post I am in deep shit."

"Trust me."

Steve gave the guard a genuine smile from ear to ear with his sunglasses still on. If looks could kill, then Steve was the poster child, hiding the truth behind those shades. The guard looked again at Steve before opening the door. He stopped and turned to Michael, who never moved the entire time. Everything seemed okay. What harm could happen with Michael locked up inside? He wasn't going anywhere. The thought never occurred to the guard that it wasn't Michael he should be concerned about.

———

Michael silently watched and listened to the entire conversation, never moving or saying a word. He needed to get out of this place, but for the moment his mind was scrambling with ideas of what to do next. If only his dad was here to help him now. He waited silently, knowing they would be asking questions about what happened. So far no one seemed to care. Sure, things looked bad, but if only he could get the chance to explain to someone with reason.

The moment he looked up and saw Steve, he realized all bets on the table changed. Michael clammed up, realizing any chance of reason was just tossed out the door. It's hard for any person to hold things inside. Michael was no different. He wanted someone to talk to. He was starting to feel comfortable with the chief and wished he was there instead. With Jenny gone, there was no one he could trust anymore. The last person in the world he would think of telling was now standing before him.

Michael felt his heart begin to race as he watched the way Steve began to pace back and forth across the room. He looked across the room to see the reflection of Steve standing behind him. Fear struck its nerve, and Michael looked at himself in the mirror. Someone was always behind the mirror—it was in all the movies—yet Michael had a funny feeling this was different. Maybe it was the way Steve was standing behind him with those sunglasses on that bothered him. His body tightened the moment Steve grabbed his shoulders and felt his chair twirl around. He looked directly into the darkness of Steve's sunglasses.

"Well, well, well, who do we have here?"

"I want my phone call."

"Oh, sure. You want a phone? Would you like dinner too?" Steve had the most cynical voice, teasing Michael.

"I want to speak to an attorney."

"You're not speaking to anyone!" Steve slapped Michael hard across the face and then grabbed both arms of the chair, pulling Michael in close. "You're going to rot in here, and I'm gonna be your newest bestest friend!"

Michael was scared and sunk down in his chair. Maybe he could have taken this little weasel, but Michael was in his territory now with hands cuffed behind him, and Steve was the one with a gun. Rule number one, the guy with the gun wins. Locked up in the room with this psycho took away so many options, like running. Rule number two, you can't outrun a bullet. He was at his mercy now and just had to survive, but surely he couldn't do anything to harm him, right? The slap was just to scare him. This guy wasn't really going to hurt him, but he couldn't be sure.

"Tell me, does your wife know you are heres?" Steve's voice hissed when he said words like "does" or finished with the word "heres" instead of "here."

"What the hell are you talking about?"

"Oh, so now the murderer wants to talk?" Steve smiled, stood up, and looked down at Michael in his chair. Michael felt like a mouse being played with before the cat ate its meal.

"I am not a murderer."

"Of course not. I am sure your wife and son aren't concerned."

"You leave my family out of this!"

"Oh my, looks like I hit a sore spot." Steve whacked Michael hard in his gut. He collapsed in the chair, bent over, and gasped for breath. "Pussy!" He grabbed Michael by the hair and pulled his head up to look into his glasses. He reached up with his free hand, and Steve pulled down the glasses to look at Michael with his own eyes.

What frightened Michael wasn't the slap or the punch or even that Steve had a gun. What really frightened him was what he saw when Steve lowered those cheap dark sunglasses. It was his eyes that frightened him the most, and Michael tried to turn to the side to barf. Steve's eyes had the biggest pupils he ever saw, like someone whose eyes were dilated, but worse was the detail in them. They were slits like a cat, and that was when he realized this police officer wasn't right. He wasn't a man but a servant of some kind to the cat. From the eyes to the way he hissed when he spoke, things were starting to make sense. "Fuck you!"

"Oh, please, let's get some things settled here." He punched Michael hard in the cheek, leaving a red mark that would eventually bruise.

Michael turned to face him, realizing he was up against someone he did not want to mess with at the moment. Vulnerable and all alone, he would listen now only to find out what it was this guy wanted.

"As long as you are in here, your ass is mine. Is that understood?" Michael sat there, not answering him, so Steve jabbed him in the side. "Is that understood?"

"Yes."

"Good. You know, as long as you are in here, your family has no one to protect them. Of course, you didn't do so well with Shawn or Krista now, did you?"

"You son of a bitch! You lay one hand on them and I'll make sure you're sorry."

"Like you did with Shawn and Krista?"

"I'm warning you."

"Just remember. As long as you are in here, your ass is mine. And as long as your ass is mine? Well, let's just say you can't be in two places at a time." Steve started to laugh.

Hell could be many things to many people, but right now hell was here for Michael. Steve was right, and Michael knew he couldn't be in two places at the same time, nor had he been able to save Shawn or Krista. Now this guy was threatening the two people he cared for more than anyone in the world, and there was nothing he could do about it but sit there and listen. He stared at Steve, and sunglasses or not, Michael's eyes burned a hole right through Steve's head. He would hunt him down, so he etched his face into his mind. One way or another Michael was getting out. He just hoped it wasn't too late.

Chief Marty Dugan stepped out of his car in front of the station. He looked up at the moon lighting up the station and noticed movement on the roof. Lifting his hat to get a better look, the chief swore he saw a cat walking on the roof.

He walked into the station and saw Becky at the board. Things seemed way too quiet for what had just happened tonight. He looked around the station, which looked like any other night. A lightbulb flashed in his head, and he knew something wasn't right.

"Becky? What the hell is going on?"

"Chief?"

"Where the hell is everyone? Come on, we just had a second murder in a week. Now what the hell is going on here?"

"Well, the phone lines have been busy, as you know, and the suspect is in the interrogation room being interviewed by Steve. The reporters have been—"

"Stop! What did you say?" He held up his palm and faced toward her.

"I was just saying the news reporters—"

"No, not that! The suspect. Where did you say he was?"

"With Steve in the interrogation—"

"Barbie! Can't anyone do things right around here?"

Dugan wasted no time and ran toward the interrogation room, knowing there would be trouble with Lieutenant Steve holding court. He had no idea what had come over Steve, with this new persona of his, but this was no time to start being a superhero. Marty grumbled about promising his wife he wouldn't swear anymore. This was a bad time to hold things like that inside.

The chief saw the guard standing outside the interrogation room, and his intuition was confirmed. Things had gone terribly wrong. He ran down the corridor as fast as he could. He told himself not to swear and hoped he wasn't late.

"What in God's name?"

"I—he—it's not what—he—"

The chief wasted no time listening to his blabber. He unlocked the door and shoved it open. He barged inside, slammed the door to the wall, and stared at Steve sitting in a chair beside Michael. Steve had his feet up on the table with hands folded across his chest. He smiled at the chief when he walked in.

"Hello, Chief."

"What the hell's going on here, Steve?"

"We're just getting to know each other."

Dugan looked at Michael, who seemed okay but was slumped a little in the chair. Steve seemed way too happy for the chief, and what was with those sunglasses? He turned to Michael again and saw the red mark on his face. This could have been from many things, but the chief knew where it came from.

"Leave me alone with Michael here," he told Steve.

"Yes, sir!" Steve leaped up all giddily and made for the door, acting like everything was great.

"And, Steve?"

"Yes, Chief?"

"Get rid of those sunglasses or I'm gonna toss you and them in a place you ain't gonna be happy about."

"Y—yes, chief." He turned to look at Michael, wanting to say something, but then turned back to the door, opened it, and left the room.

The chief watched Michael for a minute before taking a seat across from him at the table. He sat there silently for a while, looking at the red mark on his face. His clasped hands rested on the table.

"Are you okay?"

Michael nodded his head. He seemed out of it, reclusive, and he turned his eyes to the side.

"Can I get you anything?"

"Just a phone call, please?"

"A phone call? You mean you haven't made your call yet?"

"No, sir."

"Barbie! All right, son. Follow me."

---

Michael followed the chief out of the room and down a hallway to his office. Once inside the room, the chief unlocked the cuffs on

Michael's wrists. He motioned to the chair in front of his desk and turned the phone around so Michael could use it.

"Just dial nine and the number. I'll be right outside when you are finished." He stepped out of the room and closed the door behind him, leaving Michael all alone in his office.

The only person Michael could call was Jenny, and he hadn't heard from her since the day she left. What was he supposed to say to her now? Maybe he would start with "Hey, hon, killed another one," but a bell rang inside, telling him that wasn't going to work. *Be honest*, he told himself. The problem, of course, was explaining why he was with Krista. He picked up the phone and dialed Jenny's cell phone number. It rang a few times before a voice answered it.

"Hello?" It was Jenny, and her voice was so soothing. Michael had not realized how much he missed her until hearing her voice on the phone. His heart sank, and he felt his eyes begin to water. He started to daydream, nearly forgetting she was on the telephone until she snapped him out of it with her voice. "Hello? Anyone there?"

"Jen? It's me." Michael was choked up.

"Michael?"

"Jen? I miss you."

"I miss you too, Michael."

"I can't talk long. Jen?"

"You're in jail. I know, Michael. Caller ID."

"Oh."

"That and it's all over the news." She started to cry, and he could hear her sniffling.

"Jen? It's all going to work out, but I need to get bailed out."

There was a pause this time before she answered. Whether it was because she had to think about it or she was just blowing her nose, he would never know. He waited silently before she finally spoke. "I'll be there."

"Thank you, Jen. I love you."

"I love you too, Michael."

The chief was standing just outside the room, and he paused a moment before opening the door. His office was decorated with plaques, awards, and different certificates showing his status in different civic duties, confirming he was able to be a chief of a police department. The two of them looked at one another, and Michael spoke first.

"Chief? I need to get out of here."

"You're not going anywhere till I get some answers."

"I didn't kill anyone."

The chief raised an eye, as if doubting what he said. His head tilted to one side, and he moved a little closer to see the reaction on Michael's face.

"I killed a cat trying to defend Krista, and if that's a crime then arrest me. Otherwise you have no reason to hold me here."

"I have two people dead now and a million and one reasons to keep you here, boy."

"When can I make bail?"

"I don't think you understand the severity of the situation you are in, Michael. I have a dead woman in a house with you standing over her with a fire poker in your hand."

"I was defending her!"

"Now calm down." The chief motioned with his hands to settle down.

"This is insane. You saw that cat lying there, didn't you? That cat killed her, and I killed the fucking thing."

"Michael?" The chief was talking in a calm and steady voice. "We have a little history now, you and I, don't we?"

Michael didn't know exactly what he meant, but he nodded his head just the same. The two of them had bumped into one another lately, but he didn't really want to call it a history. A history with a police chief usually isn't good. The two of them were bonding, though it was the most unusual circumstance.

"Ever since that first meeting, you have been talking about cats. Even before I met you there was that incident in the forest with the dead cat in the bag. Your brother-in-law is dead because of a cat and now this woman as well. She's the same woman your wife was fighting with in the Wagon the other day. Now, I want to know what the hell is going on with these cats, and I want a straight answer, because right now I'm the only friend you've got."

"All right, but you are going to think I'm crazy."

"Try me."

Michael sat there silently for a moment, looking at the chief. He thought about everything he told him and wondered about it himself. He was right; the chief was the only person other than Jenny he could trust. He rubbed the side of his cheek, feeling it start to swell. He decided to tell the chief his story but knew once he did the chief was going to send for the guys in the white jackets to come take him away.

"It started like this . . ." Michael told the chief his story from the day he came home after work. He told him everything about how the cat always came back as another. The chief asked him how he knew it was the same cat. Michael told him it was because of the milky eye that he'd popped out the very first day under the tire of the Boss. He told the chief that every cat that he killed had something wrong with it. The neck was chopped off, so when it came back the cat's head bobbed up and down. If he crushed a leg, it would have a limp, but it was always that milky eye. He told him about the other cats, and the chief was silent about this.

"That's my story. I know it sounds crazy, but you did ask and I didn't kill anyone, Chief. They were my friends."

"I know you didn't, Michael, but this story isn't going to cut the mustard."

"Chief? I need to make bail. I am afraid for my wife, Jenny, and my kid."

"Well, I suspect you'll be out of here in a couple of days but—"

"A couple of days?" Michael was agitated now. "Chief? I need to get home now!"

"Calm down, son. Your wife and kid are safe. This isn't something we can take lightly. I'll talk things over and do the best I can, but you need to keep me informed about everything from now on. Is that a deal?"

"Deal. Now help me get out of here."

The chief helped Michael straight to his cell. He was nice about it and gave him an extra blanket but told him there wasn't much he could do until bail was set. It was a rough night in the cell, sleeping all alone. The cell was bare, with nothing but a cot and a toilet to the side. He slept on the cot with the small blanket the chief gave him but hardly slept during the night. The moonlight shone through the one small window most of the night. It was hard to sleep, having so much on his mind, yet his eyelids weighed on him after swallowing those Midol PM pills. The pills did help his neck, though, because the pain was now gone, but so was Krista. He thought about this for a moment, sad for the loss of her.

It was early Monday morning and all the lights were out. Other than the moon that shone inside his cell, everything else was dark. He was the only one in the jail, which really gave him the creeps. Locked up helplessly in the dark and all alone did nothing but unsettle his nerves.

A noise echoed down the hallway, and then all was silent again. Michael tucked himself under the covers, wishing to get some rest, but it was hard with his mind on his wife and kid. After his little episode with Lieutenant Steve, he was concerned about getting back to them as quickly as he could. His only savior was that she wasn't home yet. He ignored the noise down the hallway until he heard another noise. This one was definitely the sound of someone else who was there.

"Who's there?"

There was no answer and everything was silent again, but something inside told Michael someone else was in the cells with him now. He was safe for now, he told himself, but what if whoever or whatever was inside the cells had a key to his cell as well? Certainly whoever was inside must have had a way to get in. If that was the case, then certainly they had a way to get into his cell as well. He had no concept of time, with no light or watch, since they took everything he had.

A shadow walked along the window, and he turned to see nothing but the waxing moon shining through the barred window. Another noise came from the hall, and he turned and fought to widen his eyes, wishing he could focus in the dark.

"Who the hell is there? I know you are there."

It was an eerie sight to see the cat standing on the window with the waxing moon behind it. Like a poster of a Halloween night, the cat was posed so perfectly. The moment Michael turned to see it sitting on the ledge, the cat hissed and arched its back, clawing at the window.

Another sound came from the end of the hallway, and this time Michael heard footsteps down the hallway. Closer they came to his cell, but he still couldn't see anyone. He could sense someone maybe ten or fifteen feet away, but it was hard to judge in the dark.

"Who's there?"

A very bright light came on and shone on Michael's face. He held up his hands to block out the light. He squinted and tried to maneuver his hands to cover the light so he could look past the light that was so bright, blinding his dilated pupils.

"What do you want?"

"I want everything that's yours," the voice finally hissed, dragging out the "s" as long as it could.

"What are you talking about?"

"You took his life, and now he will take all that is yours." The voice started to laugh, and Michael recognized it. The voice behind the high-powered light was Steve, and this worried him.

"What the hell are you talking about? I know who you are. You better knock this off or—"

He heard a loud mechanical noise of metal against metal, but he still couldn't see what was happening. It sounded like a lock was opened, and now he panicked, certain it was his. Why was he opening his cage, and what was he going to do? Michael pressed his body hard against the corner of the cell, holding up both hands and waiting for another blow from Steve's hands—or maybe worse.

"You owe me," the voice hissed.

"I owe you nothing!"

"On Halloween night the moon will rise." Something crashed to the floor, and slowly the light moved back and forth. Michael held up his hands, protecting himself from an invisible force. His hands were shaking, and his eyes were searching for something beyond the light. He was able to see a dark silhouette of someone, but that was all he was able to see. "Everything you had in life will be taken, as you have taken from him. Your house, your wife, your son. Everything, including all your dreams. You won't have anything left, and in the end you will beg to serve him."

"What the hell are you talking about? Are you crazy?"

"Until then I will make sure your wife and kid are safe." There was the sound of metal creaking and then the sound of metals clanking shut. It was probably the sound of the cell door closing, but what the hell was he doing inside his cell? If Steve was inside the cell, then he had to be two feet away or closer. He smelled the air, and it reminded him of the smell when he was close to the cat. The air smelled of bile or something worse, which was something not of this earth. The light turned off, leaving Michael in total blackness again. His eyes had to refocus to the darkness once again. He heard Steve's laughter down the hallway. He was stepping away. Then he heard the sound of the door leading to the cells open and close.

Michael sat in his cot the rest of the night, waiting for Steve to come back. Afraid of what was going to happen to Jenny and JR, he was frustrated sitting in his cell. He cried most of the night, blaming himself for the mess he was in.

The rest of the night was silent other than a passing cat here and there in the window. Were they guarding him or keeping check on him? On his mind were Jenny and JR. He needed to figure a way out of here, and it had to be soon.

"Dad? I need your help."

———w·o·a·o·o·a·o·w———

The morning light lit up the room, and Michael was lying on the cot. His eyes were red and his body completely exhausted from last night's events. A sound of the door opening caught him by surprise. He leaped to his feet, certain it was Steve coming back for more. When he saw it was a guard, Michael started to cry and dropped back down to the cot. The guard walked down to his door and pulled out keys from his side.

"Michael Merlino?"

"Yes?"

"You made bail."

He was so overwhelmed with emotion that Michael started to cry again. His hands and legs were shaking, and he dropped his head into his hands. She was here! It had to be Jenny who bailed him out, and he would hold her tight and never let her go.

"Jenny."

# RUN

Most people would have been leaping for joy after being bailed out from jail, but this felt different. It was late in the morning by the time Michael was released from the station. He was allowed to collect his personal items from Becky Tomlinson, who managed the items. She handed over a small ziplock baggy with his name marked in black marker, which held his wallet, watch, and any change he'd had in his pockets.

Last night was a doozy, and he was still shaken by the events. Restless from hardly any sleep during the night, he was almost thankful Krista had given him the Midol. However, he was agitated from being held in a cell at the mercy of some madman, with no one to call for help. His biggest concern now was finding Jenny and JR. Surely they were here waiting to bail him out, and he couldn't wait to give the two of them the biggest hug and kiss.

"Can I get you any coffee?" Becky Tomlinson scared the hell out of Michael, who jumped and nearly knocked over the chair beside him.

"No, I'm fine."

"You don't look fine."

"I'm fine," he reassured her.

"Sleeping in the jail will do that to a person."

"Yeah, you can say that again."

"The chief told me to tell you he had your car dropped off in front."

"Tell him thanks."

"Oh, I will." She laughed a little. "Keys are under the mat in front."

"Hey, who bailed me out?"

"Your wife."

"Is she here?"

"Nope, said she couldn't wait."

"Well, thanks again."

He waved to her and then walked off and headed to the door, unsure why he was thanking her. But it wasn't Becky who did anything wrong. She waved back, folding her arms across one another on top of the counter. The station seemed so quiet, with no police officers hustling about or radios crackling with the latest traffic stops. It was early, after all, and Crystal Lake had more than its share of trouble lately. Michael was timid, looking around the station, unsure what to do next. His first concerns were Jenny and JR, but neither of them was there to pick him up.

It was ten o'clock by the time he was able to leave the station. His car had been impounded, but the chief was nice enough to drop it off at the front door. *What a guy.* Michael was actually starting to like the guy. He hopped inside, but before he closed the door he took a look around. Everything was peaceful now, which was the way it always was in this part of town. He felt along the worn loops of wool and pulled back the mat, finding the key to the car. What he was curious about was whether there were any cats roaming about. He paid special note to the police station, looking up and down the sides of the building, but saw nothing unusual. Then, of course, there was that cop named Lieutenant Steve, who really gave Michael the creeps. There was no sight of him around the station either, but Michael did not know whether that was a good thing or not. In fact, the more he thought about it, the more it bothered him, and he slammed the door shut and pulled away.

---

It was noon by the time he drove the Taurus into the garage, and he was completely exhausted. The parking spot to the right was empty, which meant Jenny was still gone. He stepped out of the car, noticed the Boss beside him, and ran his hand across the hood, which was covered by the tarp. This time he wasn't passing it by. He took the time to uncover it. There was something special about the car, and he stood there admiring it for a while. The smell of leather and oil reminded him of days long gone by. He thought about his dad and what he would do in the situation he was in now. What people didn't understand about the car was that it was very special to him. It was his dad's car, and there were so many memories and dreams hidden in that car—dreams that no one would ever see except him and the ones he loved.

Eventually he walked inside the empty house, half-expecting someone to leap out and welcome him home. He knew Jenny and JR were gone, but it would have made it so much easier to cope. There was no noise, and the house seemed so cold without someone to fill it up. He missed the smell of lilacs in Jenny's hair and the sounds of SpongeBob on the television with JR laughing.

If he slept ten minutes last night, that would have been more than he imagined. The day was hardly half over, and already he was ready for bed. There were things to do, though, and one of them was work, which he did not have time for lately. His boss was going to kill him if he did not show up this week.

He headed up to the bedroom, hoping a shower and new clothes would help rejuvenate him. He looked around the bedroom, hoping to find a note or something from Jenny, but there was nothing. He turned on the shower and started to undress, taking his time. The room started to fill with steam, and he turned to look at the mirror, half-expecting the name Valafar to appear, but it didn't.

He stepped out of the shower, placed his bath robe on, and walked around the house. Everything seemed normal, but that was the problem, because he knew nothing was. Everything was in place, but nothing seemed right. The rooms all looked the same, but there was no life inside the house. Without Jenny and JR, there was no reason to be here anymore. He checked each room, half-expecting a cat to leap out, but even they were gone.

He was worried about Jenny and knew he needed to speak with her. If anything, he needed to warn her about Lieutenant Steve. Somehow he had to find her. Somehow Lieutenant Steve was involved in this whole fiasco, but there was a greater danger lurking. His only hope was that if he did not know where she was, then neither did Steve or Valafar.

Sitting on the bed, he picked up the phone on the nightstand and dialed Jenny's number. Never had she not called him in all the years she knew him. Even when they were fighting, she would at least call and tell him she needed some time to think. This was really worrying him, and he just hoped everything was all right. He held the headset to the side of his head, and the phone rang four times before the answering machine picked it up.

"Hello, this is Jenny. Leave a message at the beep."

The beep came, and he left a message. "Jenny? This is Michael. Thanks for helping me today. Can you call me, please? I am at home right now. Thanks." He was about to say something else when the phone beeped again, letting him know that his message had been recorded. He held the phone in his hand, his mouth gaped open, and his eyes clenched tight for a moment. "Damn it!" There were things he wanted to tell her, like "Stay away until I settle everything around here," "I miss you but you can't come home because there is a crazy cop in town who wants to kill you and my son," and "Don't worry, babe, I am going to kill every damn cat in town." The most important words he left out of the message were "I love you," and this hurt the most.

He sat in the kitchen with his bathrobe on and opened up the refrigerator. It was slim pickings, but he was able to scrape something together. Sitting in the family room he turned the television on and watched SpongeBob while he sat on the couch with a beer in his hand and eventually fell asleep.

---

He woke up on the couch the next morning with the television still on. Still wearing the bathrobe, he walked around the house. He couldn't remember much of yesterday or when he ended up sleeping on the couch. He had slept very soundly and was still a little drowsy and found it very hard to wake up.

An infomercial was on the television about a magical mixer that was guaranteed to make anything taste great. He was thankful it wasn't the news with some story about the crazy cat killer, but this infomercial did bring back odd memories nonetheless. The man on the television had a table full of food, including fruit, potatoes, vegetables, and meat. The man on the television grabbed a banana, placed it on top of the mixer, and pushed it down. Beneath was a glass capturing the puree, and he mixed in a carrot and then some peas. The mixture was a yellowish liquid that he held up and drank, licking his lips. He took the device and started slicing up potatoes, apples, beef, and chicken. He sliced up or pureed anything on the table, telling the audience how delicious it was.

"This thing is amazing! Look at what it does. Just slice up this cat and we have a wonderful combination of puree."

Michael blinked. This did catch him off guard, watching the man fight with a cat and try to place it into the blender. Beneath was that glass of carrot juice and banana, but was he really putting a cat into it now? There was a smile on Michael's face while he watched this, waiting for the phone number to order it soon. It reminded him of the man at the Wagon with the super shake he was selling.

"And if you call this number within the next ten minutes we'll send you a free Ginsu knife as well, but you need to act fast!"

Michael was staring at the television, waiting with anticipation for the phone number, when the smoke alarm sounded and the man started running around frantically. Michael sat up in his chair, concerned because he really wanted the number to this fine gadget. The television started to fade out, and Michael held up his hands.

"No!"

The man was still there making a puree of an apple and some berries when Michael woke up from his dream. The buzzer on the alarm was going off. Rubbing his eyes, he realized he had fallen back to sleep again and the cat puree was just a dream.

He wasted no time getting up and dressed for work. It was a long day ahead of him. No more wasting time and dreaming about a wonderful gadget, but right now he could really use one of those. He made a quick pot of coffee and munched on whatever was left in the house before heading out.

———

It was Tuesday morning, and Michael was at work by 7:00 a.m. An emotional roller coaster over the weekend left his head swimming with a million thoughts.

Stacks of papers covered his desk with more stacks of manila folders and projects sitting on top of the chairs in his office. He was far behind, and it would take him weeks to recover, but if he stayed late and maybe worked weekends he should be able to pull through it. He sat down in the chair behind the desk and dropped both arms to the side.

On the credenza in front of him covered with files stacked upon files was a picture of his wife and son. He stared at it for a while, imagining her back home again like the picture of them in their backyard. This was all for them, he thought to himself. This wasn't his dream but a necessity to work here in this big downtown bank so they could all have a roof over their head. It was foolish to ever think he could do something he loved.

He decided to call Jenny again, hoping he would catch her. He dialed her number and waited, hearing the ring on the other end. He was counting the rings and holding up one finger at a time. After four rings, the familiar voice and message came on.

"Hello, this is Jenny. Leave a message at the beep."

"Jenny? It's Michael. I really need to talk to you. I'm concerned about your safety. Please call," and this time Michael did not forget "I love you."

The tail of the cat clock was above the credenza, and it kept ticking back and forth, making that mechanical noise of plastic ticking. He probably never noticed it before because the office was usually bustling with activity, but now it was so quiet. The eyes

288

stared at him with the black slits of the white eyes moving back and forth. This thing was pissing him off now, maybe more so than it ever had. He stood up, ready to beat the thing to a million pieces.

Outside his room was Franklin, pacing back and forth. For whatever reason, Michael stopped himself for the moment before smashing the cat. He was concerned, of course, because of all the turmoil. It would look pretty bad if Michael was all of a sudden inside his office smashing a plastic cat to a million pieces. Headlines would read, "Cat killer goes crazy in downtown bank, kills another cat." No, he decided to hold off for now, but why was Franklin pacing back and forth?

He decided the best thing to do was work, and there was plenty of it piled on his desk. He picked up the phone, called several branches, and cleared off many of the files on his desk. The day went on, and Michael cleared up quite a bit of business that had been left unattended during his absence. It helped to be here at work with his mind on this instead of the cats and worrying about Jenny and JR. They were safe, he was certain, and he was just letting his mind run wild with crazy thoughts.

During the day while he was busy cleaning up files, Michael noticed Franklin pacing back and forth throughout the day just outside his office. There were times he would disappear for an hour, but then he would be right back outside his door, pacing back and forth again. Michael was trying to finish up some of the neglected things, but watching Franklin pace like that was starting to annoy him.

The ticktock of the clock was agitating Michael, and Franklin pacing back and forth in the halls only made the ticking worse. The ticking never stopped, and Michael knew it was only a matter of time before that clock went to the garbage in a hundred million pieces. Franklin had been gone for at least fifteen minutes, so this looked like as good a time as any to demolish the demon on the wall.

Michael stood up and walked over to the wall with the cat clock hanging from it. He peeked around the corner to make sure Franklin was nowhere in sight. A couple people passed by, but Franklin was nowhere to be seen. This was perfect because something told him that it was better Franklin did not see. He pulled the clock from the wall and carried it back to his desk. Again he looked around to make sure no one was near and set it down by his feet. Like a happy boy jumping in mud, he stomped on the clock with both feet. The first crack was loud, but the pleasure it gave him was immeasurable. Small black pieces flew in the air behind his desk, and the tail fell off immediately. He stomped on that tail several times, enjoying the feel of the plastic parts beneath his shoe. The eyes popped and rolled to the side but were hidden behind his desk. Playfully he kicked them back and forth between his feet, like a couple of soccer balls, before smashing each one to pieces.

He was having so much fun smashing the clock that he never noticed Franklin standing at the doorway to his office. A picture is worth a thousand words, and Franklin's face was memorable. Scrunched up like never before, it was obvious there was anger ready to explode. He knocked on the door and waited for Michael to realize he was standing there, watching the cat clock get smashed under his desk. It was his cat clock, after all, and Michael had no idea. Michael looked up to see the look on Franklin's face and would never forget it. His own face flushed, and he was certain it showed guilt written all over it. So he smashed a clock. So what? What was Franklin going to do?

"Hello, Michael."

"Uh, hello, sir."

"What is it you are doing at the moment?"

"I uh . . . am, uh."

"Spit it out, boy. You're breaking the cat clock, aren't you?" Franklin was staring at him now with eyes that were red. His entire face was turning red, like he was holding his breath.

"I am."

"That was *my* clock!" He emphasized the word "my" with such ownership.

Michael stared at Franklin for a few seconds and then looked down to the shattered pieces of plastic beneath his feet. He liked the feel of the broken clock crunching beneath his feet, and just to verify this, he squished his toes back and forth, making a crunching sound that seemed to bother Franklin even more. This pleased Michael, and he smiled and did it again before answering him.

"I never liked that clock."

Franklin never answered him but stormed out of the office, walking fast with arms moving swiftly along his sides. Michael watched this and never laughed so hard, seeing the way Franklin held his chin high in the air. There was something odd going on with Franklin, and Michael had noticed it before, but with all the events going on Michael couldn't give two cents anymore about what Franklin thought of him. Something was wrong because Franklin's hair was messed up like a mad scientist today, sticking up in all directions. Franklin was really losing it, and Michael just didn't care anymore. In fact, he was losing interest in his job and turned to the photo of his family again on the credenza across the way. That was where his mind was now.

Michael stared at the picture of Jenny and JR and some thoughts occurred to him. What would he do without her? What would his life be like? He knew she meant everything to him, and all that he did was for her and JR. Then why did she leave him? The voice of his dad filled his head, and he laughed. "Don't tell your mother." He imagined him driving the Boss. Michael once had a dream of being happy with the woman he loved, but all of that was lost one day when he decided to grow up and be a man. Now everything was lost, and he wanted it back again, so what was it he had to do to get it back?

"I'm coming for ya, babe," he said to himself.

There was a good hour at least before they locked the doors to the bank and another hour for people like Michael, who wanted to put in a good day at the office. Michael stood up, grabbed his jacket, and left what work needed to be finished lying on his table. Something hit him like a lightning bolt, and he had to work fast. Time may have worked like molasses for him lately, but he was going to set things right and get Jenny and JR back into his life. He had to find that dream of his and bring it all back. If it meant working several jobs to make ends meet, then that was what he had to do. It was his dream that everyone was trying to take away, and he wanted it back. His dream of being an astronomer may have been crazy, but he would figure out a way because Jenny and JR were the most important part of his life.

———

The train was not far, but it was raining, and if Michael wanted to catch the early train he had to make up time in a hurry. He ran down the steps to the tunnels below, hoping to grab an L train up to Washington and catch his train. The blue line would be perfect to catch at LaSalle, so he ran down the tunnels, hoping one was coming soon.

He thought it was odd on a Tuesday that no one would be walking to the subway, but he figured it was because he left work a little early. When he arrived at the platform he was the only one in the tunnel. The tracks were beneath the concrete platform he stood on, and a sign lit up on the wall across the way. It was a directional sign with different colors of the trains pointing to where each train went and the stops along the way. The lights in the tunnel were yellow from the dingy lens that covered the lights, with a couple benches and concrete posts. Not a single person was waiting for a train in this busy part of the city.

He leaned up against one of the concrete posts and waited for his train. He looked down at his watch and then back down the dark tunnel, hoping he saw a light heading his way. The tracks led into a dark hole, but no light was coming toward him just yet. Paint was chipping along the cracks in the walls. The lights above flickered, and the sign across the way sparked. Michael figured it was the storm that caused the lights to lose power. The L was powered by electricity, which made him stop and wonder if the train lost power. He would miss the train, for sure. He listened for a sound of the train, hoping to hear it coming, but the only sound was a slow dripping of water somewhere from the ceiling. Every sound seemed to be magnified in the cavernous concrete tunnel.

Someone coughed nearby, but Michael couldn't see who was there. Someone was standing behind a concrete column, but Michael paid no attention because he was worried about catching the train. At least he knew someone was there, which comforted him when the lights flickered again. Footsteps started to move toward him, and Michael looked around the column, surprised at who he saw.

Franklin J. Smith had the funniest hairdo Michael ever saw. It was sticking up like he had his finger stuck in a socket. His eyes were red and saggy, like he hadn't slept in a week. The bow tie around his neck that was always perfectly tied was undone and hanging from his shirt. It may have been because Michael never left this early and had missed seeing Franklin like this, but he doubted this very much and watched as he approached him.

"Hello, Franklin." Michael gave up on the "sir." He just didn't feel like calling him that anymore. Besides, the way he was dressed hardly demanded it.

"Fuck you!"

"Excuse me?"

"You heard me, you fucktard!" The lights flickered again, and the sign across the way sparked with the lights remaining off.

"Look, I'm sorry about your clock and will—"

"You're not sorry. Master said you were a fucktard."

Now Franklin was acting weird, but this was the first time he heard Franklin swear like that. And "Master"? The last time he'd heard that word was with Lieutenant Steve, but he'd had eyes of a cat beneath cheap dark shades. Michael looked directly at him and, sure as shit, guess what. Franklin had dark eyes of a cat, too.

"Son of a bitch!"

Franklin reached out and grabbed Michael by the shirt, pulling him hard to the side. Michael was shocked at first but was quick to fight back. He pulled Franklin, grabbed his hands, and was amazed at the strength of the old man. The two of them struggled in the empty tunnel, moving closer to the drop-off to the tracks.

"I am going to fucking kill you!"

"It was a fucking clock, you asshole!"

"Valafar told me you would say that."

"Val—Valafar?"

"You know who he is, you asshole!"

Franklin took a swing and punched Michael in the jaw. It knocked him over to the side, and Michael held his jaw, bent over to the side. Franklin ran toward him and hoped to get another punch, but Michael was still younger than this old man, who stepped quickly to the side. Franklin tripped and fell to the drop-off, landing on the tracks. Michael stared at him, still holding his jaw and shocked at what was happening. Luckily Franklin hadn't landed on the third track or he would have been electrocuted already.

"You're fired!"

"Fuck you, I quit!"

Inside the tunnel a light was heading their way. Michael saw this and turned to Franklin, holding out his hand. Franklin was in another world, and who knew if Franklin was even there when the light moved closer, barreling down on him standing in the tracks? The train came swiftly once the light was close and ran over Franklin, who seemed not to even notice while it severed his body into pieces. Michael leaped back, hearing a splat and another electrical spark, while his body landed on the third track.

The train stopped and the doors opened, and Michael hopped on the train with Franklin under the tracks. Not a soul was on the train that night, and the lights in the tunnel flickered off, leaving it in total darkness. He grabbed a handle hanging from the ceiling and leaned forward when the train pulled away, feeling the gravity pull him back.

Watching all of this were dark eyes waiting in the corner of the twilight of the tunnel. Thunder clapped, and the ground shook when the train whisked away. Darkness was accompanied by emptiness, and those caliginous eyes glowed in the cavernous tunnels of the trains.

# CHEETAH

The subway ride should have been short, but things were not going as planned lately for Michael. The storm was bad, and lights flickered in the empty car. The subway was completely empty, which was odd since it was Tuesday night. He had left early, but rush hour traffic was usually between 3:00 p.m. and 6:00 p.m. He looked at his watch, which said the time was now 4:20 p.m. Rush hour definitely had begun.

The train was traveling smoothly down the tracks toward the next stop, which was Jackson. Certainly there would be many people there, since that was a part of the loop and the hub for other trains. Other than the lights inside the cars, it was dark in the tunnel. Above the small windows were advertisements and a small plan of the routes of the train. The walls of the tunnel were very close to the train, making it hard for the claustrophobic.

A large cavernous room opened up when the train entered the Jackson station. Slowly the train came to a stop, and all the doors opened. Not a single person was waiting for the train in the Jackson station. The station was larger than the LaSalle station, since it was more of a hub for the other trains. Usually this place was bustling with people, but today not a soul was near. The lights were similar to the last station; they had a soft-green or limelike color that glowed about the walls.

An alarm went off, warning everyone that the doors were closing, but it was met by another foreign sound. It was the sound of a cat roaring, which echoed in the tunnel. If anyone was in the tunnel, it would have scared the hell out of them. It certainly scared the hell out of Michael, because this sound was deeper than the other cats he had killed, and this meant only one thing. This cat was big—really big. He could feel his heart pounding in his chest, and a small trickle of sweat dripped from his forehead. *What the hell is a cat doing on the L?* he thought to himself, pressing his back up against the wall of the train. He looked up and down the train, wondering where the sound came from. It was hard to tell because the sound echoed off the walls of the tunnel. It could have been standing on the platform or far in the tunnels. What he was afraid of, though, was that it could be on the train.

The next thing that happened frightened him even more. Cats ran in the doors, leaping into the car. Hundreds of cats flowed through the doors, filling up the car. Both doors of the train became a river of cats running inside. They leaped up on the seats and walked around the floor. Rubbing against his legs, one even started to claw at his thigh like a scratching post. A white cat with a black patch on its eye leaned over and started to gag. The stomach was involuntarily heaving, and its mouth opened wide. To Michael's disgust the cat spit out a large hair ball, making him want to gag.

"Fucking cats."

The doors started to close, and his hand reached out to stop the door. In that split second he asked himself if he should stay on the train or leap off and take his chance. The door hit his hand and he pulled it back, letting the door close. He had decided to stay on the train. There were two more stops before he could get off at Washington, so he had to take the chance. The train started to move again, and he leaned his body forward again. He scanned the horizon out of the window, hoping to see the large cat on the platform or in the tunnel. The train entered the tunnel, and darkness consumed the train once again, with the lights inside the train being the only light there was. There was no sign of the large cat, but there were a hundred or so smaller cats instead. The doors leading to the attached trains were shut, and no one else was on the train. Unless this cat was able to open the doors, he was safe for now.

Light approached again when the train spurted out of the tunnel and into the Monroe station. The train started to slow again until it came to a final stop. The force of the train pushed Michael forward, so he leaned back and grabbed the strap above his head. Meowing and purring was overwhelming, and Michael wished he could have covered his ears, but he had to hold on because of the gravity pull.

Nothing seemed right about the station at Monroe. Having a wild cat on a train was certainly anything but normal, but there were other things too. Like the other stations, this one was completely empty. Considering the time and place, that was very unusual. If it wasn't for the hundreds of cats stepping across his feet, the station would have been silent. The doors to the train opened wide for any passengers who decided to join the fun. This train was filled to capacity. Michael began to laugh because he knew no one was coming on this train except himself and the cat, wherever it was. They seemed to have a meeting of destiny, but Michael didn't know why. The lime-colored lights overhead were flickering, and Michael decided it had nothing to do with the storm. He was still looking around the station, trying to decipher what else was wrong. It was starting to become a game—like Where's Waldo—but this seemed real. It was real, wasn't it? Michael pinched himself and it hurt, so it had to be, but where was everyone?

It was hard to concentrate, knowing a wild cat was on the loose. Chances were highly likely it was stalking him. He knew the beast was there, but where? It was so silent now that the smallest of sounds could be heard. Even the cats stopped purring and meowing and stood still. A gust blew from the tunnel, and a wrapper tumbled across the platform. Lights on a sign zapped and sparked, and Michael blinked and stared at the sign. It was for the little magic mixer he saw on the television he had sworn was a dream.

The doors remained open longer than they should have, adding to the things that were not right about this place. The train should have been moving on now, and the doors should have closed. It would have made him feel better, but as long as those doors were open he was vulnerable to whatever was stalking him. Above the small windows were the advertisements, but one was different from the others. He was certain it hadn't been there earlier, but now it was and Michael couldn't miss it. Lit up with flashing lights was a picture of a black-and-white cat, just like the clock in his office that he had just smashed. Standing over it was a perfect image of Michael with a knife in his hand dripping of blood and stabbing the clock. Above this was written "Cat Killer!" and Michael's name below it.

"Come on. One more station."

"Rrrrrrrrr."

Michael heard taps and a growl on the roof, and he knew exactly what it was. Claws of the beast were tapping on the roof, and that meant the cat was walking right above him. He was sweating now, because he was afraid of the unknown. What did this cat look like, and how big was it? He was completely defenseless, standing in the train, and his only hope was the doors. His chest was pounding; his heart wanting to break out. It was beating faster than it ever had before.

A large red button was next to the doors with a sign above that said, "Close Doors." How convenient. He leaped to the button, pushing it repeatedly like a little kid on an elevator. The doors never budged but remained open, and his eyes were wide, looking back and forth from the button to the doors.

"Rrrrrrrrrr rrrrrrrrrr rrrrrrrrrr," the beast purred.

The beast was near and was getting ready to pounce. Michael could smell it. That sickening smell of death and decay was so close it made his stomach turn. He reached out, grabbed the double doors, and tugged at the handles to pull them shut. Neither of them budged, and he leaned his whole weight on them, pulling and jerking, but the doors just wouldn't give in. Even if he did close these doors, there was another set of doors at the other end of the car. Suddenly all the cats in the car scattered out the door as quickly as they had come in before. He looked down past the seats and straps to the door on the other side and saw the beast for the very first time.

The cat was big, as he had sensed from the low growls, and stared at Michael from the entrance of the car. He recognized the type of cat this was by the golden fur and black spots on it. He had seen this type of wild cat before in the zoo but never thought he would actually have an encounter in person. This cat look sickly like the others, with the infamous milky eye staring at him and the other endless black eye.

The cat froze for a moment, just like Michael did, and they stared at one another. Michael knew the moment he made a move, the cat would strike, so he had to play it cool. Neither one of them moved except for Michael's eyes, which shifted back and forth and then looked up and down. The cat's eyes stared at him, never flinching, and the milky eye was simply dead.

Michael was the first to make a move and leaped out of the car, quickly running to the back of the train. His suit and polished shoes were not the best clothes to run in, but he ran this time for his life, hoping not to slip. Cats scattered when he ran, crawling into the tunnels and beneath the train.

A cheetah is the fastest animal in the world, able to run up to seventy miles per hour. Michael leaped out of the car, but catching him wasn't going to be a problem. The cat's body hunched down as it watched Michael run, with head lowered and eyes narrowing on its target before leaping after him.

Michael was able to get to the rear end of the train and turned behind it, hoping he was right. If he was fast enough there would be a ladder attached to the last car of the train, allowing workers to climb to the roof. All he had to do was get to the ladder fast enough and climb up before the cheetah was able to catch him. Once on top of the stainless steel train, he would be safe and there would be no way for a cat to catch him. He made it to the back of the train, but sometimes things don't work out the way you plan them.

"Damn it!"

There was no ladder on the back of the train—just a door leading back into the train with a few small chains swung low across the door. There was no other plan, and the cat would be on him any moment now. There was nowhere to run, nowhere to escape fast enough from a cheetah that was capable of running seventy miles an hour.

Michael ran across the tracks, leaping across the electrified third track to the far end of the tunnel. The third track made it difficult to run because he had to spot each electrified rail and then leap over each one, making sure he wasn't electrified. Each track carried 750 volts of power, certain to fry anything making contact with it. Small eyes glowed from the darkness of the tunnels, accompanied by soft meows and purring. He placed both hands on the tunnel walls, afraid to look back and knowing the cat wasn't too far behind.

The cheetah was quick when he wanted to be, but it was in control this time and took its time. It walked toward the back of the train, where Michael turned out of view. The cat had to be careful at this point, because Michael showed he was capable of coming up with solutions each time. This time was different, though, because Valafar had thought of everything. They were alone in the tunnel with no escape. Valafar was able to use whatever power he had to arrange this, and now it was just Michael and the cat. The cat was going to win this time.

He turned his back to the wall, and things seemed to move in slow motion. Walking toward him was a living hell. The spotted yellow beast stepped slowly toward him, placing each foot in front of the other. Pulling back its lip and revealing those grotesque yellowing teeth with saliva dripping, the cat was smiling. It had Michael cornered, and now it was over. Valafar was going to enjoy this kill.

A lightbulb lit up inside Michael's mind as he watched the cat step slowly toward him. One surprise after another made it hard to think, but sometimes when your back is up against the wall the best ideas in the world can happen. The cat was stepping into the pit of tracks, heading straight toward him.

"Shit!"

The third track was the answer to everything, and he watched while the cheetah stepped closer to the tracks. Michael's excited eyes widened when the cat approached the tracks, waiting for a crackling of the electricity to fry it. The cat stepped on the first track and then placed a paw in between the two. Certainly it would step on the third track and he would escape the claws of this beast.

"Come on, you son of a bitch."

The cat froze with its paw over the second rail, not moving a muscle. The black eye looked toward Michael, dropped to the rail, and stared at it. The paw lowered to the rail about an inch above it and then stopped, as if an invisible force held it.

A small black-and-white cat leaped into the tunnel, making its way down the tracks. Placing a paw on the deadly third rail, the cat was tossed in the air. Sparks flew, leaving nothing of the cat except burned, smoldering fur.

Valafar saw what happened to the cat and quickly pulled back his own paw from the deadly third rail. His head lifted and he looked straight at Michael, who swore that cat from hell with its sickly white orb was smiling at him now.

"Fuck," Michael muttered, grinding his teeth. He spoke again through clenched teeth, "Here, kitty, kitty, you fucking kitty."

The cat leaped over the second and third rails, landing safely on the other side. The smell of the roasted cat was sickening. Sparks flew, and zaps on the rail were still frying parts of what was left of the small cat. Valafar smiled, revealing those jagged teeth, but it was that fucked-up milky eye that bothered him the most. It was winking at Michael, mocking him now.

"You're kidding me, right?"

Stepping back into the tunnel, Michael was cornered now. His back was up against the wall, and his arms and hands flattened against the wall, spread out. The walls were damp and moldy with water dripping down the sides, making them slippery to the touch. This was the end, he was certain, with no escape from the cat this time.

The cat walked closer, raising its head to sniff the air. Its nose twitched back and forth, with both eyes set on Michael. Its shoulders raised, its head lowered, and it moved slowly toward him, baring sharp yellow teeth. It was so close to Michael now he could smell the vile breath of the beast, certain it was from hell itself.

What neither of them expected was the other set of tracks. There were tracks going in every direction in and out of the tunnels. The cat crossed over the first set of tracks, but there were more going through the tunnels. The cat lurched its body, pressing most of its weight on its front paws, its hind legs raised high in the air. With one fluid movement the cat rolled back on its hind legs, stretching one front paw forward to leap at Michael and end this once and for all. Long sharp claws pulled from the paw and touched the third rail of the tracks. Sparks flew everywhere, and loud zaps echoed in the tunnels. Hair stood up on the cat like static electricity rubbed against its body. It cooked every part of the cat, turning the color of its hair from golden to a dull burned black, crispy from 750 volts of electricity.

Michael screamed, figuring it was his last, as he held up his hands, ready to fight. His body tensed, and adrenaline flowed through every part of him. If this was it, he was going to give that cat one hell of a fight. When he watched the way the cat was smoldering and burning on the tracks, he nearly burst out crying. It took him by surprise as much as it did the cat, and Michael started to laugh like a lunatic, jumping up and down. "Ha ha! You son of a bitch." He pointed at the burned remains of the cat still smoldering on the tracks with sparks zapping in the air. "I beat you again."

Michael did somehow beat the cat again, but this was not the last time he would see him. He stepped out from the tunnel, careful of the tracks when he walked. He wasn't going to make the same mistake the cat made. He stepped over the third rail of every track he crossed. He looked down the tunnels to see if there were any cats in the vicinity, but there were none, and that allowed him a little breather. But he knew the next one was to come for him again. How many were there?

Seven cats were dead so far, and he started to wonder. Not counting the few odd cats he'd killed with his shotgun in his backyard and the one still roasting on the third rail, there were seven cats he had killed. How many lives does a cat really have? Is it true they have nine lives, and if so, would they come back for revenge? He turned to the cat still sparking on the tracks, knowing there were two more cats to kill.

He stepped out of the subway and walked the rest of the way to the train station. There was no need to rush for the early train, having missed that one anyways. The cat was dead for now, and there was no rush to make it home any earlier. He still couldn't contact Jenny, which worried him. He would make it home and all things would change for the good, but one question remained.

"Where are Jenny and JR?"

# NINE LIVES

It was now two days since Michael quit his job—or so he told himself. He told himself Franklin wasn't right and couldn't fire him, so quitting was the only option. Besides, it felt like the right thing to do, and since that moment he was feeling good about himself. He had a couple days to think about that horrible last day at work. There were some things that made him happy, like the smashing of the clock. The killing of Valafar's seventh life on the electrical rail came in a close second.

The loss of Franklin was hard for Michael to accept, but the person who fell beneath the train was not the same person he'd known and admired all these years. Michael had known something wasn't right but could not place his finger on it until he saw those eyes staring at him. Cold and cruel, dark and ominous, those eyes were not of the person who was his mentor. Something took over the man inside who wore the bow tie. Something evil and menacing had taken over the man who taught him well in the business world.

Halloween was only a few days away, and Michael still had not been able to contact Jenny. He tried her cell and her mother's house, but there was no answer. The last thing he wanted to do was panic, but with only a few days left and no word from her, it was getting hard not to worry. Jenny was on speed dial on both the house and Michael's cell phones. He picked up the phone in the kitchen and pressed *recall* to dial Jenny's number again. As always, the phone rang and the same message was on. He left message number twenty-four about how he missed her and really needed her to call. The thought crossed his mind to put some urgency into the message, but that would do two things that he really did not want to do: it would create panic, and it would build on the image of himself being a little crazy.

In the kitchen he opened the refrigerator and took a look inside. The top shelf had a few beers inside, a half gallon of skim milk, and a leftover sandwich from Tony's Deli in town. Since Jenny was gone, Michael ate very poorly, but Tony's had a delicious-looking Italian sub, so he had purchased the footlong, ate half, and saved the rest for later. He grabbed a beer and popped the cap on the side of the refrigerator. It was one of the fancy beers from Germany that did not get one of the easy twist-off caps.

Some things were bothering Michael about this cat, and he needed answers. Everything he knew was so far-fetched, yet all of it was coming together and making him look like a lunatic. The thought did occur to him that maybe he really was losing his mind and all of this was just a figment of his imagination.

The doorbell rang, and he went to the door to see who it was. In the driveway was a brown truck pulling away. He opened the door and on the front stoop was a small cardboard box addressed to him. He knew what the package was, brought it into the den, and sat behind the desk. Grabbing the small tag on the side, he ripped the box open and held it above the desk, shaking it a couple times until the book slid out. He held it in both hands and read the cover: *Valafar, Cats and Our Demise*. He flipped it over and saw the picture of the author with his name beneath, Mohamed Abdulah.

He spent the rest of the day lying near a fire in the family room and reading the book. He drank a couple beers and ate the leftover sandwich along with a bag of potato chips, which made for an appetizing lunch. He examined the book, flipping through the pages. The front cover had an illustration of the sphinx with the face of a cat on it. The face of the cat was white and ghoulish, like the man in the dark cloak, but it didn't do the real face justice. Perhaps it would have been better if the illustrator saw the wraith for himself, because there was nothing like it in this world. The back cover was a photo of the author. The picture of Mohamed Abdulah was black-and-white and showed he had a beard. There were no other pictures than the ones on the cover and the back, which disappointed Michael. He was hoping there would be a picture of the wraith, but he knew the chances of that were highly unlikely. In the book the author spent a lot of time describing an expedition in Egypt that took place a couple years ago. It was funded by some megamillionaire who felt the rules did not apply to him, and they dug the site with no government authorization. The author talked about his own credentials, which included attending famous universities such as Harvard and Oxford. He was a renowned archeologist in Cairo, having worked on the pyramids and Luxor, but there were no great finds other than this one. Conveniently there was no hard evidence of any of his claims, but he stated over and over again that he saw all of this firsthand. The dig site was lost in a sandstorm, the plane carrying all the evidence crashed, and all other survivors on this expedition were now dead. Michael felt sorry for him, because it was obvious why he was on the Jerry Springer show. People thought he was a quack, and it was exactly why Michael did not want to tell people of his own experience. Everything he said sounded so familiar to Michael, and as crazy as the story was, Michael was probably one of the very few who believed his story.

Eventually Michael tired of the book, because it was long and very technical. He felt like there was urgency now to figure out what this thing was that he was dealing with. He skipped many of the chapters because quite frankly he had already been through it himself. What he needed to know was who, what, where, and why.

There was a chapter on Valafar himself, so he skipped to that portion of the book. Valafar was not living, nor was he dead, it said. He was something in between and searching for a way to exist again. He had been a living being over twelve thousand years ago, although Mohamed believed he lived much longer than this. The hieroglyphics found in the tomb talked about this evil ruler who was an ancient being, but they did not say how old he was. Mohamed felt that sometimes hieroglyphics could not be taken literally, yet he did believe this ancient being lived for a very long time before his demise. Valafar was not of this world—or at least not anymore. He was overtaken and killed by men who were kept as slaves. This was, according to the hieroglyphics, the beginning of mankind and the end of Valafar.

The next chapter was filled with warnings and described more of what Michael was looking for. When they took the mummy from the tomb, it started a chain reaction that could not be undone. The ancient Egyptians were trying to warn us not to open the tomb or, worse, take Valafar out from his cell. According to the markings, there were emeralds that held some kind of power over Valafar and were buried along with his mummified remains to keep him buried forever. When they took the mummy it must have somehow managed to escape and was no longer contained in its prison. The last known location was the plane crash in St. Louis, Missouri, where all passengers were found dead—all except Valafar, who was nowhere to be found. Mohamed believed that Valafar was able to somehow leap into another life and reignite his life once again. He somehow walked the earth in the form of a man or wraith, which was not living nor dead but able to roam and somehow protect his form of a cat. He described the man in the black coat, with its grotesque white face, perfectly, though no one would believe it unless they were face-to-face with it like Michael was. This wraith, according to the markings on the tomb, was Valafar, but he was trapped in this form until a sacrifice was made on Samhain night. That was an ancient Gaelic term meaning Halloween night. Until this sacrifice took place, Valafar was trapped inside this wraithlike form to roam the earth, stuck between the living and the dead. Its only form was that of a cat, which would grow larger with every life—nine lives, to be exact, just as legend told. In each life, Valafar would become stronger, but it wasn't until a sacrifice was made on Halloween night that Valafar could truly become what he once was, and this frightened Mohamed.

There was one weakness, though Mohamed felt the chances were slim to none to defeat Valafar. On the night of his resurrection, or Halloween night, he was very vulnerable. This was because all his energy was directed toward the resurrection, leaving him exposed to an attack. Valafar needed to jump into another being or cat at this moment, and with all efforts being on his resurrection, there was no chance of leaping into another cat like he normally would have done. To do that, Valafar needed power that would all be directed toward his resurrection instead. This also had to be accomplished with Valafar's ninth life. If he were to be killed during any of his other lives, then Valafar would be able to easily transfer to his next life.

Michael decided he needed to contact Mohamed. He was the only person who would believe his story and the only one who could give him advice. He searched the book for any information to contact the author and found the name of the publisher along with an Internet site on the back cover. He looked it up, found a number, and dialed it. The phone rang a few times before it was answered by a pleasant voice.

"Good afternoon, Horizon Publishing. How can I help you?"

"Hi. I am trying to contact one of your authors. Is there someone who can help me?"

"Oh, I see. Well, which one of our authors are you trying to contact, sir? I can try and find someone to help, although we are not normally at liberty to hand out that information."

"His name is Mohamed Abdulah. He wrote the book."

"Mr. Abdulah?"

"Yes, he wrote the book."

"I'm sorry, sir, but . . ." There was a pause of uncertainty. "He's dead."

This took a moment to sink in, and Michael held the phone to his ear, stunned and certain he misunderstood the girl on the phone. "Dead? Did you say 'dead'?"

"Yes, sir. I'm very sorry but he had a tragic accident just the other day and passed away."

"I'm sorry to hear that." He could only imagine what had happened, but what bothered him even more was this was the only man who could help him. "Can you tell me how he died?"

"I am not allowed to say. I hope you understand." She was a young girl, and sometimes people just couldn't keep a secret to themselves. U2 wrote a lyric, "They say a secret is something you tell one other person, so I'm telling you, child." The girl paused before whispering into the phone, "They say he was surrounded by cats when they found his body. Odd, if you ask me, being he tried to warn people about cats."

"Cats?" A mixture of both excitement and fear filled Michael's voice.

"Yes, sir, I'm sorry. Someone is coming. I need to go."

Before Michael could say thank you, he heard a click and the phone went dead—dead just like Mohamed, the only person who would have understood and possibly the only one who could have helped. Dead like Shawn and Krista and his dog Max, too. Alone to fight this beast without a clue about what to do. Jenny and JR were missing and in terrible danger, but he did not know what to do. He sat there alone, staring at the phone and knowing what had to be accomplished, yet where did he begin? He knew everything rested on his shoulders now, to end this once and for all. Now it was up to Michael to save his family and his dreams, which had been neglected for so long.

# CAUGHT

## SUNDAY, OCTOBER 31

Halloween was finally here, but there would be no trick-or-treaters out and about. The nearest neighbor was the farmhouse, which was a hike from the house. No children would be visiting the house this year. There would be no parties, because word was out that a police officer lived here. In the past, the house was always popular on Halloween night, because kids liked to pretend the place was haunted. They may not have been too far off, considering what was going on presently.

The day started off brisk with a cool breeze blowing across the cornfields. It was a dark, cloudy day with rain in the morning, but the sun was expected to shine later. The weatherman said tonight was going to be perfect weather for everyone to enjoy Halloween.

Lieutenant Steve Case was standing in the hole he labored to dig. Stepping back and forth with his head down, he appeared to be measuring the hole. He would stop and look up sometimes, raise his hand, and point a finger, possibly calculating to himself because no one else was there.

"Who's the fucktard now?"

Placing both hands on the side of the hole, Steve pulled himself up and out of it. The hole was maybe five feet deep now, with huge piles of dirt alongside it. Inside the hole were three large wooden crates all wrapped with chains and padlocks.

"Who's the stupid one now?"

Steve was laughing alone, standing over the hole, and talking to no one other than maybe the old wooden chests lying in the hole. He seemed excited about something, waving his hands up and down, but he also seemed drunk or high on hallucinogens, talking to an imaginary person.

"We are ready for the sacrifices, master."

If someone was watching all of this, they certainly would have said Steve had completely lost his mind that night. Walking around digging holes and talking to himself was one thing, but talking about sacrifices and calling an invisible person "master" was just a little off the deep end. He looked creepy as well, with his hair slicked back and his clothes stained with dirt. Tall and skinny, he didn't walk exactly elegantly. There was an odor about Steve that would have knocked over a skunk. His hygiene was less than desirable, to say the least.

Standing in front of Lieutenant Steve was the man dressed in a black cloak. With the hood over his head, the man in black was talking to Steve, but only he could see and hear him.

"You really shouldn't be dancing on your brother's grave."

"Yes, master, but—"

"He was the smart one, after all."

"Yes, master." Steve sighed, regretting the truth.

"Your work impresses me."

"Thank you, mas—"

"But you are forgetting something, aren't you?"

Valafar—the man dressed in a black coat, the wraith or whatever he was—tonight made it a point that it was Steve who forgot something and no one else. Steve just looked around and waved his arms in the air, excited about what he had accomplished yet dumbfounded about what he had forgotten. He placed his hand to his chin, thinking to himself, but Steve was never the smartest of the bunch. He looked to the house for a moment, hearing muffled sounds before turning back to Valafar again and lowering his eyes to his feet. Even someone as dumb as Steve could feel the power oozing from beneath the cloak.

"Michael?"

"Yesssss." There was an arrogance and maybe even cynicism in his voice when he hissed. If Valafar wasn't thousands of years old, he would have rolled his eyes at Steve, but he was a loyal subject so far and Valafar was being nice.

"Uh, yeah. I was getting to that."

The man hidden beneath the cloak rolled his hand to Steve. "Continue."

"Well, let's just say I have a plan."

Steve turned to the house, which was hidden by weeds with a leaky roof and paint peeling on the warped siding. A soft wind blew, rustling the weeds, but there was another sound coming from the house. He smiled, stared at the house, and listened silently for the voices held within.

---

Five days ago Jenny was driving through town in the minivan with JR in his seat in back. She decided they would try going home, talking to Michael, and hopefully working things out. She spent her time at her mother's house, but all the while she was thinking of Michael. She missed him, of course, but needed that time to think alone. Her mother was out of town, so Jenny and JR had the house to themselves.

She looked at her phone and saw he had called, but decided it was best not to discuss things on the phone. Besides, it would be nice to see the look on his face when she was home again. Her phone was filled with missed calls from Michael, and she listened to his voice on her messages. She thought maybe it was cruel of her to be able to hear his voice and he couldn't hear her voice, but that would change soon.

She thought of preparing a nice meal for him with some nice decorations and a candlelight dinner. Jenny was missing Michael more than he would ever know. In all their time together since they'd first met, she had never been away from him this long, and it was eating her up inside. She realized Michael was going through something, and it was time she stood by his side, through thick and thin. What better place than the Wagon to gather some things for dinner.

"Mom?"

"Yes, my baby, we're going home soon."

Finding a parking spot wasn't difficult, but today something different happened. Bright red and blue lights flashed behind her, so she pulled the car over to the side. Adjusting the mirror, she looked behind to see a police car pulling her over.

"Damn! I wasn't speeding."

She pulled into a parking spot, figuring this way her car wasn't in the way. The police car conveniently parked behind her, not allowing an escape in case Jenny had some wild notion to do so. She fumbled through her purse to get out her license and turned to JR, who was sitting behind her, and smiled at him.

Lieutenant Steve stepped out of his squad car and looked all around. He adjusted the cheap sunglasses he was wearing. He stood tall and gangly and tugged his belt with both hands because his pants were two sizes too big for him. He slowly walked toward the minivan he had pulled over.

Jenny watched him walking toward her door in the side mirror. Fumbling for her driver's license, she nearly burst out laughing when she saw the thin, awkward man. He stood beside her window, tapped the glass twice, and then looked the other way. Jenny rolled the window down and looked up, forcing a smile on her flustered face.

"Hello, I'm sorry but was I speeding?"

"License?" Steve was still looking away when he held out his palm at the window, waiting for her license to drop into it.

"Uh, well sure, but . . ." She handed him her license. "What did I do?"

"Nothing." He held the license up in the air, examining it behind his shades.

"Oh good, well, can I ask why you're stopping me?" She smiled and turned to JR.

His hand lowered to his side with her license in it, and he turned his head to look at her. Leaning down to face her at eye level with his cheap sunglasses reflecting her pretty face, he stared at her silently for a moment before answering. Of course it was creepy because Steve was creepy himself. The silence was a little unsettling for Jenny, and she stirred in her seat, waiting for his answer and trying to smile innocently again. He lifted her license to the window, and she stared at it a moment before taking it back.

"It seems we have a Michael Merlino back at the station and—"

"Again?"

"Yes, and being you're his wife—"

"I'll head there right now." She took the bait, and Steve smiled down to her.

"No, no, no. That won't be necessary. We have procedures, you know?"

"Of course, but—"

"Trust me, just step out of the car and come with me." The smile on his face could have been framed.

"Well, okay, but I have my baby with me." She turned and pointed at JR.

This threw Steve for a loop, and he turned to the backseat. Lowering his glasses to inspect the backseat, he saw there definitely was a baby strapped in a car seat. He pushed up the glasses with his index finger and turned back to Jenny with a smile.

"I suppose he can come too."

Jenny laughed, having no idea of Steve's intentions, and stepped out of the car. She wore blue jeans and a tight red shirt, exposing the tight curves of her body. She was innocent and never took notice of the eyes behind the sunglasses staring at her body. Steve looked like a harmless buffoon, so she missed the tongue dangling out of the corner of his mouth. She walked around back, opened the door, and stretched out her arms to place on her jean coat. She bent over to get JR out of the back and innocently wiggled her ass, struggling to get the car seat out from the belt. When she was finally able to detach the seat, she held it up with both arms, JR strapped inside.

"Ready when you are."

Steve opened the back door of the squad car, allowing Jenny to strap her son in. Once he was in, she sat beside him and placed an arm across the top. She noticed the cage separating the front seat from the back and waited while Steve shut the door, locking her in. Taking note that the doors had no handles or locks, she just smiled and thought to herself it was just a short ride to the station. Steve stepped around the side of the car, sat in the front seat, and closed the door. He started the engine, put the car into drive, pulled out, and turned right, the opposite direction from the station.

"Wow, a real police car." Jenny tried to make some small talk, seeing the car moving in the opposite direction of the station. "The station's that way, right?"

Steve remained silent in the front seat with both hands on the wheel now. Maybe Lieutenant Steve had his reasons and would turn at the next block, but he just kept on driving away from the station. Slowly they passed the edge of town, and Jenny stared out the window, feeling her heart sink. Something was wrong, but what was she to say now? "Can you tell me where you're taking me?"

"Barrington."

"Barrington? But I thought—"

"I said Barrington. Now shut up!" Steve snapped, cutting her off. No more Mr. Nice Guy. His mood did a one-eighty, changing from a nice, helpful police officer here to serve and protect to a complete asshole.

JR started crying, and Jenny leaned over and covered him up. She wrapped her arms around the car seat, and her long hair dangled across, covering him from view. She was scared and had no idea what was going on but knew she was in trouble now.

They drove for about fifteen minutes out of town, past the subdivisions and toward the farms. With cornfields on either side, Jenny knew the police officer wasn't bringing her to Barrington or any other station nearby. They pulled into a gravel driveway, and she looked out to see his house for the very first time. The house looked more like a haunted house like all the kids rumored about. Siding was falling down, and paint was peeling. Weeds grew all around, and old shredded drapes covered the windows. Oddly she noticed the cats walking around the home. There must have been a hundred cats around the property—standing on the roof, the front stairs, the gravel driveway, and in the window. There were cats on every part of the old abandoned home.

"Where are we?"

"Home."

———·w·o·◊·◊·◊·◊·◊·◊·w·———

Michael was sitting at home in the family room all alone when the phone rang. The room was silent, with no television or voices to listen to. He was lonely sitting in the room, imagining the voices of Jenny and JR sitting beside him. When the phone rang he leaped up, certain it was Jenny finally calling him. He grabbed the phone like it was the last glass of water and he was stranded in a desert for weeks.

"Jenny?" Excitement filled his voice.

"Hello, Michael. Remember me?"

The voice was familiar, but he was expecting Jenny's voice. When he heard Lieutenant Steve's voice on the line, his whole world started spinning. Confused for a moment, Michael was still thinking it was Jenny before snapping out of it.

"Who is this?"

"Your newest bestest friend." Steve started to laugh after repeating the words he once told him when Michael was in the cell.

"Fuck you, asshole."

"Now, now, now. Don't be so harsh with your newest bestest friend. I mean after all, can't we all just get along?"

"I'm hanging up. Don't you ever call here again, asshole!"

"You might want to hold on a minute before hanging up. There's someone here I think you want to hear."

There was silence on the other end, and Michael's heart just sank. Who the hell was he talking about? With a gut-wrenching feeling deep down inside, he knew the answer already. There was a small shuffling noise but otherwise no sound at all. It was the worst feeling he could ever imagine, knowing something was wrong.

"Michael?"

Jenny's voice was shaky, and it sent chills throughout his body. He knew before she even spoke it would be her. Michael could sense her breath. He could imagine the fear and anxiety, and his hands tightened so hard around the phone that his knuckles became white. He missed her voice, but the devil had her now. His entire life came crashing down, and his eyes started to water as he stared off to nowhere.

"J—Jenny?"

"Michael! Help us! This guy's an asshole!"

Her voice trailed off, as if she was being pulled away, and there was laughter in the background. She was screaming in the background, but the sound was stifled with some noises that sounded like struggling. One word bothered him that did not register immediately, but it struck him harshly. He felt like a dagger was thrust into his heart. She had screamed "us," and that meant he had his son as well. Michael was completely helpless now and screamed into the phone, wishing he could strangle the man who held her against her will.

"Jenny!"

"I thought you wanted to hang up, fucktard." That was Steve's new word he learned from Franklin of all people. "Who's the asshole now?"

"You sick fuck! If you lay one hand on them I'm gonna kill you!"

"Oh really? Well, I might just have some fun with her until you get your ass here." Steve started to laugh again, driving Michael insane. "Now, you will meet me here alone. If you call anyone I am going to know. I'm the police, after all." He laughed again like a maniac would and then gave Michael directions on where to go. "Hurry up, fucktard. Time's running out."

The phone went dead, and he dropped it to the floor, letting it buzz on the floor. He dropped back to the couch, holding his head in his hands. A million thoughts ran through his mind on how to get her back, but the only option was to meet this creep and hope she would be safe.

Everything in his life was lost, but there was still hope to save his wife and his child. He was going to save the two of them whether he had to sacrifice himself or not. He gathered himself together and prepared to save the only two people left in his life.

———

Lieutenant Steve hung up the phone, still laughing at his conversation. He was really liking this new Steve who wielded so much power. Slowly turning to look at Jenny with his dark sunglasses on, he stared at her with the darkest of grins on his face.

"We're going to have a party."

Jenny struggled, sitting in a wooden chair. Her mouth was gagged with a cloth, and another cloth was tightly wrapped and tied at the back of her neck. She pulled both arms, which were pulled behind her and handcuffed to the chair. She looked like a mess, with tears streaking down and makeup smeared on her face. Her ankles were tied tightly to the legs of the wooden chair, restraining her body.

Steve walked around her and stood behind her back. He played with her hair softly before tugging it with one hand. He pulled her head back so she was forced to look into his eyes. He lowered the glasses, revealing the cat eyes behind them. Jenny screamed, and his other hand rubbed her shoulder. She was a very beautiful woman, and he wanted her the moment he saw her. He had not raped her yet, but it was getting hard not to. After five days of holding her in his house, it was hard to keep things in his pants any longer.

Valafar had promised Steve he could keep Jenny after the ceremony. She would be insignificant once they killed Michael and Valafar was resurrected. They would all die eventually, but what Steve did not know wouldn't hurt him. Valafar was not to be trusted, but Steve was under his spell.

Steve's hand moved down her body, about to cup her breast, when another scream was heard. It was like nails across the chalkboard. JR was strapped into his car seat, sitting to the side. He was crying most of the time, and it drove Steve absolutely nuts. That was probably the wrong word to describe an insane person, but he was not used to a baby screaming. Five days of screaming from an infant really did a number inside Steve's head. On top of the screaming, the baby needed to eat and have his diaper changed, not to mention an occasional burping—food was dribbling down JR's chin. Steve had no idea what he had gotten himself into when he took the two of them. The idea of dropping off the kid ran through his mind, but then it would cause a search for Jenny, and right now the only one who knew she was gone was Michael. So Steve would deal with it for now. Instead, Steve untied Jenny from the chair, keeping her close with a gun in his hands. He allowed her to change the diapers, feed her baby, and keep JR quiet. He left the gag in her mouth most of the time because he didn't want to hear the whining.

There were times when Steve wished this whole thing was over and he could just have fun with Jenny all alone. He would place his hands on her shoulders or run his fingers through her hair. Tonight was the night when the sacrifices would happen and Valafar would be reincarnated. Steve had waited five days, so what were a few more hours? Steve was living in an imaginary world, seeing her together with him.

---

Jenny was a strong person, but this was going to mess with her. She had to remain strong as long as Steve had her and JR. What Steve did not calculate was that a mother was the fiercest of adversaries if you messed with one of her offspring. She would be strong for JR, and when she was given the chance, Steve would pay for his mistake. In the beginning she was certain of this, but it was five days now and she was getting weak. She knew Michael was trying to call her, and she wished she had answered his calls. Now he was coming here alone, and she was worried he wouldn't tell anyone. She had one big regret—that she had not told Michael how much she loved him. They would overcome all of this nonsense, but now things were looking dim for all of them. No one knew they were here, and she prayed that someone would find them.

———————

Chief Marty Dugan had been with the police force for a very long time. During that time he learned many things, but there were some things a person could never learn. Instincts were something a person just had, and Dugan's hairs stood up when he saw the minivan parked in town.

The minivan had been parked in town for five days now in front of Tommie's Restaurant. The police marked the tires, and then the tickets started piling up on the windshield for not paying or moving the car after the two-hour parking limit during the weekdays. It was strictly enforced because people did not want anyone loitering. Besides, it was good revenue for the village, which the mayor often denied. The minivan had a stack of tickets on the windshield, and they decided to tow the car. When they reported the owner of the vehicle over the radio, the chief interrupted, taking special note himself.

"The license plate is registered to a Jenny Merlino," Becky Tomlinson reported on the police band.

"Is that Jenny Merlino married to a Michael Merlino living in Rolling Hills?" the chief asked.

"Uh, yeah. Lives in Rolling Hills, Chief."

"Where's the car again? I am going to take a look myself."

The chief pulled up behind the minivan and stepped out of the car to examine what he found. Everything seemed normal except for the pile of tickets mounting on the front windshield of the car. He checked the front, sides, and back but saw nothing unusual about the car, yet it just did not seem right. A small toy was lying underneath the rear passenger door. He picked it up and looked at it and then peeked inside the window. There was nothing inside, but he wondered if the toy fell out of the car. Grabbing the radio on his side, he called the station.

"Becky?"

"Yeah, Chief?"

"Is there any history about this car going back five days ago?"

"Lieutenant Steve stopped the car for running a red light, Chief."

"Son of a Barbie . . . Steve?" Now there was an urgency in his voice.

"Uh, yeah, Chief. Steve pulled the car over but never wrote a ticket. Said he let her go."

"Becky? Get me Steve immediately!"

"He's been sick these past few days, Chief."

"Then get me his goddamn home address now!"

———

There was not much time to prepare, so Michael had to make do with what he had. He would have one chance to do this, or everything was gone. Everyone he loved and cared for would be gone. All he had worked for, but most of all every dream he and Jenny had shared, would be lost forever if he was to fail. He could lose everything else in the world, but if he lost Jenny and JR? Nothing would matter anymore.

He had watched plenty of movies before like *Die Hard* with Bruce Willis. He loved the part when Bruce Willis strapped the gun on his back, hiding it from the bad guys, and pulled it off when he held his hands up and pretended to give up. That was his plan unless he could think of something else. Time was moving way too quickly, and Michael had no time to think. Jenny's and JR's lives were riding on him being there for them.

When he ran out to the garage a voice was inside his head. He swore it was his dad, but his mind was playing tricks on him again. He grabbed the door to the Taurus to open it. He tugged but the door would not budge. Again the voice of his dad was inside his head, but something just wasn't right. His dad was dead. Then he heard Jim Morrison from the Doors yelling, "Who's dead?" Michael was tired, and his mind wasn't right with that crazy Steve holding his wife. He turned to the Boss and saw his dad sitting in it. The car looked beautiful, as if it was straight off the floor of the dealer.

"Dad?"

"Don't tell your mother."

"Dad!"

"What are you waiting for, son?"

"Is that really you?"

"I told you I would be watching you. Have you forgotten to chase your dream?"

"No, Dad, but I have a family now. Dad, I have to save them."

"Hop in the Boss, son, and chase that dream."

"It's fast, Dad."

"You bet'cher ass it is, son. Now drive it!"

Michael held back the tears and rubbed his eyes. He was so messed up. He was seeing ghosts and now he was talking to his dad. Closing his eyes, Michael started shaking, scared of what would happen to his wife and son. They were all he had now, and he had to save them. He opened his eyes, and his dad was gone and the cover was on the Boss.

"Drive it."

The last words of his dad echoed in his head. He pulled the cover off the Boss and hopped inside the car. He turned the key in the ignition, and the car never sounded better. Slowly he pulled out of the garage and sat in his driveway with the front pointed toward the street. The Boss looked so new, like it just drove off the factory floor. Never had it looked any better. He stepped on the gas pedal a couple of times, letting everyone know the Boss was out.

The car roared out of Rolling Hills and onto the highway, leaving a trail of rubber on the road behind. The seat beside him was empty, but Michael could feel the presence of his dad sitting there beside him. Now it was Michael driving the car, and he was laughing with his dad. It was his turn now to take on life. It was Michael's turn to chase his dream, and the two of them were together again one last time to save the world.

When he pulled up to the house he sensed something evil about it. Maybe it was the hundreds of cats standing all over the property.

The place seemed deserted, but he knew better as he pulled onto the gravel drive.

Taped to the top of his shoulders was a semiautomatic 9 mm Glock 17. It held a cartridge of seventeen bullets, and he was planning on using every one. He kept this gun in the house, never telling Jenny about it. He had purchased it to protect his family in case they were ever robbed, but as time went on he forgot about it. It was locked up in the corner of his closet, where it just disappeared. His plan was simple: find Jenny and JR and then pull the gun. If he had to he would kill Lieutenant Steve, but he hoped it wouldn't go that far. He practiced the move several times, holding his hands high and then pulling the gun from his back. He would catch Steve by surprise. Michael owed him after his treatment in the jail cell.

Steve stepped out of the front door, which creaked and looked like it was going to fall off. A gun was in his hand, and this worried Michael because he was mad at himself for not thinking Steve would have one. Michael stared at him, not saying a word, when a black cat walked up to him and straddled his legs. It curled its body around him, moving in and out of his legs. Michael kept his eyes on Steve when he kicked the cat ten feet from where he stood. Then he tilted his head and smiled up at Steve.

"Hello." Steve waved the gun in his hand.

"Where's my family?"

"You were smart coming alone." He looked out to the road, checking to see if there were any cars following him.

"I did what you asked. Now where's my family?"

Steve said nothing but motioned with the gun for Michael to follow inside the house. He stood at the door and held it open with one hand, the other pointing the gun at Michael.

Michael stepped up the stairs, hearing them creak and feeling them ready to break. He looked right at Steve, knowing what was behind those dark sunglasses he wore. Hands clenched at his side, fighting everything inside to punch him.

The anger inside Michael changed the moment he entered the house. Sitting handcuffed and tied to a chair with a gag in her mouth was Jenny, and his son was strapped into a car seat on the floor. She looked up at him and moaned with tears in her eyes, but she was weak and hardly able to move. He looked at his son, who started to cry and reached his hands out for him, wanting to get out of the chair. Michael felt tears in his eyes, seeing the two of them, and the rage inside was about to erupt.

"Let them go."

"Turn around, fucktard, and put your hands in the air."

This was the moment he was waiting for. He had practiced it a few times, raising his hands in the air. Now the moment was here, and his nerves suddenly seemed frazzled. He hadn't expected Steve to have a gun, which meant Michael was going to have to shoot him. Worse was the fact that his wife and son were sitting there. If anything went wrong, the consequences would be bad. He turned his back to Jenny and JR and looked straight at Steve, raising his hands in the air.

"Like this?"

Michael froze as he stood before Steve. This wasn't something he was born to do. Steve, on the other hand, practiced every day for this type of situation. With a gun in his hand, Steve had the advantage. Surprise was the only thing Michael had going for him. He counted to five inside his head, deciding he had no other choice. This was the moment and it had to work, so he reached farther behind his back to feel the gun in his hand.

Steve moved closer to Michael now that his hands were raised above his head. One hand held the gun while the other patted down his sides, checking for any hidden weapons he may have. Michael could smell the pungent body odor of Steve, who probably hadn't taken a shower in a week. Steve had worked on the hole in the back, and his skin was covered in dirt. His hands tightened around the gun, and Michael watched Steve closely, waiting for the moment when he leaned down and turned away from him.

The tape was very secure on his back, and maybe more so than it needed to be. The moment Michael tried to pull the gun out, the tape pulled at the skin on his back. He had practiced this so many times but was worried it would drop from his body, because he was sweating just thinking about what he was going to do. So he had put extra tape on his body to hold the gun in place, not realizing that was a big mistake. The gun was stuck, and he pulled but by the time he was able to snag it from his back Steve had already noticed and was standing up again. Michael jerked his body back and forth until the gun finally pulled from his back.

Steve saw what was happening and slapped Michael hard across the back of the head with his gun. He knocked him out with a heavy blow to the back of his head. From that point on, Michael could remember nothing, as the entire room suddenly went black.

# PANTHER

## HALLOWEEN NIGHT

Everything was blurry when Michael opened his eyes. The side of his head was pounding, but he couldn't remember why. Sounds were amplified, hurting his ears like large drums beating next to him. He tried to move his hands but they were held tight by something that felt like concrete. Slowly opening his eyes, he strained to see before him because the room was spinning. He tried to stand but felt dizzy and dropped back to the chair.

"Welcome back, fucktard."

As if cold water was splashed in his face, he shook his head and focused his eyes. Now he saw Jenny tied beside him and his child before him on the floor in his car seat. He had no idea how long he had been knocked out. Judging by the darkness of the room, it was very late at night. He looked at the one window covered with filth and flies buzzing around. Everything was still spinning while he tried to focus. He looked up at Steve standing before him.

"Who do you think you are, Bruce Willis?" Steve asked cynically and started to laugh.

"Fuck you, asshole."

"Now that isn't the way you should be talking to me."

"You're sick."

Steve slapped Michael hard across the face, jerking his head to one side. He walked over to Jenny and stood behind her, watching

Michael's reaction in the chair. Michael was cuffed to the chair like Jenny was, with his hands locked behind his back and to the chair. His legs were tied to the chair, but he was allowed to speak, unlike Jenny, who was gagged. The side of his head was pounding, and he felt a warm sensation that must have been blood.

"Would you like to hear how this all ends?" Steve asked.

Michael watched him walk around behind his wife, who he loved more than anyone in this world. He had failed his family, and now he sat there helpless and ashamed. He looked down to his son, strapped in his little chair, and wondered if he would ever say "Dad." What would his little boy do without him? And he thought about his own dad. What did Michael do when he lost his dad? He was to follow his dream, but during that time he was lost, and now there was no hope of ever chasing it.

"Sure. Tell me everything. Tell me how you got so fucked up."

"Well, this is all thanks to you. It all started when you killed the cat. Don't you know cats have nine lives?" Steve laughed again.

"Seven down, two more to go."

"Ah, but see? You'll be too late. In a few short hours it will be midnight. You will be dead, and Valafar will be resurrected. You took his life, and from that moment on, he has taken everything that was yours."

"Do you have any idea what you are talking about?"

"Yessssss, I do," Steve hissed and grabbed the dark sunglasses, tossing them to the side. His dark catlike eyes stared at Michael, and one hand grabbed Jenny by the hair and pulled her head back hard so her body arched. She strained in the chair, staring at Michael with wide blue eyes. She was crying. "And she will be mine!"

"You're an idiot. Let her go!" Michael tugged his hands.

Steve wasted no more time and dropped Jenny's hair from his hands. Quickly he walked over to Michael and stood before him with his right hand reaching down to his gun. He pulled out his police-issue Glock like he'd practiced so many times. Holding it to Michael's forehead, he grinned and held the trigger.

"Enough of this bullshit. Time for you to die."

Chief Marty Dugan wasted no time and headed out to Steve's house. He drove his large Ford Expedition with the lights flashing red and blue. Traffic pulled over when the car passed. Once out of the village limits and more into the country, he turned off the lights on top. He did not want to warn Steve or anyone else.

Driving as fast as he could through red lights, Marty knew there wasn't much time left. Five days was a long time for someone to be missing, but he had one of those instinctive feelings inside that he wasn't too late. But if he did not get there soon things were going to get bad, instinct or not.

The sun was just setting when he first arrived, and he drove past slowly, seeing something else that disturbed him. It was the Boss sitting in Steve's driveway. There was something odd going on with Steve lately, and there was friction between him and Michael. He had had to pull the two of them apart a couple of times now. He was beginning to like this kid Michael, but something was happening in his life that he couldn't quite put a finger to just yet. Marty kept driving about a half a mile past the house and pulling into the farmhouse down the road. He pulled off to the side so no one could see his car.

He called the station on his cell phone to let them know where he was. The thought occurred to him to call on the radio, but then Steve might have heard it as well. What if he'd heard the call earlier? Marty had to take that chance.

"Hello, this is Crystal Lake Police, what's your emergency?"

"Becky? It's the chief."

"Chief? Why are you calling me on a landline?"

"No time for questions, Becky. Listen to me. I am out at Steve's place on the farm. If you don't hear from me in about an hour, send the cavalry."

"Got it, Chief, but—"

"Just do it!"

He clicked the *off* button and slipped the phone in his pocket. Reaching into the Expedition he pulled out a rifle off the back rack and placed it over his shoulder. The house was a ways off, and he could walk it fast enough. Just beyond the cornfield with a light on in one room, Marty started to walk toward the house. He thought about protocol because he did not have a search warrant, but then again Steve worked for him. The hell with protocol and a search warrant—there wasn't time.

It was about a fifteen-minute walk from the farm to the small house. He walked through mud and the ruts of the cornstalks. Rain started to drizzle, making it wet, cold, and sloppy. Damn weatherman was wrong again, not that it surprised the chief. He brushed back the cornstalks that made it hard to walk and grabbed at the rifle strapped across his shoulder. Mud caked on the bottoms of his boots, weighing his feet down, made it feel like he was walking through molasses. Finally he stepped out of the cornfield and into an opening with the house right before him. He was cautious and kept close to the cornfield, making sure his cover wasn't blown before moving closer. The pitter-patter of rain on the roof and the cornfields helped disguise the sound of his own footsteps. One small light was on inside the house, and then he saw movement across the room.

He ran toward the house, tripping in a pile of dirt. He fell down about four feet, landing on top of some old wooden crates with a loud thud. The rifle fell off his shoulder, and he was thankful it didn't accidentally fire. He lay there for a few minutes, trying not to move a muscle and certain someone would have heard him fall into the hole. Once he was satisfied no one was coming, he lifted his head to peek at the house. There was a large pile of dirt surrounding the hole, which helped muffle the thud. Reaching out with both hands, he searched for his rifle. There were several crates he found, and he wondered what they were doing in this hole. Steve was definitely up to no good, but there wasn't time for that now. He strapped the rifle over his shoulder again, climbed up out of the hole, and stepped closer to the house.

He was able to make it to the house and kneel just beneath the window with the one light on. Careful not to be seen, he waited and listened for any sounds. He looked up to the window for any sort of movement before leaning up to peek inside.

There before his eyes was Steve with his back to the window. In front of him were Michael and Jenny, tied up and sitting in chairs, and off to the side was a baby strapped into a chair. The chief couldn't believe what he was seeing. Steve was holding his gun up against Michael's temple. Quickly pulling out his revolver from his side and raising it in the air, Marty had to fight back every urge to shoot. He had no idea what was going on, but if he was to shoot he might not get any answers. Yet if he didn't, it could be too late.

Marty waited but his finger was ready to pull the trigger the moment he sensed Steve was going to pull his trigger. He saw the faces of Michael and Jenny, wondering if the two of them could see his. Raising his own body higher so his face could be seen fully in the window, he got the response he wanted.

Jenny was the first to notice the face in he window, darting her eyes toward the face and then back toward Michael. The chief was quick to put his finger to his lips, telling her to be quiet even if she did have a gag in her mouth. She nodded her head up and down, turning her eyes back toward Michael. The gun was pointed toward his head.

The chief could hear muffled talk but that was all. He was uncertain what Steve was going to do. Steve turned toward the window and Marty quickly dropped to the ground, pressing his back up against the house. It was all the time Steve needed, and things happened so fast. Chief Marty Dugan wished he had fired his gun when he had the chance.

He heard a shout from inside, but it was the small voice that followed that worried him more. Scrambling noises and a large crash came from inside, and his heart sank. Gunfire exploded inside the house, and a flash of light accompanied the sound.

---

The last thing Michael wanted his wife and son to see was him tied up helpless in a chair, shot and killed by a madman right in front of them. He turned to Jenny, put a smile on his face, and whispered to her. "I love you."

The look in Jenny's eyes was not the look he expected of someone who was just given final words of affection. Instead she was motioning with her head back and forth, almost like she was trying to tell him something. Tilting his head to one side, he was about to question her, but that instinct inside told him not to. Instead he turned and looked toward the empty window. Raindrops slowly drizzled down the dirty pane of glass. Lightning lit up far away, and he saw his own reflection in the window.

"Dad!" JR screamed for the very first time the one word that Michael would have waited a lifetime to hear. A surge went through his body like nothing he had ever felt before. Adrenaline raced through his veins like fire searching for air. All things flashed before him, from the day he was born until now. There was an instant he swore his dad was standing there before him. So strong was that little voice that it sent shock waves through Michael's entire body. Every muscle strained as he pulled at his hands and leaning forward in order to move the chair.

Steve was busy looking at the reflection of himself in the window when the scream of the child caught him off guard. The gun was held loosely in one hand, still pointed at Michael's forehead. Steve swore he saw movement outside but was distracted by the scream of JR, and a jolt to his side sent him falling.

Michael was able to rock the chair hard into the side of Steve's body. Like new life surging through Michael's body, the sound of JR screaming his name brought about a resurgence in him. With the power of a dozen men, Michael was able to knock Steve over with the chair.

The gun fell from Steve's hand to the ground and fired accidentally. The bullet ricocheted safely, not hitting anything. Jenny screamed into her gag, certain she just lost a husband. Watching all of this was JR, who screamed again and again.

"Dad! Dad!"

Chief Marty Dugan was a perfect shot and stood up the moment he heard the gunfire. He was certain he was late when he fired the gun into the window, hitting Lieutenant Steve right between the eyes. One-shot Dugan never missed, but was he too late?

Lying on the ground with the chair tied to his body was Michael, staring at the floor laughing. Never had words sounded as sweet as his son's voice shouting out his name for the very first time. He turned his head to one side and saw Steve staring directly at him with dead eyes and mouth agape. Blood dripped down from the hole in his forehead, making a large puddle of crimson beneath him.

"Dad! Dad!"

"You saved my life, Chief." Michael laughed hysterically.

"Wasn't me. It was your son that saved your life," the chief responded, brushing back the shards of shattered glass from the window. He tugged himself in through the window, moving his gun and holster to the side. Stepping past Michael, he went directly to Jenny and untied her first because she looked like she needed help more than anyone. "Sorry, Michael, but ladies first."

"Absolutely! Take your time." Michael just lay there laughing while the chief untied Jenny. He couldn't remember the last time he laughed so hard.

The chief pulled down the gag from Jenny's mouth and then knelt at her side to untie her ankles from the chair. He pulled out some keys from his side and uncuffed her wrists from behind her back. She was weak. Michael could see her face was pale and her body was limp.

"Don't get up just yet," the chief told Jenny, holding up a hand before her. He looked over to JR and then back to her. "I'll get him for you."

She was very weak but wanted her baby so badly she didn't want to listen and tried to stand. Her legs gave way, and she fell back to her chair. Marty rushed to unbuckle her baby from the chair and handed him to her.

"My baby!" Jenny held out her arms and started to cry, tugging JR close to her body and rocking him back and forth.

"Now for my friend."

Michael lay there feeling his hands and legs being untied from the chair. Steve was dead beside him, but it wasn't Steve who was the enemy. The cat was still out there, and there were still two left. This night wasn't over by a long shot.

"What time is it?" Michael asked.

"Huh? Don't worry, son, everything is okay now. It's over." The chief pulled off the cuffs, freeing Michael from the broken chair. Lightning struck, crackling through the air. Rain burst from the skies above, and it started to pour. Rain started to trickle from the rotting ceiling. The chief stood up and smiled at Michael, shook his head, and then looked at the sunglasses that Steve wore, lying in the corner. "It's really over."

Timing was everything, and the way the cat leaped through the window was frightening. Broken glass was hanging from the edges, and there was a flash of lightning in the distance. Every muscle of the cat was highlighted from the bolt of lightning. Black fur like midnight stood straight up in the air. Front paws stretched forward with claws like razors, ready to rip something or someone apart. It was the milky eye that Michael recognized that made him want to shout, but it happened so fast he could barely open his mouth.

The chief never knew what took him when the claws dug into his side. A warm flash filled his body when the cat landed on him. Pinning the chief down with all four paws, the cat looked down to him with its mouth half open and jagged yellow teeth showing. Saliva dripped down to the chief, who stared up into the eyes of the cat. The chief hardly had time to scream when the cat lurched down and bit his neck, sinking those nasty jagged teeth into his flesh and ripping his body apart.

Michael recognized the cat immediately because of the milky eye, but it was the black fur standing straight up in the air that he thought was odd. It was a black panther this time, but never had he seen a picture of one with hair frizzled like this one. It took a moment before he realized the last cat was electrocuted. This one looked like it still had its claws stuck in the electrical socket, with its hair standing up. Michael would have laughed at this if it were under different circumstances. Instead his eyes darted from side to side, looking for a gun. There were three guns in the room now, one of them being his. His first instinct was to protect his wife and son. He ran to his wife, and then his eyes went wide.

It was Jenny who had been tied up for days but who reacted the swiftest. Maybe motherly instincts took over and she was protecting her baby. The black panther was standing over the chief, taking another bite out of his arm and figuring this time he had the upper hand. Michael was unarmed now, and the cat had the only other person capable of attacking underneath its paws. Certainly Jenny wasn't going to do anything, and the cat would save her for last. That was its mistake. Jenny grabbed the gun lying beside Lieutenant Steve's dead body. Never had she touched a gun, much less pulled the trigger of one. She hated guns and would have been very upset if she ever knew Michael had one in the house. Yet, like a pro, something inside her took over and she grabbed the gun in both hands. She aimed it directly at the cat, which was about to take another bite of the chief's neck. She pulled the trigger, firing it four times into the fuzzy black fur of the cat. Each shot hit vital organs, and the cat dropped on the spot.

"I hate cats."

Michael stared at Jenny in disbelief, and his jaw dropped to the floor. She was standing there holding the gun with both hands, like Annie Oakley, smoke coming out of the end of the barrel. She was frozen in a state of shock, and he ran to her and took the gun from her hands. He slowly pried her fingers apart to take the gun, and she finally started to shake. He took her into his arms, holding her there with her head on his shoulder.

"It's okay, it's okay." He stroked her hair with one hand and looked at her. "Jenny? We don't have time. Things will be okay, but you need to call the police. Take care of our boy."

Jenny looked up at him with eyes wide with fear. "What do you mean?"

"I have to finish this."

She knew what he meant and leaned down to pick up their son, who had been silent the entire time. Holding him in her arms, she turned to the chief and sighed. "Go. Do what you have to do, but after this we are getting a large dog." Although what she said was funny, she did not laugh. She cried instead. She went to the side of the chief and stared down at his torn, bloody body. "Is he dead?"

"Dad!"

Again that voice from his little boy resonated in his ears, and adrenaline pumped in Michael's veins. He didn't answer Jenny's question but just smiled, hearing his name called by his son again. It gave him hope and strength and a reason to finish what needed to be done. He turned back to Jenny, who had just gone through hell. She was safe for now, but he had to finish this with Valafar, or all of this was for nothing. He stepped closer to her side and took her hand in his.

"Call the police. I'll be back. I promise."

"Wait." She held his hand tight in hers, and Michael knew it was all the strength she had. She was tired and weak, but the two of them gave each other strength. She kissed his lips gently, looking up at him. "That's for good luck."

"Thanks, I'm going to need it."

# Showdown

## Halloween Night

When Michael stepped out of the house he never felt the rain falling down on his face. The weatherman was wrong about tonight. It was dark outside with just a small amount of light from the full moon, which was partially hidden behind the storm clouds scattered across the sky. The ground was slick, with mud sliding down from the weed-covered lawn. Small rivers flowed down the driveway, cutting paths into the ground like little valleys.

The Boss was sitting in a pool of rainwater when lightning lit it up. Beads of water rolled along its waxed surface to the muddy ground below. In that instant the car looked like it had a life of its own. It called Michael to the front seat because they had a mission to finish. The car was a beast itself, ready to devour the road or anything else in its way.

Strapped across his shoulder was a large canvas bag he'd found inside the house. He prepared himself with a few little things, like his Glock 17. He'd brought plenty of ammo in his car, and Steve had plenty of items as well inside his house. Stuffing what he could grab into the bag, he hoped it was enough. There was no way of telling what he was about to face this time, but so far he'd beaten them all.

He stepped into the front seat of the Boss, soaked in rain, and tossed the bag in back. The key was already in the ignition, and

336

he reached for it and turned it once. That roar sounded, and he gunned the engine with his foot on the pedal. It was a very distinct sound that only this car could make. One hand was on the steering wheel and the other was on the shift, tossing it into gear. He stepped on the gas pedal again, and the car spit the gravel beneath it and swerved a little to one side before grabbing the road and pulling out. Headlights shone on the slick pavement with rain pouring down. Lightning flashed, illuminating the road with a ghostly bluish color.

There was one purpose to this ride, and one alone would end this. It was between a young ambitious man searching his way toward his dream but ended up lost, and something or someone who wanted to take it all away. This was his chance now to find it again, and one stubborn beast stood in his way. Of course, it could be said that Michael stood in the way of the beast as well, so the showdown had to happen. It was Halloween night and nearly midnight when the Boss hit the road, and whether Michael knew it or not he was driven to his destiny—no pun intended.

He drove through the night with no plan for where he was going, yet somehow he knew something would show him the way. The road was empty with not a soul anywhere. Outside of town there was nothing except cornfields and a few farmhouses scattered around. The night sky flickered with lightning far off in the clouds.

Along the way he passed a few road signs, such as the speed limit and no pass zones, which he thought was funny since he was going well over the limit. But one sign caught his interest. It was larger than the rest and lit up with a green neon light flashing in a circular motion. It was a picture of himself with a dagger in his hands, standing over a small bloodied cat in neon red. On top of the sign was written in neon light, "This Way, Cat Killer." It was the first sign he was heading in the right direction, so he stepped on the gas and buried the needle beyond the limit on the dial.

One after another, road signs started to appear. Some were in neon lights and others were just painted in red. The ones in red looked like they were painted in blood, and Michael never doubted that they weren't. Most of the signs had something or another about the cat killer, but the closer he came the more lifelike the signs suddenly became. One sign nearly made him drive off the road. It was a picture of a large cat reaching out with an arm clawing at his car.

"Michael."

The strangest thing happened. He looked around, certain he heard a voice. Alone in the car, the only sound was the pitter-patter of rain on the windshield. The radio had been dead for so many years. The sound was so familiar, yet that voice had been gone a long time and now he was all alone.

"Dad?"

"What did I tell you?"

"Dad? Is that really you?"

"Drive, Michael."

"I am, but—"

"Take care of your dreams, Michael."

"Dad! I know, but—"

"And never give them up."

"Dad!"

"I'll be watching you from above."

"Wait! Dad, wait!"

"Drive it."

"Dad! Dad!"

"And don't tell your mother."

"I won't, Dad."

"Then drive it."

"Dad, I'm going as fast as I can." He turned to look beside him, but no one was there except the empty seat. "Dad? You there?"

Then the voice was gone, or was it ever there? There was no time to think anymore. He had to keep his eyes on the road ahead. Trees and telephone posts zipped by at blinding speeds as his foot pressed the gas pedal to the floor. The car never went so fast since his father drove the car. As quick as the voice appeared, it was suddenly gone. Was he hallucinating? Michael was certain he wasn't this time. It wasn't a crazy dream, but it was his dad giving him one final word of advice. His presence could still be felt inside the car. There was something there beside him, and Michael just held onto the steering wheel, driving straight on the rain-covered road. He turned to see if his dad would appear, but he never did.

Straight ahead, standing in the middle of the road, was a large lion staring directly at the oncoming car. Michael hit the brakes, and the wheels locked up, sliding on the slick pavement. Both hands braced, holding tight on the steering wheel for the collision about to happen. The tires squealed on the asphalt. The lion stood as still as a statue, and the car slid along the pavement, but this was an old sixty-six, and they did not make antilock braking systems back then. The car slid to the side, losing control and hydroplaning on the road. It turned sideways with the wheels locked up, sliding along the asphalt. The car skidded into the side of the road, spraying gravel. The engine stopped, and all was silent while he sat there, waiting for things to clear.

The lion was a magnificent one, with beautiful brown hair and a large mane around its head. Weighing at least five hundred pounds, it was a massive animal and the biggest one Michael had ever seen. The muscles were very well defined underneath the animal's smooth brown fur. The first thing Michael noticed about this one that was different from the rest of the cats was the eyes. The eyes were big, black, and endless, but there was no milky eye. Both of them were staring directly at Michael, so there was no mistake this one was perfect, with no faults of past events. The head did not wobble and jerk up and down, nor did it have any noticeable limps. This was the king of cats, and that meant just one thing.

"Valafar."

He immediately thought of the lion in the story his dad once told him as a kid. Was this the Nemean lion? He remembered sitting there in the grass with his dad, who told him, "Never be afraid to enter that cave alone." Michael understood what he meant for the first time and quickly reached back to gather his gun.

"Rrrrrrrrrrrrrrr!"

The growl of Valafar—or the Nemean lion—was louder than any animal he had ever heard before. No beast could roar like a lion. Of all the wild cats, only four could roar, and the lion was the strongest of them all. Whatever the reason, this beast was close. Michael twisted in his seat, trying to find the canvas bag in the backseat. Panic consumed him and he slapped the backseat and the floor, searching for the bag of goodies he'd brought with him.

"Son of a bitch!"

A loud thump landed on the top of the car, and claws dug into the roof like nails on a chalkboard—only this was amplified tenfold. Along the side windows, a long tan tail curled and slithered back and forth. The roof caved in with the weight of the animal standing on top, and Michael crouched down lower, feeling his body squeezed. Rain started to drizzle in and, looking up, Michael could see why. A large ivory claw dug into the metal roof, piercing it from above.

Michael couldn't find the canvas bag full of tricks to kill Valafar. His hand was searching the floor of the backseat, but it was nowhere to be found. After the spinout and all the commotion with the cat, the bag seemed to be lost. He was too preoccupied with the cat above and where he might be at any given moment. He had been expecting to have some time to organize before the lion appeared. Watching the way the roof caved in and listening to the sounds of the nails, Michael tried to follow the location of Valafar.

The lion slid down the windshield from the roof, front paws stretched out first, and turned on the hood of the car to face Michael. His long tail wagged back and forth with the tassel at the tip whipping around in circles. It stepped closer to the windshield, breathing through its nostrils, and the glass fogged over from its breath.

Michael grabbed the key in the ignition and turned it over to start the car. The engine turned over and made a grinding sound, but it would not start. "Come on, Boss, don't fail me now," he said, looking up nervously at the giant lion about to wreak havoc on his body. Again he turned the ignition, but the car wouldn't start. The tail of the lion bounced up and down on the hood of the car, and the tassel lit up with sparks.

Valafar turned his head and opened that massive mouth of his with a fierce roar that nearly shattered the glass. Huge white teeth, sharp and straight, still drooled with saliva, but this was no longer the mangy-looking cat he saw in the others. This was a killing machine unlike anything he saw before. Perfect in every way, it no longer had jagged yellow teeth or one milky eye. The transformation was nearly complete, and now it just needed a body. It licked its lips, staring at the only flesh and meat around, which was sitting in the seat before him.

Michael pounded the dashboard, trapped inside the Boss. "Why won't you start?" The car always started on the first click, but now nothing happened. Was it the dirt in the carburetor or a jostle of some wires? He looked at the lion outside his window and saw the tassel of his tail flicker with sparks again. It was Valafar's powers that surged cutting off the power to the Boss, just like the train stations with no one there and the electrical signs that short-circuited when he was near. Somehow he managed to control mechanical things that required power, and now Michael sat helplessly in his car.

The lion raised an arm, baring its long, sharp, ivory claws. Every muscle in its arm flexed like five of the strongest men all rolled together in one. It swatted at the front windshield, and the glass shattered into a million pieces. Lightning struck so close that thunder clapped instantaneously, and the sound mixed with the noise of glass shattering all over the front seat of the Boss.

Michael was stunned when lightning struck, lighting up the face of the lion. Standing before him was a beast so gruesome he could only wish it away. The face of the lion transformed for that brief instant of blue light to a white grotesque face of jagged yellow teeth before transforming back to the beast once again.

The lion reached in and clawed at Michael's chest, slashing more than just the shirt on his chest. Bright-red blood poured from his body, and the two of them screamed simultaneously. The lion roared, and Michael shouted in pain, the two sounds so very different but it was the two somehow tied together that mixed the sound into one.

Michael crawled back into the farthest part of the car, knowing there was no other escape. There was no rear door or back door to escape out of. The sloped back roof of the Boss made it quite uncomfortable, but it was all he had now. He frantically gave the backseat one final search for the bag of goodies but found none.

Valafar seemed content knowing he had Michael cornered and trapped like a rat. Reaching in farther, he swatted at Michael again. He cut his arm this time, and more blood splattered in the backseat of the Boss. Cats liked to play with their meal before eating it. He would not just weaken Michael, but he was going to make him suffer until he begged him to kill him.

"Dad!" It was his last shout for hope.

The radio had not worked for at least thirty years, but a small light came on, filling the car with an eerie green glow. Music started to play an oldie from 1966. It was a song from the Troggs, a hard banging of both guitars and drums with a voice shouting over the speakers very loud: "Wild thing." Both the lion's and Michael's eyes widened larger than ever before when they heard the sound of the music screaming out of the speakers. "You make my heart sing!"

The cat had no idea what to make of this when the car rumbled to a start on its own. Gears somehow shifted into drive, and the car screamed forward all alone. Michael watched from the backseat. The cat was sitting on the hood when the car came to an immediate stop before hitting a tree. The cat fell off the car, slammed into the tree, and fell down at the base. The Boss then reversed about twenty feet and stopped shining its bright lights on the cat.

"Get off the Boss, you son of a bitch." Michael cheered from the rear of the car.

At this point Michael realized the Boss really was alive. Magic was inside, but it took both him and his dad to make it come true. Cats did have nine lives, but Michael found out he too had more than one. Incapacitated at the base of the tree was his nightmare, and to make his dream come true the beast had to be gone. The taking of one life for another was the oldest ritual ever, and now the table had been turned on Valafar.

"Time to go back to hell."

The gas pedal of the Boss slammed to the floor with the help of a ghostly foot pressed hard to the metal. No one was sitting there, but Michael was certain it was his dad riding the Boss one last time before he had to go. The tires skidded at first, peeling off mud and gravel behind it before lurching forward with all the power it had. The lion tried to stand, but it was still stunned from slamming hard into the tree. The cat barely had time to look up at the headlights coming closer before it slammed into the tree. The beast roared before the car hit, but it ended abruptly when the car hit the tree. The horn started to wail, and smoke poured and swirled out of the radiator, but the Boss wasn't finished with this beast from hell just yet. It backed up once again, pointing its headlights directly into its eyes, and there sitting crushed up against the tree was Valafar. It was the man with the white face holding up one weak hand toward the car, pleading not to run over him again.

"Stop," the thing hissed. "I will give you everything if you let me live."

Michael wasn't buying it, knowing this thing had killed so many people he loved. And who knew what other death it brought on? He had always been taught never to trust the devil, and that was who was pleading with him now. Instead, he just shook his head and pointed to the beast with one final word to him.

"Step on it."

Valafar's eyes widened, seeing the Boss slam into his body. Hands reached out helplessly trying to stop it. Every animal it ever was suddenly appeared before the crash—from the smallest of kittens to the great lion he was now. In that moment Michael also saw life. He saw the lives of his friends who had departed. The car slammed into Valafar, severing his body. The tree had a gouge that would be scarred forever.

The Boss had been the first one to kill the cat, and in the end it was the one that would finish it. Valafar was always after the one who killed him, not realizing it was always the Boss that ran it over and not Michael. Either way, Michael had the pleasure of riding with the Boss on both occasions.

Michael stepped out of the car, which was wrapped around the tree now, and saw what remained of Valafar pressed tightly against the tree. His hands touched the badly damaged Boss, and he felt something warm against his hands. It wasn't the heat of the engine but something soft, like a human. His heart started to beat hard, and he knew what it was. A tear fell down from his eyes because he was so happy to have one last chance to say a final good-bye.

"Thanks, Dad."

# FINALE

Life is good but sometimes you have to swim through frigid shark-infested waters with weights chained to your waist to get there. Michael was able to survive that swim, hoping to never return. Things were different now, and he promised never to look back, although a joy ride in the Boss would certainly be one thing worth breaking the rules for.

Michael drove the Taurus to pick up Jenny and JR at the hospital. If the Boss wasn't so damaged, he would have driven that instead. He remembered his dad's words to drive it, which were now embedded in his head. He promised his dad he would.

On his way to the hospital he thought about how many lives everyone had. If you asked him how many lives a cat had, Michael would have told you nine. The real question, though, was how many lives do we have? It was what you did with the one life that mattered, and Michael was going to live his dream just like his dad told him. He was back on track, but now it was time to settle things at home.

He walked into the hospital with a dozen red roses under his arm, a stuffed dog in one hand, and a small wrapped box in the other hand. Jenny was seated in a wheelchair with JR in her lap. The two of them were smiling, and Michael ran to them. Bandages covered the claw marks that had nearly ripped Michael's body apart.

"Dad!" JR shouted.

Michael never felt as good when he heard those words from his son again. It was happiness, hope, and strength he felt all wrapped up in one. He leaned down on one knee, handed JR the stuffed dog, and then kissed him and rubbed his head. He sensed that the torch had just been passed from his dad to him.

"Dog." JR hugged the stuffed animal.

"That's right. Dog. No cat." He winked at JR. He handed Jenny the flowers from under his arm, kissing her lips, and it felt like he hadn't kissed them in years. The smell of roses lingered in the air.

"Thank you, Michael."

"May I wheel you to our friend's room?"

"You may."

Michael pushed the wheelchair toward the room down the hall. Something was bothering him, so he said, "You never told me what the great Zara told you that night."

Jenny bit into her lip but couldn't hold back the laugh. "She told me the scent of perfume was a sign that you loved me and not to worry."

The wheelchair stopped, and Michael felt his face flush. "You knew?"

"Mmhmm."

Michael kissed her on the lips. "I love you, Jenny."

"I love you too, Michael."

Lying there in the hospital bed was Chief Dugan. Nearly every part of his body was wrapped with gauze. His head, hands, neck, and torso were all wrapped up, making him look very much like a mummy. Nothing moved but his eyes when they stepped into his room.

"Chief, you're alive!" Michael said with excitement.

"I better be. Someone has to protect this town," he grumbled back.

"I brought you a present for all your troubles." Michael handed him the small wrapped box. Everyone started to laugh, including JR. It was good to laugh. Each one of them was injured and, although in pain, Michael knew it would pass.

"Aw, you shouldn't have." He held up both wrapped hands, showing he couldn't grab the box.

"Oh, sorry, Chief." Michael placed it on the table near his bed.

"Don't be sorry. Just explain to me one thing."

"Sure, what is it?"

"Where in Barbie land did you go?"

"What's Barbie land?" Jenny was so confused.

"I'll explain later. Trust me, you don't want to hear the alternative." Michael was laughing.

"Well? You going to tell me, or do I have to give you a ticket?" Chief Dugan joked.

"I just had to say good-bye to an old friend of mine."

"While I laid on my deathbed?" Dugan said incredulously and then laughed.

"Well, let's just say, he was on his bed too." Michael left it at that and just smiled at the chief.

"Well, I found a hole with some old chests in it, but my crew tells me when they got there nothing was in the hole except dirt." He eyed Michael, looking at him like he always did. He searched for the slightest of lies on his face or something to detect. "You wouldn't happen to know where those chests are, would you?"

"No, sir, I wouldn't," Michael answered.

The chief knew he would never get a straight answer about the chests, nor did he care anymore since none of it mattered. All that mattered to him was that this case was closed. They talked a little longer, and of course the chief told him he would keep an eye on him, but Michael just laughed, happy to see him alive. The two of them became the best of friends.

---

The three of them were home again, pushing JR back and forth on the swing set. Everything was back to normal at the Merlinos' once again. Winter was coming soon, and snow would be covering the ground, so they took this short time to enjoy the outdoors while they could.

Michael and Jenny were silent, happy with each other, home at last. Michael softly stroked Jenny's hair. They watched JR playing, but there were still some things to talk about. What was their future now that Michael had quit his job?

"We can manage somehow. I'll ask for a bigger territory," Jenny said.

Michael laughed, hugged her tight, and kissed her. "You don't have to do that."

"But I want to," Jenny told him.

"I lost myself, but someone reminded me and brought me back. We have nothing to worry about anymore." Michael winked at JR.

Michael pulled out a small box wrapped in paper and a ribbon across the top. Jenny stared at it before looking back up to him.

"Michael? You didn't have to do this."

"I wanted to."

She opened it and froze, staring at the large emerald inside. It was the prettiest ring she ever saw. The emerald was huge, and her head whipped back and forth from the ring to him. She was unable to speak before finally putting the box back into his hands.

"We can't afford this."

Now it was Michael's turn to just laugh, and he watched her face. She looked at him, confused by his laughter. He was full of surprises lately and wanted to drag this one on for a while. His life had changed for the better—one life gone for another. He just took in every part of the woman who he loved, recording every detail of her inside his head.

"Michael! We are in debt. We can never pay the Sullivans and the Wagon for the damages we caused. You have no job, and we have a small baby to feed, with another on the way."

This caught Michael off guard, and he nearly fell back on the floor. He was so sly, setting up the ring, that he never thought she had something to hide as well. She was always full of surprises that made him smile for a lifetime.

"A . . . baby?"

"Mmhmm." She smiled, rubbing her belly.

Michael reached over and placed his hand on her belly. This threw him off his agenda, but for now he was content. He would wait until later to tell her of the chests he'd found at the bottom of the hole. Another baby was coming into his life, and he wondered if his dad knew already. He looked up to the sky and knew the answer already.

He thought back to the other night when he was leaving the farmhouse to kill the final cat. His car wouldn't start for the first time, so he'd stepped out to open the hood. The rain had been pouring down when he was standing to the side of the car, looking down inside the engine and having no idea what to do next, when something glimmered off to the side. At the time it happened, he did not think anything of it and walked over to the hole. Down inside were three chests, and a ringing in his head told him to take every single one. He placed all three chests inside his car, forgetting the car wouldn't start. He sat inside, turned the key, and magically the car started on the first turn. What made him turn and find the chests, he did not know at the time, but now the more he thought about it the more he knew who it was. Later he would open the chests and find them all filled with thousands of the brightest emeralds.

"You okay?" Jenny asked, looking up at Michael.

"Uh, yeah. I'm feeling great!"

He picked up JR to carry him to the front yard. Tickling his sides and making him laugh, Michael kissed the side of his neck.

"I have one more thing to do." He smiled at Jenny and took JR around the side of the house, holding him tight.

There in the front driveway was a black pickup truck. A man stepped out and smiled at Michael, who waved to the man with one hand and carried JR in the other.

"You take care of them now," the man told him.

"Don't you worry about a thing." Michael smiled and then walked back to the end of the truck.

There sitting in the back of the pickup truck were two of the prettiest rottweilers a person ever saw—two puppies maybe eight to ten weeks old. The man opened the back, grabbed both of them, and placed them gently on the grass. Michael sat with them and placed JR on the grass as well.

"A present for you too, JR," he told his son.

"Dogs!" JR took to them immediately, pointing to both of them.

"Yep! Dogs." Michael was laughing when the dogs curled up against JR and rested their eyes. Already they were his buddies, and Michael knew his child was safe. Of course, he did have one word of advice for his son as he watched him, happy to have two dogs, two brand-new buddies. Although they wouldn't replace his old buddy Max, they would begin a new friendship. Michael found out we all have more than one life. He stood rubbing his son's head and told him his final words of advice.

"Don't tell your mother."

CPSIA information can be obtained at www.ICGtesting.com
Printed in the USA
LVOW052314040612

284632LV00006B/23/P